THE
SILENT WAR

THE
SILENT WAR

Book III of The Asteroid Wars

BEN BOVA

TOR®

A TOM DOHERTY ASSOCIATES BOOK
NEW YORK

THE SILENT WAR: BOOK III OF THE ASTEROID WARS

Copyright © 2004 by Ben Bova

This book is printed on acid-free paper.

Edited by Patrick Nielsen Hayden

A Tor Book
Published by Tom Doherty Associates, LLC
175 Fifth Avenue
New York, NY 10010

www.tor.com

Tor® is a registered trademark of Tom Doherty Associates, LLC.

Library of Congress Cataloging-in-Publication Data

Bova, Ben, 1932-
    The silent war / Ben Bova.— 1st ed.
      p. cm. — (The asteroid wars ; bk. 3)
    "A Tom Doherty Associates book."
    ISBN 0-312-84878-1 (alk. paper)
    EAN 978-0312-84878-1
    1. Mines and mineral resources—Fiction. 2. Space colonies—Fiction. 3. Space warfare—Fiction. 4. Asteroids—Fiction. I. Title.

  PS3552.O84S55 2004
  813'.54—dc22

                          2003071145

First Edition: May 2004

Printed in the United States of America

0 9 8 7 6 5 4 3 2 1

To the memory of Stephen Jay Gould,
scientist, writer, baseball fan,
and an inspiration to all thinking people

Everything is very simple in war, but
the simplest thing is difficult. . . . War is
the province of uncertainty; three-fourths
of the things on which action in war is
based lie hidden in the fog of a greater or
lesser certainty.

—Carl von Clausewitz,
On War

THE
SILENT WAR

ASTEROID 67-046

was a soldier," he said. "Now I am a priest. You may call me Dorn."

Elverda Apacheta could not help staring at him. She had seen cyborgs before, but this . . . person seemed more machine than man. She felt a chill ripple of contempt along her veins. How could a human being allow his body to be disfigured so?

He was not tall; Elverda herself stood several centimeters taller than he. His shoulders were quite broad, though; his torso thick and solid. The left side of his face was engraved metal, as was the entire top of his head: like a skullcap made of finest etched steel.

Dorn's left hand was prosthetic. He made no attempt to disguise it. Beneath the rough fabric of his shabby tunic and threadbare trousers, how much more of him was metal and electrical machinery? Tattered though his clothing was, his calf-length boots were polished to a high gloss.

"A priest?" asked Martin Humphries. "Of what church? What order?"

The half of Dorn's lips that could move made a slight curl. A smile or a sneer, Elverda could not tell.

"I will show you to your quarters," said Dorn. His voice was a low rumble, as if it came from the belly of a beast. It echoed faintly off the walls of rough-hewn rock.

Humphries looked briefly surprised. He was not accustomed to having his questions ignored. Elverda watched his face. Humphries was as handsome as regeneration therapies and cosmetic nanomachines could make a person appear: chiseled features, straight of spine, lean of limb, athletically flat midsection. Yet his cold gray eyes were hard, merciless. And there was a faint smell of corruption about him, Elverda thought. As if he were dead inside and already beginning to rot.

The tension between the two men seemed to drain the energy from Elverda's aged body. "It has been a long journey," she said. "I am very tired. I would welcome a hot shower and a long nap."

"Before you see it?" Humphries snapped.

"It has taken us more than a week to get here. We can wait a few hours more." Inwardly she marveled at her own words. Once she would have been all fiery excitement. Have the years taught you patience? No, she realized. Only weariness.

"Not me!" Humphries said. Turning to Dorn, "Take me to it now. I've waited long enough. I want to see it now."

Dorn's eyes, one as brown as Elverda's own, the other a red electronic glow, regarded Humphries for a lengthening moment.

"Well?" Humphries demanded.

"I am afraid, sir, that the chamber is sealed for the next twelve hours. It will be imposs—"

"Sealed? By whom? On whose authority?"

"The chamber is self-controlled. Whoever made the artifact installed the controls, as well."

"No one told me about that," said Humphries.

Dorn replied, "Your quarters are down this corridor."

He turned almost like a solid block of metal, shoulders and hips together, head unmoving on those wide shoulders, and started down the central corridor. Elverda fell in step alongside his metal half, still angered at his self-desecration. Yet despite herself, she thought of what a challenge it would be to sculpt him. If I were younger, she told herself. If I were not so close to death. Human and inhuman, all in one strangely fierce figure.

Humphries came up on Dorn's other side, his face red with barely suppressed anger.

They walked down the corridor in silence, Humphries's weighted shoes clicking against the uneven rock floor. Dorn's boots made hardly any noise at all. Half-machine he may be, Elverda thought, but once in motion he moves like a panther.

The asteroid's inherent gravity was so slight that Humphries needed the weighted footgear to keep himself from stumbling ridiculously. Elverda, who had spent most of her long life in low-gravity environments, felt completely at home. The corridor they were walking through was actually a tunnel, shadowy and mysterious, or perhaps a natural chimney vented through the metallic body by escaping gases eons ago when the asteroid was still molten. Now it was cold, chill enough to make Elverda shudder. The rough ceiling was so low she wanted to stoop, even though the rational side of her mind knew it was not necessary.

Soon, though, the walls smoothed out and the ceiling grew higher. Humans had extended the tunnel, squaring it with laser precision. Doors lined both walls now and the ceiling glowed with glareless, shadowless light. Still she hugged herself against the chill that the two men did not seem to notice.

They stopped at a wide double door. Dorn tapped out the entrance code on the panel set into the wall, and the doors slid open.

"Your quarters, sir," he said to Humphries. "You may, of course, change the privacy code to suit yourself."

Humphries gave a curt nod and strode through the open doorway. Elverda got a glimpse of a spacious suite, carpeting on the floor and hologram windows on the walls.

Humphries turned in the doorway to face them. "I expect you to call for me in twelve hours," he said to Dorn, his voice hard.

"Eleven hours and fifty-seven minutes," Dorn replied.

Humphries's nostrils flared and he slid the double doors shut.

"This way." Dorn gestured with his human hand. "I'm afraid your quarters are not as sumptuous as Mr. Humphries's."

Elverda said, "I am his guest. He is paying all the bills."

"You are a great artist. I have heard of you."

"Thank you."

"For the truth? That is not necessary."

I was a great artist, Elverda said to herself. Once. Long ago. Now I am an old woman waiting for death.

Aloud, she asked, "Have you seen my work?"

Dorn's voice grew heavier. "Only holograms. Once I set out to see The Rememberer for myself, but—other matters intervened."

"You were a soldier then?"

"Yes. I have only been a priest since coming to this place."

Elverda wanted to ask him more, but Dorn stopped before a blank door and opened it for her. For an instant she thought he was going to reach for her with his prosthetic hand. She shrank away from him.

"I will call for you in eleven hours and fifty-six minutes," he said, as if he had not noticed her revulsion.

"Thank you."

He turned away, like a machine pivoting.

"Wait," Elverda called. "Please—how many others are here? Everything seems so quiet."

"There are no others. Only the three of us."

"But—"

"I am in charge of the security brigade. I ordered the others of my command to go back to our spacecraft and wait there."

"And the scientists? The prospector family that found this asteroid?"

"They are in Mr. Humphries's spacecraft, the one you arrived in," said Dorn. "Under the protection of my brigade."

Elverda looked into his eyes. Whatever burned in them, she could not fathom.

"Then we are alone here?"

Dorn nodded solemnly. "You and me—and Mr. Humphries, who pays all the bills." The human half of his face remained as immobile as the metal. Elverda could not tell if he were trying to be humorous or bitter.

"Thank you," she said. He turned away and she closed the door.

Her quarters consisted of a single room, comfortably warm but hardly larger than the compartment on the ship they had come in. Elverda saw that her meager travel bag was already sitting on the bed, her worn old drawing computer resting in its travel-smudged case on the desk. She stared at the computer case as if it were accusing her. *I should have left it home,* she thought. *I will never use it again.*

A small utility robot, hardly more than a glistening drum of metal and six gleaming arms folded like a praying mantis's, stood mutely in the farthest corner. Elverda studied it for a moment. At least it was entirely a machine; not a self-mutilated human being. To take the most beautiful form in the universe and turn it into a hybrid mechanism, a travesty of humanity. Why did he do it? So he could be a better soldier? A more efficient killing machine?

And why did he send all the others away? she asked herself while she opened the travel bag. As she carried her toiletries to the narrow alcove of the lavatory, a new thought struck her. *Did he send them away before he saw the artifact, or afterward? Has he even seen it? Perhaps . . .*

Then she saw her reflection in the mirror above the wash basin. Her heart sank. Once she had been called regal, stately, a goddess made of copper. Now she looked withered, dried up, bone thin, her face a geological map of too many years of living, her flight coveralls hanging limply on her emaciated frame.

You are old, she said to her image. *Old and aching and tired.*

It is the long trip, she told herself. *You need to rest. But the other voice in her mind laughed scornfully. You've done nothing but rest for the entire time it's taken to reach this piece of rock. You are ready for the permanent rest; why deny it?*

She had been teaching at the University of Selene, the Moon being the closest she could get to Earth after a long lifetime of living in low-gravity environments. Close enough to see the world of her birth, the only world of life and warmth in the solar system, the only place where a person could walk out in the sunshine and feel its warmth soaking your bones, smell the fertile earth nurturing its bounty, feel a cool breeze plucking at your hair.

But she had separated herself from Earth permanently. She had stood on the ice crags of Europa's frozen ocean; from an orbiting spacecraft she had watched the surging clouds of Jupiter swirl their overpowering colors; she had carved the kilometer-long rock of The Rememberer. But she could no longer stand in the village of her birth, at the edge of the Pacific's booming surf, and watch the soft white clouds form shapes of imaginary animals.

Her creative life was long finished. She had lived too long; there were no friends left, and she had never had a family. There was no purpose to her life, no reason to do anything except go through the motions and wait. She refused the rejuvenation therapies that were offered her. At the university she was no longer truly working at her art but helping students who had the fires of inspiration burning fresh and hot inside them. Her life was one of vain regrets for all the things she had not accomplished, for all the failures she could recall. Failures at love; those were the bitterest. She was praised as the solar system's greatest artist: the sculptress of The Rememberer, *the creator of the first great ionospheric painting,* The Virgin of the Andes. *She was respected, but not loved. She felt empty, alone, barren. She had nothing to look forward to; absolutely nothing.*

Then Martin Humphries swept into her existence. A lifetime younger, bold, vital, even ruthless, he stormed her academic tower with the news that an alien artifact had been discovered deep in the Asteroid Belt.

"It's some kind of art form," he said, desperate with excitement. "You've got to come with me and see it."

Trying to control the long-forgotten yearning that stirred within her, Elverda had asked quietly, "Why do I have to go with you, Mr. Humphries? Why me? I'm an old wo—"

"You are the greatest artist of our time," he had answered without an eyeblink's hesitation. "You've got to see this! Don't bullshit me with false modesty. You're the only other person in the whole whirling solar system who deserves to see it!"

"The only other person besides whom?" she had asked.

He had blinked with surprise. "Why, besides me, of course."

So now we are on this nameless asteroid, waiting to see the alien art-work. Just the three of us. The richest man in the solar system. An elderly artist who has outlived her usefulness. And a cyborg soldier who has cleared everyone else away.

He claims to be a priest, Elverda remembered. A priest who is half machine. She shivered as if a cold wind surged through her.

A harsh buzzing noise interrupted her thoughts. Looking into the main part of the room, Elverda saw that the phone screen was blinking red in rhythm to the buzzing.

"Phone," she called out.

Humphries's face appeared on the screen instantly. "Come to my quarters," he said. "We have to talk."

"Give me an hour. I need—"

"Now."

Elverda felt her brows rise haughtily. Then the strength sagged out of her. He has bought the right to command you, she told herself. He is quite capable of refusing to allow you to see the artifact.

"Now," she agreed.

Humphries was pacing across the plush carpeting when she arrived at his quarters. He had changed from his flight coveralls to a comfortably loose royal blue pullover and expensive genuine twill slacks. As the doors slid shut behind her, he stopped in front of a low couch and faced her squarely.

"Do you know who this Dorn creature is?"

Elverda answered, "Only what he has told us."

"I've checked him out. My staff in the ship has a complete file on him. He's the butcher who led the Chrysalis massacre, six years ago."

"He . . ."

"Eleven hundred men, women and children. Slaughtered. He was the man who commanded the attack."

"He said he had been a soldier."

"A mercenary. A cold-blooded murderer. He worked for me once, *long ago, but he was working for Yamagata then. The* Chrysalis *was the rock rats' habitat. When its population refused to give up Lars Fuchs, Yamagata put him in charge of a squad to convince them to cooperate. He killed them all; slashed the habitat to shreds and let them all die."*

Elverda felt shakily for the nearest chair and sank into it. Her legs seemed to have lost all their strength.

"His name was Harbin then. Dorik Harbin."

"Wasn't he brought to trial?"

"No. He ran away. Disappeared. I always thought Yamagata helped to hide him. They take care of their own, they do. He must have changed his name afterwards. Nobody would hire the butcher, not even Yamagata."

"His face . . . half his body . . ." Elverda felt terribly weak, almost faint. "When . . .?"

"Must have been after he ran away. Maybe it was an attempt to disguise himself."

"And now he is working for you again." She wanted to laugh at the irony of it, but did not have the strength.

"He's got us trapped on this chunk of rock! There's nobody else here except the three of us."

"You have your staff in your ship. Surely they would come if you summoned them."

"His security squad's been ordered to keep everybody except you and me off the asteroid. He gave those orders."

"You can countermand them, can't you?"

For the first time since she had met Martin Humphries, he looked unsure of himself. "I wonder," he said.

"Why?" Elverda asked. "Why is he doing this?"

"That's what I intend to find out." Humphries strode to the phone console. "Harbin!" he called. "Dorik Harbin. Come to my quarters at once."

Without even a microsecond's delay the phone's computer-synthesized voice replied, "Dorik Harbin no longer exists. Transferring your call to Dorn."

Humphries's gray eyes snapped at the phone's blank screen.

"Dorn is not available at present," the phone's voice said. "He will call for you in eleven hours and thirty-two minutes."

"What do you mean, Dorn's not available?" Humphries shouted at the blank phone screen. "Get me the officer on watch aboard the Humphries Eagle.*"*

"All exterior communications are inoperable at the present time," replied the phone.

"That's impossible!"

"All exterior communications are inoperable at the present time," the phone repeated, unperturbed.

Humphries stared at the empty screen, then turned slowly toward Elverda Apacheta. "He's cut us off. We're trapped in here."

SIX YEARS EARLIER

SELENE: ASTRO CORPORATION HEADQUARTERS

Pancho Lane tilted back in her sculpted chair, fingers steepled in front of her face, hiding any display of the suspicion she felt for the man sitting before her desk.

One of the two major things she had learned in her years as chief of Astro Corporation was to control her emotions. Once she would have gotten out of her chair, strode around the desk, hauled this lying turkey buzzard up by the scruff of his neck and booted his butt all the way back to Nairobi, where he claimed to come from. Now, though, she simply sat back in cold silence, hearing him out.

"A strategic alliance would be of great benefit to both of us," he was saying, in his deeply resonant baritone. "After all, we are going to be neighbors here on the Moon, aren't we?"

Physically, he was a hunk and a half, Pancho admitted to herself. If he's here as bait, at least they sent something worth biting on. Strong, broad cheekbones and a firm jawline. Deeply dark eyes that sparkled at her when he smiled, which he did a lot. Brilliant white teeth. Skin so black it almost looked purple. Conservative gray business cardigan, but under it peeped a colorfully patterned vest and a soft yellow shirt opened at the collar to reveal a single chain of heavy gold.

"Your base is going to be more'n four thousand kilometers from here, way down at Aitken Basin."

"Yes, of course," he said, with that dazzling smile. "But our base at Shackleton will be only about a hundred klicks from the Astro power facility down in the Malapert Range, you see."

"The Mountains of Eternal Light," Pancho murmured, nodding. The Japanese called them the Shining Mountains. Down near the lunar south pole there were several peaks so tall that they were perpetually in sunlight. Astro had established a solar power center there, close to the deposits of frozen water.

"The facility that we are building will be more than a mere base," the Nairobi representative added. "We intend to make a real city at Shackleton Crater, much like Selene."

"Really?" Pancho said, keeping her expression noncommittal. She had just been informed, a few minutes earlier, that another Astro freighter had disappeared out in the Belt: the second one in as many weeks. Humphries is at it again, she thought, nibbling away. And if this guy isn't a stalking horse for Humphries, I'll be dipped in deep dung.

The other major thing that Pancho had learned was to maintain herself as physically youthful as possible. Rejuvenation therapies that were once regarded as expensive extravagances for the vain and video personalities were now commonplace, especially among the viciously competitive power brokers of the giant corporations. So Pancho looked, physically, much as she had when she'd been thirty: tall, leggy and slim. She had even had the tattoo on her buttocks removed, because board room politics sometimes evolved into bedroom antics, and she didn't want a teenaged misjudgment to become a whispered rumor. She hadn't done anything about her face, though, which she considered to be forgettably ordinary except for its unfortunate stubborn, square jaw. Her only concession to the years was that she'd allowed her closely cropped hair to go totally white. The beauticians told her it made a stunning contrast to her light mocha skin.

Pancho made a point of going counter to the fashionable styles of the moment. This season the emphasis was on bulky pullovers and heavy-looking sweaters with strategic cutouts to make them interesting to the eye. Instead, Pancho wore a tailored pantsuit of pale ivory, which accented her long, lean figure, with highlights of asteroidal jewelry at her wrists and earlobes. Her office wasn't particularly large, as corporate suites went, but it was sumptuously decorated with modern furniture, paintings that Pancho had personally commissioned, and holowindows that could display scenery from half a dozen worlds.

"Pardon me for asking a foolish question, I've never been to the Moon before. Is that real wood paneling?" her visitor asked, wide-eyed.

Aw, come on, Pancho groused silently. You can't be that much of a rube.

"And your desk, too? Did you have it flown all the way here to the Moon?"

"In a sense," Pancho answered evenly, wondering how much of this guy's naïveté was an act. "Our biotech division sent up a shipload of gengineered bacteria that produce cellulose. Same things tree do, at the cellular level."

"I see," he said, his voice still somewhat awed. "The bacteria produce bioengineered wood for you."

Pancho nodded. "All we bring up from Earth is a small sample of bugs, and they reproduce themselves for us."

"Marvelous. Nairobi Industries doesn't have a biotechnology division. We are only a small corporation, compared to Astro or Humphries Space Systems."

"Well, we all had to start at the beginning," Pancho said, thinking that it sounded fatuous.

Her visitor didn't seem to notice. "However, in exchange for help in building our base here on the Moon we offer a unique entry into the growing markets of Africa and the Indian subcontinent."

The Indian subcontinent, Pancho thought grimly; between their nukes and their biowar there isn't much left for those poor bastards. And Africa's still a mess, pretty much.

"We are also developing strong ties with Australia and New Zealand," he went on. "They still hesitate to deal with Africans, but we are overcoming their prejudices with sound business opportunities for them."

Pancho nodded. This guy's a stalking horse, all right. Whoever he's really working for thinks he's damned smart sending a black man to make this offer. Thinks I'll get all gooey and not see past the trap they're setting up.

Humphries. It's gotta be Martin Humphries, she reasoned. The old Humper's been after Astro for years. This is just his latest maneuver. And he's started knocking off our freighters again.

As if he could read her thoughts, the Nairobi representative added, in a confidential near-whisper, "Besides, an alliance between your corporation and mine will outflank Humphries Space Systems, so to speak. Together, we could take a considerable amount of market share away from HSS."

Pancho felt her eyebrows hike up. "You mean the asteroidal metals and minerals that Earthside corporations buy."

"Yes. Of course. But Selene imports a good deal from Humphries's mining operations in the Belt, too."

The big struggle, Pancho knew, was to control the resources of the Asteroid Belt. The metals and minerals mined from the asteroids were feeding Earthside industries crippled by the environmental disasters stemming from the greenhouse cliff.

"Well," said the Nairobi executive, with his gleaming smile, "that's just about the whole of it. Does it strike any interest in you?"

Pancho smiled back at him. "'Course it does," she said, thinking about how the kids she grew up with in west Texas would cross their fingers when they fibbed. "I'll give it a lot of thought, you can believe me."

"Then you'll recommend a strategic alliance to your board?"

She could see the eagerness on his handsome young face.

Keeping her smile in place, Pancho replied, "Let me think it over, get my staff to run the numbers. Then, if everything checks out, I'll certainly bring it up before the board."

He fairly glowed with pleasure. Pancho thought, Whoever sent this hunk of beefcake didn't pick him because he's got a poker face.

She got to her feet and he shot up so quickly that Pancho thought he'd bounce off the ceiling. As it was, he stumbled slightly, unaccustomed to the low lunar gravity, and had to grab a corner of her desk to steady himself.

"Easy there," she said, grinning. "You only weigh one-sixth of Earth normal here."

He made a shamefaced smile. "I forgot. The weighted boots aren't all that much help. Please forgive me."

"Nothing to it. Everybody needs a little time to get accustomed to lunar gee. How long will you be staying at Selene?"

"I leave tomorrow."

"You won't be talking to anybody from HSS?"

"No. Mr. Humphries has a reputation for swallowing up smaller corporations rather than helping them."

Maybe he's not from Humphries after all, Pancho thought.

She asked, "So you came up here just to see me?"

He nodded. "This alliance is very important to us. I wanted to speak to you about it face-to-face, not by videophone."

"Good thinking," Pancho said, coming around her desk and gesturing toward her office door. "That three-second lag in phone communication is enough to drive me loco."

He blinked. "Loco? Is that lunar slang?"

With a laugh, Pancho answered, "West Texas, for crazy."

"You are from Texas?"

"Long time ago."

Pancho played it cool, watching how he tried to maneuver their conversation into a dinner invitation before she could shoo him out of her office. He smelled good, she noticed. Some sort of cologne that reminded her of cinnamon and tangy spices.

Finally he got to it. "I suppose a person of your importance has a very full calendar."

"Yep. Pretty much."

"I was hoping we might have dinner together. Actually, I don't know anyone else in Selene City."

She made a show of pulling up her schedule on the wallscreen. "Dinner engagement with my PR director."

He looked genuinely crestfallen. "Oh. I see."

Pancho couldn't help smiling at him. "Hell, I can talk to her some other time. Let's have dinner together."

His smile grew even wider than before.

And he was good in bed, too, Pancho discovered. Great, in fact. But the next morning, once he was on his way back Earthside and Pancho had fed herself a breakfast of vitamin E and orange juice, she called her security director from her kitchen and told him to check the guy out thoroughly. If he's not from Humphries, maybe somebody else wants to move into the territory.

She chuckled to herself as she headed for her office that morning. She had forgotten the man's name.

TORCH SHIP *NAUTILUS*

The ship had once been a freighter with the unlikely name of *Lubbock Lights*, plying the Asteroid Belt, picking up ores mined by the rock rats and carrying them back to the factories in Earth orbit and on the Moon. Lars Fuchs and his ragtag crew of exiles had seized it and renamed it *Nautilus*, after the fictional submersible of the vengeance-seeking Captain Nemo.

Over the years, Fuchs had changed the spacecraft. It was still a dumbbell shape, rotating on a buckyball tether to provide a feeling of gravity for the crew. It still could carry thousands of tons of ores in its external grapples. But now it also bore five powerful lasers, which Fuchs used as weapons. And it was armored with thin layers of asteroidal copper fixed a few centimeters outside the ship's true hull, enough to absorb an infrared laser beam for a second or more. *Nautilus's* fusion propulsion system was among the most powerful in the Belt. Speed and maneuverability were important for a pirate vessel.

In the ship's cramped bridge Fuchs leaned over the back of the pilot's chair and scowled at the scanner display.

"It is a freighter, nothing more," said Amarjagal, his pilot. She was a stocky, stoic woman of Mongol ancestry who had been with Fuchs since he'd fled from the mining center at Ceres to take up this life of exile and piracy.

"With a crew pod?" Fuchs sneered.

Nodon, the ship's engineer, had also been part of Fuchs's renegade team since the earliest days. He was rail-thin, all bone and sinew, his head shaved bald, spiral scars of ceremonial tattoos swirling across both cheeks. A menacing black moustache drooped down to his jawline, yet his dark brown eyes were big and expressive, soulful.

"A crew pod means that the ship carries food," he pointed out as he studied the image on the display screen.

"And medical supplies," added Amarjagal.

"Both of which we could use," said Nodon.

Fuchs shook his head ponderously. "It could be a trap."

Neither of his crew replied. They glanced at each other but remained silent.

Fuchs wore a black pullover and shapeless black slacks, as usual. He was a short-limbed, barrel-chested little bear of a man, scowling with anger and implacable in his wrath. His broad, jowly face was etched with hatred, thin slash of a mouth set in a permanent glower, deepset eyes looking far beyond what the others saw. He looked like a badger, a wolverine, small but explosively dangerous.

For nearly a decade Lars Fuchs had been a pirate, an outcast, a renegade who cruised through the vast, silent emptiness of the Belt and preyed on ships owned by Humphries Space Systems.

Once he had considered himself the luckiest man in the solar system. A love-struck student riding the first crewed exploratory ship into the Asteroid Belt, he had actually married the most beautiful woman he'd ever seen, Amanda Cunningham. But then he became ensnarled in the battle over the riches of the Belt, one man pitted against Martin Humphries, the wealthiest person off-Earth, and his Humphries Space Systems' hired thugs. When the HSS mercenaries finally cornered him, Amanda begged Humphries to spare his life.

Humphries was merciful, in the cruelest manner imaginable. Fuchs was banished from Ceres, the only permanent settlement in the Belt, while Amanda divorced him and married Humphries. She was the price for Fuchs's life. From that time on, Fuchs wandered through the vast dark emptiness of the Belt like a Flying Dutchman, never touching down at a human habitation, living as a rock rat, sometimes prospecting among the asteroids in the farthest reaches of the Belt and digging metal ores and minerals to sell to refinery ships.

More often he swooped down on HSS freighters like a hawk attacking a pigeon, taking the supplies he needed from them, even stealing the ores they carried and selling them clandestinely to other rock rats plying the Belt. It was a pitiful way to maintain his self-respect, telling himself that he was still a thorn in Humphries's flesh. Merely a small thorn, to be sure, but it was the only thing he could do to keep his sanity. While he almost always attacked automated drone freighters toting their ores back toward the Earth/Moon system, often enough he hit ships that were crewed. Fuchs did not consider himself a killer, but there were times when blood was spilled.

As when he wiped out the HSS mercenaries' base on Vesta.

Now he frowned at the image of the approaching freighter, with its crew pod attached.

"Our supplies are very low," Nodon said in a soft voice, almost a whisper.

"They won't have much aboard," Fuchs muttered back.

"Enough for us and the rest of the crew for a few weeks, perhaps."

"Perhaps. We could grab more supplies from a logistics ship."

Nodon bowed his head slightly. "Yes, that is so."

Despite its name, the Asteroid Belt is a wide swath of emptiness between the orbits of Mars and Jupiter, populated by millions of tiny, cold, dark lumps of metal and rock tumbling around the Sun, leftover bits from the creation of the solar system. The largest, Ceres, is barely a thousand kilometers across. Most of the asteroids are the size of boulders, pebbles, dust motes. Trash, Fuchs thought. Chunks of matter that never became part of a true planet. Leftovers. God's garbage.

But the "garbage" was a treasure trove for desperate, needy humankind. Earth had been hit hard by climate change, a greenhouse cliff that struck suddenly, viciously, over a few decades. Glaciers melted down, ocean levels rose, coastal cities worldwide were flooded out, the global electrical power net collapsed, hundreds of millions lost their homes, their livelihoods, even their lives. Farmlands dried to dust in perpetual droughts; deserts were swamped with rain; monster storms lashed the frightened, starving refugees everywhere.

In the distant stretches of the Asteroid Belt there were metals and minerals beyond reckoning, raw materials to replace the lost mines of Earth. Factories built in orbit and on the Moon depended on those raw materials. The salvation of the battered, weary Earth lay in the resources and energy of space.

Fuchs gave all this hardly a thought. He concentrated on that freighter plying its way through the Belt, heading at a leisurely pace inward, toward Earth.

"If there's a crew aboard, why are they coasting on a Hohmann ellipse? Why not light their fusion drive and accelerate toward Earth?"

"Perhaps their engines malfunctioned," Amarjagal said, without looking up from her control board.

"She's not beaming out a distress call."

The pilot lapsed into silence.

"We could hail her," Nodon proposed.

"And let her know we're on her tail?" Fuchs snarled.

"If we can see her, she can see us."

"Then let her hail us."

"She isn't transmitting anything except a normal tracking beacon and telemetry data," said Amarjagal.

"What's her name and registration?"

The pilot touched a key on the board before her, and the information superimposed itself on the ship's image: *John C. Frémont*, owned and operated by Humphries Space Systems.

Fuchs sucked in a deep breath. "Get us out of here," he said, gripping the pilot's shoulder in his broad, thick-fingered hand. "That ship's a trap."

Amarjagal glanced at the engineer, sitting in the right-hand seat beside her, then obediently tapped in a course change. The ship's fusion engines powered up; *Nautilus* swung deeper into the Belt.

Aboard the *John C. Frémont*, Dorik Harbin watched the radar screen on his control panel, his ice-blue eyes intent on the image of Fuchs's ship dwindling into the vast emptiness of the Asteroid Belt.

His face was like a warrior of old: high cheekbones, narrow eyes, a bristling dark beard that matched the thick black thatch that tumbled over his forehead. His gray coveralls bore the HSS logo over the left breast pocket, and symbols of rank and service on the sleeves and cuffs; he wore them like a military uniform, immaculately clean and sharply pressed. Yet those glacier cold eyes were haunted, tortured. He only slept when he could no longer force himself to stay awake, and even then he needed sedatives to drive away the nightmares that screamed at him.

Now, though, he smiled—almost. He had tangled with Fuchs several times in the past, and the wily outlaw always escaped his grasp. Except once, and that had required a small army of mercenaries. Even then, Humphries had allowed Fuchs to get away alive. It was Fuchs's wife that Humphries was after, Harbin had learned.

But now Humphries had ordered Harbin to find Fuchs and kill him. Quietly. Out in the cold darkness of the Belt, where no one would know for many months, perhaps years, that the man was dead. So Harbin hunted his elusive quarry alone. He preferred being alone. Other people brought complications, memories, desires he would rather do without.

Harbin shook his head, wondering what schemes played through Humphries's mind.

Better not to know, he told himself. You have enough old crimes to fill your nightmares for the rest of your life. You don't need to peer into anyone else's.

SELENE: WINTER SOLSTICE PARTY

I t was the social event of the year. Everyone who meant anything in Selene City was invited and everyone who was invited dressed up and came to the party. Douglas Stavenger, the scion of the lunar nation's founding family, brought his wife. The ambassador from the Global Economic Council, Earth's world government in all but name, brought two of his four wives. Pancho Lane, head of the rival Astro Corporation, came unescorted. Nobuhiko Yamagata, head of the giant Japanese corporation, made a special trip to Selene for the occasion. Even Big George Ambrose, the shaggy red-maned chief of the rock rats' settlement at Ceres, traveled on a torch ship all the way from the Belt to be at Martin Humphries's Christmas party.

The invitations called it a Winter Solstice Party, artfully avoiding any religious sensitivities among the Moslems, Buddhists, Hindus and die-hard atheists on the guest list. Some of the Christian conservatives grumbled at the lack of proper piety, but then Martin Humphries never pretended to be a believer. Big George complained, with a mug of beer in each beefy paw, that back in his native Australia this time of the year marked the onset of winter darkness, not the gradually longer days that led to springtime.

One of the reasons for the full turnout was that Humphries gave the party in his palatial home, built deep in the lowest level of Selene City. He rarely invited anyone to his mansion, and curiosity—more than holiday good cheer—impelled many of the hundreds of guests.

Technically, the sprawling, low-roofed mansion was the property of the Humphries Trust Research Center, a legal fiction that was a monument to the ingenuity of Martin Humphries.

The airless surface of the Moon is exposed to temperature swings of four hundred degrees between sunlight and shadow, drenched in hard radiation from the Sun and deep space, and peppered with a constant infall of microscopic meteoroids. Human settlements are built underground, and the deeper below the surface, the more prestigious and expensive the habitation.

Humphries built his home in the deepest grotto below the original Moonbase, seven levels beneath the surface. He established an extensive garden that filled the grotto with the heady scents of roses and lilacs, irrigated by water manufactured from oxygen and hydrogen smelted out of the lunar surface rocks, lit by long strips of broadspectrum lamps fixed to the rough rock ceiling to simulate sunshine. The garden was a little over one square kilometer in extent, slightly more than ten hectares. It cost a fortune to maintain this improbable paradise, with its showy azaleas and peonies always in bloom, its alders and white-boled birches and graceful fronds of frangipani. Flowering white and pink gardenia bushes grew tall as trees. Humphries had established a research trust to finance his garden, and had even gotten the government of Selene to accept the slightly absurd justification that it was a long-term study in maintaining a man-made ecology on the Moon.

The truth was that Humphries wanted to live on the Moon, as far away as he could get from his coldly crusty father and the storm-racked world of his birth. So he built a mansion in the middle of his underground Eden, half of it taken up by research laboratories and botanical workshops, the other half an opulent home for none other than Martin Humphries.

The residential half of the mansion was big enough to take a couple of hundred guests easily. The big living room accommodated most of them, while others roamed through the formal dining room and the art galleries and outdoor patios.

Pancho headed straight for the bar built into the book-lined library, where she found Big George Ambrose with one hand wrapped around a frosty-looking beer mug, deep in intent conversation with a slinky, low-cut blonde. George was unconsciously worming a finger of his free hand in his collar, obviously uncomfortable in a tux. Wonder who did the bow tie for him, Pancho asked herself. Or maybe it's a clip-on.

Grinning, Pancho worked her way through the chattering crowd and ordered a bourbon and ginger ale from one of the three harried-looking men working behind the bar. Dozens of conversations buzzed around her; laughter and the tinkle of ice cubes filled the big, beam-ceilinged room. Pancho leaned both her elbows against the bar and searched the crowd for Amanda.

"Hey, Pancho!" Big George had disentangled himself from the blonde and pushed toward her, the crowd parting before him like sailboats scampering out of the way of a lumbering supertanker.

"How're the bots bitin', old gal?" George asked, in his surprisingly high, sweet tenor.

Pancho laughed. While she had worked for years to smother her West Texas accent as she climbed the slippery ladder of Astro Corporation, George's Aussie argot seemed to get thicker every time she saw him.

"Some bash, isn't it?" she shouted over the noise of the crowd.

George nodded enthusiastically. " 'Nuff money in this room to finance a trip to Alpha Centauri."

"And back."

"How's it goin' with you, Panch?"

"No major complaints," she lied, unwilling to talk about the missing freighters. "What's new with the rock rats?"

"Closed down the last warehouse on Ceres," George said. "Everything's up in *Chrysalis* now."

"You finally finished the habitat?"

"Naw, it'll never be finished. We'll keep addin' to it, hangin' bits and pieces here and there. But we don't have to live down in the dust anymore. We've got a decent gravity for ourselves."

Searching the crowd as she spoke, Pancho asked, "A full one g?"

"One-sixth, like here. Good enough to keep the bones producin' calcium and all that."

"You seen Mandy?"

George's shaggy-bearded face compressed into a frown. "You mean Mrs. Humphries? Nope. No sign of her."

Pancho could hear the scorn in the big redhead's voice. Like most of the other rock rats, he loathed Martin Humphries. Is he sore at Amanda for marrying the Hump? Pancho wondered.

Before she could ask George about that, Humphries appeared in the doorway that led to the living room, clutching Amanda by the wrist at his side.

She was splendidly beautiful, wearing a sleeveless white gown that hung to the floor in soft folds. Despite its slack cut, anyone could see that Amanda must be the most beautiful woman in the solar system, Pancho thought: radiant blond hair, a face that would shame Helen of Troy, the kind of figure that makes men and even other women stare in unalloyed awe. With a slight grin, Pancho noticed that Amanda's hairdo, piled high atop her head, made her a centimeter or so taller than Humphries, even with the lifts he always wore in his shoes.

When Pancho had first met Humphries, more than a decade earlier, his face had been round and puffy, his body soft, slightly potbellied. Yet his eyes were hard, piercing gray chips of flint set into that bland face. Since he'd married Amanda, though, Humphries had become slimmer, straighter; his face thinned down, too. Pancho figured he had partaken liberally of nanotech therapies; no need for cosmetic surgery when nanomachines could tighten muscles, smooth skin, erase wrinkles. Those gray eyes of his were unchanged, though: brutal and ruthless.

"Can I have your attention, please?" Humphries called out in a strong baritone.

The room fell silent and everyone turned to face their host and hostess.

Smiling broadly, Humphries said, "If you can tear yourselves away from the bar for a minute, Amanda and I have an announcement to make, in the living room."

The guests dutifully trooped into the living room. Pancho and George lingered at the bar, then at last followed the others. George even put his beer mug down. The living room was packed now with women in opulent gowns and dazzling jewelry, men in formal black attire. Peacocks and penguins, Pancho thought. Only, the women are the peacocks.

Despite the room's great size it felt slightly uncomfortable with that many bodies pressed together, no matter how well they were dressed. Pancho's nostrils twitched at the mingled scents of perfume and perspiration.

Humphries led Amanda by the hand to the grand piano in the middle of the spacious room, then climbed up on its bench. Amanda stood on the floor beside him, smiling, yet to Pancho's eyes she looked uncomfortable, unhappy, almost frightened.

"My friends," Humphries began.

Friends my blistered butt, Pancho said to herself. He hasn't got any friends, just people he's bought or bullied.

"It's so good to see all of you here. I hope you're enjoying yourselves."

Some sycophant started clapping and in a flash the whole crowd was applauding. Even Pancho slapped her hands together a few times.

Humphries smiled and tried to look properly humble.

"I'm so glad," he said. "I'm especially happy to be able to tell you our good news." He hesitated a moment, savoring the crowd's obvious anticipation. "Amanda and I are going to have a son. The exact delivery date hasn't been determined yet, but it should be in late August."

The women cooed, the men cheered, then everybody applauded and shouted congratulations. Pancho was tall enough to see past the heads bobbing in front of her. She focused on Amanda. Mandy was smiling, sure enough, but it looked forced, without a trace of happiness behind it.

The crowd formed an impromptu reception line, each guest shaking Humphries's hand and congratulating him and the expectant mother. When Pancho's turn came, she saw that Amanda's china-blue eyes looked bleak, miserable.

She had known Amanda since they'd both been astronauts working for Astro Corporation. Pancho had been there when Mandy had first met Lars Fuchs, and when Fuchs proposed to her. They were old friends, confidants—until Amanda had married Humphries. For the past eight years she had seen Mandy only rarely, and never alone.

"Congratulations, Mandy," Pancho said to her, grasping her hand in both of her own. Amanda's hand felt cold. Pancho could feel it trembling.

"Congratulate me, too, Pancho," said Humphries, full of smiles and good cheer. "I'm the father. She couldn't have done it without me."

"Sure," Pancho said, releasing Amanda's hand. "Congratulations. Good work."

She wanted to ask him why it had taken eight years, but held her tongue. She wanted to say that it didn't take skilled labor to impregnate a woman, but she held back on that, too.

"Now I've got everything a man needs to be happy," Humphries said, clutching Amanda's hand possessively, "except Astro Corporation. Why don't you retire gracefully, Pancho, and let me take my rightful place as chairman of the Astro board?"

"In your dreams, Martin," Pancho growled.

With a brittle smile, Humphries said, "Then I'll just have to find some other way to take control of Astro."

"Over my dead body."

Humphries' smile turned brighter. "Remember, you said that, Pancho. I didn't."

Frowning, Pancho left them and drifted off into the crowd, but kept an eye on Amanda. *If I can just get her alone, without the Humper hanging onto her . . .*

At last she saw Amanda disengage herself from her husband's hand and make her way toward the stairs that led up to their bedroom. She looked as if she were fleeing, escaping. Pancho slipped back through the bar, into the kitchen and past the busy, clanging, complaining crew that was already starting to clean up the plates and glasses, and went up the back stairs.

Pancho knew where the master suite was. More than eight years ago, before Mandy married Fuchs and the Humper was pursuing her fervently, Pancho had broken into Humphries's mansion to do a bit of industrial espionage for Astro Corporation. With the noise of the party guests filtering up from below, she slipped along the upstairs corridor and through the open double doors of the sitting room that fronted the master bedroom.

Holding her long skirt to keep it from swishing, Pancho went to the bedroom door and looked in. Amanda was in the lavatory; she could see Mandy's reflection in the full-length mirror on the open lavatory door; she was standing in front of the sink, holding a small pill bottle. The bedroom was mirrored all over the place, walls and ceiling. *Wonder if the Humper still keeps video cameras behind the mirrors,* Pancho asked herself.

"Hey, Mandy, you in there?" she called as she stepped into the plushly carpeted bedroom.

She could see Amanda flinch with surprise. She dropped the vial of pills she'd been holding. They cascaded into the sink and onto the floor like a miniature hailstorm.

"Jeeps, I'm sorry," Pancho said, coming up to the open lavatory door. "Didn't mean to scare you."

"It's all right, Pancho," said Amanda, her voice trembling almost as much as her hands. She began to scoop the pills out of the sink and tried to return them to the little bottle. She dropped as many as she got in.

Pancho knelt down and started scooping the oval, blood-red lozenges. No trademark embossed on them.

"What are these?" she asked. "Somethin' special?"

Leaning on the sink, trying to hold herself together, Amanda said, "They're rather like tranquilizers."

"You need tranquilizers?"

"Now and again," Amanda replied.

Pancho took the bottle from Amanda's shaking hands. There was no label on it.

"You don't need this shit," Pancho growled. She pushed past Amanda and started to pour the pills down the toilet.

"Don't!" Amanda screeched, snatching the bottle from Pancho's hands. "Don't you dare!"

"Mandy, this crap can't be any good for you."

Tears sprang into Amanda's eyes. "Don't tell me what's good for me, Pancho. You don't know. You have no idea."

Pancho looked into her red-rimmed eyes. "Mandy, this is me, remember? You can tell me whatever troubles you got."

Amanda shook her head. "You don't want to know, Pancho."

She clicked the bottle's cap back on after three fumbling tries, then opened the medicine chest atop the sink to return the bottle to its shelf. Pancho saw the chest was filled with pill bottles.

"Jeeps, you got a regular drug store," she murmured.

Amanda said nothing.

"You need all that stuff?"

"Now and again," Amanda repeated.

"But why?"

Amanda closed her eyes and took a deep, shuddering breath. "They help me."

"Help you how?"

"When Martin wants some special performances," Amanda said, in a voice so low that Pancho could barely hear her. "When he invites other women to help us in bed. When he wants me to take aphrodisiacs to enhance my response to him and his friends. Some of them are video stars, you know. You'd recognize them, Pancho. They're famous."

Pancho felt her jaw drop open.

"And when Martin brings one or two of his strange young male friends to join us, I really need pills to get through that. And for watching the videos he projects on the ceiling. And for trying to sleep without seeing all those nasty, horrible scenes over and over again . . ."

Amanda was sobbing now, tears streaming down her cheeks, her words incomprehensible. Pancho wrapped her long arms around her and held her tightly. She didn't know what to say except to whisper, "There, there. It'll be all right, Mandy. You'll see. It'll be all right."

After several minutes, Amanda pulled away slightly. "Don't you see, Pancho? Don't you understand? He'll kill Lars if I don't satisfy him. He's got me completely under his control. There's no way out for me."

Pancho had no response for that.

"That's why I agreed to have the baby, Pancho. He's promised to stop the sex games if I bear his son. I'll have to quit the drugs, of course. I'm already started on a detox program."

Pointing to the bottle of red capsules, Pancho said, "Yeah, I can see."

"I'm weaning myself off them," Amanda protested. "It's just that tonight . . . I need one."

"What the news nets would give for this story," Pancho muttered.

"You can't! You mustn't!" Desperate alarm flashed in her tear-filled eyes. "I only told you—"

Pancho gripped her quaking shoulders. "Hey, this is me, remember? I'm your friend, Mandy. Not a peep of this gets past that door."

Amanda stared at her.

"Not even if it could save Astro from being taken over by the Humper. This is between you and me, Mandy, nobody else. Ever."

Amanda nodded slowly.

"But I'll tell you one thing. I'd like to go downstairs and punch that smug sonofabitch so hard he'll never be able to smile again."

Amanda shook her head slowly, wearily. "If only it were that simple, Pancho. If only—"

The phone in the bedroom buzzed. Amanda took a deep breath and walked to the bed. Pancho swung the lavatory door halfway shut, hiding her from the phone camera's view.

"Answer," said Amanda.

Pancho heard Humphries's irritated voice demand, "How long are you going to stay up there? Some of the guests are starting to leave."

"I'll be down in a moment, Martin."

Amanda returned to the lavatory and began repairing the makeup on her face. Pancho thought that if the Humper even noticed she'd been crying, it wouldn't make any difference to him.

Then a new thought struck her. If Lars knew about this he'd kill Humphries. He'd fight his way past all the armies in the solar system to get to Humphries and rip his throat out.

SELENE: HOTEL LUNA RESIDENTIAL SUITE

Pancho could not sleep that night. She roamed the rooms and corridors of her residential suite, her mind in a turmoil over Amanda and Humphries.

It had taken Pancho years to realize that, as the top executive of one of the largest corporations in the solar system, she could afford luxuries. It wasn't until her younger sister left on the five-year expedition to Saturn that it finally hit her: Sis is on her own now, I'm not responsible for her anymore. I can start living any way I want to.

She changed her lifestyle, but only minimally. Her wardrobe improved, although not grandiosely so. She didn't become a party-goer; she *never* got mentioned in the tabloid shows. She still worked nearly every waking moment at her job as chief executive officer of Astro Corporation, still spent as much time in the factories and research labs as in the corporate offices and conference rooms, still knew each of the division heads and many of the lower-echelon managers on a first-name, drinking buddy basis.

Her one obvious change was her domicile. For years Pancho had lived with her sister in a pair of adjoining two-room units on Selene's third level. When she traveled to Earth she stayed at corporate-owned suites. After her sister left, Pancho spent several months feeling lonely, betrayed by the sister she had raised from infancy—twice, since Sis had died and been cryonically preserved for years while Pancho watched over her sarcophagus and waited for a cure for the cancer that took her first life.

Once Sis was revived from her liquid-nitrogen immersion, Pancho had to train her all over again to walk, to use the toilet, to speak, to live as an adult. And then the kid took off for distant Saturn with a team of scientists and their support personnel, starting her second life in independence, as far from her big sister as she could get.

Eventually Pancho realized that now she could live in independence, too. So she splurged for the first time in her life. She leased several units from the nearly bankrupt Hotel Luna and brought in contractors who broke through walls and floors to make her a spacious, high-ceilinged, thoroughly modern home that was perfectly suited to her personality. The double-height ceilings were a special luxury; no one else in Selene enjoyed such spaciousness, not even Martin Humphries in his palatial mansion.

Some said she was competing with Humphries, trying to show that she too could live in opulence. That thought had never occurred to Pancho. She simply decided to build the home of her dreams, and her dreams were many and various.

In every room, the walls and floors and ceilings were covered with smart screens. Pancho could change the décor, the ambiance, even the scent of a room with the touch of a button or the mere utterance of a word. She could live in the palace of the Caliph of Baghdad, or atop the Eiffel Tower, or deep in the fragrant pine forest of the Canadian Rockies, or even out in the flat dusty scrubland of her native west Texas.

This night, though, she walked on the barren, pockmarked surface of the Moon, as the cameras on the floor of the crater Alphonsus showed it in real time: silent, airless, the glowing blue and white crescent of Earth hanging in the black star-strewn sky.

Mandy doesn't want Lars to know what she's been going through, Pancho finally realized, because he'd go wild and try to kill Humphries, but Humphries's people would kill Lars long before he got anywhere near the Humper.

She stopped her pacing and stared out across the dark uneven floor of Alphonsus, dotted with smaller craterlets and cracked here and there by rilles. Maybe that's what Humphries wants. He promised Mandy he wouldn't try to kill Fuchs if Mandy married him, but now he's making her life so miserable that Lars'll come after him. And get himself killed.

That's just like the Humper. Make the other guy jump to his tune. He won't go after Lars; he'll make Lars come after him.

What'll Lars's reaction be when he finds out Mandy's going to have a baby? Will that be enough to set him off? Is that why Humphries impregnated Mandy? He's got one son already, somebody to carry on his gene line. Rumor is the kid's his clone, for cripes sake. Why's he need another son?

To kill Lars, that's why, Pancho answered herself.

What should I do about it? Should I do anything? Warn Lars? Try to help Mandy, show her she's got somebody she can depend on? Or just stay the hell out of the whole ugly mess?

Pancho gazed out at the tired, worn, slumped ringwall mountains of Alphonsus. They look like I feel, she said to herself. Weary. Worn down.

What should I do? Without thinking about it, she called out, "Décor scheme, deep space."

The lunar surface abruptly disappeared. Pancho was in the midst of empty space, stars and glowing nebulas and whirling galaxies stretching out into the blackness of infinity.

"Saturn vicinity," she called.

The ringed planet appeared before her eyes, hovering in emptiness, a splendid, eye-dazzling oblate sphere of delicate pastel colors with those impossible bright-white rings floating around its middle.

That's where Sis is, Pancho thought. Hundreds of millions of kilometers away.

Abruptly, she shook her head, as if to clear it. "Versailles, Hall of Mirrors," she called. And instantly was in the French palace, staring at her own reflections.

What should I do about Mandy? she asked herself again. Then a new thought struck her: What do I want to do?

Me. Myself. What do I want to do?

Once Pancho had been a roughneck astronaut, a tomboy who dared farther and played harder than all the others. But ever since her younger sister was struck down by cancer, so many years ago—so many lifetimes ago—Pancho had lived her life for others. Her sister. Then Dan Randolph came along, hired her as an astronaut and, as he lay dying, bequeathed his share of Astro Corporation to her. Ever since, she had been fighting Dan's fights, striving to hold Astro together, to make it profitable, to keep it out of Humphries's clutching paws. And now— Amanda?

What about me? she wondered. What do I want to be when I grow up?

She studied her reflection in the nearest mirror and saw beyond the floor-length party skirt and glittering lamé blouse, beyond the cosmetic therapies, to the gawky, gangling African-American from west Texas that lay beneath the expensive exterior. What do you want out of life, girl?

Her reflection shook its head at her. Doesn't matter. You inherited this responsibility from Dan Randolph. It's on your shoulders now. Mandy, Humphries, even this guy from Nairobi Industries, it's all part of the game you're in. Whether you like it or not. What you want doesn't matter. Not until this game is finished, one way or the other. Especially not now, with the Humper starting to peck away at Astro again. He's starting the war again. I thought it was all finished and over with eight years ago, but Humphries is starting again. Third freighter in as many weeks, according to this morning's report. He's only knocked off unmanned freighters so far, but this is just the beginning. He's probing to see how I'm gonna react.

And it's not just Humphries, either, Pancho reminded herself as she walked slowly along the mirrored corridor. It's the whole danged world. Earth's just starting to recover from the greenhouse cliff a li'l bit. Raw materials from the Belt are so blasted cheap they're providing the basis for an economic comeback. But if Humphries gets complete control of the Belt he'll jack up prices to wherever he wants 'em. He doesn't care about Earth or anybody besides himself. He wants a monopoly. He wants a goddam empire for himself.

You've got responsibilities, lady, she said to her reflection. You got no time to feel sorry for yourself.

"Acropolis," she commanded, striding back to her bedroom through colonnades of graceful fluted columns, the ancient city of Athens visible beyond them, lying in the hot summer sun beneath a sky of perfect blue.

Once in her bedroom Pancho made two phone calls: one to the investment firm in New York that she always used to check out potential business partners or rivals; the other was a personal call to Big George Ambrose, in his room in the very same Hotel Luna.

She was surprised when the phone's synthesized voice told her that George Ambrose had already left Selene; he was returning to Ceres.

"Find him, wherever he is," Pancho snapped at the phone. "I want to talk to him."

EARTH: CHOTA MONASTERY, NEPAL

The first thing Nobuhiko Yamagata did once he returned to Earth following Humphries's party was to visit his revered father, which meant an overnight flight in a corporate jet to Patna, on the Ganges, and then an arduous haul by tilt-rotor halfway up the snowy slopes of the Himalayas.

Saito Yamagata had founded the corporation in the earliest years of the space age and made it into one of the most powerful industrial giants in the world. It had been Saito's vision that built the first solar power satellites and established factories in Earth orbit. It had been Saito who partnered with Dan Randolph's Astro Corporation back in those primitive years when the frontier of human endeavor barely reached to the surface of the Moon.

When Nobuhiko was a young man, just starting to learn the intricacies of corporate politics and power, Saito was stricken with an inoperable brain tumor. Instead of stoically accepting his fate, the elder Yamagata had himself frozen, preserved cryonically in liquid nitrogen until medical science advanced enough to remove the tumor without destroying his brain.

Young Nobu, then, was in command of Yamagata Corporation when the greenhouse cliff plunged the world into global disaster. Japan was struck harder than most industrial nations by the sudden floods that inundated coastal cities and the mammoth storms that raged out of the ocean remorselessly. Earthquakes shattered whole cities, and tsunamis swept the Pacific. Many of the nations that sold food to Japan were also devastated by the greenhouse cliff. Croplands died in withering droughts or were carved away by roaring floods. Millions went hungry, and then tens of millions starved.

Still Saito waited in his sarcophagus of liquid nitrogen, legally dead yet waiting to be revived and returned to life.

Under Nobuhiko's direction, Yamagata Corporation retreated from space and spent every bit of its financial and technical power on rebuilding Japan's shattered cities. Meanwhile, he learned that he could use nanomachines to safely destroy the tumor in his father's brain; the virus-sized devices could be programmed to take the tumor apart, molecule by molecule. Nanotechnology was banned on Earth; fearful mobs and acquiescent politicians had driven the world's experts in nanotech off the Earth altogether. Nobu understood that he could bring his father's preserved body to Selene and have the nanotherapy done there. But he decided against it.

He did not stay his hand because of the horrendous political pressures that would be brought to bear on Yamagata Corporation for using a technology that was illegal on Earth, nor even because of the moral and religious outcry against such a step—although Nobuhiko publicly blamed those forces for his decision. In truth, Nobu dreaded the thought of his father's revival, fearing that his father would be displeased with the way he was running the corporation. Saito had never been an easy man to live with; his son was torn between family loyalty and his desire to keep the reins of power in his own hands.

In the end, family loyalty won. On the inevitable day when the corporation's medical experts told Nobu that his father's tumor could be safely removed without using nanomachines, Nobu felt he had no choice but to agree to the procedure.

The medical experts had also told him, with some reluctance, that although persons could be physically revived from cryonic suspension, their minds were usually as blank as a newborn baby's. Long immersion at cryogenic temperature erodes the synaptic connections in the brain's higher centers. No matter that the person was physically an adult, a cryonic reborn had to be toilet trained, taught to speak, to walk, to be an adult, all over again. And even then, the *mind* of the reborn would probably be different from the mind of the person who had gone into the cryonic suspension. Subtly different, perhaps, but Nobuhiko was warned not to expect his father to be exactly the same personality he'd been before he had died.

With some trepidation, Nobu had his father revived and personally supervised his father's training and education, wondering if the adult that finally emerged from all this would be the same father he had known. Gradually, Saito's mind returned. He was the same man. And yet not.

The first hint of Saito's different personality came the morning that the psychologists finally pronounced their work was finished. Nobu brought his father to his office in New Kyoto. It had once been Saito's office, the center of power for a world-spanning corporation.

Saito strode into the office alongside his son, beaming cheerfully until the door closed and they were alone.

He looked around curiously at the big curved desk, the plush chairs, the silk prints on the walls. "You haven't changed it at all."

Nobuhiko had carefully returned the office to the way it had been when his father was declared clinically dead.

Saito peered into his son's eyes, studied his face for long, silent moments. "My god," he said at last, "it's like looking into a mirror."

Indeed, they looked more like twin brothers than father and son. Both men were stocky, with round faces and deep-set almond eyes. Both wore western business suits of identical sky blue.

Saito threw back his head and laughed, a hearty, full-throated bellow of amusement. "You're as old as I am!"

Automatically, Nobu replied, "But not as wise."

Saito clapped his son on the shoulder. "They've told me about the problems you've faced. And dealt with. I doubt that I could have done better."

Nobu stood in the middle of the office. His father looked just as he remembered him. It was something of a shock for Nobu to realize that he himself looked almost exactly the same.

Feeling nervous, uncertain, Nobu gestured toward the sweeping curve of the desk. "It's been waiting for you, Father."

Saito grew serious. "No. It's your desk now. This is your office."

"But—"

"I'm finished with it," said Saito. "I've decided to retire. I have no intention of returning to work."

Nobu blinked with surprise. "But all this is yours, Father. It's—"

Shaking his head, Saito repeated, "I'm finished with it. The world I once lived in is gone. All the people I knew, all my friends, they're all gone."

"They're not all dead."

"No, but the years have changed them so much I would hardly recognize them. I don't want to try to relive a life that once was. The world moves on. This corporation is your responsibility now, Nobu. I don't want any part of it."

Stunned, Nobuhiko asked, "But what will you do?"

The answer was that Saito retired to a monastery high in the Himalayas, to a life of study and contemplation. Nobu could not have been more shocked if his father had become a serial killer or a child molester.

But even though he filled his days by writing his memoirs (or perhaps *because* he began to write his memoirs) Saito Yamagata could not entirely divorce himself from the corporation on which he had spent his first life. Whenever his son called him, Saito listened greedily to the events of the hour, then offered Nobuhiko the gift of his advice. At first Nobu was wary of his father's simmering interest in the corporation. Gradually, however, he came to cherish his father's wisdom, and even to rely upon it.

So now Nobuhiko flew to Nepal in a corporate tilt-rotor. Videophone calls were all well and good, but still nothing could replace a personal visit, face to face, where no one could possibly eavesdrop.

It was bitingly cold in the mountains. Swirls of snow swept around the plane when it touched down lightly on the crushed gravel pad outside the monastery's gray stone walls. Despite his hooded parka, Nobu was thoroughly chilled by the time a saffron-robed lama conducted him through the thick wooden door and into a hallway paneled with polished oak.

Saito was waiting for him in a small room with a single window that looked out on the snow-clad mountains. A low lacquered table and two kneeling mats were the only furniture, but there was a warm fire crackling in the soot-blackened fireplace. Nobu folded his parka neatly on the floor and stood before the fireplace, gratefully absorbing its warmth.

Wearing a kimono of deep blue, decorated with the flying crane emblem of the Yamagata family, his father waited in patient silence until Nobu grew uneasy and turned from the fireplace. Then Saito greeted his son with a full-bodied embrace that delighted Nobu even though it squeezed the breath out of him. Altitude and bear hugs did not mix well.

"You've lost a kilo or two," said the elder Yamagata, holding his son at arm's length. "That's good."

Nobuhiko dipped his chin in acknowledgment.

Saito slapped his bulging belly. "I've found them! And more!" He laughed heartily.

Wondering how his father could gain weight in a monastery, Nobu said, "I spoke with Martin Humphries. He apparently does not know that we are backing the Africans."

"And Astro?"

"Pancho Lane launched an investigation of Nairobi Industries. It has found nothing to tie us to them."

"Good," said Saito as he knelt slowly, carefully on one of the mats. It rustled slightly beneath his weight. "It's better if no one realizes we are returning to space operations."

"I still don't understand why we must keep our interest in Nairobi Industries a secret." Nobu knelt on the other mat, close enough to his father to smell the older man's aftershave lotion.

Saito patted his son's knee. "Humphries Space Systems and Astro Corporation are fighting for control of the Belt, aren't they? If they knew Yamagata will soon be competing against them, they might combine their forces against us."

Nobu shook his head. "Pancho Lane despises Humphries. And he feels the same about her."

With a knowing grin, Saito countered, "They might hate each other, but their personal feelings wouldn't stop them from uniting to prevent us from establishing ourselves in the Belt. Personal emotions take a back seat to business, son."

"Perhaps," Nobu conceded.

"Work through the Africans," Saito counseled. "Let Nairobi Industries establish a base on the Moon. That will be our foothold. The prospecting ships and ore carriers they send to the Asteroid Belt will return profits to Yamagata."

"One-third of our profits go to Humphries," Nobu reminded his father.

The hardest thing that Nobuhiko had been forced to tell his father was that Humphries had bought into Yamagata Corporation back in the days when the greenhouse cliff had struck so hard that the corporation was teetering on the edge of bankruptcy. Humphries owned a third of

Yamagata Corporation, and was constantly scheming to gain more. It had taken every gram of Nobu's courage to tell his father that. He feared it would break the old man's heart.

Instead, Saito had accepted the news stoically, saying only, "Humphries took advantage of the situation."

With some heat, Nobu growled, "He took advantage of the catastrophes that struck Japan."

"Yes," Saito said, his voice a low rumble. "We'll have to do something about that, eventually."

Nobu had never felt so relieved, so grateful.

Now, Saito sat back on his heels and gazed out at the snowy mountains.

"Our first objective is to make certain that neither Humphries nor Astro Corporation learns that we aim to establish ourselves in the Belt."

Nobu nodded his acknowledgment.

"The best way to accomplish that," Saito went on, "is to keep them both busy fighting each other."

"We've already destroyed a few automated freighters of both corporations, as you suggested. Pancho Lane blames Humphries, of course, and he blames her."

"Good," Saito grunted.

"But they're not actually fighting. There's a bit of piracy in the Belt, mainly by the man Fuchs, but he is one lone madman, without support from anyone except a few of the rock rats."

"He may be the key to the situation, then."

"I don't understand how," said Nobu.

"Let me think about it," Saito replied. "Our objective remains to keep HSS and Astro focused on each other. Fuchs could be an important element in this. Properly exploited, he could help us to stir this simmering enmity between Pancho Lane and Martin Humphries into a major conflict."

"A major conflict?" Nobu asked, alarmed. "You mean actual fighting? War?"

"Business is a form of warfare, son. If Astro and Humphries fight each other out there in the Belt, it can only be to our benefit."

Nobuhiko left his father with his mind whirling. Set Humphries and Astro against each other. Yes, he decided, it would be in Yamagata Corporation's best interest to do so. And this exile Fuchs could be the pivot that moves the stone.

By the time he landed in the family's estate near New Kyoto, Nobuhiko was lost in admiration for the depth of his father's thought. A war between HSS and Astro. Nobu smiled. Living in a monastery hasn't softened the old man's heart. Or his brain.

HABITAT *CHRYSALIS*

O
riginally, the prospectors and miners who came out to the Belt lived inside the largest of the asteroids, Ceres. Honeycombed by nature with lava tubes and caves, Ceres offered solid rock protection against the hard radiation that constantly sleets through the solar system. But at less than half the size of Earth's Moon, the asteroid's minuscule gravity presented problems for long-term residents. Muscle and bone deteriorate in microgravity. And every movement in the asteroid's caves and tunnels, every footfall or hand's brush against a rock wall, stirred up fine, powdery, carbon-dark dust that lingered in the air, hovering constantly in the light gravity. The dust was everywhere. It irritated the lungs and made people cough. It settled in fine black coatings on dishes in cupboards, on furniture, on clothing hanging limply in closets.

It was Lars Fuchs who had started the ramshackle habitat that eventually was named *Chrysalis* by the rock rats. When he lived in Ceres with his wife, Amanda, before he was exiled and she divorced him to marry Humphries, Fuchs got his fellow rock rats to start building the habitat.

All the rock rats knew that Fuchs's real motive was to start a family. A habitat in orbit around Ceres, rotating to produce an artificial gravity, would be a much safer place to have babies. So they started buying stripped-down spacecraft and old junkers that had been abandoned by their owners. They connected them, Tinkertoy fashion, and slowly built a wheeled station in orbit around Ceres that could house the growing population of rock rats. It looked like a rotating junkyard, from the outside. But its interior was clean, efficient, and protected by the electromagnetic radiation shields that each individual ship had built into it.

By the time the residents of Ceres moved to their orbital habitat and named it *Chrysalis*, Fuchs had lost his one-man war against

Humphries Space Systems, been exiled from the habitat he himself had originated, and lost his wife to Martin Humphries.

Big George Ambrose was thinking about that sad history while his torch ship approached Ceres. As he packed his toiletries in preparation for docking, he cast an eye at the wallscreen view of the habitat. *Chrysalis* was growing. A new ring was being built around the original circular collection of spacecraft. The new ring looked more like a proper habitat: the rock rats had enough money now to invest in real engineering and the same quality of construction that went into the space habitats in the Earth/Moon region.

One day we'll abandon the old clunker, George told himself, surprised at how rueful he felt about it. It's been a good home.

The big, shaggy-bearded, redheaded Aussie had started his career as an engineer at Moonbase, long before it became the independent nation of Selene. He had lost his job in one of the economic wobbles of those early days and became a fugitive, a non-person who lived by his wits in the shadowy black market of the "lunar underground." Then he'd run into Dan Randolph, who made George respectable again. By the time Randolph died, George was a rock rat, plying the dark and lonely expanse of the Belt in search of a fortune. Eventually he was elected chief administrator of Ceres. Now he was returning home from Humphries's winter solstice party.

He had spent the six days of his return voyage in a liaison with the torch ship's propulsion engineer, a delightful young Vietnamese woman of extraordinary beauty who talked about fusion rocket systems between passionate bouts of lovemaking. George had been flabbergasted by the unexpected affair, until he realized that she wanted a position on a prospecting ship and a fling with the chief of the rock rats' community looked to her like a good way to get one.

Well, thought George as he packed his one travel bag, it was fun while it lasted. He told her he'd introduce her to a few prospectors; some of them might need a propulsion engineer. Still, he felt sad about the affair. I've been manipulated, he realized. Then, despite himself, he broke into a rueful grin. She's pretty good at manipulatin', he had to admit.

Once his travel bag was zipped up, George instructed the ship's computer to display any messages waiting for him. The wall screen instantly showed a long list. He hadn't been paying attention to his duties for the past several days, he knew. Being chief administrator means bein' a mediator, a decision-maker, even a father/confessor to everyone and anyone in the fookin' Belt, he grumbled silently.

One message, though, was from Pancho Lane.

Surprised and curious, George ordered her message on-screen. The computer displayed a wavering, eye-straining hash of colored streaks. Pancho's message was scrambled. George had to pull out his personal palmcomp and hunt for the combination to descramble it.

At last Pancho's lean, lantern-jawed face filled with screen. "Hi George. Sorry we didn't get to spend more time together before you had to take off. Lemme ask you a question: Can you contact Lars if you need to? I might hafta talk to him."

The screen went blank.

George stared at it thoughtfully, wondering: Now why in all the caverns of hell would Pancho need to talk to Lars Fuchs?

HELL CRATER

Pancho always grinned when she thought about Father Maximilian J. Hell, the Jesuit astronomer for whom this thirty-kilometer-wide lunar crater had been named. Wily promoters such as Sam Gunn had capitalized on the name and built a no-holds-barred resort city at Hell Crater, complete with gambling casinos and euphemistically named "honeymoon hotels."

Astro Corporation had made a fair pocketful of profits from building part of the resort complex. But Pancho wasn't visiting Hell to check on corporate interests. She had received a message from Amanda to meet her at the medical center there. Mandy's message had come by a tortuously circuitous route, imbedded in a seemingly innocuous invitation to Selene's annual Independence Day celebration, sent by none other than Douglas Stavenger.

Ever since the Christmas party Pancho had been trying to see Amanda, to renew the friendship that had come to a screeching halt once Mandy had married Humphries. Amanda replied politely to each of Pancho's invitations, but somehow always had an excuse to postpone a meeting. Mandy never replied in real time; her messages were always recorded. Pancho studied Amanda's face each time, searching for some hint of how Mandy was and why she wouldn't—or, more likely, couldn't—get away from Humphries long enough to have lunch with an old pal.

So when Stavenger's video invitation popped up on Pancho's screen, she was staggered to see his youthful face morph into Amanda's features.

"Please meet me at the Fossel Medical Center, Pancho, next Wednesday at eleven-thirty."

Then her image winked out and Doug Stavenger's was smiling at her again. Pancho couldn't recapture Mandy's message, either. It was gone completely.

Curiouser and curiouser, Pancho thought as she rode the cable car from Selene. The cable lines were the cheapest and most efficient transportation system on the Moon. Rockets were faster, and there was a regular rocket shuttle between Selene and the growing astronomical observatory complex at Farside. But the cable cars ran up and over the Alphonsus ringwall mountains and out to Copernicus, Hell, and the other budding centers being built on the Moon's near side. There were even plans afoot to link Selene with the bases being built in the lunar south polar region by cable systems.

A corporate executive of Pancho's stature could have commandeered a car for herself, or even flown over to Hell in her own rocket hopper. But that wasn't Pancho's style. She enjoyed being as inconspicuous as possible, and found it valuable to see what the ordinary residents of Selene—the self-styled Lunatics—were thinking and doing. Besides, she didn't want to call the attention of Humphries's ever-present spies to the fact that she was going, literally, to Hell.

So she whizzed along twenty meters above the flat, pockmarked, rock-strewn surface of Mare Nubium, wondering what Amanda was up to. The cable car's interior was almost exactly like a spacecraft's passenger cabin, except that Pancho could feel it swaying slightly as she sat in her padded chair. Small windows lined each side of the cabin, and there was a pair of larger curving windows up forward, where tourists or romantics could get a broad view of the barren lunar landscape rushing past. What'd that old astronaut call it? Pancho asked herself. Then she remembered: "Magnificent desolation."

Those front seats were already taken, so Pancho slouched back in her chair and pulled out her palmcomp. Might's well get some work done, she told herself. But she couldn't help staring out at the mountains of the highlands rising beyond the horizon, stark and bare in the harsh unfiltered sunlight.

At last the car popped into the yawning airlock at Hell Crater. Pancho hurried through the reception center and out into the main plaza. The domed plaza was circular, which made it seem bigger than the plaza at Selene. Pancho marveled at the crowds that bustled along the shrubbery-lined walkways: elderly couples, plenty of younger singles, whole families with laughing, excited kids. Most of the tourists were stumbling in the low lunar gravity, even in the weighted boots they had rented. Despite the catastrophes that had smitten Earth, there were still enough people with enough wealth to make Hell a profitable resort.

Shaking her head ruefully as she walked toward the medical center, Pancho thought about how Hotel Luna back at Selene was practically bankrupt. It wasn't enough to a offer first-rate hotel facility on the Moon, she realized. Not anymore. But give people gambling, prostitution, and recreational drugs and they'll come up and spend their money. Of course, nobody accepted cash. All financial transactions were computerized, which helped keep everybody reasonably honest. For a modest percentage of the gross, the government of Selene policed the complex and saw to it that visitors got what they paid for, nothing more and nothing less. Even the fundamentalists among Selene's population appreciated the income that kept their taxes low, although they grumbled about the sinful disgrace of Hell.

As Pancho pushed through the lobby door of the Fossel Medical Center, she immediately saw that the center's clientele consisted almost entirely of two types: senior citizens with chronic complaints, and very beautiful prostitutes—men as well as women—who were required to have their health checked regularly. Pancho was wearing a well-tailored business suit, but still the "working women" made her feel shabby.

She strode up to the reception center, which was nothing more than a set of flat screens set into the paneling of the curved wall. Pancho picked the screen marked VISITORS and spoke her name slowly and clearly.

"You are expected in Room 21-A," said a synthesized voice, while the screen displayed a floor plan with Room 21-A outlined in blinking red. "Follow the red floor lights, please."

Pancho followed the lights set into the floor tiles and found 21-A without trouble. A couple of security people were in the corridor, a man at one end and a woman at the other, both dressed in ordinary coveralls, both trying to look unobtrusive. HSS flunkies, Pancho guessed.

When she opened the door and stepped into the room, though, she was surprised to see not Amanda, but Doug Stavenger.

"Hello, Pancho," he said, getting up from the chair on which he'd been sitting. "Sorry for all the cloak and dagger business."

The room was apparently a waiting area. Small, comfortably upholstered chairs lined its walls. A holowindow displayed a view of the Earth in real time. A second door was set into the back wall.

"I was expecting Mandy," said Pancho.

"She'll be here in a few minutes."

Doug Stavenger's family had created the original Moonbase, the lunar outpost that eventually grew into the nation of Selene. He had been the leader in Moonbase's brief, successful war against the old United Nations and their Peacekeeper troops, which established the lunar community's independence from Earth. Stavenger himself had chosen the name Selene for the fledgling lunar nation.

Although he was fully a generation older than Pancho, Stavenger looked no more than thirty: a handsome, solidly built middleweight whose tawny skin was only a shade lighter than Pancho's. His body was filled with therapeutic nanomachines that destroyed invading microbes, cleared away fats and arterial plaque, rebuilt his tissues to keep him physically youthful. They had saved his life, twice. Officially Stavenger had been retired for many years, although everyone knew he was still a political power broker in Selene. His influence was even felt in the Asteroid Belt and at the fusion-scooping operation in orbit around Jupiter. But he was exiled from Earth; the worldwide ban on nanotechnology meant that no nation on Earth would allow him within its borders.

"What're you doin' here?" Pancho asked as she sat in the chair next to Stavenger.

He hesitated a heartbeat, then replied, "I'll let Amanda tell you."

"What's she here for?"

Stavenger smiled sphinxlike.

If it had been anyone else Pancho would have fumed. She felt her brows knitting. "Some sort of game going on?"

Stavenger's smile faded. "Some sort, indeed."

The inner door swung open and Amanda stepped into the room. She was wearing the latest style of baggy blue-gray sweatshirt that stopped short of her rumpled, darker slacks so that her midriff was bare. In keeping with the current fashion, she had an animated decal sprayed around her waist: a procession of colorful elves and trolls, their endless marching powered by Amanda's body heat. Her golden hair was slightly disheveled. Even though she smiled at Pancho, the expression on her face seemed far less than happy. She looked pale, tense.

Stavenger got to his feet, but Pancho went like a shot to Amanda and wrapped her arms around her and held her close.

"Cripes almighty, Mandy, it's great to see you." *Without your sumbitch husband between us*, Pancho added mentally.

Amanda seemed to understand exactly how Pancho felt. She rested her head on Pancho's shoulder for a moment and murmured, "It's good to see you, too, Pancho."

They disentangled and sat down next to each other. Stavenger pulled a third chair over to sit facing them.

"The room's clean," he said. "Whatever we say here won't go beyond these walls. And all the other waiting rooms along this corridor are unoccupied."

Pancho realized that the security people out in the hallway were from Selene, not Humphries Space Systems.

"What's this all about?" she asked.

"I need to tell you something, Pancho," said Amanda.

"Must be important."

"Life or death," Stavenger muttered.

"Martin is planning some sort of move against Astro," Amanda said. "He's furious with you, Pancho. He believes you've been supplying Lars, helping him to prey on HSS ships."

"That's bullshit," Pancho snapped. "Hell, he's knocked off three of Astro's robot freighters in the past month. First one, I thought maybe Lars had done it, but not three."

"Lars wouldn't attack your ships, Pancho," Amanda said.

Stavenger agreed. "There's something in the wind, that's for sure. Someone's pumping money into this new African corporation."

"Nairobi Industries," said Pancho. "They're building a facility at Shackleton Crater, near the south pole."

"And Martin is backing them?"

"Either Humphries or a third player that's staying behind the scenes so far," said Stavenger.

"The Hump's always planning some sort of move," Pancho said lightly. "He's wanted to get his paws on Astro from the git-go."

"If he gains control of Astro Corporation, he'll have a monopoly on space operations from here to the Belt. He'll have the rock rats at his mercy."

"I think whatever Martin is planning could become violent," Amanda said. "He's rebuilding the base on Vesta that Lars destroyed. He's hiring a small army of mercenary troops."

Pancho had heard the same from her own intelligence people.

"But why is he going to all that expense?" Stavenger wondered aloud.

"To get control of Astro. To get control of everything," said Amanda.

"Including Lars," said Pancho.

"He's promised not to harm Lars," Amanda said. Without much conviction, Pancho thought.

"You believe him?"

Amanda looked away for a moment, then said bitterly, "I did once. I don't anymore."

Pancho nodded. "Neither do I."

"I thought we had this all settled eight years ago," Stavenger said. "You both agreed to stop the fighting."

"Astro's lived up the agreement," Pancho said.

"So has Humphries," replied Stavenger. "Until now."

"But why?" Pancho demanded again. "Why start all this crap again? Is he so damn crazy he really wants to be emperor of the whole solar system?"

"It's Lars," Amanda said. "He wants to kill Lars. He thinks I still love him."

"Do you?"

Amanda pressed her lips together tightly. Then she said, "That's why I'm here."

"Here? You mean this med center?"

"Yes."

"I don't understand, Mandy."

She took a deep breath. "The baby I'm carrying is Lars's, not Martin's."

Pancho felt as if someone had punched her in the solar plexus. "Lars's? How in hell did you—"

"We stored frozen zygotes years ago," said Amanda, "back when Lars and I first went out to the Belt on the old *Starpower*. We knew we could be exposed to dangerous radiation doses, so we fertilized some of my eggs and stored them at Selene."

"And now you've implanted yourself with one of 'em," Pancho said, her voice hollow.

Nodding slowly, Amanda said, "Martin thinks I'm carrying his son. But it's Lars's."

"If he finds out he'll kill you both."

"That's why I had it done here. Doug made the arrangements for me, brought together the proper medical personnel, even provided security."

Pancho glanced at Stavenger with new respect. "That's one way to spit in Humphries's eye," she muttered.

He shrugged. "I did it for Amanda, not to spite Humphries."

Yeah, sure, Pancho retorted silently.

Aloud, she said, "You're playin' with nitroglycerine, Mandy. If Humphries even suspects—"

Amanda silenced her with a flash of her eyes. "He won't rest until he's killed Lars," she said, her voice low but hard, determined. "But even if he does, I'll bear Lars's son."

Pancho let the breath sag out of her.

"It's the only way I can get back at him," Amanda said. "The only way I can express my love for Lars."

"Yeah, but if Humphries even suspects—"

"He won't," Stavenger said flatly. "Amanda's traveled here as part of my team, completely incognito."

"Only the three of us know about it," said Amanda.

"What about the medics?"

Stavenger answered, "They don't know who Amanda is. I fly the team up from Earth and then back again. They don't stay here."

"Only the three of us know about it," Amanda repeated.

Pancho nodded, but she thought about Ben Franklin's dictum: *Three people can keep a secret—if two of them are dead.*

LUNAR CABLE CAR 502

P ancho had to grin as she walked up to the cable car along with the other passengers returning to Selene. Above the car's front windows someone had stenciled the car's route in blood-red letters: To HELL AND BACK. None of the other tourists or resident Lunatics seemed to pay any attention to the lettering. Pancho shook her head at their indifference to the unknown graffitist's sense of humor.

Amanda had left the Hell Crater complex as she had arrived, as part of Douglas Stavenger's small, private entourage. She had slipped a beige snood over her golden hair, and an equally bland, shapeless mid-calf coat over her dress. No one would see the parade of animated figures circling her waist. She blended in with the rest of Stavenger's people. Unless someone was specifically searching for her, no one would notice her among the others who boarded Stavenger's special cable car.

Pancho had decided not to go with them. The lantern-jawed face and tall, long-limbed figure of Astro Corporation's board chairwoman were known well enough that there was a small but real chance that she might be recognized by news reporters—or snoops from Humphries Space Systems. No sense taking unnecessary risks, she decided. So Pancho spent the rest of the afternoon playing in the casinos, enjoying herself. For an hour or so she piled up a considerable score on one of the computer games, but eventually the law of averages caught up with her. When she sank back to break-even, Pancho called it a day and strolled over to one of the better restaurants for a solitary dinner. Gambling was fun, she thought, but losing wasn't. And the longer you play, the better the odds favor the house.

She always ate too quickly when she was alone. Feeling full yet unsatisfied, Pancho made her way back to the cable car airlock. "To Hell and back," she muttered to herself as she climbed through the cable car's hatch and strapped herself into a seat up front. She looked forward to watching the lunar scenery whipping past, and besides, with her back to most of the other passengers there was less chance of her being recognized. I'll get a good look at the Straight Wall, she thought.

The overweight Asian-American who settled into the seat beside her, though, stared at her for a few moments after he clicked his safety harness over his bulky shoulders. Then, as the car jerked into motion and glided past the airlock doors, he said, "Pardon me, but aren't you Pancho Lane? I saw your picture in the financial news net a few days ago and . . ."

Pancho didn't have to say a word. She couldn't. The man prattled on nonstop about his own small company and his great admiration for an executive as lofty as Pancho and how he had come up to Selene from the big refugee center at SeaTac, in the States, to try to clinch a deal with Astro Corporation.

Pancho was almost grateful when the cable car suddenly lurched violently and then began to fall, slowly, with the inexorable horror of a nightmare, to crash nose-first into the dusty, cracked, crater-pocked ground.

Martin Humphries leaned back as his desk chair molded itself to the contours of his spine. He sat alone in his office, just off the master bedroom in his mansion, squinting at the string of numbers and accompanying text that hovered in midair above his wide, expansive desk. He steepled his fingers before his face as he studied the reports from his accounting department. Profits were down slightly, but he had expected that. Four ships had been lost in the past quarter, three of them automated ore freighters, one of them a logistics ship that had been seized, looted, and then gutted by Lars Fuchs. The crew had been set adrift in their escape pod. The attack had taken place close enough to Ceres for them to be rescued within forty-eight hours.

Humphries snapped his fingers and the report dissolved.

"Fuchs," he muttered. The sonofabitch is still out there in the Belt, drifting around like some Flying Dutchman, getting his pitiful little jolts out of knocking off HSS vessels. And that damned greasemonkey Pancho is helping him.

Humphries smiled to himself. Well, enjoy yourself while you can,

Fuchs. The end is near. And meanwhile, I've got your ex-wife pregnant.

Pancho is a different problem. Tougher nut to crack. But I'll get her. I'll bleed Astro white until their board of directors boots her ass out the door. Then I'll offer them a merger deal that they can't afford to refuse. I'll take Astro Corporation; it's only a matter of time.

Getting up from the chair and walking slowly around his desk, Humphries laughed out loud. As soon as Amanda gets home from her shopping or whatever the hell she's doing today, I'll pop her into bed. Just because she's carrying my son doesn't mean I can't enjoy her.

"Holowindow," he called out, "give me a view of the Asteroid Belt."

The window on the left wall of the office immediately displayed a painting by Davis of a lumpy, potato-brown asteroid with a smaller chip of rock floating near it.

"No, a photo. Real-time telescopic view."

The holowindow went blank for a second, then showed a stretch of star-flecked darkness. One of the pinpoints of light was noticeably brighter than any of the others. The single word CERES flashed briefly next to it.

"He's out there somewhere," Humphries muttered to himself. "But not for much longer."

Humphries went back to his desk and called up the latest progress report from his special security detail in the Belt. The base on Vesta was complete, and twenty-four attack craft were on their way to take up stations around the Belt. All of HSS's freighters were being equipped with military crews and weapons. The costs were draining the corporation's profits, but sooner or later Fuchs would be found and destroyed.

In the meantime, Humphries thought, it's time to make my move against Astro. Time to take Pancho down. That greasemonkey's blocked my takeover of Astro long enough.

She doesn't understand the first principles of economics, Humphries told himself. Supply and demand. Astro is cutting our throats, undercutting our price for raw materials from the asteroids. And that damned guttersnipe will keep on undercutting me until I wipe her off the board completely. There isn't room for two players out in the Belt. The only way to make economic sense out there is to have just one corporation in charge of everything. And that one's got to be Humphries Space Systems.

Yet his thoughts returned to Fuchs. I've given the sonofabitch eight years. I promised Amanda I wouldn't harm him, and for eight years I've lived up to that promise. And what has Fuchs done? He sticks it to me every time he can. Instead of being grateful that I didn't kill him, he kicks me in the balls every chance he gets. Well, eight years is long enough. It's damned expensive trying to track him down, but I'm going to *get* that bastard, the sooner the better.

He's smart, though. Clever enough to hide out in the Belt and let his fellow rock rats help him. And Pancho, too; she's helping him all she can. I've got to get him out of hiding. Out into the open, where my people can destroy him.

Maybe the news that Amanda is pregnant will bring him out, goad him into making a mistake.

Looking at his own faint reflection in the holowindows, Humphries thought, I'd like to see the expression on his shitty face when he finds out Amanda's carrying my son.

MARE NUBIUM

Passengers screamed as the cablecar plunged in lunar slow motion toward the ground, twenty meters below. It was like a nightmare. Strangely, Pancho felt no fear, only an odd sort of fascination. While she watched the ground coming up toward the car's windows she had time to think, If the windows crack we'll lose our air and die in less than a minute.

The cable car's nose plowed into the ground with a grinding, screeching groan. Pancho was thrown painfully against the shoulder straps of her safety harness, then banged the back of her head against her seat's headrest.

For a second or two there was complete silence. Then people began to moan, sob. Pancho's head buzzed painfully. Automatically, she started to unclick the safety harness. The Asian-American seated next to her was already out of his straps.

"You okay?" he asked.

Pancho nodded tentatively. "I think so."

"They designed these cars to withstand a crash," he said.

"Yeah."

"They'll have a rescue team here shortly. There's enough air to keep us breathing for several hours, plus emergency tanks."

Pancho stared at him. "Sounds like you swallowed the emergency procedures book."

He grinned weakly, looking slightly ashamed. "I'm always a little nervous about traveling, so I read everything I can find about the vehicles I'm going to travel in."

Pancho tapped on the glassteel window. "Ain't even cracked."

"Good thing. There's no air outside."

"What's going to happen?" a woman's voice demanded sharply.

Pancho turned in her seat. The car's floor slanted upward, but otherwise everything inside seemed close to normal. A couple of the passengers had even stood up, legs a little shaky, looking around with wide, staring eyes.

"Better to stay in your seats," Pancho said, in her most authoritative voice. "The car's got an automatic emergency beacon. They've prob'ly already started a rescue team from Selene."

"How long will it take?"

"Will our air hold out?"

"The lights are dimmer, aren't they?"

"We must be on battery power," said the Asian-American. "The batteries are designed to last for six hours or more."

"Six hours? You mean we'll be stuck here for six hours?"

"No, it's just—"

The speakers set in to the overhead suddenly announced, "Cable car five-oh-two, this is the Safety Office headquarters. We will be launching a rescue hopper in less than thirty minutes. What is your situation, please?"

A babble of voices rose from the passengers, some frightened, some angry.

"*Shut Up!*" Pancho commanded. Once they were stilled, she said loudly and clearly, "We've crashed, but we're intact. All systems functioning. No major injuries."

"My back is hurt!" a woman said.

"I think I sprained my wrist," said one of the male passengers.

The loudspeakers replied, "We'll have a medic aboard the rescue hopper. Please stay calm. Help is on the way."

Pancho sat on her seat's armrest so she could look up the car's central aisle at the other passengers. They had all gotten back into their seats. No blood in sight. They looked shaken; a few of them were definitely angry, glaring.

"How long is this going to take?" one of the men asked no one in particular. "I've got a flight back to Kansas City to catch."

Pancho smiled inwardly. If they're in good enough shape to complain, she thought, we've got no major problems. Then she added, As long as the rescue team gets here before the batteries go flat.

The Asian-American pressed his fingertips against the curved inner wall of the car's hull. "Diamond construction," he said, as much to himself as to Pancho. "Built by nanomachines."

It sounded to Pancho as if he were trying to reassure himself. Then she noticed that he had a plastic packet in his lap. It contained two breathing masks and a small tank of compressed oxygen.

Lordy lord, Pancho thought. He really came prepared for a calamity.

LOGISTICS SHIP *ROEBUCK*

still don't like it," said Luke Abrams as he studied the radar display.

"You'll like the money," replied his partner, Indra Wanmanigee.

Abrams shot her a sour look. They were sitting side by side in the cockpit of *Roebuck*'s crew module. Normally the ship carried supplies from the habitat in orbit around Ceres to the miners and prospectors scattered around the Belt. This time, however, they were sailing deeper into the Belt than normal. And instead of supplies, *Roebuck* carried a team of mercenaries, armed with a pair of high-power lasers.

Tired of eking out a living as a merchant to the rock rats, Wanmanigee had made a deal with Humphries Space Systems to use *Roebuck* as a Trojan horse, drifting deep into the Belt in the hope that Lars Fuchs would intercept the ship to raid it for supplies. Fuchs would find, of course, not the supplies he and his crew wanted, but trained mercenaries who would destroy his ship and kill him. The HSS people offered a huge reward for Fuchs's head, enough to retire and finally get married and live the rest of her life like a maharanee and her consort.

"I still don't like it," Abrams muttered again. "We're sitting out here like a big, fat target. Fuchs could gut our crew module and kill us both with one pop of a laser."

"He hardly ever kills independents," she replied mildly. "More likely he will demand to board us and steal our cargo."

Abrams grumbled something too low for her to understand. She knew he worried about the six roughnecks living in the cargo hold. There were two women among them, but still Abrams feared that they might take her into their clutches. Wanmanigee kept to the crew module; the only mercenary she saw was their captain—a handsome brute, she thought, but she wanted no man except her stoop-shouldered, balding, potbellied, perpetually worried Abrams. She could control him, and he genuinely loved her. No other man would be worth the trouble, she had decided years earlier.

Suddenly Abrams sat up straighter in his copilot's chair. "I've got a blip," he said, tapping a fingernail against the radar screen.

Aboard *Nautilus* Lars Fuchs sat in his privacy cubicle, staring bitterly at Big George's image on the screen above his bunk.

Over the years of his exile, Fuchs had worked out a tenuous communications arrangement with Big George, who was the only man outside of his ship's crew that Fuchs trusted. It was George who had commuted Fuchs's death sentence to exile; the big Aussie with the brick-red hair and bushy beard had saved Fuchs's life when Humphries had been certain that he'd seen the last of his adversary.

Fuchs planted miniaturized transceivers on tiny, obscure asteroids. From time to time, George squirted a highly compressed message to one of those asteroids by tight-beam laser. Each coded message ended with the number designation of the asteroid to which the next message would be beamed. In this way Fuchs could be kept abreast of the news from the rest of civilization. It was a halting, limping method of communication; the news reports Fuchs received were always weeks out of date, sometimes months. But it was his only link to the rest of the human race, and Fuchs was grateful to Big George for taking the trouble and the risk to do it.

Now, though, as he glowered at George's unhappy countenance, Fuchs felt considerably less than grateful.

"That's what his fookin' party was for," George was saying, morosely. "He got up on the fookin' piano bench to tell all those people that he was gonna be a father. Pleased as a fat snake, he looked."

Fuchs wiped George's image off the screen and got up from his chair. His compartment was only three strides across, and he paced from one side of it to the other twice, three times, four . . .

It was inevitable, he told himself. She's been married to him for eight years. She's been in his bed every night for all that time. What did you expect?

Yet a fury boiled within him like raging molten lava. This is Humphries's way of taunting me. Humiliating me. He's showing the whole world, the whole solar system, that he's the master. He's taken my wife and made her pregnant with his son. The bastard! The crowing, gloating, boasting filthy swine of a bastard! I've been fighting him for all these years and he fights back by stealing my wife and making her bear his son. The coward! The gutless shit-hearted spineless slimy coward.

His hands balled into fists, Fuchs advanced to the blanked screen, the image of George's shaggy-maned face still burning in his eyes. He had to hit something, anything, had to release this fury somehow, *now*, before it exploded inside him.

"Contact," sang Nodon's voice over the intercom. "We have radar contact with a vessel."

Fuchs's head jerked to the speaker built into the bulkhead.

"It appears to be a logistics ship," Nodon added.

Fuchs's lips curled into a humorless smile. "I'm coming up to the bridge," he said.

By the time he got to the compact, equipment-crammed bridge, Nodon had the approaching logistics ship on the main screen. Amarjagal was in the pilot's seat, silent and dour as usual. Fuchs stood behind her and focused his attention on the ship.

"What's a logistics ship doing this deep in the Belt?" he wondered aloud.

Nodon shifted his big, liquid eyes from the screen to Fuchs, then back again. "Perhaps it is off course," he suggested.

"Or a decoy," Fuchs snapped. "Any other ships in sight?"

"Nosir. The nearest object is a minor asteroid, less than a hundred meters across."

"Distance?"

"Four hundred kilometers. Four thirty-two, to be precise."

"Could it be another ship, disguised?"

Amarjagal spoke up. "There could be a ship behind it. Or even sitting on it."

The communications receiver's light began blinking amber.

"They're trying to speak to us," Nodon said, pointing to the light.

"Listen, but don't reply," Fuchs commanded.

"This is the *Roebuck*," the comm speaker announced. A man's voice; it sounded a little shaky to Fuchs. He's excited, maybe nervous.

"We have a full cargo of supplies for you. Be willing to accept credit if you don't have hard goods to trade."

"Is *Roebuck* an HSS vessel?" Fuchs asked Nodon.

His fingers flicked across the keyboard set into the control panel. "Nosir. It is registered as an independent."

"Are the lasers ready?"

Pointing to the green lights of the weapons board, Nodon replied, "Yessir. The crews are all in place."

In *Roebuck*'s cargo bay the team of trained mercenaries was already in their spacesuits and warming up the laser weapons.

"Don't open the hatches until I give the word," their captain said from his post on the catwalk that ran around the interior of the spacious bay. "I don't want to give Fuchs any hint that we're ready to fry his ass."

Fuchs rubbed his broad, stubbled chin as he stared at the image of the logistics vessel on the bridge's main screen.

"Why would an independent logistics ship be this deep in the Belt?" he repeated. "There aren't any miners or prospectors out here."

"Except us," agreed Amarjagal.

"Fire number one at their cargo bay," Fuchs snapped.

Nodon hesitated for a fraction of a moment.

"Fire it!" Fuchs roared.

The first laser blast did little more damage than puncturing the thin skin of *Roebuck*'s cargo bay hull. As the air rushed out of the bay, their spacesuited commander gave the order to open the hatches and begin firing back at *Nautilus*.

In the cockpit Abrams felt cold sweat break out all over his body. "He's shooting at us!"

Wanmanigee tensed, too. "We should get into our space suits! Quickly!"

Those were her last words.

His eyes glued to the main screen, Fuchs saw *Roebuck*'s cargo bay hatches open.

"They're firing back," reported Amarjagal, her voice flat and calm.

"All weapons fire," Fuchs said. "Tear her to shreds."

It was a totally unequal battle. *Roebuck*'s laser beams splashed off *Nautilus*'s copper armor shields. *Nautilus*'s five laser weapons slashed through *Roebuck*'s thin hull, shredding the cargo bay and crew pod within seconds. Fuchs saw several space-suited figures tumble out of the wreckage.

"Cease firing," he said.

Jabbing a finger at the image of the space-suited people floating helplessly, Nodon asked, "Shall we pick them up?"

Fuchs sneered at him. "Do you want to share your rations with them?"

Nodon hesitated, obviously torn.

"And if we take them aboard, what do we do with them? How do we get rid of them? Do you think we can cruise back to Ceres and land them there?"

Nodon shook his head. Still, he turned back to watch the helpless figures floating amidst the wreckage of what had been a vessel only a few moments earlier. His finger hovered over the communications keyboard.

"Don't tap into their frequency," Fuchs commanded. "I don't want to hear them begging."

For several moments Fuchs and his bridge crew watched the figures slowly, silently drifting. They must be screaming for help, Nodon thought. Beseeching us for mercy. Yet we will not hear them.

At last Fuchs broke the silence. "One-third g acceleration," he ordered. "Back on our original course. Let's find a real logistics ship and fill up our supplies."

"But . . ."

"They're mercenaries," Fuchs snapped. "Hired killers. They came out here to kill us. Now they'll be dead. It's no great loss."

Nodon's face still showed his desolation. "But they'll die. They'll float out there . . . forever."

"Think of it this way," Fuchs said, his voice iron-hard. "We've added a few more minor asteroids to the Belt."

SELENE: ASTRO CORPORATION HEADQUARTERS

Sabotaged." Pancho knew it was true, even though she did not want to believe it.

Doug Stavenger looked grim. He sat tensely before Pancho's desk, wearing light tan slacks and a micromesh pullover. Only the slight sparkling in the air around him betrayed the fact that his image was a hologram; otherwise he looked as solid and real as if he were actually in Pancho's office, instead of his own office, up in one of the towers that supported the Main Plaza's dome.

"It could have been worse," he said. "A solar storm broke out just hours after you were rescued. We had to suspend all surface operations because of the radiation. If it had come a little earlier you would have fried out there in the cable car."

"Nobody can predict solar flares that fine," Pancho said.

"No, I suppose not."

"But—sabotage?" she repeated.

"That's what our investigation showed," Stavenger replied. "Whoever did it wasn't even very subtle about it. They used an explosive charge to knock out the trolley wheels that the cable car rides on. The blast damaged one of the poles, too."

Pancho leaned both elbows on her desk. "Doug, are you telling me we've got terrorists in Selene now?"

Stavenger shook his head. "I don't believe so."

"But who would want to knock out a cable car? That's the kind of random violence a terrorist would do. Or a nutcase."

"Or an assassin."

Pancho's insides clenched. There it was. The same conclusion her own security people had swiftly come to. Yet she heard herself ask, "Assassin?"

"Selene's security investigators think somebody was trying to kill you, Pancho."

And twenty-three other people who happened to be aboard the car, she added silently.

Stavenger asked, "What do your own security people think?"

"Exactly the same," she replied.

"I'm not surprised," said Stavenger.

"Neither am I, I guess," she said. Then she admitted, "I just didn't want to believe that he'd try to kill me."

"He?"

"Humphries. Who else?"

And she remembered their exchange at Humphries's party:

"Why don't you retire gracefully, Pancho, and let me take my rightful place as chairman of the Astro board?"

"In your dreams, Martin."

"Then I'll just have to find some other way to take control of Astro."

"Over my dead body."

"Remember, you said that, Pancho. I didn't."

The sonofabitch! Pancho thought.

Stavenger took a deep breath. "I don't want you fighting here in Selene."

Pancho understood his meaning. If Astro and Humphries are going to war, let it be out in the Belt.

"Doug," she said earnestly, "I don't want a war. I thought we had ended all that eight years ago."

"So had I."

"The sumbitch wants control of Astro, and he knows I won't step aside and let him take over."

"Pancho," said Stavenger wearily, rubbing a hand across his eyes, "Humphries wants control of the Belt and all its resources. That seems clear."

"And if he gets the Belt, he'll have control of the whole solar system. And everybody in it."

"Including Selene."

Pancho nodded. "Including Selene."

"I can't allow that to happen."

"So what're you going to do about it, Doug?"

He spread his hands in a gesture of uncertainty. "That's just it,

Pancho. I don't know what I can do. Humphries isn't trying to take political control of Selene. He's after economic power. He knows that if he controls the resources of the Belt, he'll have Selene and everyone else under his thumb. He can let us continue to govern ourselves. But we'll have to buy our water and most of our other raw materials from him."

Pancho shook her head. Once Selene had been virtually self-sufficient, mining water from the deposits of ice at the lunar poles, and using the raw materials scraped from the Moon's surface layers of regolith. Selene even exported fusion fuels to Earth and supplied the aluminum and silicon for building solar power satellites in Earth orbit.

But once Selene's government decided to allow limited immigration from the devastated Earth, the lunar nation's self-sufficiency ended. Selene became dependent on the metals and minerals, even the water, imported from the asteroids. And the trickle of immigration from Earth had become an ever-increasing stream, Pancho knew.

"What're you going to do?" Pancho repeated.

Looking decidedly unhappy, Stavenger said, "I'll have a talk with Humphries. Not that it'll do much good, I expect."

Pancho heard his unspoken words. It's up to me to stop Humphries, she realized. I've got to fight him. Nobody else can.

"Okay," she said to Stavenger. "You talk. I'll act."

"No fighting here," Stavenger snapped. "Not here."

"Not here, Doug," Pancho promised. Already in her head she was starting to figure how much it would cost to go to war against Humphries Space Systems out in the Asteroid Belt.

Flying in the rattling, roaring helicopter from SeaTac Aerospaceport, the Asian-American who had been assigned to make certain that Pancho Lane survived the sabotage of the cable car looked forward to returning to his home in the mountains of Washington State's Olympic peninsula. His family would be waiting for him, he knew. So would the fat stipend from Yamagata Corporation.

The helicopter touched down on the cleared gravel area at the foot of the path that led up to his cabin. Strangely, no one was there to greet him. Surely his wife and children heard the copter's throbbing engines. He walked to the edge of the helipad, clutching his travel bag in one hand, squinting in the miniature sandstorm of gravel and grit from the helicopter's swirling rotors.

From the gravel pad he could see downslope to the drowned city of Port Townsend and the cluster of scuba-diving camps huddled around it. On a clear day, he could gaze through binoculars at the shattered remains of Seattle's high-rise towers poking up above the waters of Puget Sound.

It had been a curious assignment, he thought. Fly to the Moon as a tourist—at a cost that would have emptied his life savings—and ride in a certain cable car at a certain time, carrying emergency survival equipment to make certain that Ms. Lane would not be killed by the "accident."

He shrugged his heavy shoulders as he watched the helicopter dwindle into the cloudy sky, then turned and headed up the winding path toward his home.

He never saw his wife and children, who lay in their bloody beds, each of them shot through the head. Two men grabbed him as he stepped through the front door of his cabin and put a gun to his temple. By the time the local police arrived on the scene, several days later, it seemed obvious to them that the man had slaughtered his family and then committed suicide.

"He must've gone nuts," said the police chief. "It happens. A guy just snaps, for no apparent reason."

Case closed.

At Selene, the maintenance technician who had planted the tiny explosive device that knocked the car off its cable was also found dead: of an overdose of narcotics. His papers showed that although he was an employee of Selene's maintenance department, he had recently received a sizeable amount of money from some unknown benefactor. The money was untraceable; apparently he had used it to buy the drugs that killed him.

Rumors quickly bruited through Selene that the money had come from Humphries Space Systems. There was no hint that it had actually been provided by Yamagata Corporation.

HUMPHRIES MANSION

Somebody tried to kill Pancho?" Martin Humphries could barely hide his elation. "You mean there's somebody else who wants that guttersnipe offed?"

Grigor Malenkovich was not smiling. Humphries sometimes wondered if the man knew how to smile. The chief of HSS's security department, Grigor was a lean, silent man with thinning dark hair combed straight back from his forehead, and dark, probing eyes. He said little, and moved like a furtive shadow. He habitually wore suits of slate gray. He could fade into a crowd and remain unnoticed by all except the most discerning eye. Humphries thought of him as the ultimate bureaucrat, functioning quietly, obeying any order without question, as inconspicuous as a mouse, as dangerous as a plague bacillus.

He stood before Humphries's desk, sallow-faced, humorless.

"You are being blamed for the attempt on her life," he said, his voice low and soft as a lullaby.

"Me?"

Grigor nodded wordlessly.

"I didn't order her killed," Humphries snapped. "If you freelanced this—"

"Not me," said Grigor. "Nor anyone in my department."

"Then who?"

Grigor shrugged.

"Find out," Humphries commanded. "I want to know who tried to kill Pancho. Maybe I'll give him a reward."

"This is not funny, sir," Grigor replied. "An order has gone out from Astro Corporation headquarters to arm Astro's vessels in the Belt."

Humphries could feel his cheeks flush with anger. "That damned greasemonkey! She wants a war, does she?"

"Apparently she believes that you want one."

Humphries drummed his fingers on his desktop. "I don't," he said at last. "But if she wants to fight, by god I'll flatten her! No matter what it costs!"

Long after Grigor had left his office, Humphries's phone said in its synthesized voice, "Incoming call from Douglas Stavenger."

Humphries glared at the phone's blinking amber light. "Tell him I'm not available at present. Take his message."

Humphries knew what Stavenger's message would be. He wants to be the peacemaker again, just as he was eight years ago. But not this time, Humphries decided. Pancho wants to go to war, and I'm going to accommodate her. I'll get rid of her and take control of Astro in one swoop.

What was it that German said, he wondered silently, the guy who wrote about war? Then he remembered: War is a continuation of politics by other means.

Other means. Humphries smiled, alone in his office, and told his phone to instruct Grigor to contact that mercenary, Dorik Harbin. He's a one-man Mongol horde, Humphries remembered. A madman, when he's high on drugs. Time to get him onto Pancho's trail.

Amanda kept her eyes closed and her breathing deep and regular. Humphries lay beside her in their sumptuous bedroom, twitching slightly in his sleep. Nightmares again, she thought. He's such a powerful and commanding person all day long, demanding and imperious, but when he sleeps he whimpers like a whipped little boy.

She couldn't hate Martin Humphries. The man was driven by inner demons that he allowed no one to see, not even his wife. He was alone in his torments, and he kept a high wall of separation around the deepset fears that haunted his dreams. Even his sexual excesses were driven by a desperate need to prove himself master of his world. He says he does it to excite me, Amanda told herself, but we both know it's really to control me, to make me obey him, to prove that he's my master.

At least that's ended, she thought. For the time being. He won't do anything that might harm my baby.

If he knew it wasn't his. If he knew this life growing inside me is Lars's son, Martin would kill me and the child both. He mustn't know! He mustn't find out!

It had been simple enough to hack into Humphries's medical records and replace his genetic profile with Lars's. Amanda had done that herself, no accomplices, no chance of anyone revealing to her husband what she had done. To the doctors and medical technicians in Humphries's employ the baby's genetic profile seemed consistent with those of its parents. And it was.

Yet she knew it would be bad enough, once the baby was born. Humphries wanted a perfect child, healthy and intelligent. His six-year-old son was like that: bright, athletic, talented, strong.

The baby Amanda was carrying would not be so.

"It's a rather minor defect," the doctor had told her, after her examination at the Hell medical center. The somber expression on his face said it was worse than minor. "Thank god that the genetic screening revealed it. We can prepare for it and take steps to control his condition."

A minor genetic defect. The baby would be born with a form of chronic anemia. "It can be controlled with proper medication," said the doctor, trying to reassure Amanda. "Or we could replace the defective gene, if you choose to undergo the procedure."

They could operate on the fetus while it's in my womb, Amanda was told. But that would mean a major medical procedure and I'd never be able to keep that secret from Martin. Just getting the genetic screening tests done was difficult enough. If it weren't for Doug Stavenger's help I wouldn't have been able to do it.

"It might be just a random mutation," said the doctor, trying to look optimistic. "Or perhaps there was some chromosomal damage due to the zygote's long immersion in liquid nitrogen. We just don't know enough about the long-term effects of cryogenic temperatures."

It's the drugs, she knew. All those years and all those uppers and aphrodisiacs and designer specials. They must have done the damage, carried to the poor helpless embryo through my bloodstream. My son will pay for my weakness.

So the baby will be born with chronic anemia, Amanda thought. Martin will just have to accept that. He'll be unhappy about it, but he'll have to accept it. As long as he believes it's his son he'll do whatever is necessary for the baby.

The doctor had hesitated and stammered until he finally worked up the courage to suggest, "There's nanotechnology, of course, should you choose to use it. It's banned on Earth, and I couldn't recommend it there. But here on the Moon you might be able to use nanotherapy to correct the baby's faulty gene. And your own."

Amanda thanked him for being so open. But she knew that nano-therapy was impossible for her. Martin would find out about it. Not even Doug Stavenger could keep it a secret if she went to the nanotech lab in Selene. The news that Martin Humphries's wife wanted nano-therapy for her unborn child would flash to Martin's ears with the speed of light. The only nanotechnologist Amanda could trust was Kris Car-denas, and she'd been living in Ceres for years in self-imposed exile from Selene. Now she was on the Saturn mission, going even farther away. No, nanotherapy is out, Amanda swiftly decided. I've got to han-dle this without using nanotech.

I've got to protect my baby, she said to herself as she lay in the dark-ness next to her sleeping, dreaming husband. I've got to protect him from Martin.

Which means I've got to live through the birth. Unconsciously, Amanda clenched her fists. Women don't die in childbirth. That hasn't happened in years, not in a century or more. Not in a modern medical facility. Not even women with weak hearts.

She had known that the years of living in low-gravity environments had taken a toll on her heart. All those years living in Ceres, practically zero gravity. Even here on the Moon it's only one-sixth g. Bad for the heart. Deconditions the muscles. It's so easy to enjoy low g and let your-self go.

Amanda had exercised regularly, mainly to keep her figure. Martin had married a beautiful woman and Amanda worked hard over the years to remain youthfully attractive. But it wasn't enough to strengthen her heart.

"Perhaps you should consider aborting this pregnancy," the doctor had suggested, as tentatively as a man suggesting heresy to a bishop. "Work to get your heart into proper condition and then try to have a baby again."

"No," Amanda had replied softly. "I can't do that."

The doctor had thought she had religious scruples. "I know abortion is a serious issue," he had told her. "But even the Catholics permit it now, as long as it's not simply to terminate an illegitimate pregnancy. I can provide medical justification—"

"Thank you," Amanda had said, "but no. I can't."

"I see." The doctor had sighed like a patient father faced with an intractable child. "All right, then we can use an auxiliary heart pump during the delivery."

It's very simple, he had explained. Standard procedure. A temporary ventricular assist pump, a slim balloon on the end of a catheter is inserted into the femoral artery in the thigh and worked up into the lower aorta. It provides extra cardiovascular pumping power, takes some of the workload off the heart during labor.

Amanda had nodded. When I go for my prenatal checkup at the hospital here in Selene, they'll find out about my heart and make the same recommendation. Martin will know about it but that's perfectly all right. He'll call in the best cardiovascular experts. That's fine, too. As long as no one realizes I've switched Martin's genetic profile for Lars's. That's what I've got to avoid. Martin thinks his genes are perfect. He's got a six-year-old son to prove it.

We've already done a genetic screen on me, of course. I passed that test. It's just the baby, my poor helpless little baby, that has a problem.

I've got to make certain that Martin doesn't know. He mustn't find out.

Amanda lay in her bed for hours while Humphries thrashed and moaned in his sleep next to her. She stared at the darkened ceiling, watched the digital clock count the minutes and hours. At last, well after four A.M., still wide awake, she sat up and softly slipped out of bed. On bare feet she tiptoed across the thick carpeting past the lavatory, into the walk-in closet that was lined with the finest clothes money could buy. Only after she had gently closed the closet door did she grope for the light switch on the wall. Months earlier she had disconnected the sensor that automatically turned on the overhead lights. Squinting in the sudden brightness, she stepped deeper into the closet, ignoring the gowns and frocks and slacks and precious blouses. She went to one of the leather handbags hanging in the rear of the closet and, after rummaging in it for a few moments, came out with a handful of soft blue gelatin capsules.

Tranquilizers, Amanda told herself. They're nothing more than good, strong tranquilizers. I need them, if I want to get any sleep at all. She stared at the capsules in her palm; her hand was shaking so hard she feared she would drop them. She closed her fingers around them. They won't hurt the baby. They can't, that's what the chemist told me. And I need them. I need them badly.

ASTEROID VESTA

orik Harbin hid the discomfort he felt from all the others, but he could not hide it from himself. A man who preferred solitude, a lone wolf who tracked his prey silently, without help, he now was in command of nearly five hundred men and women, mercenaries hired by Humphries for the coming assault against Astro Corporation.

Most of them were engineers and technicians, not warriors. They were building a base on Vesta, burrowing deep into the asteroid's rocky body, tunneling out hardened silos to hold missiles that could blast approaching ships out of the sky. Harbin remembered HSS's first attempt to build a base on Vesta's surface. Fuchs had wiped it out with a single blow, dropping a freighter's load of asteroidal ores that smashed buildings and people in a deadly avalanche of falling rocks.

So now we dig, Harbin said to himself as he glided down one of the dusty tunnels toward the smoothed-out cave that would be his headquarters. He wore a real uniform now, complete with epaulets on his shoulders and an uncomfortable high choke of a collar. And insignias of rank. Harbin was a colonel now, with four-pointed stars at his throat and cuffs to show it. The emblems disturbed Harbin. They reminded him of crosses. He'd seen too many crosses over the years, in churches and more often in cemeteries.

Humphries paid someone to design these stupid uniforms, he knew. He also knew that a man's ability to command comes from what is in his head and in his guts, not from fancy uniforms and polished boots.

But Humphries pays the bills, Grigor constantly reminded him. And Humphries is in a sweat to complete this base and begin the assault that will wipe Astro out of the Belt.

But Fuchs is still out there, somewhere, hiding himself deep in the dark emptiness of the Belt. It's a mistake to stop hunting him, Harbin thought. Humphries thinks that once he's eliminated Astro, Fuchs will fall into his lap easily enough. But I wonder. The man is wily, tough, a survivor. He's dangerous, too dangerous to be permitted to live.

Despite its being the third-largest of all the asteroids, Vesta is still only slightly more than five hundred kilometers across. Its gravity is minuscule. Harbin and all the others working inside the tunnels and caves had to wear uncomfortable breathing masks and goggles clamped to their faces constantly because every step they took stirred up fine powdery dust that hung in the air endlessly, floating in the infinitesimal gravity like an eternal, everlasting mist. Still, the people he passed as he glided along the tunnel all snapped salutes at the stars on his uniform. Harbin dutifully returned each salute even though he loathed the necessity.

At least his office was clean. It was a small chamber carved by plasma torches out of the metallic rock and then sprayed with thick layers of plastic to hold down the dust. With the air blowers working, Harbin could take off his goggled mask and breathe normally once the door to the tunnel outside was shut.

The office was little more than a bare cubicle containing a desk and a few chairs. No decorations on the walls. Nothing to remind Harbin of his past. Even the desk drawers were mostly empty, except for the locked one that contained his medications. He slumped tiredly onto his desk chair and commanded his computer to display the day's incoming messages. I shouldn't be sitting behind a desk, he told himself. I should be in a ship, tracking down Fuchs. It's a mistake to let him live.

Then he smiled bitterly at himself. Not that I've been so successful at getting him. Fuchs is a wily old badger, Harbin admitted to himself. Almost, he admired the man.

The list of incoming messages took form in the air above Harbin's desk. Most of them were routine, but there was one from Grigor, Harbin's direct superior in the HSS chain of command, the only man between him and Martin Humphries himself.

Harbin told the computer to display Grigor's message.

Grigor's gloomy image appeared immediately. He was seated at his own desk. It was as if Harbin were looking into the man's office. To his surprise, the dour, cold-eyed chief of HSS security was actually smiling; it looked as if it pained him to stretch his thin lips that way.

"I have good news for you, Dorik," said Grigor, almost jovially. "A dozen attack ships are on their way to you, plus supply and logistics vessels. They are not sailing together, of course. That would attract unwelcome attention from Astro and even from the International Astronautical Authority. But they will start arriving at your base within the week. A detailed schedule of their courses, cargoes and arrival times are attached to this message."

Harbin stopped Grigor's message and checked the attachment. Impressive. Within two weeks he would have a small armada of warships, ready to ravage the Belt.

He turned Grigor back on. "From the reports you've been sending, I can see that the base will be fully operational within three weeks or less. Mr. Humphries wants to make absolutely certain that the base is protected properly. He wants to take no chances that Fuchs or anyone else will attack it before it is completed. Therefore, you are to use the attack vessels as a defensive screen around Vesta. Keep them in orbit around the asteroid and keep them on high alert, prepared to intercept any unauthorized vessel. Is that clear?"

The question was rhetorical, of course. Harbin wouldn't be able to get a reply to Grigor at Selene for a half-hour or more.

"One final order," Grigor went on, without waiting for a reply. "Once the entire battle fleet has been assembled, you will hold it in readiness until an attack plan is sent to you through me. Mr. Humphries wants no moves made until he has approved a complete campaign plan."

Then Grigor smiled again, obviously forced. "Of course, we will expect your inputs for the plan. We won't finalize it until you have made your contribution."

The image winked off and Harbin was staring at the empty chairs in front of his desk once again.

"A plan of campaign," he muttered to himself. Humphries thinks he's a field marshal now, planning battle strategy. Harbin groaned inwardly. He's amassing all these weapons, all these people, and he's sitting back in the safety of that underground mansion of his, playing armchair general. I'll have to follow his orders, no matter how stupid they might be.

Harbin scrupulously avoided sexual liaisons with any of the people under his command. A commander doesn't take advantage of his troops, he told himself sternly. Besides, he had medications and virtual reality simulations that satisfied his needs, in part. In some ways they were better than sex; he didn't have to deal with a real, living person. Better to be alone, he told himself. Better to avoid entanglements.

Yet there was one slim young woman among the engineering staff who attracted him. She looked almost Asian, but not quite: tall, willowy, soft of speech, her skin smooth and the color of burnt gold, with high sculpted cheekbones and almond eyes that he caught, several times, watching him through lowered lashes.

She reminded him of someone, someone he had taken months of rehabilitation treatments to forget. Someone who haunted the edges of his dreams, a woman that not even his drugs could erase completely from his memory. A woman who had claimed to love him, a woman who had betrayed him. A woman he had murdered, ripping the lying tongue out of her throat with his bare hands.

Harbin woke nights sobbing over her. And now this Eurasian engineer watched him furtively when they were in the same room together, smiled at him seductively when he caught her staring at him.

Harbin tried to ignore her, but he couldn't. Over the weeks and months of building the base, he could not avoid her. And every time he saw her, she smiled and watched him in silence, as if waiting for him to smile back at her, to speak to her, to ask her what her name was or where she was born or why she was here on this godforsaken outpost in the depths of nothingness.

Instead of speaking to her, Harbin brought up her personnel dossier on his office computer. Her name was Leeza Chaptal, born in Selene, her father a French medical doctor, her mother a Japanese-American biologist. She herself was a life-support engineer, and had a year-to-year contract with Humphries Space Systems. She had not volunteered for this job at Vesta; she had been faced with accepting the position or being fired for breach of contract.

She's not happy here, Harbin thought, scanning her dossier. Yet she seems pleasant enough. Her supervisor rates her work highly, he saw.

It wasn't until his phone buzzed that Harbin realized he'd been staring at her dossier photograph for more than fifteen minutes.

HUMPHRIES'S DREAMS

He was a child again, being led by the hand through the majestic marble-walled building where people stood in quiet little groups gazing at the pictures on the walls and speaking in hushed murmurs. The paintings meant nothing to him, nor did the names that his tutor whispered to him: da Vinci, Raphael, Degas, Renoir. Then he saw the picture of the beautiful sailboats gliding across a calm blue sea beneath the summer sun. When he refused to leave it, his tutor sniffed, "Monet. Quite overly popular."

Suddenly it was Christmas, and instead of the painting he wanted, his father presented him with a new computer. When he started to cry with disappointment, his father loomed over him and said sternly, "You can look at all the paintings you want through the web."

And then he was on the boat, the trimaran, and the storm was coming up fast and the boat was heaving wickedly in the monstrous waves and one of the waves broke over the bow and swept him off his feet. He felt the numbing cold water clutching at him, dragging him under, while his father watched from the tossing deck, his arms folded sternly across his chest, his face set in a scowl of disappointment. He doesn't care if I drown! young Martin realized as he thrashed helplessly in the icy water. He doesn't care if I live or die.

"That was foolish of you, Marty," his father growled at him after a crewman had fished him out of the ocean. "Nine years old and you still don't have the brains that god gave to a rabbit."

Martin Humphries, aged nine, dripping wet and shivering with cold, understood from that moment onward that he had no one on Earth to protect him, no one to help him, no one that could ever love him. Not even his mother, drunk most of the time, gave a damn about him. He was alone, except for what and who he could buy.

"This is a dream," he told himself. "This all happened long ago.

Mother's been dead for ages and father died years ago. It's all over. He can't humiliate you anymore."

But others could. He saw himself at the board meeting of the Astro Corporation, everyone seated at the long table staring at him.

Sitting at the head of the table in the chairman's seat to which she'd just been elected, Pancho Lane was pointing her accusing finger at him.

"How long are we going to allow the head of our biggest rival to sit on our board of directors?" she demanded. "How long are we going to let Judas sit among us? All he wants is to take control of Astro Corporation, and he'll keep on screwing us every chance he gets, if we don't get rid of him here and now."

The vote was close, but not close enough.

"That's it, then," said Pancho, barely able to conceal the satisfied smirk that played at the corners of her lips. "Martin, you've been kicked off this board. And high time, too."

He saw how white his face was, how his hands trembled no matter how hard he struggled to control them. The others tried to hide their emotions, but he could see they were secretly laughing at him. All of them, even the ones he had thought were on his side.

Feeling cold sweat beading his forehead, his upper lip, he rose shakily to his feet, the blood thundering in his ears, his mind pulsing with ringing, defiant declarations.

But all he could manage to choke out was, "You haven't seen the last of me."

As he stumbled out of the richly carpeted boardroom he could hear muffled laughter behind his back. I'll get them, he swore to himself. Each and every one of them. Especially Pancho, that guttersnipe. I'll get her if it takes every penny, every ounce of sweat, every drop of blood that I've got. I'll get her. I'll see her dead. I'll dance on her grave.

HABITAT *CHRYSALIS*

ig George was at the airlock to greet her when Pancho left her private torch ship *Starpower III* and stepped aboard the rock rats' habitat in orbit about Ceres.

"Welcome to our humble home," George said, with an exaggerated flourish.

Pancho grinned at him. "Good to be here, Georgie. Gonna give me the ten-dollar tour?"

"Sure will."

George led her almost halfway through the rotating complex of connected spacecraft bodies. Pancho enjoyed teasing George about how the habitat looked like a floating junkyard, but once inside the linked vessels she had to admit that the habitat was clean, comfortable, and even attractive. Each interconnected craft was painted in a distinctive color scheme, mostly restful pastels, although there were some bolder, brighter hues here and there, and striking designs decorating some of the bulkheads. The place smelled new, fresh, a far cry from the dust-choked caves and tunnels of Ceres.

As they stepped through the hatches from one spacecraft to another, George proudly showed Pancho the living quarters, common rooms, laboratories, workshops, warehouses and business offices that made up the growing complex.

"Got nearly a thousand people livin' here now," he declared, "with more comin' every week."

"I'm impressed," Pancho said. "I really am. You guys've done a terrific job."

George smiled boyishly behind his thick red beard.

The tour ended at a closed metal door marked NANOTECH LAB. Pancho felt a pang of hopeful surprise.

"Don't tell me Kris is back!"

"Nah," George replied, tapping out the combination on the door's security keypad. "Dr. Cardenas is still off on the Saturn expedition."

As he pushed the door open he added, "But she's not the only nano-tech genius in the world, y'know. We've got a few of our own, right here."

The nanotechnology lab was eerily quiet. Pancho saw gleaming cabinets of white and stainless steel lining the walls, and a double row of workbenches that held more metal boxes and instruments. She recognized the gray metal tubing of a scanning field micro-scope off in one corner, but the rest of the equipment was unfamil-iar to her.

"Is anybody working here?" she asked. The lab seemed empty of people, except for the two of them.

"Should be," George said, frowning slightly. "I told 'im we'd be here."

"Excuse me," said a soft voice behind them.

Pancho turned to see an overweight young man with dark hair tied back in a ponytail, a neatly trimmed beard, and a slightly bemused ex-pression on his roundish face. His thick dark brows were raised, as if he were puzzled. His lips were curled slightly into a half smile that seemed apologetic, defensive. He was wearing plain gray coveralls, but had a bright plaid vest over them. No tattoos or jewelry, except for a heavy square gold ring on his right hand.

"I had to take a break," he said in a gentle, almost feminine voice. "I'm sorry I wasn't here when you came in."

George clapped him on the shoulder lightly, but it was enough to make the young man totter. "That's okay, Lev. When you gotta go, you gotta go."

He introduced Pancho to Levi Levinson, then added, "Lev here's from MIT. Brightest lad we've got. Boy genius and all that."

Levinson didn't seem at all embarrassed by George's praise. "I learned a lot from Dr. Cardenas before she left."

"Such as?" Pancho challenged.

Levinson's smile turned slightly superior. "I'll show you. I've got a demonstration all set up." He gestured toward the nearer of the two workbenches.

George dragged over a couple of high stools and offered one to Pancho as he explained, "I was after Kris for years to figure out how we could use nanomachines to separate metals from the ores in the asteroids. Lev here thinks he's solved the problem."

Pancho felt impressed. Turning to Levinson, she asked, "Have you?"

He looked quietly confident, almost smug. All he said was, "Watch."

Pancho watched. Levinson took a dark, lumpy, potato-sized chunk of a metallic asteroid and deposited it into one of the big metal cubicles on the workbench. Half a dozen transparent plastic tubes led from the container to smaller bins farther down the bench. Pancho saw that a digital timer started counting seconds when Levinson clicked the lid closed.

"It's not much of a trick to program nanomachines to separate a specific element from a gross sample," he said. "Nanos are quite capable of taking specific atoms from a sample of material. It's just a matter of programming them properly."

"Uh-huh," said Pancho.

"The problem's always been to separate *all* the different elements in a 'roid simultaneously, without the nanos interfering with one another."

"And in a high-UV environment," George added.

Levinson shrugged his rounded shoulders. "That part was easy. Just harden the nanos so UV won't dissociate them."

Pointing to the sealed container, Pancho asked, "You mean these nanomachines won't be knocked out by ultraviolet light?"

"That's why I keep them sealed inside the container," Levinson answered. "If they got loose they'd start taking the habitat apart, atom by atom."

"Jeeps," Pancho muttered.

"It's perfectly safe," Levinson calmly assured her. "The container is lined with diamond surfaces and none of the nanos are programmed to separate carbon."

"So they can't attack people," George said.

Levinson nodded, but Pancho thought that people also contain iron, phosphorus and a lot of other elements that those nanomachines were programmed to separate. Maybe that's why Kris dragged her feet on this project, she thought.

A bell pinged. An electric motor whirred. Pancho saw little trickles of what looked like dirt or dust sliding down the six transparent tubes toward the bins on the workbench. As she looked closer, though, several of the growing piles seemed to glitter in the light from the overhead lamps.

"The transport tubes are also pure diamond," Levinson said. "Just a precaution, in case a few of the nanomachines are still present in the differentiated samples."

Pancho nodded wordlessly.

Levinson applied a handheld mass spectrometer to each of the piles of dirt, in turn. Pure iron, pure nickel, gold, silver, platinum and lead.

With a wave of one hand, he said, "Voila!"

George clapped his beefy hands together. "Y'see, Pancho? With nanomachines we can mine the metals outta the 'roids easy as pie. All the slugwork gets done by the nanos. All the miners hafta do is sit back and let the little buggers do all the fookin' work!"

"It can be done for minerals, too," Levinson said, in an offhand manner. "Easier, in fact. The nanos work at the molecular level there, rather than atomic."

Pancho looked at each of them in turn. She stood up and planted her hands on her hips. "Fine work," she said. "Only one problem I can see."

"What's that?"

"This'll knock the price of metals and minerals down pretty close to zero."

"Huh?" George grunted.

"You're gonna make it so easy to mine the asteroids that we'll get a glut on the market," Pancho said. "And most of the miners will be thrown out of work, to boot."

George frowned. "I didn't think of that. I was just tryin' t'make their work easier."

"Too easy," said Pancho.

Levinson looked completely unconcerned. "New technology always brings some economic dislocations. But think of the benefits of cheaper raw materials."

"Yeah, sure," said Pancho. Then it hit her with the force of a body blow. "Holy cripes! Once Humphries finds out about this there's gonna be hell to pay!"

"Whattaya mean?" George asked.

"Once this nanotechnology starts being used, there won't be room for two competing companies in the Belt. The only way to make economic sense out of this is for one company to run the whole damned Belt, keep production of raw materials under control and set prices for the buyers. *That's* what he's after!"

"But Humphries doesn't know anything about this," George said.

"Wanna bet?" Pancho snapped.

HUMPHRIES MANSION

t really works?" Humphries asked. "They've done it?"

"It really works," said Victoria Ferrer, his latest administrative assistant. "Their top nanotech expert, this man Levinson, demonstrated it to Ms. Lane two days ago. She's on her way back here with him now."

Ferrer was a small, light-boned young woman with large, limpid eyes, full sensuous lips and lovely large breasts. When he had first interviewed her for the job, Humphries had wondered if her breasts were siliconed. They seemed oversized for the rest of her. Soon enough he found that they were natural, although enhanced by a genetic modification that Victoria's stagestruck mother had insisted upon when she was pushing her teenaged daughter into a career in show business. Young Vickie went to university instead, and earned honors in economics and finance. Eventually Humphries learned that, as good as Victoria was in bed, she was even better in the office. Ferrer's best asset, he eventually realized, was her brain. But that didn't prevent Humphries from bedding her now and then.

At the moment, though, she was bringing him disturbing news about the nanotechnology work going on at the rock rats' habitat in the Belt.

"That tears it," he said thoughtfully, leaning back in his self-adjusting desk chair. "I should have seen it coming. It's going to knock the bottom out of the market for asteroidal commodities."

"Not necessarily," said Ferrer. She was seated in the plush chair in front of his desk, looking very trim and businesslike in a tailored off-white blouse and charcoal gray slacks.

His brows knitting, Humphries said, "Don't you see? Once they start using nanomachines to get pure metals out of the asteroids, the price for those metals will sink out of sight. Minerals, too. Same thing. The major price factor will be the cost of transportation."

"Only if the rock rats actually use nanos," Ferrer countered.

Humphries sat up a little straighter. "You think they won't?"

With a slight smile, she replied, "I think Ambrose is smart enough to realize that nanomachines could throw most of the miners out of work. I think he'll suppress the idea."

"Buy off the scientist? What's his name, this kid from MIT."

"Levinson," said Ferrer. "I doubt that he can be bought off. He's the kind who'll want the whole world to know how brilliant he is. But Ambrose and the rest of the governing council at Ceres could easily claim that nanomachines are too dangerous to use on the asteroids."

"That sounds farfetched."

She shook her head, just slightly, but enough to let Humphries see that she thought he was wrong. "To operate on the asteroids the nanos would have to be hardened against ultraviolet light. That means the main safety feature that Cardenas built into the nanos years ago would be disabled. Ambrose could argue that the nanos are too dangerous to use."

"And let the rock rats keep on operating the way they have been since the beginning."

"Exactly."

Humphries drummed his fingers on the desktop. "That would avoid a collapse of the market."

"Which is to the rock rats' best interests."

"Sort of like the Luddites smashing the steam-powered looms, back at the beginning of the first industrial revolution."

Ferrer looked puzzled for a moment, and Humphries smiled inwardly. Score one for the boss, he said to himself. I know more than you do.

Aloud, he asked, "You really think Ambrose and the others will suppress this?"

"My information is that he and Ms. Lane have already discussed it. I'm sure he will."

"And use safety precautions as the excuse."

"It's a very good excuse."

Humphries glanced up at the ceiling's smooth cream-colored expanse, then at the holowindow on the far wall that displayed a view of Mount Kilimanjaro when it still had snow on its summit.

"Doesn't matter," he said at last. "In the long run, this development of nanotech mining will be the last straw. I've got to get control of Astro *now*, before that greasemonkey Pancho realizes she can use the nanomachines to undercut my prices and—"

"But if Astro starts using nanomachines for mining the asteroids," Ferrer interrupted, "we could do the same."

"Yeah, and drive the price for asteroidal commodities down to nothing, or close to it," Humphries snapped. "No, I've got to get Astro into my hands now, no more delays or hesitations. Once I've got Astro we can use nanomachines to drive down the cost of mining, but we'll have a monopoly in the damned Belt so we can fix the selling prices!"

Ferrer started to nod, then thought better of it. "What about this new company, Nairobi Industries?"

"They don't have anything going in the Belt."

"They might move that way, eventually."

Humphries made a snorting, dismissive laugh. "By the time they get their base built here on the Moon and start thinking about expanding to the Belt, I'll have the whole thing in my hands. They'll be shut out before they even start."

She looked dubious, but said nothing.

Humphries smacked his hands together. "Okay! The gloves come off. All the preparations are in place. We knock Astro out of the Belt once and for all."

Ferrer still looked less than enthusiastic. She rose from her chair and started for the door.

Before she got halfway across the office, though, Humphries said, "Tell Grigor I want to see him. In half an hour. No, make it a full hour."

And he crooked his finger at her. Dutifully, she turned around and headed back to him.

TORCH SHIP *STARPOWER III*

Like most torch ships, *Starpower III* was built like a dumbbell, bulbous propellant tanks on one end of a kilometer-long buckyball tether, habitation module on the other, with the fusion rocket engine in the center. The ship spun lazily on the ends of the long tether, producing a feeling of gravity for the crew and passengers.

Pancho's quarters aboard her personal torch ship were comfortable, not sumptuous. The habitation module included the crew's quarters, the bridge, work spaces and storage areas, as well as Pancho's private quarters plus two more compartments for guests.

Pancho was afraid that her lone guest on this trip from Ceres to Selene would become obstreperous. Levi Levinson was flattered almost out of his mind when Pancho told him she wanted to bring him to Selene to meet the top scientists there. "Two of 'em are on the Nobel committee," Pancho had said, with complete truthfulness and a good deal of artful suggestion.

Levinson had immediately packed a travel bag and accompanied her to the torch ship.

Now, though, as they approached Selene, Pancho broke the unpleasant news to him. She invited him to dinner in her private quarters and watched with secret amusement as he goggled at the array of food spread on the table between them by the ship's two galley servers.

"You've made a terrific scientific breakthrough," she told Levinson, once the servers had left. "But I'm not sure the rock rats are gonna take advantage of it."

Levinson's normal expression reminded Pancho of a deer caught in an automobile's headlights. Now his brows shot even higher than usual.

"Not take advantage of it?" he asked, a spoonful of soup trembling halfway between the bowl and his mouth. "What do you mean?"

Pancho had spent most of the day talking with Big George via a tight-beam laser link. George had hammered it out with the rock rats' governing council. They were dead-set against using *anything* that would drop the prices of the ores they mined.

"Fookin' prices are low enough," George had growled. "We'll all go broke if they drop much more."

Now Pancho looked into Levinson's questioning eyes and decided to avoid the truth. The kid's worked his butt off to make this breakthrough, she told herself, and now you've got to tell him it was all for nothing.

"It's the safety problem," she temporized. "The rock rats are worried about using nanos that can't be disabled by ultraviolet light."

Levinson blinked, slurped his soup, then put the spoon back into the bowl. "I suppose some other safety features could be built into the system," he said.

"You think so?"

"Trouble is, the nanos have to work in a high radiation environment. They've got to be hardened."

"And that makes them dangerous," said Pancho.

"Not really."

"The miners think so."

Levinson took a deep, distressed breath. "But if they handle the nanos properly there shouldn't be any problems."

Pancho smiled at him like a mother. "Lev, they're miners. Rock rats. Sure, most of 'em have technical degrees, but they're not scientists like you."

"I could work out protocols for them," he mumbled, half to himself. "Safety procedures for them to follow."

"Maybe you could," Pancho said vaguely.

He stared down into his soup bowl for several moments, then looked back up at her. "Does this mean I can't publish my work?"

"Publish?"

"In *The Journal of Nanotechnology*. It's published in Selene and I thought I'd meet the editors while I'm there."

Pancho thought it over for all of a half-second. A scientific journal. Maybe a hundred people in the whole solar system read it. But one of them will bring the news to Humphries, she was sure. Hell, she said to herself, the Hump prob'ly knows about it already. Not much goes on anywhere that he doesn't know about.

"Sure you can publish it," she said easily. "No problem."

Levinson broke into a boyish smile. "Oh, that's okay then. As long as I can publish and get credit for my work, I don't care what the stupid rock rats do."

Pancho stared at him, struggling to hide her feelings. Like so many scientists, this kid's an elitist. She felt enormously relieved.

Dorik Harbin knew all about addiction. He'd started taking narcotics when he was a teenager, still in his native Balkan village. The elders fed a rough form of hashish to the kids when they sent the youths out on missions of ethnic cleansing. As he progressed up the ladder of organized murder and rape, his need for drugs became deeper, more demanding. As a mercenary in the employ of Humphries Space Systems he had been detoxed several times, only to fall back into his habit time and again. Ironically, HSS medics supplied the medications as part of the corporation's "incentive program."

Their meds were much better, too: designer drugs, tailored for specific needs. Drugs to help you stay awake and alert through long days and weeks of cruising alone through the Belt, seeking ships to destroy. Drugs to enhance your battle prowess, to make you fiercer, angrier, bloodier than any normal human being could be. Most of all, Harbin needed drugs to help him forget, to blot out the images of helpless men and women screaming for mercy as they floated into space from their broken spacecraft to drift in their survival pods or even alone in their spacesuits, drift like flailing, begging, terrified dust motes until at last death quieted their beseeching voices and they wafted through space in eternal silence.

A lesser man would have been driven to madness by the hopelessness of it all. Humphries's medical specialists took pains to detoxify Harbin's body, to purge his blood stream of the lingering molecules of narcotics. Then other Humphries specialists fed him new medications, to help him do the killings that the corporation paid him to do. Harbin smiled grimly at the irony and remembered Kayyam's words:

> And much as Wine has play'd the Infidel,
> And robb'd me of my Robe of Honor—well,
> I often wonder what the Vintners buy
> One half so precious as the Goods they sell.

No matter which of the laboratory-designed drugs he took, though, nor how much, they could not erase his dreams, could never blot out the memories that made his sleep an endless torture of punishment. He saw their faces, the faces of all those he had killed over the years, distorted with pain and terror and the sudden realization that their lives were finished, without mercy, without hope of rescue or reprieve or even delay. He heard their screams, every time he slept.

The revenge of the weak against the strong, he told himself. But he dreaded sleep, dreaded the begging, pleading chorus of men and women and babies.

Yes, Harbin knew about addiction. He had allowed himself to become addicted to a woman once, and she had betrayed him. So he had to kill her. He had trusted her, let his guard down and allowed her to reach his innermost soul. He had even dared to dream of a different life, an existence of peace and gentleness, of loving and being loved. And she had betrayed him. When he ripped the lying tongue out of her mouth, she was carrying another man's baby.

He swore never to repeat that mistake. Never to allow a woman to get that close to him. Never. Women were for pleasure, just as some drugs were. Nothing more.

Yet Leeza intrigued him. She went to bed with Harbin easily enough; she even seemed flattered that the commander of the growing base on Vesta took enough notice of her to bring her to his bed. She was compliant, amiable, and energetic in her lovemaking.

Don't get involved with her! Harbin warned himself sternly. Yet, as the weeks slipped by in the dull, cramped underground warrens of Vesta, he found himself spending more and more time with her. She could make him forget the past, at least for the duration of a pleasant dinner together. She could make time disappear entirely when they made love. She could even make Harbin laugh.

Still he refused to allow her into his private thoughts. He refused to hope about the future, refused even to think about any future at all except completing this military base on Vesta and following Martin Humphries's command to hunt down Lars Fuchs and kill him.

But the new orders superseded the old. Grigor told him that Humphries wanted an all-out attack on Astro Corporation ships.

"Forget Fuchs for the moment," Grigor's prerecorded message said. "There are bigger plans in the works."

Harbin knew he was becoming addicted to Leeza when he told her how dissatisfied he was with the new orders.

She lay in bed beside him, her tousled head on his bare shoulder, the only light in the room coming from the glow of starlight from the wallscreen that displayed the camera view of deep space from the surface of Vesta.

"Humphries is preparing to go to war against Astro?" Leeza asked, her voice soft as silk in the starlit darkness.

Knowing he shouldn't be revealing so much to her, Harbin said merely, "It looks that way."

"Won't that be dangerous for you?"

It was difficult to shrug with her head on his shoulder. "I get paid for taking risks."

She was silent for several heartbeats. Then, "You could get paid much more."

"Oh? How?"

"Yamagata Corporation would equal your salary from HSS," she said.

"Yamagata?"

With a slight, mischievous giggle, Leeza added, "And you could still be drawing your pay from Humphries, at the same time."

He turned toward her, brows knitting. "What are you talking about?"

"Yamagata wants to hire you, Dorik."

"How do you know?"

"Because I work for them."

"For Yamagata?"

Her voice became almost impish. "I do the job I was hired to do for Humphries and draw my HSS salary for it. I report on what's happening here to Yamagata, and they pay me the same amount that HSS does. Isn't that neat?"

"It's treason," Harbin snapped.

She raised herself on one elbow. "Treason? To a corporation? Don't be silly."

"It's not right."

"Loyalty to a corporation is a one-way street, Dorik. Humphries can fire you whenever he chooses to. There's nothing wrong with feathering your own nest when you have the opportunity."

"Why is Yamagata so interested in me?"

"They want to know what Humphries is doing. I'm too low in the organization to give them the whole picture. You're the source they need."

Harbin leaned back on his pillow, his thoughts spinning.

"You don't have to do anything against HSS," Leeza urged. "All Yamagata wants is information."

For now, Harbin added silently. Then he smiled in the darkness. She's just like all the others. A traitor. He almost felt relieved that he didn't have to build an emotional attachment to her.

SEVEN MONTHS LATER

How is she?" Martin Humphries asked, his voice tight with a mixture of anticipation and apprehension.

The holographic image of the obstetrician sitting calmly on a chair in front of Humphries's desk looked relaxed, unruffled.

"It's going to take another hour or so, Mr. Humphries," she said. "Perhaps longer. The baby will arrive when he's good and ready to enter the world."

Humphries drummed his fingers on the desktop. First the brat is three weeks premature and now he's taking his time about being born.

"There's nothing to do but wait," the doctor warned. "Mrs. Humphries is pretty heavily sedated."

"Sedated?" Humphries was instantly alarmed. "Why? By whose order? I wanted a natural childbirth. I told you —"

"Sir, she was sedated when your people wheeled her in here."

"That's impossible!"

The obstetrician shrugged inside her loose-fitting green surgical gown. "I was surprised, too."

"I'm coming over," Humphries snapped.

He clicked off the phone connection before the obstetrician could reply and pushed himself up from his desk chair. He had set up the birthing facility for Amanda down the hall from his office. He had no desire to be present during the mess and blood and pain of childbirth, but the obstetrician's claim that Amanda was heavily sedated alarmed him. She was supposed to be off all the drugs. She promised me, Humphries reminded himself, anger rising inside him. She promised me to stay clean while she was carrying my son.

Humphries raced down the short corridor between his office and the birthing facility.

She's been doing drugs again, he realized. I've had her detoxed three—no, four times, and she went right back onto them, pregnant or not. She doesn't give a damn about my son, about me. Her and her damned habit. If she's harmed my son I'll kill her.

In his frenzy he forgot that Amanda was the only woman he had ever loved. After two earlier wives and no one knew how many other women, he had fallen truly in love with Amanda. But she never loved him. He knew that. She loved that bastard Fuchs, probably still does, he thought. She's just having this baby to placate me. Fury boiling in him, he swore that if his son wasn't perfect he'd have it terminated before it left the birthing room.

And her with it, Humphries snarled inwardly.

He banged through the door of the birthing facility, startling the green-gowned nurse sitting in the anteroom, her mask pulled down from her face, calmly reading from a palmcomp screen, a cup of coffee in her other hand.

The woman jumped to her feet, sloshing coffee onto the carpeted floor. "Mr. Humphries!"

He strode past her.

"I wouldn't go in there, sir. There's nothing—"

Humphries ignored her and pushed through the door to the birthing room. Amanda lay on the bed, unconscious or asleep, soaked with perspiration, pale as death. Three women in green surgical gowns and masks stood to one side of the bed. Humphries saw that Amanda wore not a trace of makeup. Her china-blue eyes were closed, her lustrous blonde hair matted with sweat. And still she looked so beautiful, so vulnerable, like a golden princess from a fairy tale. His anger melted.

One of the women came up before him, burly, square-shouldered, blocking his view of his wife. "You're not gowned!" she hissed from behind her mask.

Fuming, Humphries went out to the anteroom and demanded that the nurse out there find him a surgical gown and mask. In less than five minutes he was dressed, with plastic booties over his shoes, a mask, gloves, and a ridiculous cap pulled down over his ears.

He went back into the birthing room. It was ominously quiet. Amanda had not moved. The only sound in the room was the slow clicking of one of the monitors clustered around the head of the bed. Humphries stared at the machines. The clicking seemed to be coming from the heart monitor, counting off Amanda's heartbeats. It sounded terribly slow.

"Well," he whispered to the obstetrician, "how is she doing?"

The woman drew in a breath, then replied, "There are some complications."

"Complications?"

"Her heart. The strain of labor has placed an unusually severe workload on her heart."

"Her heart?" Humphries snapped. Pointing a finger like a pistol at the cardiologist, he demanded, "What about the auxiliary pump?"

"It's doing its job," the cardiologist said firmly. "But there's a limit to how much workload it can carry."

"Will she be all right? Will she get through this all right?"

The obstetrician looked away from him.

He grabbed her shoulder. "My son. Is he all right?"

She looked back at him, but her eyes wavered. "The baby will be fine, Mr. Humphries. Once we get him out of his mother."

Humphries suddenly understood. *She's going to die. Amanda's going to die! The only woman I've ever loved in my whole life is going to die giving birth to my son.*

His knees gave way. He almost collapsed, but the same burly medic who had pushed him out of the room now grasped his arm in a powerful grip and held him on his feet.

"We're doing everything we can," the obstetrician said as the medic walked Humphries through the door and deposited him on a chair in the anteroom. The nurse out there sprang to her feet again.

Humphries slumped down onto the chair, barely hearing the whispered words between the nurse and medic. The nurse put a cup of steaming coffee in his hand. He ostentatiously poured it onto the carpeting. She looked surprised, then backed away and remained standing by the door to the birthing room. Humphries sat there, his thoughts darker and darker with each passing moment.

Fuchs. He's the cause of all this. This is all his fault. She still loves him. She's only having this baby to keep me happy, to save his putrid ass. Well, if she dies then all my promises are finished. I'll find that sonofabitch and kill him. I'll get Harbin and every ship I've got out there in the Belt to hunt him down and kill him. I don't care if it takes a thousand ships, I'll see him dead. I'll have him skinned alive. I'll have his balls roasted over a slow fire. I'll —

The squall of a baby's first cry stopped his litany of rage.

Humphries shot to his feet. The nurse was still standing in front of the door.

Which opened slowly. The obstetrician came out, pulling the mask off her face. She looked tired.

"My son?" Humphries demanded.

"The boy's fine," said the woman, unsmiling. "We'll run him through the usual tests in a day or so, but he appears to be normal. A little scrawny, but that's not unusual for a preemie."

Scrawny, Humphries thought. But he'll be all right. He'll grow. He'll be a healthy son.

"Your wife . . ." the obstetrician murmured.

"Is she all right?"

The doctor shook her head slowly.

"Amanda?"

"I'm afraid she didn't make it, sir. Her heart stopped and we couldn't revive her."

Humphries gaped at the woman. "She's dead? Amanda's dead?"

"I'm very sorry, Mr. Humphries," the obstetrician said, her eyes avoiding his. "We did everything that's humanly possible."

"He killed her," Humphries muttered. "The bastard killed her."

"It's not the baby's fault," said the obstetrician, looking alarmed.

"He killed her," Humphries repeated.

HABITAT *CHRYSALIS*

ancho dropped everything and flew on a full-g burn to Ceres, completing the trip from Selene in slightly less than thirty hours.

As her torch ship made rendezvous with the orbiting habitat and docked at one of its airlocks, it felt good to Pancho to get back down to one-sixth gravity. Been living in lunar grav so long it feels normal to me, she thought as she strode through the central passageway of the interlinked spacecraft bodies, heading for Big George's quarters.

When he'd first been elected chief administrator for the rock rats, George had insisted that he would not establish a fancy office nor hire any unnecessary staff personnel. Over the years he had stuck to that promise—in a manner of speaking. His office was still in his quarters, but George's quarters had expanded gradually, steadily, until now they spanned the entire length of one of the spacecraft modules that composed *Chrysalis*.

"Only one side of the passageway," George grumbled defensively when Pancho kidded him about it. "And I haven't hired a single staff member that I didn't absolutely need."

George's "office" was still the sitting room of his quarters. He had no desk, just comfortable furniture scavenged from junked spacecraft. Now he sat in a recliner that had once been a pilot's chair. Pancho was in a similar seat, sitting sideways, her long legs draped over its armrest.

"Looks to me like you're buildin' yourself an empire, George," Pancho teased. "Maybe only a teeny-weeny one, but still an empire."

George glowered at her from behind his brick-red beard. "You di'n't come battin' out here to twit me about my empire, didja?"

"No," said Pancho, immediately growing serious. "I surely didn't."

"Then what?"

"I gotta see Lars."

"See 'im? You mean face to face?"

Pancho nodded somberly.

"What for?"

"Amanda," said Pancho, surprised at how choked up she got. "She's . . . she died."

"Died?" George looked stunned.

"In childbirth."

"Pig's arse," George muttered. "Lars is gonna go fookin' nuts."

"Acute anemia?" Humphries echoed, his eyes narrowing. "How can my son have acute anemia?"

The man sitting in front of Humphries's desk was the chief physician of Selene's hospital. He was a cardiovascular surgeon, a large, imposing man with strangely small and delicate hands, wearing an impeccably tailored business cardigan of ash gray. His expression was serious but fatherly; he was accustomed to dispensing information and wisdom to distressed, bewildered patients and their families. He knew he had to maintain the upper hand with Humphries. Such a powerful man could be troublesome. None of the hospital's lower ranking physicians dared to accept the task of breaking this news to Martin Humphries.

He spread his hands in a placating gesture. "That's not an easy question to answer, Mr. Humphries. The baby has a defective gene, a mutation."

Humphries glanced sharply at Victoria Ferrer, seated to one side of his desk. She kept her face impassive.

"It might have been caused by some stray bit of ionizing radiation," the doctor went on condescendingly, "or even by the low gravity here. We simply don't know enough about the long-term effects of low gravity."

"Could it have been caused by drug use?" Ferrer asked.

Humphries glowered at her. The doctor's self-confidence slipped noticeably for a moment, but he swiftly regained his composure. "We did find an elevated level of barbiturates in Mrs. Humphries's blood, post-mortem. But I doubt—"

"Never mind," Humphries snapped. "It doesn't matter. The question now is, how will this affect my son?"

"Chronic anemia is treatable," the doctor answered smoothly. "It can be controlled with medication. He'll be able to lead a completely normal life as long as he takes his medication."

"No problems at all?"

"Not as long as he takes his medication," said the doctor, with his patented reassuring smile. "Oh, there might be some incidents of asthmatic attacks, but they should be amenable to antihistamines or adrenaline therapy. In severe cases we can even—"

"What else? Humphries snapped.

"I beg your pardon?"

"What else is wrong with him?"

The doctor's smile dimmed, then reappeared at full wattage. "His genetic screening looks perfectly normal, otherwise. With proper diet he should get to the sixth or seventh percentile, size-wise. And if he—"

"You mean he'll be a runt," said Humphries.

Startled, the doctor stammered, "I, eh . . . I wouldn't put it that way, Mr. Humphries. The boy will be well within normal standards."

"Will he be six feet tall?"

"Six feet . . . that's about one point eight meters, isn't it? No, I doubt that he'll get that tall."

"Will he be athletic?"

"Well, that all depends. I mean, the anemia will certainly be a factor in his athletic abilities, of course. But it's much too early . . ."

Humphries let him stumble on, half apologizing, half lecturing on what it takes to be a good father. Leaning back in his chair, keeping his hands deliberately in his lap to avoid drumming his fingers impatiently on the desktop, Humphries saw once again in his mind's eye his newborn son: a scrawny, red-skinned, squalling little rat-like thing, eyes shut, mouth open and gasping, miserable little toothpick arms and legs waving pathetically. A runt. A helpless, useless runt.

He had seen the baby only once, just after Amanda had died. As he stared down at it, struggling to breathe in its incubator, Humphries had said silently to it, You killed her. You killed my wife. She died giving life to you.

He had walked out of the nursery and hadn't seen the baby since that moment. He knew that if he did, if he went back into the nursery, he'd want to kill the brat. Smother it in its incubator. Turn off its air. Get rid of it.

He couldn't do it. There were too many nurses and pediatricians and servants constantly hovering over the little monster.

Besides, it wasn't really the baby's fault, Humphries told himself. It's Fuchs. Remember that. It's his fault. He's killed Amanda. He drove her to use the drugs that killed her and ruined my son. He's hidden behind her protection all these years. Well, that's over now. Over and done with.

". . . and later on, in a year or two, we can attempt gene replacement therapy," the doctor was saying. "Or even nanotherapy, since it's legal up here."

Ferrer was nodding as if she were interested.

"Thank you so much for explaining everything, doctor," Humphries said, getting to his feet.

The physician looked startled, then a flash of anger crossed his face momentarily, but he quickly recovered and got up from his chair.

"Please feel free to call on me at any time, Mr. Humphries. The entire services of the hospital are at your disposal."

"Certainly."

Neither man extended his hand to the other.

Once the physician left the office, Ferrer turned to Humphries. "Should I arrange a christening ceremony?"

"Christening?"

"It's expected for a newborn baby."

"Which comes first," Humphries asked bleakly, "her funeral or the brat's christening?"

Ferrer took a deep breath. Normally it would have roused Humphries but at the moment he ignored it.

"I'll make the arrangements for both," she said softly. "What do you want to name the baby?"

"Name?"

"He's got to have a name."

"Van. It's an old family name. My great-grandfather was named Van. He ran off to South America to avoid being drafted by the U.S. Army. A coward. That's an appropriate name for the little runt, don't you think?"

"I still don't see why you've gotta meet Lars face to face," said Big George.

Pancho swung her legs off the recliner's armrest and got to her feet. "Got something to tell him. Something personal."

"Somethin' more than Amanda's death?"

"Yep."

"Must be fookin' important."

"It is."

"Well," George said, getting up from his chair to stand beside her, "I can try gettin' a message to him. Dunno if he'll respond, though."

"He knows me."

"He *knew* you," George corrected. "Ol' Lars isn't the same man he was back then."

Pancho gave him a long unhappy look, then muttered, "Who the hell is?"

ASTEROID VESTA

arbin studied the image of Grigor on the wallscreen of his private quarters. A Russian, Harbin said to himself, recalling the way the village elders had spoken of the Russians when he'd been a lad. The Russians are our friends, they intoned, as long as they stay far away from our village.

Grigor's normally dour, downcast features looked almost happy as he gave Harbin the latest orders from Selene. An important executive of the rival Astro Corporation was at Ceres. Probably she would go deeper into the Belt, seeking a meeting with the renegade Fuchs.

"We will receive tracking data from our informant in the IAA facility at Ceres. You will intercept her vessel and eliminate it. Quite possibly you'll be able to eliminate Fuchs at the same time. You are to take as many ships as you deem necessary, but in any event no fewer than five. Humphries wants this job done without fail."

Harbin wanted to answer, "Then let Humphries come out here and do it himself." But he knew that it would take more than half an hour for any reply from him to reach the Moon. Besides, it wouldn't be wise to be so disrespectful to the man who pays all the bills.

So he wiped Grigor's image from his wallscreen and replied merely, "Message received. Will comply."

Five ships. Grigor thinks that more ships will guarantee success. He has no idea of how difficult it is to coordinate a multiship attack out here. And the more ships we use, the sooner the prey will realize it's being tracked.

Harbin shook his head in mild disgust. I could do it alone, one ship with a crew of one. Give me the coordinates of the Astro vessel's course and I'll intercept it and terminate it. And if Fuchs is in the area I'll handle him, too.

Leaning back in his padded chair, Harbin locked his fingers behind his head and thought it over. Fuchs is smart, though. Wily, like a badger. He can sniff out danger a thousand kilometers away. Five ships might make sense. Maybe a few more, to go out ahead of me and take up stations that will cut off his line of retreat. Then I'd have him, finally.

He sat up straight, nodded once at the blank wallscreen, then got to his feet and headed for the command center. He needed the latest tracking data on the Astro vessel.

Big George was staring at a wallscreen, too. Pancho sat beside him in his informal office, her eyes glued to the grainy image of Lars Fuchs.

"I received Pancho's message," Fuchs said, his broad, jowly face downcast, sour-looking. "Unfortunately, I can't risk a meeting. Too many of Humphries's spies might learn of it. Whatever you have to tell me, Pancho, send it in a message."

The image winked off.

Pancho blinked, then turned to George. "That's it? That's his whole message?"

"He doesn't waste words," George replied. " 'Fraid somebody might intercept the beam and get a fix on his location."

"I've got to talk to him," Pancho said, feeling frustrated. "Face to face."

George said, "Lots o' luck."

Getting to her feet, Pancho said, "I can't tell him Mandy's dead over a comm link."

Shaking his unshorn head, George replied, "He's not gonna meet with you, Pancho. I di'n't think he would."

"I'm not going to lead him into a trap, for cripes sake!"

"Not knowingly."

She frowned at him.

"Lars hasn't survived out there for so long by bein' naive," George said. "Humphries has had mercenaries tryin' to bag him. Freelancers, too; the word's gone 'round the Belt that Humphries'll pay a bounty for Lars's head."

Pancho grimaced. "Mandy told me he promised to leave Lars alone."

"Sure he did," George replied, scorn dripping from each syllable.

"I've got to see him."

"It's not gonna happen, Pancho. Face it. Lars is cautious, and I can't say I blame him."

Pancho took a deep breath, telling herself, When you're faced with a stone wall, find a way around it. Or over it. Or tunnel under it, if you have to. What did Dan Randolph always say: When the going gets tough, the tough get going—to where the going's easier.

"George," she asked, sitting down next to him again, "how do you get messages to Lars?"

He hesitated a moment. Then, "He's got a half-dozen or so miniaturized transceivers scattered around on minor asteroids out there. When I squirt a message to one of 'em, I tell him which one I'll be aimin' at on the next message."

"And the transceivers stay on the same 'roids all the time?"

"Naw. Lars moves 'em around. He tells me where they'll be next when he answers me back."

Pancho was silent for a few moments, thinking. At last she said, "So you could send him a message and tell him where you'll be sending the next one."

"And when," George added.

"And then he goes to that rock to pick up your message."

"Right."

"I could be waiting for him at the asteroid where the transceiver is. When Lars shows up, I'll be there to greet him."

George huffed. "And he'll blow you to bits before you can say hello."

"Not if—"

"Count on it," George said.

"I'll take that chance."

Shaking his head, George replied, "Pancho, I can't give you the fookin' coordinates! Lars'll think I betrayed him, for cryin' out loud!"

"I've got to see Lars face to face. I'm willing to take the chance that he'll attack my ship. It's on my head."

George remained adamant for hours. Pancho wheedled, pleaded, begged.

"What's so fookin' important?" George asked. "What is it you've got to tell him to his face?"

Pancho hesitated for a fraction of a second. Then she answered,

"George, if I could tell you, I would. But it's for Lars's ears only."

He scratched at his thick beard. "That big, huh?"

Pancho nodded wordlessly.

"All right," he said uneasily. "Tell you what I'll do. I'll go out on the ship with you."

"But you said it'd be dangerous!"

"Yeah. And it will be, believe it. But I think I can work out a scheme that'll keep Lars from blasting us on sight. Besides, I'd rather be there to face him than have him think I ratted him out."

TORCH SHIP *SAMARKAND*

arbin sat in *Samarkand*'s command chair, his pilot and navigator seated on a level of the bridge slightly below his. The data screens showed a confusing array of ship trajectories heading toward Ceres and away from the asteroid. The ship's computer was sorting out all the information, seeking the one ship that carried Pancho Lane.

She's too clever to use her own vessel, Harbin thought, as one by one the curving lines indicating individual ships' courses winked out. She'll hitch a ride aboard some prospector's ship, or maybe an Astro logistics vessel.

The tracking information came straight from the IAA controllers in the *Chrysalis* habitat orbiting Ceres. Harbin wished that Humphries had enough spies aboard the habitat to watch Pancho Lane and see which vessel she entered, but that kind of information was not available to him.

So he dispatched three armed ships out into the Belt, and kept three more in a very loose formation centered on his own vessel. To an untrained eye it looked like a few more prospectors' ships heading outward. Harbin hoped that's what Fuchs would see.

The welter of curving lines slowly diminished on the screen until only one ship's planned trajectory was displayed. Harbin shook his head, muttering, "Stupid computer." The ship's manifest said it belonged to the government of Ceres and carried none other than their chief administrator, who was going out on an inspection tour of various mining operations in the Belt. The chief rock rat going to visit his little rock rat brethren, Harbin thought.

Then his eyes narrowed. Why is their chief administrator traipsing through the Belt? Has he ever done that before? he asked the computer. The answer returned almost before he finished uttering the question. Never. This was the first inspection tour on record.

Harbin smiled grimly. *Maybe the computer isn't so stupid, after all.* He sent a message to Grigor, all the way back at Selene. "Do you have any way of finding out who's on the torch ship *Mathilda II* with the rock rats' chief administrator?"

Grigor replied in little more than an hour. "No passenger list is available. Apparently the vessel carries only its crew of three, and the man Ambrose."

Harbin nodded and remembered that Pancho Lane had once been a professional astronaut. She could probably take the place of a crewman on Ambrose's ship.

To his own navigator he commanded, "Set a course to follow the vessel shown on the computer display. Stay well behind it. I don't want them to know we're following them."

Mathilda II was a great deal more comfortable than the original *Waltzing Matilda*. That old bucket had been a mining ship before it was shot to shreds in the first asteroid war. *Mathilda II* was a comfortably fitted torch ship capable of carrying important passengers while serving as a mobile office for the chief administrator of the Ceres settlement.

Sitting in a swivel chair in the galley, George was explaining, "I left the message for Lars and told him where we'll be waitin' for him. This way we don't surprise him."

Pancho was seated across the galley table from George. They were in the middle of dinner, Pancho picking at a salad while George wholeheartedly attacked a rack of ribs.

"And the spot you picked to rendezvous with him isn't where one of the transceivers is stashed?" she asked.

"Naw," said George, dabbing at his sauce-soaked beard with a napkin. "We'll rendezvous in dead-empty space. I gave him the coordinates. If anybody's followin' us we'll both be able to see 'em long before they can cause any trouble."

Pancho nodded. "And you send all your messages to Lars over a tight laser link?"

"Yup. Just about impossible for anybody to intercept 'em or eavesdrop. If somebody does get into the beam we see it right away as a drop in received power."

"Pretty cute."

"Pretty necessary," George said, picking up another sauce-dripping barbecued rib.

In the weeks since his encounter with the disguised logistics ship *Roebuck*, Lars Fuchs had added a new wrinkle to his *Nautilus*.

Ships operating in deep space required radiation shielding. When solar flares erupted and spewed planet-engulfing clouds of deadly ionizing particles through interplanetary space, a ship without shielding was little more than a coffin for its crew. The powerful protons in such clouds were particularly dangerous, capable of killing humans and frying electronics systems within minutes unless they were properly protected.

Most spacecraft shielded themselves by charging their outer skins to a very high positive electrical potential. This diverted the deadly high-energy protons of the radiation cloud. The cloud also contained electrons, however, which were less energetic but capable of discharging the ship's positive electrical field. To keep the electrons at bay, the ships surrounded themselves with a magnetic field, generated by lightweight superconducting wires. Thus spacecraft operating beyond the Earth/Moon system were wrapped in an invisible but powerful magnetic field of their own, and charged their outer skins to high positive potential when a solar storm broke out.

Fuchs, once a planetary geochemist, used *Nautilus*'s electron guns to charge up his craft's skin, then covered the spacecraft with pebbles and dust from a loosely aggregated chondritic asteroid. A radar probe of his spacecraft gave a return that looked like the pebbly surface of a small "beanbag" type of chondritic asteroid. Moreover, the dust and pebbles would scatter a laser beam and absorb its energy even better than the copper shields he had affixed earlier to *Nautilus*'s hull.

If he let his ship drift in a Sun-centered orbit, Fuchs felt confident that *Nautilus* would look to a casual probe just like a small, dumbbell-shaped asteroid. He felt less confident, though, about responding to Big George's latest message.

Pancho wants to meet me face to face, he mused. Why? What's so important that she's coming out here into the Belt to find me?

"I don't like it," he muttered to himself.

Sanja, on duty in the pilot's chair, the son of a former Mongol tribesman, turned his shaved head toward Fuchs and asked, "Sir?"

"Nothing, Sanja," said Fuchs. "Nothing. Once you've reached orbital velocity, cut power and let the ship coast."

W e have arrived at the designated position," said the pilot.

Pancho was sitting in the copilot's chair of *Mathilda II*'s snug, efficiently laid-out bridge. The pilot, seated on her left, was a youngster she had met when she'd come aboard for this flight. He looked like a kid to Pancho, blond and soft-cheeked and scrubbed pink, but he ran the vessel well enough. Good square shoulders, she noticed. Pancho's piloting skills were rusty, she knew, but inwardly she longed for a chance to fly this bucket, just for a little larking around. She couldn't ask, of course. The chairman of the board of Astro Corporation isn't supposed to be a fly-girl. One of the epithets that Humphries often threw at her was "greasemonkey." Pancho had no intention of giving the Humper any ammunition.

Still, she thought as she watched the young man play his fingers over the control panel's keyboard, it'd be fun to goose up the engines and see what this flying machine can do.

"This is the spot, is it?" George asked. Standing behind the pilot's seat, he bent forward slightly to peer out the forward window. Nothing visible except the desert of dark empty space spangled with solemn, unblinking stars.

The pilot's name was Oskar Johannson. Despite his youthful appearance, he was stiffly formal with George and Pancho.

"Yes, sir," he said, pointing to the control panel's main display screen. "These are the coordinates, in yellow, and this is our position, the blinking red cursor. As you can see, sir, they overlap. We are at the proper position."

George nodded. Pancho admired Johannson's strong jaw and gleaming white teeth. Wish he'd smile, she thought. I wonder what it'd take to ruffle his composure a bit.

"No ships in sight?"

"Nothing in view, sir, except a small asteroid about five hundred klicks off, in about the four o'clock position." He tapped the keyboard once. "Five hundred seventeen kilometers, one hundred twenty-two degrees relative to our position, eight degrees elevation."

Pancho grinned at the kid's earnestness. "I thought this position was clear of rocks for at least a thousand klicks all round," she said.

George scratched at his beard, answering, "Rocks get kicked into new orbits all the time, Pancho. Gravity resonances from Jupiter and the other planets are always scrambling the smaller chunks."

Resisting the urge to run the display herself, she said, "An unnumbered rock. Might's well claim it."

"To do that one of us would hafta suit up and go out there and plant a marker on it."

"Why not?" Pancho said, pushing herself up from her seat. "I'll do it. Claim it for Astro."

"Gimme a closer look at it, Oskar," George said.

The radar image showed a dumbbell-shaped chondritic asteroid, slowly tumbling end over end.

"A peanut," George said. "Just like what's-'is-name."

"Ida," said Johannson. "Asteroid number 243."

"Showin' off your college education, Ossie?" asked George.

Johannson actually blushed.

Pushing past George, Pancho said, "I'll go out and claim it. Give me something to do while we're waiting for Lars to show up."

George turned and ducked through the hatch after her. "I'll give you a hand, Pancho."

"I can do it myself," she said, heading up the narrow passageway toward the main airlock, where the space suits were stored.

"You'll need help gettin' into a suit," George called after her. "I'll hafta suit up meself, too, y'know."

"You don't have to—"

"Safety regs," George said firmly. "Somebody's gotta be suited up and ready to go out in case of an emergency."

Pancho hmmphed but didn't object. Safety regulations had saved more than one astronaut's butt, she knew. She allowed George to help her into the suit and check out her seals and systems. Then she helped George and checked him out.

"What's funny?" George asked as he pulled the fishbowl helmet over his wild red mane.

Pancho hadn't realized she was grinning. George seemed about to burst his suit's seams. "Georgie, you look like a red-headed Santa Claus, you know that?"

"Ho, ho, ho," he answered flatly.

Pancho was ready to step into the airlock when Johannson's voice came over the ship's intercom:

"A ship's approaching," he called out. "It's coming up fast."

"Lasers armed and ready, sir," said the weapons technician.

Harbin nodded curtly, his eyes focused on the image of *Mathilda II* on the main screen of *Samarkand*'s bridge. Nothing else in range except a minor asteroid, some five hundred klicks away.

Samarkand carried two powerful continuous-wave lasers, adapted from the cutting tools the rock rats used, plus a high-energy pulsed weapon capable of blowing a centimeter-sized hole in the metal skin of a spacecraft from a distance of a thousand kilometers.

Mathilda's crew module was out of position, Harbin saw; it had rotated away from his fast-approaching ship and was partially shielded by the bulk of the propulsion system, engines and big spherical fuel tanks.

"Stand by," Harbin ordered quietly. The three crew personnel on the bridge with him sat tensely, waiting for the order to fire.

Just a little closer, Harbin said under his breath to the slowly rotating *Mathilda*. Just turn a little bit more.

There. The crew module was clearly visible.

"Fire," Harbin said to the weapons tech. To make certain, he pressed the red button on the keypad set into his command chair's armrest.

"We got her," he whispered triumphantly.

Pancho was inside the airlock, ready to go out and claim the unnamed asteroid, when she heard a gurgling scream in her earphones and warning sirens begin an ear-piercing howl.

"What's that?" she yelled into her helmet microphone.

"Dunno," George's voice replied. "Sounds like the emergency hatches slammed shut."

Pancho banged the airlock control panel, stopping its pumps, then reopened the inner hatch. George was in his space suit, peering down the passageway, his shaggy face frowning with worry.

"Can't get Johannson on the intercom," he muttered.

Pointing to the control panel on the emergency hatch a few meters up the passageway, Pancho said, "We've lost air pressure."

"Better stay in the suits, then," said George as he started toward the closed hatch.

Pancho followed him through three hatches, past the ship's galley and up to the hatch that opened onto the bridge. Red warning lights showed there was no air pressure along the entire way.

"Jesus!" George yelped once he pushed the hatch open.

Looking over the shoulder of George's suit, Pancho saw that the bridge's forward window had been punctured with a fist-sized hole and the control panel was spattered, dripping with bright red blood. Johannson was slumped in his seat, arms hanging, blood-soaked head lolling on his shoulders. George went to him and turned the pilot's chair around slightly. Johannson's eyes had blown out, and blood was still cascading from his open mouth.

For the first time in her long career as an astronaut and executive of a space-based corporation, Pancho vomited inside her fishbowl helmet.

"Hit!" said the weapons tech.

Harbin saw that they had indeed hit the crew module dead-on, probably at the bridge. Good.

"Slow to match the target's velocity," he commanded. "Move in closer."

Now to slice the ship to pieces and make sure no one survives.

Suddenly the lights on the bridge went out. As the dim emergency lights winked on, Harbin saw that his pilot's control board was glaring with red lights.

"What's wrong?" he demanded.

"Malfunction in the weapons pod," said the pilot, his fingers playing over the console keypads. "Electrical failure and—"

The lights blinked. This time Harbin felt the ship shudder slightly.

"We've been hit!" he snapped.

"*Mathilda* isn't firing at us," the navigator said, staring at the main screen. "That vessel isn't armed. It's only a—"

Samarkand lurched noticeably.

"We're spinning!" the pilot shouted. "Number two propulsion tank's been ruptured!"

"They're firing at us," Harbin shouted.

"But they can't!"

"*Somebody's* firing at us!" he insisted. "Get us out of here! Now!"

"I'm trying to bring the ship under control," the pilot yelled, her voice edgy, nearing panic.

We should get into our suits, Harbin knew. But there's no time for that now.

"Get us out of here!" he repeated, trying to sound calm, measured.

That asteroid, he realized. Somebody's on that asteroid and shooting at us. It must be Fuchs.

Lars Fuchs stood behind his pilot's chair, legs spread slightly, fists on his hips, eyes blazing with anger as he studied the display screen.

They fired on George's ship, he said to himself. Why? Did they think I was aboard? Or were they trying to kill Pancho? Probably both.

"The enemy is escaping," Nodon said. He spoke softly, keeping his tone neutral, making as certain as he could not to anger Fuchs.

"Let them go," Fuchs said. "The dog is whipped, no sense daring him to turn back and snap at us."

None of the crew on the bridge raised any objection.

"Sanja," Fuchs said to the man on the communications console, "see if you can contact the ship they attacked."

Within a few minutes Big George's face appeared on the screen, his brick-red hair and beard still stuffed inside the fishbowl helmet of his space suit.

"We lost one man," George said grimly. "No damage to the ship's systems."

Past George's broad shoulder Fuchs could see space-suited personnel smearing epoxy across the bridge's forward window.

"We'll have air pressure back in half an hour, maybe less," said George.

"Pancho is with you?" Fuchs asked.

"Yep. She's okay."

"You said she wanted to speak with me."

"I'll get her on the line," said George.

Fuchs waited impatiently, fighting the urge to pace the narrow confines of *Nautilus*'s bridge. Within a few minutes Pancho's face replaced George's on his screen. She was apparently in a privacy compartment, still in her space suit.

"He tried to assassinate you," Fuchs said without any preliminaries.

"Humphries?" she replied.

"Who else."

"Maybe he was trying to get you," Pancho said.

"He promised Amanda he wouldn't try to harm me," Fuchs answered, his voice heavy with irony.

An odd expression crossed Pancho's face. He could not determine what was going through her thoughts.

"It might've been a freelancer," she said at last. "Plenty people are after your scalp, Lars."

He shook his head, scowling. "That was no freebooter. He knew where you would be and he knew you were attempting to make a rendezvous with me. Only one of Humphries's agents would have access to such intelligence."

Pancho nodded inside her space-suit helmet. "I guess."

Taking a deep breath, Fuchs said, "Well, Pancho, you wanted to speak with me. Here I am. What is it that's so important?"

That strange expression clouded her face again. "Lars, I need to talk to you face to face about this. Not over a comm link."

"Impossible. You can't come aboard my ship and I won't leave it. Talk now. What is it?"

She hesitated, obviously torn between conflicting emotions.

"Well?" he demanded.

"Lars . . . it's about Amanda. Before she died she—"

"She died?" Fuchs felt his heart constrict beneath his ribs. "Amanda is dead?"

Pancho looked stricken. "I didn't want to tell you like this. I wanted to—"

"She's dead?" Fuchs repeated, his voice gone hollow. He felt as if he needed to sit down, but he couldn't show that weakness here on the bridge, in front of his crew.

"She died in childbirth, Lars."

"Giving birth to his son," Fuchs muttered.

"No, not—"

"He killed her. Humphries killed her just as certainly as if he put a gun to her head and pulled the trigger."

"Lars, you don't understand," said Pancho, almost pleading.

"I understand everything," he growled. "Everything! Now that she's dead even his lying promise to her is gone. Now he'll bend every effort, send every murdering thug he can buy, to kill me. But it won't work, Pancho. He'll never kill me."

"Lars, please. Let me explain—"

"I'll kill him!" Fuchs bellowed, raising his clenched fists above his head. "I'll wipe that smug smile off his face and kill him with these bare hands! I'll repay him for Amanda! I'll kill him!"

He lurched between the two pilots' chairs and punched the communications console so hard that glass broke. Pancho's image disappeared from the display screen.

"I'll kill you, Humphries!" Fuchs screamed to an uncaring universe.

e got away again?" Humphries squawked.

Standing before his desk, Victoria Ferrer nodded glumly. She wore a plain business suit of dove gray: knee-length skirt and collarless jacket, cut low, with no blouse under it.

Humphries glowered at her. "And Harbin missed Pancho, too?"

"I'm afraid so," Ferrer admitted. "I've had our top military advisor analyze the engagement. Apparently Fuchs has disguised his ship to look like an asteroid—superficially, at least."

"And that psychopath Harbin fell for it."

"As far as the reports show, yes, that's apparently what happened. He damaged *Mathilda II* but not badly enough. The vessel limped back to Ceres. Pancho Lane was not injured."

"And Fuchs got away again," Humphries muttered darkly.

Ferrer said nothing.

"Fire that lunatic Harbin," he snapped. "I don't want him on my payroll for another microsecond."

"But—"

"Fire him!" Humphries shouted. "Get rid of him! Kill him if you have to, just get him out of my way!"

Ferrer sighed patiently. "If you insist."

Noting the way her cleavage moved, Humphries allowed a small grin to creep across his face. "I insist."

"Very well." But instead of turning to leave his office, she remained standing in front of his desk.

"What else?" Humphries asked warily. He knew from long experience that when he had to ask an aide what was on her mind, it wasn't going to be pleasant.

"About your son . . ."

"Alex?"

"No. The baby. Van."

"The runt."

"He's your son, Mr. Humphries, and he needs medical attention."

"See to it, then."

"Don't you want to know—"

"The less I hear about that runt the better I like it. Don't bother me about him. Just do what needs to be done."

She sighed again. This time with disappointment, Humphries could clearly see. "Yes, sir," she said.

Humphries pushed himself up from his desk chair and crooked a finger at her. "Come with me, Victoria. Business hours are finished for this afternoon. Time for fun."

She gave him a look somewhere between surprised and reluctant. "But there's still—"

Coming around the desk, he held out his hand to her. "Vickie, if you wear such enticing clothes you can't blame me for reacting."

She shrugged, which made her even more enticing to him.

Pancho was still steaming by the time she got back to her home in Selene. That's twice the bastard's tried to kill me, she said to herself as she paced through the suite's front corridor to her bedroom. I can't let him have a third shot at me.

She tossed her travel bag onto the bed and told the phone to get her chief of security. Abruptly she canceled the call.

"Find Nobuhiko Yamagata," Pancho said. Silently, she added, Time to fight fire with fire.

It took several minutes for Pancho's computerized communications system to work its way through the Yamagata Corporation's computerized communications system, but at last the wall of Pancho's bedroom seemed to dissolve and she was looking at a three-dimensional image of Nobuhiko. He was on his feet, in a quilted winter parka, its hood pulled down off his head. Pancho could see snow-covered mountains and a crisp blue sky in the background.

"Jeeps," she said, "I hope I haven't busted into your vacation."

Nobuhiko smiled and shook his head. "Only a weekend getaway, Ms. Lane. Your call sounded important."

"It's important to me," Pancho said. "Martin Humphries has tried to murder me again."

"Again?" Nobu's brows rose.

As he listened to Pancho's story, Nobuhiko was thinking that his father's strategy was working perfectly. *She believes Humphries has tried to kill her twice. The first time was our doing, of course. But Humphries is playing his role, too, just as Father predicted.*

". . . so I was thinking that a strategic alliance between our two corporations would make a lot of sense. Together, we could outmaneuver Humphries, and outmuscle him if we have to."

Nobu pretended to be impressed. "The problem is," he said slowly, "that Yamagata Corporation has confined its activities to Earth ever since the greenhouse cliff devastated Japan and so many other nations."

"I know," Pancho said, after the nearly three-second lag that bedeviled communications between the Earth and Moon. "But if our two companies work together, Yamagata can get back into space industries as Astro's partner."

Stroking his chin thoughtfully, Nobu replied, "That is something worth considering, naturally. I will take it up with my board of directors. I'll call a special meeting, as early as I can."

Almost three seconds later Pancho nodded. "Okay. I appreciate that. In the meantime, though, I need some advice. Military advice. Can you recommend someone to me?"

Ahh, thought Nobuhiko, *now we come to the real reason for her call. She is going to war with Humphries and she needs a military force.*

"There are several organizations of mercenaries that might be of service to you."

"I want the best," Pancho said.

"I will send you complete dossiers on the best three organizations," Nobu said, while thinking, *Father will be very impressed. His plan is moving well. Let Astro and Humphries destroy each other. Yamagata Corporation will even help them to do so.*

"Terminated?" Harbin stared at Grigor's message on his screen. "Just like that, they kick me out?"

He was in his quarters in Vesta while the damaged *Samarkand* was undergoing repairs. Leeza Chaptal was in bed with him when Grigor's stinging message came through. Simply one line: Your services for Humphries Space Systems are hereby terminated. Period.

Harbin knew it would take at least half an hour for him to get a message back to Grigor. But what could he say? Ask why he'd been cut loose? That was obvious. He'd failed to get Fuchs, and failed to carry out his assignment about Pancho Lane. They were finished with him.

How many have I killed for them? Harbin asked himself. For more than eight years I've done their bidding, and now they kick me out. Terminated. Like some bug they squash under their boots.

Leeza saw the frozen expression on his face, realized that Harbin was raging beneath his mask of icy indifference.

"It's all right," she said, sliding her arms around his neck. "Yamagata will hire you."

"How can you be sure?" he muttered.

"They've wanted to hire you for months. Now there's nothing to prevent you from accepting their offer."

"But if I'm no longer with HSS, why would they hire me? They only wanted me to spy on Humphries for them."

"They'll hire you," she repeated. "I know they will."

"Why?"

Leeza smiled at him. "Because there's going to be a war here in the Belt, and you are a warrior."

ASTRO CORPORATION HEADQUARTERS

echnically, the principal offices of Astro Corporation were still at La Guaira, off the drowned coast of Venezuela. But Pancho had moved almost all of the corporate headquarters staff to Selene. Most of the board of directors lived in the lunar city, and those who didn't attended board meetings electronically. The three-second communications lag made the meetings tedious to some extent, but Pancho was perfectly willing to accept that. Astro's business was off-Earth; even shipping asteroidal ores Earthside was almost entirely a space operation, and Pancho had always insisted on being where the action was.

Now she sat in the richly paneled boardroom, in her usual place at the head of the long polished conference table. The only other person in the room at this moment was Jacob Wanamaker, known as "Hard-Ass Jake." A retired commander of the International Peacekeeping Force, Wanamaker was a big-shouldered, heavy-bellied, genial-looking older man with a wry, lopsided smile and sad, pouchy brown eyes that had seen much more than their share of death and destruction.

Nobuhiko Yamagata had recommended three military advisors to Pancho: a Japanese mercenary who had fought in miniwars from Indonesia to Chiapas, in Mexico; a Swedish woman who had organized the multinational force that pacified the turmoil in southern Africa; and Hard-Ass Jake. The first two had never been off-Earth; Wanamaker had served several tours aboard a missile-defense space station in Earth orbit. Besides, Jacob Wanamaker had been an admiral in the U.S. Navy before accepting a commission with the IPF, and Pancho figured that fighting in space would be more closely akin to naval warfare than land campaigns.

Once she had personally interviewed the three candidates, Jake won hands down. He was open, easily admitting his lack of experience in space, but the toughness he was famous for showed through his veneer of polite sociability. Pancho had seen men like him when she'd been growing up in west Texas.

"So the trick is," he told her in his rough, sandpaper voice, "to control the lanes of communication. And to do that, you need vessels that are armed and bases for them to be supplied and repaired."

Pancho nodded. "Sounds expensive."

Wanamaker's weather-seamed face was a geological map of hard experience. "War is never cheap, Ms. Lane. The cost is always high: high in blood and high in money. Lots of money."

"It must be exciting, though," she said, probing for his reaction.

Wanamaker cocked a cold eye at her. "Exciting? If you think shitting your pants because you could get killed in the next millisecond is fun, yeah, then I guess you could call it exciting."

It was at that moment that Pancho decided to hire Jacob Wanamaker.

Now they sat in the otherwise empty boardroom, planning strategy.

"HSS has a major base on Vesta," Pancho said. "What do we do about that, attack it?"

Wanamaker pursed his lips for a moment, then replied in his gravelly voice, "Why attack them where they're dug in with solid defenses? That'd cost too many lives."

"But that base is the center of all their operations in the Belt."

"Neutralize it, then. Keep a squadron of ships in the vicinity, close enough to knock off vessels going to or from Vesta, but far away enough to avoid the asteroid's dug-in defenses."

Pancho nodded.

Warming to his subject, Wanamaker gesticulated with his big hands, cupping them together to form an imaginary sphere.

"Matter of fact," he said, "why can't you put three or four of your armed ships together, armor them with asteroidal rock, and keep them on station at a decent distance around Vesta? They'd have more firepower than any individual HSS vessel and more staying power."

"It'd be like a blockade, wouldn't it?" Pancho said.

Wanamaker grinned lopsidedly at her. "You catch on pretty quick."

The rush of pleasure Pancho felt from his praise quickly faded.

"But then Humphries'll send out his ships in groups, 'stead of individually, won't he?"

"Yep, convoying would be the countermove."

"It just makes the battles bigger."

"And more expensive."

Suddenly she felt gloomy.

Wanamaker immediately picked up on her mood. "Look, Ms. Lane—"

"Pancho," she corrected absently.

"Okay, Pancho, then. Sherman was right: war is hell, pure and simple. It costs so much in money and blood that if there's any other way to settle your differences with Humphries—any way at all—take it and avoid the bloodshed."

She looked into his earnest brown eyes and said, "I've been trying to avoid this for more'n eight years, Jake. There's no way to get around it, short of giving Humphries total control of the Belt, which means total control of the whole solar system. I won't allow that. I can't."

He puffed his cheeks out in a king-sized sigh. "Then we'll have to fight."

"Guess so," Pancho said morosely.

"You know, battles are won first of all on the morale of the people doing the fighting. Hardly any unit fights to the last man or the last cartridge. Especially mercenaries, such as you'll be using. Somebody decides it's hopeless and gives up before he gets killed."

"Or she," said Pancho.

He acknowledged that with a nod. "Battles are won in the mind and the heart, Pancho. Wars too. The winner is always the guy who won't admit defeat."

She leaned back in her chair, stretched her long legs and stared up at the boardroom's smooth white ceiling.

"Humphries is a stubborn SOB," she said. "And he's not doing the fighting. He sits safe and snug in his house down at the bottom level and gives the orders."

"And pays the bills," Wanamaker added.

Pancho stared at him.

"The way to win this war is to make it too expensive for him to keep on fighting it."

"That means it'll be expensive for Astro, too, and I've got a board of directors to answer to. Humphries can walk all over his board."

With an understanding nod, Wanamaker replied, "Then you're going to have to do some fighting, too, with your board. Just because you're at the top of the chain of command doesn't mean you don't have to put your butt on the line, Pancho."

She tried to smile. "I guess the price of commodities from the Belt is gonna go up."

George was surprised at Pancho's message.

"Go full speed ahead on the nanoprocessing," she said, her lantern-jawed face deadly serious. "It's important that we bring down the costs of mining the rocks."

George studied her image on the wallscreen of his sitting room, thinking, First she says nanoprocessing is gonna knock the bottom outta the market and now she's hot to trot with it. What's goin' on with her?

Pancho's next sentence explained it, at least partially. "Astro's got some big expenses coming up, Georgie. Anything we can do to lower our costs will let us squeeze some extra profits out of the mining operations and help us pay for what's coming up."

"What's coming up?" George asked Pancho's image.

She couldn't answer, of course, not for an hour or so, but George was afraid he already knew. They're gonna fight it out, he figured. No more pokin' here and there, they're gonna fight a fookin' full-scale war. And they're gonna do it right here in the Belt.

"One more thing," Pancho was going on, with hardly a pause for breath. "It's going to be more dangerous out there for Lars than ever before. Tell him it's time for him to come in from the cold. I can give him a new identity, let him live here in Selene if he wants to or even back on Earth. He's got to get out of the Belt, for his own safety."

George nodded at Pancho's image. She looked grave, somber. Like a woman about to go to war, George thought. Then he realized, No. She looks more like a fookin' avenging angel.

Victoria Ferrer watched Humphries's reaction to the latest reports from his far-flung intelligence network.

"Astro's arming ships," he muttered, staring at the display hovering in midair above his desk. "And she's pushing the nanoprocessing scheme."

"She's preparing to go to war," Ferrer said. "Against you."

He looked up at her, his face cold with fury. "With nanoprocessing, Pancho can cut her costs and give Astro an extra layer of profits to finance her war."

"Then we've got to get into nanoprocessing, too."

"Damned quick," Humphries snapped.

"The scientist who perfected the process is here in Selene," Ferrer pointed out. "He came in with Pancho."

"Hire him away from Astro," Humphries said immediately.

"He's not an Astro employee," she said. "Not legally, at least."

"Then hire him. Give him whatever he wants. If he won't come along with us, kidnap him. I want him working for me!"

"I understand," Ferrer said.

Humphries rubbed his hands together. "By god, with nanoprocessing we'll cut the costs of mining down to nothing, almost. Down to the cost of transportation, just about."

"Nanotechnicians don't come cheap."

He sneered at her. "Cheap enough. We'll only need a handful of them. We'll have those little buggers not only mining the ores out of the asteroids, but refining them into pure metals while they do it. What more could you ask for?"

Ferrer looked less enthusiastic. "Lots of miners are going to be thrown out of work."

"So what?" Humphries said offhandedly. "More recruits for the mercenaries."

More cannon fodder, Ferrer thought.

Still in his quarters inside the asteroid Vesta, Dorik Harbin tried to think of the French phrase about the more that things may change, the more they remain the same. Instead, a quatrain from the *Rubaiyat* came to his mind:

> Yesterday, *this* day's madness did prepare:
> Tomorrow's silence, triumph or despair;
>   Drink! for you know not whence you came, nor why;
> Drink! for you know not why you go, nor where.

The irony is almost cosmic, Harbin thought. Humphries fires me because I've failed to kill Fuchs. Yamagata hires me to lead a squadron of mercenaries. Humphries hires Yamagata's mercenaries and bases their ships on Vesta. I didn't have to move, didn't even have to pack a travel bag. Here I am in the same quarters, lower in rank but higher in pay. All I have to do is lead three ships into battle against Astro Corporation. Fuchs has become a sideshow.

His relationship with Leeza Chaptal had changed, though. She had emerged as Yamagata's senior officer among the mercenaries hired by Humphries Space Systems. Now she outranked Harbin, and had little time for him. Which was just as well, Harbin thought. He had no enthusiasm for sleeping with a senior officer. It was one thing to take orders from a woman in battle; in bed, it was a totally different matter.

But Harbin had his consolations. In the travel bag that he didn't have to pack rested a flat gray oblong medical kit that contained a subcutaneous microspray syringe and an array of specially designed medications.

Something for every mood, Harbin thought as he went to the bag and pulled out the kit. Sitting on his bed, he clicked open its lid and examined the vials lined up neatly, each in their clasps. Something to alleviate depression. Something to enhance sexual performance. This one smothers fear. That one speeds reaction times. Each one designed specifically for my metabolism. And Leeza says Yamagata can supply as much as I need.

Drink! for you know not why you go, nor where. He repeated the line over and again in his mind as he took a vial from the neat little row and inserted it into the syringe. Something to make me forget everything, he thought. Something for oblivion.

He rolled up the sleeve of his uniform and pressed the syringe to the bare skin of his forearm. Heard its gentle, soothing, reptilian hiss.

He looked up and saw that the wallscreen was displaying a view from the surface of Vesta. A sliver of bare rock, and then the black emptiness of infinity. Stars upon stars, all silent and grave, staring back at him. A barren wilderness of cold and dark.

The drug started to take effect quickly. Harbin lay back on his bed, thinking, *Oh, wilderness were paradise enow.*

He closed his eyes and begged the silent stars to keep him from dreaming.

SELENE: EARTHVIEW RESTAURANT

evi Levinson had never seen such a luxurious restaurant, except in videos. The main eating establishment of Hotel Luna, the Earthview was three levels deep beneath the floor of the crater Alphonsus, big enough to hold a hundred tables covered with heavy damask tablecloths and glittering with silver tableware and sparkling wine glasses and lit by real, actual flickering candles. The spacious room buzzed softly with muted conversations and the barest hint of elegant classical music purring from the overhead speakers. Real, live waiters moved among the tables wearing formal evening clothes. Levinson never gave a thought to the fact that he was wearing his usual coveralls; he had nothing better in his meager wardrobe. Nor did he realize that most of the restaurant's tables were empty. His eyes went to the wide holoscreens mounted on the walls, each showing a real-time view of Earth, glowing blue and white against the endless blackness of space as it hung in the sky above Alphonsus's ringwall mountains.

He was more than a quarter-hour early for his appointment with Victoria Ferrer, so the table that the maitre d' led him to was empty. He sat ogling the well-dressed tourists and executives at the few other occupied tables, while a waiter poured water for him and left a wine list on the table. Levinson was satisfied with the water. He really wanted a beer, but he felt too self-conscious to ask for one.

After so many weeks in Selene, living in an apartment provided by Astro Corporation, Levinson felt a little guilty about accepting an invitation to dine with an executive from the rival Humphries Space Systems. But what the hell, he thought, I'm not an Astro employee and Pancho Lane has just totally ignored me since she brought me here. It's like she wants me out of the way, hidden like some witness against a crime syndicate back on Earth. I've got nothing better to do until the

Journal of Nanotechnology publishes my paper. And even there, they've been dragging their feet, like they don't really want to publish it.

Those were the thoughts tumbling through his mind when Victoria Ferrer came up to his table and said:

"You're Dr. Levinson? I'm Vicki Ferrer."

Something in the back of his mind told Levinson he should get to his feet, that's the polite thing. But all he could do was gape at this splendidly beautiful woman standing before him. Ferrer wore a dress of some gold metallic stuff that gleamed in the candlelight and clung to her enticingly.

The waiter held her chair as she sat down, smiling at Levinson. He felt breathless.

Dinner was like some romantic dream. Vicki did the ordering while Levinson simply stared at her, entranced. As they worked their way through the several courses, each accompanied by a special wine, Levinson found himself telling her the story of his life. It sounded plain and dull and boring to him, but she seemed vitally interested in every word.

"And you actually have programmed nanos to process the ores from asteroids?" she asked, her wide brown eyes gleaming with respect, maybe even fascination, he thought.

He went into details about it, but inevitably ended with the disappointing information that the rock rats refused to use his process because they considered it too dangerous.

"It's not really dangerous," Levinson insisted. "I mean, it could be, but I could work out procedures for them that would bring the risk down to a manageable level."

"I'm sure you could," said Vicki, reaching for the sauterne that had been served with dessert.

"But they're not interested in it," Levinson said unhappily.

"Aren't they?"

"No."

She leaned slightly closer to him. "Then why has Pancho Lane ordered her people at Ceres to go ahead with nanoprocessing?"

Levinson blinked at her. "She what?"

"Astro Corporation is preparing to use nanomachines to mine asteroids."

"But that's my work! I published it! I mean, I've got it to the journal and—"

"I'm sure Astro will pay you a royalty of some sort," Ferrer said. "Probably a pittance, just to avoid a lawsuit."

Levinson felt as if someone had stabbed him in the heart.

Ferrer reached across the table and touched his hand. "Lev, how would you like to work for Humphries Space Systems? How would you like to be in charge of a whole operation out in the Belt?"

"Me?"

"You. You're the man we want, Lev. You'll be in charge of nanoprocessing operations at the salary level of a senior executive."

He didn't even bother to ask how much money that meant. He knew it was astronomically more than a laboratory scientist made.

"I'd be very grateful if you said yes, Lev," Victoria Ferrer told him, her voice a whisper, her eyes lowered shyly.

He nodded dumbly. She smiled her warmest at him. Levinson walked on air all the way back to his quarters, with Vicki at his side. She allowed him to give her a fumbling peck on the lips, then left him standing there in the corridor, slightly drunk with wine, more intoxicated with thoughts of being in charge of a major corporate operation and maybe even having this beautiful woman fall in love with him.

He watched her walk down the corridor, then turned to his door and fumbled with the electronic combination lock. Finally stumbling into his apartment, he told himself, This was just our first date. It went pretty damned well. I think she really likes me.

Victoria Ferrer rode the powered stairs down to her own quarters, a quiet smile of accomplishment playing across her lips. We've got him, she said to herself. Martin will be pleased.

SELENE: FACTORY NUMBER ELEVEN

Douglas Stavenger's youthful face was frowning with a mixture of anger and dread as he paced slowly down the length of the factory. Like most lunar manufacturing facilities, Factory Eleven was built out on the surface, open and exposed to the vacuum, protected against the constant rain of micrometeoroids only by a thin dome of honeycomb metal.

"Not much to see, actually," said the factory manager, waving a gloved hand toward the vats where microscopic nanomachines were constructing spacecraft hulls of pure diamond, built atom by atom from carbon soot mined out of asteroids.

Stavenger was wearing one of the new so-called "softsuits" of nanomachined fabric rather than the cumbersome space suit of hardshell cermet that the factory director wore. The softsuit was almost like a pair of kiddie's pajamas, even down to the attached boots. It was easy to pull on and seal up. The nanomachines held almost-normal air pressure inside the suit without ballooning the way older fabric suits did when exposed to vacuum. Even the gloves felt comfortable, easily flexed. A transparent fishbowl helmet completed the rig, with a small air recycler and even smaller communications unit packed into the belt that went around Stavenger's waist.

"How's the suit feel?" the factory director asked. Her voice sounded a bit uneasy, edgy, in Stavenger's earplug.

"Fine," he said. "I'll bet I could do handsprings in it."

The woman immediately said, "I wouldn't advise that, sir."

Stavenger laughed. "Please call me Doug. Everybody does."

"Yes, sir. I mean, uh, Doug. My name's Ronda."

Stavenger knew her name. And her complete dossier. Although he had not held an official position in Selene's government for decades, Doug Stavenger still kept a steady finger on the lunar nation's pulse.

He had the advantage of prestige and the even bigger advantage of freedom. He could go anywhere, see anything, influence anyone. And he did, although usually only in the subtlest manner.

But the time for subtlety was ending quickly. He had asked for this tour of Selene's newest factory because it had been built to supply new torch ships for the corporations competing in the Belt: torch ships armed with powerful lasers, warships built of diamond hulls constructed by nanomachines.

They're killing each other out in the Belt, Stavenger knew. He also knew that sooner or later, one way or the other, the war would come to Selene. What he didn't know was how to prevent it; how to stop the fighting.

"How many orders for ships do you have?" he asked the factory manager.

"Six," she replied. "Three from Astro and three from HSS." She hesitated a beat, then added, "Funny how the orders always come paired up. We never make a ship for one of the corporations without making a ship for the other at the same time."

That had been Stavenger's doing. He had exerted every gram of influence he possessed to keep both Humphries and Pancho from outproducing the other. If they want to fight, Stavenger had reasoned, it's up to us to keep the competition equal. As soon as one of them gets the upper hand they'll be able to dictate the prices for raw materials to us. Selene will have to pay whatever the winner asks for its natural resources. Whoever wins this war in the Belt will win control of Selene as well.

That, Stavenger was determined, would not be allowed to happen.

To the factory manager, he asked as casually as he could manage, "Suppose a third party started ordering spacecraft. Could you supply them on the same schedule you're working now?"

He couldn't see her face through the visor of her hard-shell helmet, but he could sense her nodding. "Sure. We'd have to set up another facility, but that's easy to do: Just pour another concrete pad and roof it over. The nanos do all the real work."

Stavenger nodded. "I see."

Curiosity got the better of the manager. "But who'd be ordering more ships? Who'd this third party be?"

With a soft shrug, he replied, "Oh, I don't know. Maybe Selene."

The manager could not have been more surprised if Stavenger had actually turned a handspring there on the factory floor.

Less than twenty kilometers from the new lunar factory, Lars Fuchs was passing through customs at Selene's Armstrong Spaceport.

He had come to the Moon by a circuitous route, leaving the Belt weeks earlier to return to his native Switzerland, using the passport that Pancho had sent to him through Big George. Although exiled from Ceres and persona non grata at Selene, neither Switzerland nor any other nation of Earth had outlawed Fuchs. Customs officials at the spaceport in Milan had subjected him to a quick but thorough medical examination, including a full-body scan and a blood sample to make certain he did not bear nanomachines.

Thus Lars Fuchs, citizen of Switzerland, returned to his native land. He had spent weeks working out in a centrifuge he'd built aboard *Nautilus*, but still the heavy gravity of Earth made him feel tired, depressed. Even worse was the sight of the sprawling tent city that he glimpsed outside of Milan from the high-speed train as it raced toward the Alps. From the city's newly walled and guarded borders, past Brescia and all the way to the shores of Lake Garda he could see nothing but the shacks and shanties of the homeless, the dispossessed, the haunted, hopeless victims of the greenhouse warming.

After all these years, Fuchs thought, staring through the train window, and still they live like animals.

Then he caught his first glimpse of the Alps. Bare rock, stark and barren as the Moon. Where's the snow? he asked himself, knowing that it was gone, perhaps for centuries, perhaps forever.

His world, the world he had known, was gone also. He didn't realize how much he had loved it, how much he missed it, until he realized that he would never see it again.

As the train plunged into the tunnel at the Brenner Pass, Fuchs stared at his own grim reflection in the window. He looked away, squeezed his eyes shut, and determined to stop thinking about the past. Only the future. Think only of the day when you kill Martin Humphries.

To do that he had to return to Selene, and to accomplish *that* he had to change his identity. Pancho thought she was saving Fuchs's life, protecting the man she had known since he'd first left Earth as an eager graduate student more than a decade earlier. She had provided Fuchs with a new identity and enough money to live comfortably for a few years. At his insistence, she had also done as much for the nine men and women of his crew. *Nautilus* was parked in a Sun-circling orbit deep in the Belt, still disguised to resemble a smallish asteroid. It will be waiting for me when I finish my business with Humphries, Fuchs thought.

He knew what that business was, what it had to be. Pancho hasn't brought me to Earth merely out of friendship. She wants me to get back to Selene. She can't trust any communications link to say it in so many words, but her intention is clear. She wants me to kill Humphries. She knows that's what I want to do, and she's willing to help me do it. It will be a great help to her, of course. But it will be a joy to me. Even if it costs my own life, I will snuff out Humphries.

His thirst for vengeance kindled him for the remainder of his train ride to Bern.

But once in his native Bern he became sad and dispirited, depressed at how the old city had become so shabby, so filled with aimless, homeless men and women, even children, wandering the streets, begging for handouts when the police weren't looking. Fuchs was shocked that the streets were littered with trash; the city that had once sparkled was now grimy, obviously decaying. And at night the streets could even be dangerous, he was warned by the weary-eyed concierge at his hotel.

A week was more than enough for him. Fuchs used the identity Pancho had provided for him to book passage back to Selene. He rented a modest suite for himself at the Hotel Luna, with an expense account to be paid by Astro Corporation. Closer to Humphries, he told himself. Within arm's reach, almost. Close enough to kill. But you must be patient, he thought. You must be careful. Humphries is surrounded by guards and other employees. Pancho can't openly help me to reach him; she can't allow herself to be seen as aiding an assassin. I'll have to act alone. I'll have to get through to Humphries on my own. I don't know how, not yet, but I will do it. Or die in the trying.

He had to disguise his appearance, of course. Lifts in his shoes made him slightly taller. Rigid, spartan dieting had slimmed him somewhat, but no fasting could reduce his barrel chest or thickly muscled limbs. He had grown a thick black beard and wore molecule-thin contact lenses that Astro's people had clandestinely sent him; they altered his retinal pattern enough to fool a computer's simple comparison programming.

Still, Fuchs could not help sweating nervously as he shuffled through the line leading to the customs inspection booth at Selene's Armstrong Spaceport. He had taken a mild tranquilizer but it didn't seem to be helping to calm his growing apprehension.

When he came to the inspection station the computer's synthesized German sounded slightly strange to him, until he realized the machine was not programmed to speak in his own Swiss dialect. He answered its questions as briefly as he could, knowing that the system did not have the voice print of Lars Fuchs in its memory, yet still worried that somehow it might. It didn't. He followed instructions and looked into the retinal scanner for the required five seconds, slowly counting them off in silence.

The automated systems built into the archway directly in front of the inspector's booth scanned his one travel bag and his body without a problem. Fuchs had nothing with him or on him that would trigger an alarm. The human inspector sitting in the booth behind the automated machinery looked bored, his thin smile forced. Fuchs handed him his falsified identity chip and the inspector slipped it into his desktop.

"Karl Manstein?"

"Ja," Fuchs answered.

The inspector asked, "Purpose of your visit?" in standard English; the booth's synthesized computer voice translated his words into German.

"Vacation."

For a heart-stopping moment the inspector studied his screen display, his eyes narrowing. Then he popped Fuchs's thumbnail-sized chip out of his computer and slid it over the countertop to him.

"Welcome to Selene, Herr Manstein. Enjoy your vacation."

"Thank you," Fuchs replied gratefully, scooping up the chip in one meaty hand and hurrying past the inspector, toward the electric-powered cart that would carry him into Selene.

His first task, once he was safely in his suite at the Hotel Luna, would be to send innocuous-seeming messages to his three most trusted crew members, waiting at Ceres. "I have arrived at Selene, and everything is fine." That was the code phrase that would tell them to head for Selene also. Fuchs intended to kill Humphries, and he knew he could not do it alone.

ORE FREIGHTER *SCRANTON*

Chick Egan was mildly surprised to find a ship approaching *Scranton* at high speed. The ore freighter was almost clear of the inner fringe of the Belt, heading toward Selene, carrying a full load of asteroidal metals under contract to Astro Corporation. Astro's people were busily auctioning off the metals on the commodities market at Selene, desperately hoping to get prices high enough to make a minimal profit.

Sitting sideways in the pilot's seat, his legs dangling over the armrest, Egan had been talking with his partner, "Zep" Zepopoulous, about the advisability of getting a laser weapon for the old, slow *Scranton*.

"Makes about as much sense as giving Santa Claus a six-shooter," Zep argued. He was a lean, wiry Greek with thick jet black hair and a moustache to match. "We're in the freight-hauling business, we're not fighters."

Egan's strawberry-blond hair was shorn down to a military buzz cut. "Yeah, but all the other ships are puttin' on lasers. For self-defense."

"This tub isn't worth defending," Zep replied, gesturing around the cramped, shabby cockpit with its scuffed bulkheads and worn-shiny seats. "Somebody wants what we're carrying, we just give it to them and let the insurance carrier worry about it."

"HSS is going after Astro ships," Egan said. "And vice versa."

"We're only under contract to Astro for this one flight. We could sign up with HSS next time out."

"Sam Gunn's arming all his ships," Egan countered. "Astro, HSS, a lot of the independents, too."

"Let 'em," said Zepopoulous. "The day I start carrying weapons is the day I quit this racket and go back to Naxos."

"What's left of it."

"The flooding's stabilized now, they say. I'll be a fisherman, like my father."

"And starve like your father."

That was when the radar pinged. Both men looked at the screen and saw a ship approaching at high speed.

"Who the hell is that?" Zep asked. The display screen showed only blanks where a ship's name and ownership would normally appear.

"Lars Fuchs?" Egan suggested.

"What would he want a load of ores for? We're not an HSS ship, and we don't have any supplies he'd want to take."

Feeling decidedly nervous, Egan turned to the communications unit. "This is *Scranton*. Independent inbound for Selene. Identify yourself, please."

The answer was a laser bolt that punched a hole through the skin of the cockpit. Egan's last thought was that he wished he had armed *Scranton* so he could at least die fighting.

George Ambrose listened to the reports in gloomy silence. The six other members of Ceres's governing council sitting around the oval conference table looked even bleaker.

Eight ships destroyed in the past month. Warships being built at Selene and sent to the Belt by Astro and Humphries Space Systems.

"The HSS base on Vesta has more than two dozen ships orbiting around it," said the council member responsible for relations with the two major corporations. She was a Valkyrie-sized woman with sandy hair and a lovely, almost delicate fine-boned face that looked out of place on her big, muscular body.

"Everybody's carrying weapons," said the councilman sitting beside her.

"It's damned dangerous out there," agreed the woman on the other side of the table.

"What's worrying me," said the accountant, sitting at the table's end, "is that this fighting is preventing ships from delivering their ores to the buyers."

The accountant was a red-faced, pop-eyed overweight man who usually wore a genial smile. Now he looked apprehensive, almost grim.

"Our own economy," he went on, "is based on the business that the miners do. With that business slumping, we're going to be in an economic bind, and damned soon, too."

"Worse than that," said the Valkyrie. "It's only a matter of time before one of the corporations—either Astro or HSS—tries to take over our habitat and make it a base of their own."

"And whichever one takes *Chrysalis*," said the accountant, "the other one will try to take it from them."

"Or destroy us altogether."

Big George huffed out a heavy sigh. "We can't have any fighting here. They'll kill us all."

All their faces turned to him. They didn't have to say a word; George knew the question they wanted answered. *What can we do about it?*

"All right," he said. "I'm gonna send a message to Astro and Humphries. And to Selene, too." Silently he added, With a copy to Doug Stavenger.

"A message?"

"What are you going to say?"

"I'm gonna tell them all that we're strictly neutral in this war they're fightin'," George replied. "We want no part of it. We'll keep on sellin' supplies and providin' R&R facilities for anybody who wants 'em, HSS, Astro, independents, anybody."

The others glanced around the table at one another.

George went on, "But we won't deal with warships. Not from anybody. Only mining ships, prospectors, logistics vessels and the like. We will not supply warships with so much as a toilet tissue."

"A declaration of neutrality," said the accountant.

"Do you think that will be enough?"

"What else can we do?"

"Arm the habitat. Be ready to fight anybody who tries to take us over."

George shook his head ponderously. "This habitat is like an eggshell. We can't fight. It'd just get us all killed."

"We could armor the habitat," the Valkyrie suggested. "Coat the outer hulls with powdered rock, like some of the warships do."

"That'd just postpone the inevitable," George said. "A half-dozen ships could sit out there and pound us into rubble."

"A declaration of neutrality," someone repeated.

"Do you think it would work?"

George spread his big hands. "Anybody got a better idea?"

Silence fell over the conference room.

George drafted his declaration over the next twenty-four hours, with the help of an assistant who had been a history major before coming out to the Belt. The council met again in emergency session, tore the draft to tatters and rewrote it extensively, then—sentence by sentence, almost—wrote a final draft that was quite close to George's original. Only after that did they agree to allow George to send the declaration to Pancho Lane at Astro, Martin Humphries of HSS, and the governing board of Selene. George added a copy for Douglas Stavenger, and then released the statement to the news media of the Earth/Moon region.

For the next several days Big George Ambrose was a minor media attraction. Ceres's neutrality was the first realization for most of the people on battered old Earth that there was a war going on in the Belt: a silent, furtive war taking place far, far away in the dark and cold depths of the Asteroid Belt.

For a few days the Asteroid War was a trendy topic on the news nets, even though no executive of Humphries Space Systems or Astro Corporation deigned to be interviewed or even offer a comment. Sam Gunn, the fast-talking independent entrepreneur, had a lot to say, but the media was accustomed to Gunn's frenetic pronouncements on the evildoings of the big corporations. Nobuhiko Yamagata agreed to a brief interview, mainly to express his regrets that lives were being lost out in the Belt.

Then a major earthquake struck the California coast, with landslides that sent a pair of tsunamis racing across the Pacific to batter Hawaii and drown several Polynesian atolls. Japan braced for the worst, but the hydraulic buffers that Yamagata had built—and been ridiculed for—absorbed enough of the tsunamis' energy to spare the major Japanese cities from extensive destruction. The Asteroid War was pushed to a secondary position in the news nets' daily reporting. Within a week it was a minor story, largely because it was taking place far from Earth and had no direct impact on the Earthbound news net producers.

George Ambrose, however, received a personal message from Douglas Stavenger. It was brief, but it was more than George had dared to hope for.

Seated at the desk in his comfortable home in Selene, Stavenger said simply, "George, I agree that *Chrysalis* could be endangered by the fighting in the Belt. Please let me know what I—or Selene—can do to help."

COMMAND SHIP *ANTARES*

Reid Gormley was a career soldier. He had served with the International Peacekeeping Force in Asia and Africa and had commanded the brilliant strike that had wiped out the paramilitary forces of the Latin American drug cartel. He was widely known in military circles as an able commander: a tough, demanding bantam cock who instilled a sense of pride and invincibility in his troops. He was also vain, cautious, and unwilling to move until he was certain he had an overwhelming superiority of force on his side.

He had come out of retirement to accept a commission with Astro Corporation. Fighting in space was new to him, but then it was new to every commander that the big corporations were hiring. The only experienced space fighters were a handful of mercenaries and renegades like Lars Fuchs. Like most of the other experienced officers who were suddenly finding new careers for themselves, Gormley was certain that a well-motivated, well-trained and well-equipped force could beat mercenaries, who were fighting only for money. As for lone renegades, well, they would be rounded up and dealt with in due time.

It took him nearly six months to bring his force up to the peak of efficiency that he demanded. Like himself, most of the men and women in this Astro Corporation task force were either retired military or younger types who had taken a leave of absence from their regular duties to take a crack at the better pay and more exciting duty offered by the Asteroid War.

Gormley stressed to his troops that while the HSS people were mercenaries, fighting for nothing more than money, they themselves were serving in the best traditions of the military, going into battle to keep the Asteroid Belt free from the dictatorship of one corporation, fighting to save the miners and prospectors scattered through the Belt from virtual slavery. It never occurred to him that Humphries's mercenaries could say the same thing about him and his troops, with the same degree of truth.

Now he led a force of fourteen ships, armed with high-power lasers and armored with rocky debris crushed from asteroidal stone. His mission was to clear HSS ships from the inner Belt, and then take up a position near Vesta to begin the blockade and eventual strangulation of the major Humphries base.

He had no idea that he was sailing into a trap.

Nobuhiko Yamagata noted that even though it was high summer in Japan, here at the Roof of the World the monastery was still cold, its stone walls icy to the touch of his fingertips. He looked out through the room's only window and consoled himself that at least the Himalayas were still snowcapped. The greenhouse warming had not yet melted them bare.

His father entered the small chamber so silently that when he said, "Hello, son," Nobu nearly hopped off his feet.

Turning, Nobu saw that although his father was smiling, the old man did not look truly pleased. Saito wore his usual kimono. His round face seemed even more youthful than the last time Nobu had visited. Is Father taking youth treatments? Nobuhiko asked himself. He dared not ask aloud.

Kneeling on the mat nearer the window, Saito said, "I just learned that one of our loyal agents was assassinated, together with his wife and children."

Nobu blinked with surprised confusion as he knelt beside his father.

"Assassinated?"

"The man who was assigned to make certain that Pancho Lane was not killed in the cable car incident," Saito explained curtly.

"That was months ago."

"His wife and children?" Saito demanded.

Kneading his thighs nervously, Nobu said, "Our security people felt it was necessary. To make certain there would be no possibility of Astro Corporation learning that we caused the accident."

"He was a loyal employee."

"I did not approve the move, Father. I didn't even know about it until after the fact."

Saito gave a low, growling grunt.

"The incident achieved its purpose," Nobu said, trying to get his father's approval. "It started the chain of events that has led to out-and-out war between Astro and Humphries Space Systems."

Saito nodded, although his displeased expression did not change.

"Both Astro and HSS are actually hiring our own people to help them in the fighting," Nobu added. "We're making money from their war."

A slight hint of a smile cracked Saito's stern visage.

Encouraged, Nobu went on, "I believe it's time to consider how and when we step in."

"Not yet."

"If we throw our support to one side or the other, that side will win the war, undoubtedly."

"Yes, I realize that," said the older man. "But it is too early. Let them exhaust themselves further. Already both Astro and HSS are running up huge losses because of this war. Let them bleed more red ink before we make our move."

Nobu dipped his chin in agreement. Then he asked, "Which of them do you think we should support? When the time comes, of course."

"Neither."

"Neither? But I thought—"

Saito raised an imperious hand. "When the proper moment comes, when both Astro and Humphries are tottering on the brink of collapse, we will sweep in and take command of the Belt. Our mercenary units now serving them will show their true colors. The flying crane of Yamagata will stretch its wings across the entire Asteroid Belt, and over Selene as well."

Nobu gasped at his father's grand vision.

He should have been enjoying a restful vacation at Hotel Luna, but Lars Fuchs was not.

In his guise as Karl Manstein, Fuchs was spending the expense-account money Pancho had advanced him as if there was a never-ending supply of it. In truth, it was dwindling like a sand castle awash in the inrushing tide. Hotel Luna may have been threadbare, narrowly avoiding bankruptcy on the trickle of tourists coming to Selene, but its prices were still five-star. Fresh fish from the hotel's own aquaculture ponds; rental wings for soaring like an eagle in the Grand Plaža on one's own muscular strength; guided walks across the cracked and pitted floor of the Alphonsus ringwall, where the wreckage of the primitive *Ranger 9* spacecraft sat beneath a protective dome of clear glassteel; all these things cost money, and then some.

Even though Fuchs/Manstein took in none of the tourist attractions and ate as abstemiously as possible, a suite at Hotel Luna was outrageously expensive. He spent every waking moment studying the layout of Selene, its tunnels and living spaces, its offices and workshops, the machinery systems that supplied the underground city with air to breathe and potable water. In particular, he tried to find out all he could about the lowermost level of Selene, the big natural grotto that Martin Humphries had transformed into a lush garden and luxurious mansion for himself.

About the mansion he could learn nothing. Humphries's security maintained a close guard over its layout and life support systems. Fuchs had to be satisfied with memorizing every detail of the plumbing and electrical power systems that led to the grotto. There was no information available on the piping and conduits once they entered Humphries's private preserve. Perhaps that will be enough, Fuchs thought. Perhaps that will do.

He kept at his task doggedly, filling every moment of each day with his studies, telling himself a hundred times an hour that he would find a way to kill Martin Humphries.

In the night, when he was so exhausted from his work that he could no longer keep his eyes open, the rage returned anew. He and Amanda had roomed at the Hotel Luna once. They had made love in a bedroom like the one he now was in. During the rare moments when he was actually able to sleep he dreamed of Amanda, relived their passion. And awoke to find himself shamed and sticky from his brief dreams.

I'm only a kilometer or so from Humphries, Fuchs told himself over and again. Close enough to kill him. Soon. Soon.

TORCH SHIP *SAMARKAND*

Fourteen ships, sir. Confirmed," said Harbin's pilot. The bridge of *Samarkand* was crowded with the pilot, communications technician, weapons tech, the executive officer, and Harbin, seated in the command chair, all of them in bulky, awkward space suits. The navigation officer had been banished to a rearward cabin, connected to the bridge by the ship's intercom.

"A formidable fleet," Harbin murmered.

His own force consisted of only three ships. Although he by far preferred to work alone, Harbin realized that the war had escalated far beyond the point where single ships could engage in one-on-one battles. He was now the leader of a trio of ships, a Yamagata employee, working for Humphries under a contract between HSS and Yamagata.

"They've detected us," the comm tech sang out. "Radar contact."

"Turn to one-fifteen degrees azimuth, maintain constant elevation. Increase acceleration to one-quarter g."

"They're following."

"Good."

Lasers were the weapons that spacecraft used against one another. From a distance of a thousand kilometers their intense beams of energy could slash through the unprotected skin of a spacecraft's hull in a second or less. Defensive armor was the countermove against energy weapons: Warships now spread coatings of asteroidal rubble over their hulls. Newer ships were being built at Selene of pure diamond, manufactured by nanomachines out of carbon soot.

But there was a countermeasure against armored ships, Harbin knew, as he led Astro Corporation's armada of fourteen ships toward the trap.

HSS intelligence had provided Harbin with a very detailed knowledge of the Astro ships, their mission plan, and—most importantly—their commander. Harbin had never met Reid Gormley, but he knew that the pint-sized Astro commander liked to go into battle with a clear preponderance of numbers.

Fourteen ships against three, Harbin thought. Clearly superior. Clearly.

"Don't let them get away!" snapped Gormley as he leaned forward tensely in the command chair of his flagship, *Antares*.

"We're matching their velocity vector, sir," said his navigation officer.

Like their quarry, Gormley's crews had donned their individual space suits. A ship may get punctured in battle and lose air; the suits were a necessary precaution, even though they were cumbersome. Gormley didn't like being in a suit, and he didn't think they were really necessary. But doctrine demanded the precaution and he followed doctrine obediently.

"I want to overtake them. Increase our velocity. Pass the word to the other ships."

"We should send a probe ahead to see if there are other enemy vessels lying outside our radar range," said Gormley's executive officer, a broomstick-lean, coal-black Sudanese who had never been in battle before.

"Our radar can pick up craters on the moons of Jupiter, for god's sake," Gormley snapped back. "Do you see anything out there except the three we're chasing?"

"Nosir," the Sudanese replied uneasily, his eyes on the radar screen. "Only a few small rocks."

Gormley took a quick glance at the radar. "Pebbles," he smirked. "Nothing to worry about."

The Sudanese stayed silent, but he thought, Nothing to worry about unless we go sailing into them. He made a mental note to stay well clear of those pebbles, no matter where the quarry went in its effort to escape.

Wearing a one-piece miniskirted outfit with its front zipper pulled low, Victoria Ferrer had to scamper in her high-heeled softboots to keep pace with Martin Humphries as he strode briskly along the corridor between the baby's nursery and his office.

"Send the brat to Earth," he snapped. "I don't want to see him again."

Ferrer could count the number of his visits to the nursery on the fingers of one hand. She had to admit, though, that the room looked more like a hospital's intensive care ward than an ordinary nursery. Barely more than six months old, little Van Humphries still needed a special high-pressure chamber to get enough air into his tiny lungs. The baby was scrawny, sickly, and Humphries had no patience for a weakling.

"Wouldn't it be better to keep him here?" she asked, hurrying alongside Humphries. "We have the facilities here and we can bring in any specialists the baby needs."

Humphries cast a cold eye on her. "You're not fond of the runt, are you?"

"He's only a helpless baby . . ."

"And you think that getting him attached to you will be a good career move? You think you'll have better job security by mothering the runt?"

She looked genuinely shocked. "That never crossed my mind!"

"Of course not."

Ferrer stopped dead in her tracks and planted her fists on her hips. "Mr. Humphries, *sir:* If you believe that I'm trying to use your son for my own gain, you're completely wrong. I'm not that cold-blooded."

He stopped, too, a few paces farther along the corridor, and looked her over. She seemed sincere enough, almost angry at him. Humphries laughed inwardly at the image of her, eyes flashing with righteous indignation, fists on her hips. Nice hips, he noted. She breathes sexy, too.

"We'll see how warm-blooded you are tonight," he said. Turning, he started along the corridor again. "I want the brat sent Earthside. To my family estate in Connecticut, or what's left of it. That's where his brother is. I've got enough staff and tutors there to start a university. Set up a facility for him there, get the best medical team on Earth to take care of him. Just keep him out of my sight. I don't want to lay eyes on him again. Ever."

Ferrer scurried to catch up with him. "Suppose they can cure him, make him healthy. Maybe nanotherapy or—"

"If and when that happy day arrives, I'll reconsider. Until then, keep him out of my sight. Understand?"

She nodded unhappily. "Understood."

Feeling nettled, fuming, Humphries ducked into his office and slammed the door shut behind him. Send the runt to Connecticut. Alex is down there. My real son. My clone. He's growing up fine and strong. I should've gotten rid of that miserable little brat his first day, the day his mother died. I've got a son; I don't need this other little slug.

Once he got to his desk, Humphries saw that a message from Grigor was waiting for him. He slid into his desk chair and commanded the phone to call his security chief.

Grigor appeared in front of Humphries's desk, seated at his own desk in his own office, a few meters down the hall, dark and dour as usual.

"What is it?" Humphries asked without preamble.

"The Astro flotilla that has been assembled in the Belt is pursuing our Yamagata team, as predicted."

Humphries dipped his chin a bare centimeter. "So the computer wargame is working out, is it?"

"The simulation is being followed. Gormley is rushing into the trap."

"Good. Call me when it's over." Humphries was about to cut the connection when he added. "Send me the video record as soon as it's available."

Grigor nodded. "I think you'll enjoy it," he said, mirthlessly.

"They're veering off," Gormley said, his eyes riveted to the navigation screen. "Follow them! Increase speed. Don't let them get away!"

The Sudanese executive officer noted with some relief that the three fleeing enemy ships had turned away from the sprinkling of small rocks that they had been approaching. They want no more to do with that danger than I do, he said to himself.

"We're well within range," said the weapons officer.

"Locked on?"

Without even glancing at her console, the weapons officer said, "Five lasers are locked onto each of the enemy's vessels, sir."

"Get on their tails," Gormley said. "They may be armored, but they can't armor their thruster nozzles. Hit their thrusters and we've got them crippled."

Of course, thought the Sudanese. But his attention was still on those small rocks off to their starboard. Strange to see such small objects without a larger asteroid that gave birth to them. They're like a reef in the ocean, a danger lurking, waiting to smash unsuspecting ships. Then he thought, For a man who was brought up far from the sea, you've become quite a mariner.

Harbin heard the alarm in the voice of his pilot. "They're firing at us! Firing at all three of us."

"They can't do much damage at this range," he said calmly.

"If they hit our thrusters . . ." The pilot turned in his chair and saw the set of Harbin's jaw. "Sir," he added lamely.

"All ships," Harbin commanded, "increase elevation three degrees, now."

To his exec he said, "Activate the rocks."

"They're maneuvering!" sang out the weapons officer.

Gormley saw it on the nav screen. "Keep locked onto them. Don't let them get away!"

Even the Sudanese had turned his attention away from the small rocks that were now fairly far off to their starboard to concentrate on the battle action. The enemy ships were maneuvering in unison, which was foolish. Far better, when being chased, to maneuver independently and set up a more difficult targeting problem for the attackers.

The collision-avoidance radar began to bong loudly.

"What in blazes is that?" Gormley shouted.

The navigation screen automatically switched to show several dozen meter-sized rocks hurtling toward Gormley's ships. The Sudanese could see glowing plumes of exhaust plasma thrusting the rocks toward them.

How simple! he realized. Set up small rocks with plasma thrusters and guidance chips, lure your enemy toward them, and then fire the rocks into your enemy's ships. How simple. And how deadly.

The rocks were moving at high velocity when they smashed into the Astro Corporation ships. They tore the ships apart, like high-speed bullets fired through tin cans. One of them blasted through the bridge of *Antares*, ripped through the helmeted head of the ship's pilot and plowed out the other side of the bridge while the woman's decapitated body showered blood everywhere. Screams and cries of horror filled the Sudanese's helmet earphones. Cursing wildly, he cut off the suit radio as his chair ripped free of its mounting on the ship's deck and crashed through the gaping hole in the bridge where the rock had gone through. He felt his left arm snap, and a dizzying wave of excruciating pain shot down his spine. Then he felt and heard nothing.

He was spinning slowly, slowly through empty space, still strapped into his broken chair. He could feel nothing below his neck. He could hardly breathe. Through tear-filled eyes he saw the shattered remnants of Gormley's fleet, broken and smashed pieces of spacecraft, bodies floating in their space suits, a proud armada reduced in a few seconds to a slowly spreading patch of debris. Flotsam, he thought idly. We are going to die in this empty wilderness.

"My god," whispered someone on the bridge of *Samarkand*.

Harbin also stared at the destruction. The Astro fleet looked as if it had gone through a shredder. A meatgrinder. Bodies and wreckage were strewn everywhere, spinning, tumbling, coasting through space.

"Should we pick up the survivors?" his pilot asked, in a hushed voice.

Harbin shook his head. "There are no survivors."

"But maybe some—"

"There are no survivors," he repeated harshly. But his eyes lingered on the display screen. A few hundred new asteroids have been added to the Belt, he told himself. Some of them were once human beings.

ASTRO CORPORATION HEADQUARTERS

W iped out?" Pancho asked, her insides suddenly gone hollow.

"Every ship," said Jake Wanamaker. "No survivors." He looked grim, beaten.

"What happened?"

Wanamaker was standing before her desk like a man facing a firing squad. Pancho pushed herself to her feet and gestured him to one of the comfortably padded chairs arranged around the small oval table in the corner of her office. Feeling shaky, her knees rubbery, she went to the table and sat next to her military commander.

"We're not certain. We got a brief signal that they used small asteroids—some of them no bigger than a man's fist—and rammed them into Gormley's ships."

"How could they do that?" Pancho asked.

"Attach a plasma rocket and a simple guidance system to the rock," said Wanamaker. "It doesn't have to be fancy. Just juice the rocks up to very high velocity and ram them into our ships. Like buckshot hitting paper bags."

"And they're all dead?"

Wanamaker nodded bleakly.

Jesus sufferin' Christ, Pancho thought. Thirteen ships. A hundred and fifty people, just about.

"I think I should tender my resignation," said Wanamaker.

Pancho glared at him. "Giving up?"

He flinched as though she'd slapped him. "No. But a defeat like this . . . you'll probably want a better man to head your war."

Shaking her head slowly, Pancho said, "No, I want you, Jake. One battle doesn't mean we've lost it all."

But inwardly she thought, I want you to keep on heading the military operations. But I'll take charge of this goddamned war. Humphries might have the edge on us militarily, with more mercenaries and more ships and better experience. But there's more than one way to fight a war.

To Wanamaker, she said, "I'm not giving up. Far as I'm concerned, this war's just started."

"'I have not yet begun to fight,'" he muttered.

"I heard that one," Pancho said. "John Paul Jones, wasn't it?"

Wanamaker nodded.

"Okay. You recruit more mercenaries, I'll buy more ships. For the time being, Humphries has the run of the Belt. He's gonna attack any Astro vessels he can find out there, try to drive us out of the Belt altogether."

"Convoy them."

"Convoy?"

"Don't let them sail alone. Put them in groups. It's harder to attack a formation of armed ships than a single ship."

"Makes sense," Pancho agreed. "I'll send out the word right away."

"I think Yamagata Corporation can provide us with reliable mercenaries."

"Good. Go get 'em."

It took a moment for Wanamaker to realize he'd been dismissed. It only hit him when Pancho pushed her chair back from the conference table and got to her feet. He shot up and started to salute, then caught himself and reddened slightly.

"I've got a lot of work to do," he said, as if excusing himself for leaving the room.

"Me too," said Pancho.

Wanamaker left, and Pancho returned to her desk. She called up reports on where the Astro ships were, and where Humphries's vessels were. A holographic representation of the vast space between Earth and the Belt took form in the air beyond her desk, a huge dark expanse with flickering pinpoints of light showing the positions of the ships, Astro's in blue, HSS's in red. There was a cluster of ships between the Earth and Moon; Pancho blanked them out to simplify the three-dimensional picture.

Cripes, there's a lot of red ones out in the Belt, she said to herself. And those are just the ones we know about. The Humper's prob'ly got a lot more out there, moving around the Belt without any telemetry or identification beacons for the IAA to pick up.

She had the computer identify the ore freighters, logistics carriers, and ships carrying miners to specific asteroids. Then she added the freelancers, the prospectors and miners who worked on their own, independent of the big corporations.

Minutes ticked into hours as she studied the situation. We're outnumbered in the Belt two, three to one, Pancho saw. The Hump's been building up his fleet out there for years now. We've gotta play catch-up.

But why should we play their game? she asked herself. That's what we were doing with Gormley and look what it got us.

She leaned back in her softly yielding desk chair and closed her eyes briefly. What's the point of all those ships out in the Belt? To bring ores to the factories on Earth, or in Earth orbit, or here at Selene, she answered her own question.

She stared at the hologram imagery again. Flickering red dots representing HSS ships were spread through the Belt, with a particular clustering around Vesta. But a thinner trickle of red dots was plying the lanes between the Belt and the Earth/Moon vicinity.

They've gotta bring the goods back here, Pancho saw. That's the whole point of mining the rocks. If we can knock off their ships coming Earthward, we can hit Humphries in the pocketbook, strangle his cash flow, cut his profits down to nothing.

She sat up straight in the desk chair and said aloud, "That's the way to do it! Let him have the Belt for now. Stop him from bringing the ores to market."

We don't need naval tactics, she realized. We don't need battles between fleets of warships. What we need is more like a gang of pirates. Like the old Sea Hawks from Queen Elizabeth I's time. Privateers. Pirates.

And she knew just the man who could lead such a campaign. Lars Fuchs.

"All of them?" Humphries asked, as if the news was too good to be true.

Vicki Ferrer was not smiling, but it was clear from the pleased expression on her face that she was happy to be able to bring her boss a positive report.

"Every Astro ship was destroyed," she repeated.

They were in the big library/bar on the ground floor of Humphries's mansion, alone except for the robot bartender, which stood at its post, gleaming stainless steel reflecting the ceiling lights.

"You're sure?" Humphries asked.

"The report came directly from the Yamagata team. Their idea about using the rocks worked perfectly. The Astro fleet charged right into them. No survivors."

"This calls for champagne!" Humphries strode to the bar. The robot did not move. Nettled slightly at the machine's obtuseness, Humphries called out, "Bartender! Champagne!"

The gleaming dome-topped robot trundled sideways along the bar and stopped precisely at the wine cooler. Two slim arms extruded from its cylindrical body, opened the cooler, and pulled out a bottle of Veuve Cliquot. It trundled back to Humphries and held up the bottle so he could inspect the label.

"Fine," said Humphries. "Open it and let me sample it."

"How does it find the right bottle?" Ferrer asked, coming over to sit on the stool next to him. Even though it was dinner time for most people, she was still in her office attire, a miniskirted baby pink suit that hugged her curves artfully.

"There's a sensor in each hand," said Humphries, watching the dumb machine gripping the cork. If he drops that bottle, Humphries thought, I'll run him through the recycler.

The cork came out with a satisfactorily loud pop and the robot set two champagne flutes on the bar top in front of Humphries, then poured a thimbleful of wine for him to taste.

Humphries tasted, nodded, told the robot to pour. Once it had, he lifted his glass to Ferrer and toasted, "To victory!"

She made a smile and murmured, "To victory."

"We've got them on the run now," Humphries said happily. "I'm going to drive Astro completely out of the Belt!"

Ferrer smiled again and sipped. But she was thinking, Thirteen ships destroyed. How many people did we kill? How many more have to die before this is over?

HOTEL LUNA: RESIDENTIAL SUITE

Pancho could not locate Fuchs. For two days she had her people search for him. They learned that under the false identity she had provided, Fuchs had spent a few days in his native Switzerland, then flown to Selene.

"He's here in Selene?" she asked her security chief.

The man looked uncomfortable. "Apparently."

"Find him," she snapped. "Wherever the hell he is, find him. You got twenty-four hours."

She had just returned to her suite when the phone told her the report on Fuchs came in. She glanced at her wristwatch. Eight minutes before midnight, Pancho saw. They're working overtime.

The suite's décor was set to Camelot, Pancho's fantasy of what King Arthur's fabled castle might have been like. She sat herself on one of the sofas in her bedroom and told the phone to play the report. Through a mullioned window she could see knights jousting on a perfect greensward beneath a cloudless blue sky, watched by a cheering throng standing before tented pavilions complete with colorful pennants that fluttered in the breeze of an eternal springtime.

The young man whose hologram image appeared in the middle of the room might have been one of knights of the Round Table, Pancho thought idly. He was a good-looking blond, strong shoulders, honest open face with sky-blue eyes, his hair stylishly long enough for ringlets to curl around the collar of his jacket. He was sitting at a desk in what appeared to be a smallish office somewhere in the Astro headquarters. The data line hovering to one side of the image identified him as Frederic Karstein, Astro security department.

Pancho listened to the brief report with growing incredulity. And annoyance.

"You mean he was right here in the Hotel Luna?" she asked the image.

The image flickered momentarily. Then the handsome Frederic Karstein said, "Ms. Lane, I'm live now. I can answer your questions in real time, ma'am."

"Are you telling me that Fuchs was living just a couple hundred meters from my own quarters?" she demanded.

"Yes, ma'am, apparently he was."

"And where is he now?"

Karstein shrugged his broad shoulders. "We don't know. He seems to have disappeared."

"Disappeared? How can he disappear?"

"If we knew that, Ms. Lane, we'd probably know where he is."

"You can't just disappear! Selene's not that big, and the whole dog-gone place is under surveillance all the time."

Karstein looked embarrassed. "We're certain he hasn't left Selene. We've checked the passenger lists for all the outgoing flights for the past two weeks, and examined the surveillance camera records."

"So he's someplace here in Selene?"

"It would appear so."

Pancho huffed. "All right. Stay on this. I want him found, and right away, too."

"We'll do our best, Ms. Lane."

She cut the connection and Karstein's image winked out. Dumb blond, Pancho groused to herself.

"Privateers?" Jake Wanamaker asked, his rasping voice croaking out the word. "You mean, like pirates?"

Pancho had invited him to a breakfast meeting in her suite. They sat in the tight little alcove off the kitchen, but the holowalls made it seem as if they were outdoors, beneath a graceful elm tree, with softly rolling grassy hills in the distance and the morning sun brightening a clear sky. She could hear birds chirping happily and almost felt a cool breeze ruffling their table linen.

Pancho took a sip of grapefruit juice, then replied, "Yep. Yo-ho-ho and all that stuff. Cut off Humphries's ships as they're bringing their payloads here to the Moon. Or to Earth."

Wanamaker took a considerable bite out of the sticky bun he was holding in one big hand, chewed thoughtfully for a few moments, then swallowed. "They've beaten the crap out of us in the Belt, sure enough. It'll be some time before we can build up enough forces to challenge them again."

"But a few ships operating closer to home, outside the Belt . . ." Pancho let the suggestion hang in the air between them.

Wanamaker muttered, "Cut HSS's pipeline to the market. Hit Humphries in the pocketbook."

"That's where it'd hurt him the most."

After washing down his cake with a gulp of black coffee, Wanamaker said, "Set up a blockade."

"Right."

Absently wiping his sticky fingers with his napkin, Wanamaker broke into a wicked grin. "We wouldn't even need crewed ships for that. Just automate some small birds and park them in wide orbits around the Earth/Moon system."

"You can do that?"

He nodded. "They'd be close enough to be remotely operated from here at Selene. It'd be cheaper than using crewed ships."

Pancho had only one further question. "How soon can we get this going?"

Wanamaker pushed his chair back from the table and got to his feet. "Real soon," he said. "Very damned real soon."

Pancho watched him hurry away, thinking, So I won't need Lars after all. Doesn't matter where he's hiding. I won't need him now.

Later that morning, with some reluctance, Pancho slipped on the soft-suit and sealed the opening that ran the length of the torso's front. Doug Stavenger was already in his suit. To Pancho he looked as if he'd been packed into a plastic-wrap food container, except for the fishbowl helmet he held cradled in his arms.

"This thing really works?" she asked, picking up her helmet from the shelf in the locker.

Stavenger nodded, smiling at her. "It's been tested for months now, Pancho. I've worn it outside myself several times. You're going to love it."

She felt totally unconvinced. Never fly in a new airplane, she remembered from her first days as a pilot. Never eat in a new restaurant on its opening day.

Plucking at the transparent nanomachined fabric with gloved fingers, she said, "Kinda flimsy."

"But it works like a charm."

"That mean you gotta say prayers over it?"

Stavenger laughed. "Come on, Pancho. Once we're outside you'll wonder how you were ever able to stand those clunky cermet suits."

"Uh-huh." She could see the enthusiasm in his eyes, his smile, his whole demeanor. He's like a kid with a new toy, she thought.

But he was right. It took roughly ten minutes to walk from the airlock at Selene to Factory Number Eleven, out on the floor of the giant crater Alphonsus. Before even five minutes were up, Pancho had fallen in love with the softsuit.

"It's terrific," she said to Stavenger, shuffling along beside her, his boots kicking up gentle clouds of dust. "It's like being without a suit, almost."

"I told you, didn't I?"

Pancho held both hands before her and flexed her fingers. "Hot spit! Even the gloves are easy to work. This is like magic!"

"Not magic. Just nanotechnology."

"And the radiation protection?"

"About the same as a hard-shell suit," Stavenger said. "We could add electromagnetic shielding, but that would probably attract a lot of dust from the ground."

She nodded inside her helmet.

"You're okay for short time periods on the surface," Stavenger went on. "Off the Moon an electromagnetic system can be added to the suits easily enough."

Pancho asked, "Doug, ol' pal, how'd you like to sign a contract with Astro to manufacture and distribute these softsuits?"

He laughed. "No thanks, Pancho. Selene's going to develop this product. We'll sell them at pretty close to cost, too."

Pancho understood the meaning behind his words. If Selene signed up with Astro for selling the suits, Humphries would complain. If Selene gave a contract to HSS, Astro would fight it. She nodded again inside the fishbowl helmet. Better to keep this out of either corporation's hands. Better to let Selene handle this one themselves.

The low curving roof of the factory loomed before them. Stavenger and Pancho climbed the stairs to the edge of the factory's thick concrete slab, then stepped through the "car wash," the special airlock that scrubbed their suits free of dust and other contaminants before they were allowed to enter the ultra-pure domain of the factory itself. Pancho felt the jets and scrubbers pummeling her brutally.

"Hey Doug," she gasped. "You gotta reset these things to go easier."

His voice in her helmet earphones sounded bemused. "We did reset them, Pancho. They would've knocked you flat if we'd left them at the same power level we used for the hard-shell suits."

It took Pancho a few moments to catch her breath once she had stepped out of the "car wash" and onto the factory floor. As Stavenger came up beside her, also breathing heavily, she looked out at the two completed spacecraft. Their diamond hulls looked dark, like ominous shadows lurking beneath the curved roof of the factory.

"There they are," Stavenger said tightly. "One for you and one for Humphries."

She understood the tension in his voice. "Two brand-new warships. So we can go out and kill some more mercenaries."

Stavenger said nothing.

"We've got six more under contract, right?" she asked.

After several heartbeats, Stavenger said, "Yes. And we're building the same number for Humphries."

"So no matter who wins, Selene makes money."

"I don't like it, Pancho. I don't like any of this. If I could convince the governing council to renege on these contracts, I would."

"I don't like it either, Doug. But what else can we do? Let the Humper take over the whole danged solar system?"

He fell silent again.

As they trudged back in silence toward the airlock at Selene, Pancho said to herself: Deadlock. Selene doesn't want either one of us to win. They don't want one side to beat the other and become master of the whole solar system. Even if Astro wins, if I win, Selene's scared shitless that they'll be under my thumb. Doug wants to see Humphries and Astro fight ourselves into exhaustion, and then he'll step in and be the peacemaker again.

So they're doing their best to keep us even. They won't make a warship for Humphries without making one for Astro. Keeps them neutral, Doug says. Keeps us in a deadlock, that's what it keeps.

There's gotta be some way out of this, some way to break through and beat the Humper before we're both so broke and dead-flat exhausted that both our corporations go bust.

If I could get Lars to help us, she thought. He might just be able to tip the scales in our favor. But the l'il bugger has disappeared. What's he up to? Why's he gone to ground on me?

Shaking her head inside the fishbowl helmet, Pancho considered: We need an outside force, a partner, an ally. Somebody who can tip the scales in Astro's favor. Outmaneuver Humphries. Overpower him. Some way to outflank HSS.

Then it hit her. Nairobi! That guy from Nairobi Industries wanted a strategic alliance with Astro. I wonder if he's still interested? I'll have to look him up soon's I get back to the office, whatever his name was.

ASTRO CORPORATION COMMAND CENTER

Jake Wanamaker's command center was a cluster of offices set slightly apart from the rest of Astro Corporation's headquarters. With wry humor, Wanamaker mused that Humphries could do more damage to Astro, at far less cost, by attacking these offices and wiping out the corporation's military command. But even war has its rules, and one of the fundamental rules of this conflict was that no violence would be tolerated anywhere on the Moon. The side that broke that rule would bring Selene and its considerable financial and manufacturing clout into the battle as an enemy.

So despite the purely perfunctory guards stationed at the double doors of the command center, armed with nothing more than sidearms, Wanamaker had little fear of being attacked here in Selene. He went through the doors and down the central corridor, heading for his own office to a chorus of "Good morning, Admiral" accompanied by military salutes. Wanamaker returned each salute scrupulously: good discipline began with mutual respect, he felt.

Wanamaker's office was spartan. The battleship-gray metal furniture was strictly utilitarian. The only decorations on the walls were citations he had garnered over his years of service. The wallscreens were blank as his staff filed in and took their chairs along the scuffed old conference table that butted against his desk. Wanamaker had salvaged them both from his last sea command, an amphibious assault command vessel.

He spent the morning outlining Pancho's idea of setting up a blockade against incoming HSS ore carriers.

"Unmanned craft?" asked one of his junior officers.

"Uncrewed," Wanamaker corrected, "remotely operated from here."

One of the women officers asked, "Here in Selene? Won't that get Stavenger and the governing council riled up?"

"Not if we don't commit any violent acts here in Selene," Wanamaker replied, smiling coldly. Then he added, "And especially if they don't know about it."

"It won't be easy to build and launch the little robots without Stavenger's people finding out about it."

"We can build them easily enough in Astro's factories up on the surface and launch them aboard Astro boosters. No need for Selene to get worked up over this."

The younger officers glanced at each other up and down the conference table, while Wanamaker watched from behind his desk. They get the idea, he saw. I'm not asking for their opinions about the idea, I'm telling them that they've got to make it work.

"Well," his engineering chief said, "we can build the little suckers easily enough. Nothing exotic about putting together a heavy laser with a communications system and some station-keeping gear."

"Good," said Wanamaker.

Gradually the rest of the staff warmed to the idea.

At length he asked, "How long will it take?"

"We could have the first ones ready to launch in a couple of weeks," said the engineer.

Wanamaker silently doubled the estimate.

"Wait," cautioned the intelligence officer, a plump Armenian with long, straight dark hair and darker eyes. "Each of these birds will need sensors to identify potential targets and aim the lasers."

"No worries," said the Australian electronics officer. "We can do that in two shakes of a sheep's tail. Piece of cake."

"Besides," pointed out the engineer, "the birds will be operated from here, with human brains in the loop."

The intelligence officer looked dubious, but voiced no further objections.

"All right, then," said Wanamaker at last. "Let's get to work on this. Pronto. Time is of the essence."

That broke up the meeting. But as the staff officers were shuffling toward the door, Wanamaker called the intelligence officer back to his desk.

"Sit down, Willie," he said, gesturing to the chair on the desk's left side. He knew she disliked to be called by her real name, Wilhelmina. The things parents do to their kids, Wanamaker thought.

She sat, looking curious, almost worried.

Wanamaker took a breath, then said, "We need a diversion."

"Sir?"

"Humphries has beat the hell out of us in the Belt, and it's going to be months before we can start fighting back."

"But Jess said he'd have the first robots on station in two weeks," the intelligence officer countered.

"Two weeks plus Murphy's Law," Wanamaker said.

Her dark eyes lit with understanding. "If anything can go wrong, it will."

"Especially in a wartime situation. I know the staff will push as hard as they can, but I don't expect to be able to hit back to HSS with these robot systems for at least a month, maybe more."

"I see," she said.

"Meanwhile, we need a diversion. Something to knock the HSS people off their feet a little, shake them up, make them realize we're not going to lay down and die."

"Such as?"

He grinned lopsidedly at her. "That's what I want you to figure out, kid."

She did not smile back. "I'll do my best, sir."

evinson felt distinctly uneasy in the space suit. It was bad enough to have to fly out to this remote piece of rock in the middle of nowhere, carrying the heavily armored flask of nanomachines he had produced in the HSS lab at Selene. Now he had to actually go out of the ship like some superjock astronaut and supervise the crew he had brought with him.

"Me?" he had asked, alarmed, when Vickie Ferrer had told him that Martin Humphries himself wanted Lev to personally supervise the experiment.

"You," she had replied, silky smooth. "It's to your advantage to handle the job yourself. Why let someone else take the credit for it?"

As he hung weightlessly between the slowly spinning torch ship and the lumpy dark asteroid, clipped to the tether that was anchored to the ship's airlock, Lev realized that Vickie had played him like a puppet. Her alluring smiles and promising cleavage, her smoky voice and tantalizing hints of what would be possible after he had succeeded with his nanomachines had brought him out here, to this dark and cold emptiness, face to face with a pitted, ugly chunk of rock the size of a football field.

Well, he told himself, when I get back she'll be waiting for me. She said as much. I'll be a big success and she'll be so impressed she'll do whatever I want her to.

Prodded by Ferrer's implicit promises, Levinson had rushed through the laboratory work. Producing nanomachines that were not damaged by ultraviolet light was no great feat; the trick was to keep them contained so they couldn't get loose and start eating up everything in sight. It was after he'd accomplished that that Ferrer had told him he must go out to the Belt and personally supervise the experiment.

So here I am, he said to himself, shuddering inside the space suit.

It's so absolutely *empty* out here! Despite his cerebral knowledge that the Asteroid Belt was mostly empty space, he found the dark silence unsettling. It's like being in a football stadium with only one seat occupied, he thought. Like being all alone in an empty city.

There were the stars, of course, but they just made Levinson feel spookier. There were millions of them, countless myriads of them crowding the sky so much that the old friendly constellations he knew from Earth were blotted out, swamped in the multitudes. And they didn't twinkle, they just hung up there as if they were watching, solemn unblinking eyes staring down at him.

"We're ready to unseal the bugs." The voice of one of his technicians grated in his earphones, startling Levinson out of his thoughts.

"They're not bugs," he replied automatically. "They're nanomachines."

"Yeah, right. We're ready to open the jug."

Levinson pulled himself slowly along the tether to its other end, anchored in the solid rock of the little asteroid. His two technicians floated above the rock, able to flit back and forth on the minijet thruster units attached to their backpacks. Levinson, a novice at extravehicular activities, kept himself firmly clipped to the tether. He carried the "jug," a sealed bottle made of pure diamond, on the utility belt around the waist of his space suit.

He planted his feet on the asteroid and, much to his consternation, immediately bounced off. In his earphones he heard one of his techs snicker softly.

"Newton's laws work even out here," he said, to cover his embarrassment.

He approached the rock more slowly and, after two more tries, finally got his boots to stay on the surface. He could see the puffs of dust where he first landed still hanging in the asteroid's minuscule gravity.

The technicians had marked concentric fluorescent circles across the surface of the rock, like a glowing bull's-eye. Cameras back in the ship would record how quickly the nanomachines spread from the release point, chewing up the rock as they went. Levinson went to the center of the circles, tugging on his tether, bobbing up and off the asteroid's surface with each step he took. He heard no giggling from his technicians this time. Probably they've turned their transmitters off, he thought.

It was clumsy working in the space suit's gloves, even with the tiny servomotors on the backs to help him flex the fingers. Finally Levinson unsealed the bottle and placed it, open end down, on the exact center of the bull's-eye. Again, the light gravity worked against him. The bottle bobbed up from the surface as soon as he took his hand off it. Frowning, he pushed it down and held it for a moment, then carefully removed his hand. The bottle stayed put.

Looking up, he saw that both his technicians were hovering well clear of the rock. Scared of the nanomachines, Levinson thought. Well, better to be safe than sorry. He grabbed the tether with both hands and hauled himself off the asteroid, then started his hand-over-hand return to the ship.

The tether suddenly went slack, and for a fearful moment Levinson thought something had gone wrong. Then he saw that it was still fastened to the ship's airlock and remembered that the techs were supposed to set off an explosive charge that released the end of the tether attached to the asteroid. In the vacuum of space he couldn't hear the pop of the explosive bolt. It took a surprisingly tough effort to turn around, but once he did he saw the other end of the tether hanging limply in empty space.

And the asteroid was vanishing! Levinson's eyes goggled at how fast the nanomachines were chewing up the asteroid, leaving a rising cloud of dust that grew so rapidly the solid rock itself was quickly obscured. It's like piranhas eating up a chunk of meat, he thought, recalling videos he had seen of the voracious fish setting a South American stream a-boil as they attacked their prey.

"Start the spectrometer!" Levinson called excitedly as he resumed tugging his way back to the ship.

In less than a minute he could see the sparkling dazzle of a laser beam playing over the expanding dust cloud.

Puffing with exertion, he saw as he approached the airlock that its hatch was closed. His two assistants had jetted to the ship ahead of him, he realized.

"What're you getting?" he asked into his helmet microphone.

The technician running the spectrometer aboard the ship answered, "Iron, lead, platinum, silver—"

"Pure elements or compounds?" Levinson demanded, watching

the asteroid dissolve like a log being chewed up by a wood chipper.

"Atomic species mostly. Some compounds that look pretty weird, but most of it is pure atomic species."

The weird stuff must be the nanos, Levinson thought. He had programmed them to shut down after forty-eight hours. At this rate there wouldn't be anything left of the asteroid in forty-eight hours except a cloud of individual atoms.

Wow! he thought. It works even better than I expected. Vickie's going to be impressed, all right.

ADMIRAL WANAMAKER'S OFFICE

The spare, austere office was empty except for Wanamaker himself and Wilhelmina Tashkajian, his intelligence officer. She was short, round, dark, and, according to the scuttlebutt that floated around the office, a pretty good amateur belly dancer. All Wanamaker knew for certain was that she had a fine, sharp mind, the kind that can analyze information and draw valid conclusions more quickly than anyone else on his staff. That was all he wanted to know about her.

They sat on opposite sides of the conference table that extended from the admiral's desk. Like all of Wanamaker's officers, Tashkajian wore plain gray coveralls with her name and rank spelled out on a smart-chip badge clipped to the flap of her breast pocket. Wanamaker himself wore the same uniform.

He looked up from the report on the display screen built into the table's top. "They're testing nanomachines?"

She nodded, her dark eyes somber. "Humphries recruited the scientist that Pancho brought back here from Ceres. Snatched him right out from under our noses."

Wanamaker grimaced. "She should have kept him on Astro's payroll."

"Too late for that, sir."

"And they're already in test phase?"

Another nod. "From the information we've gathered, they went through the laboratory phase very quickly, and then sent this Dr. Levinson and a crew of technicians out to the Belt. Conclusion: They're testing nanomachines on an asteroid."

"Does Pancho know this yet?"

"She gets a copy of my reports automatically."

"Any response from her?"

"Not yet, sir. I just put out the report this morning. Not everyone reacts as fast as you." She smiled slightly, then added, "Sir."

He allowed himself to smile back at her a little.

"The real question," she said, "is whether HSS is developing nanomachines for processing ores out of the asteroids or as weapons."

"Weapons?" Wanamaker's gray brows rose.

"If they can chew up rocks, they can chew up spacecraft, buildings, even people."

He sank back in the stiff metal chair. "Weapons," he muttered. "My god."

"It's a possibility, isn't it?" she asked.

"I suppose it is."

Tashkajian waited a heartbeat, then said, "I've been thinking about your request for a diversion, sir."

"Is this a change of subject?"

"Not entirely, sir."

Looking slightly puzzled, Wanamaker said, "Go ahead."

"Suppose we attacked HSS's base at Vesta," she began.

"Most of it's underground," said Wanamaker. "They're well dug in. And well defended."

"Yes, sir, I understand. But they have certain facilities on the surface of the asteroid. Communications antennas. Launchpads. Airlocks to the interior. Even their defensive laser weapons. They're all up on the surface."

"So?"

"So we strew the surface with nanomachines that eat metals."

Wanamaker's eyes flickered. She couldn't tell from his stony expression whether he was impressed or disgusted.

She plunged on, "The nanomachines would destroy metal structures, even eat into the asteroid itself. It might not wipe out the base but it would certainly disrupt their operations. It would be the diversion you've asked for."

He was silent for several moments. Then he asked, "And how do you get a ship close enough to Vesta to accomplish this raid? They'd blast the ship into molecules before it got close enough to be dangerous to them."

"I think I've got that figured out, too, sir."

He saw that she was deadly serious. She wouldn't bring this up unless she thought she had the entire scheme in hand, he realized.

"Go ahead," he said.

"We send the ship in when there's a solar flare."

Wanamaker blinked. "Do you think . . ." His voice trailed off.

"I've checked out the numbers, sir." With growing confidence she went on, "A category four solar flare emits a huge cloud of ionized particles. Scrambles communications on all frequencies, including radar! A ship could ride inside the cloud and get close enough to Vesta to release the nanomachines."

Immediately, he countered, "Solar flare clouds don't block laser beams."

"Yessir, I know. But laser sweeps aren't generally used for spotting spacecraft unless the radar scans have found a bogie. They use laser scans to identify an unknown radar blip."

"Riding inside a radiation cloud is pretty damned hazardous."

"Not if the ship is properly shielded, sir."

He fell silent once again, thinking.

"The radiation storm would drive all HSS personnel off the surface of Vesta. They'd all be deep underground, so our nanomachines would destroy their surface facilities without killing any of their personnel."

Wanamaker tried to scowl and wound up almost smiling, instead. "A humane attack on the enemy."

"A diversion that could cripple the HSS base on Vesta, at least temporarily, and check their domination of the Belt, sir."

"If there's a big enough flare to give you the cloud you need," he cautioned.

"That's what got me thinking about this idea in the first place," she said, clearly excited. "We're in the middle of a solar maximum period. Plenty of sunspots and lots of flares."

He nodded curtly. "Let me see the numbers."

"Yes, sir!"

HABITAT *CHRYSALIS*

Victoria Ferrer felt distinctly uneasy in the rock rats' habitat, in orbit around the asteroid Ceres. Although she dressed as modestly as she could, she still felt that every move she made was being watched by men — and women — who focused on her the way a stalking leopard stares at its prey.

The habitat itself was comfortable enough. The gravity was the same as the Moon's, or so close that she couldn't notice any difference. As a visitor Ferrer had a small but well-appointed compartment to herself, and the adjoining cabin to use as an office. There was a galley in the next segment of the structure, and even a passably decent restaurant on the other side of the wheel-shaped assemblage. With her expense account, she could afford to take most of her meals in the restaurant.

Ferrer had expected the rock rats to be scruffy, feisty, hard-rock types. Prospectors and miners, existing at the edge of human civilization, independent individualists eking out their living in the vast dark emptiness of the Belt, surviving in a world of danger and loneliness. To her surprise, she found that most of the residents of *Chrysalis* were shopkeepers, accountants, technicians employed in the service industries. Even the actual miners and prospectors had technical educations. They operated complex equipment out in the Belt; they had to know how to keep a spacecraft functioning when the nearest supply or maintenance depot was millions of kilometers away.

But they stared at her. Even in plain coveralls buttoned up to her chin, she felt their eyes on her. Fresh meat, she thought. A new face. A new body.

Her mission at Ceres was twofold. She was recruiting more hands for the army of mercenaries that the war demanded out of the growing numbers of unemployed miners and prospectors. And she was waiting for the return of Levinson and his nanotech team, to see firsthand the results of their experiment on an actual asteroid.

It had been pathetically easy to keep Levinson on a string. Every time they met he stared at her with hungry puppy eyes. If he comes back with a success he'll expect me to reward him, Ferrer thought. It won't be so easy to put him off then. But if he's successful I can let him down gently and maneuver him off to some other woman. God knows there are plenty here at Ceres who would be happy to get connected with a scientist who can take her back to Earth.

She tried to clear her mind of worries about Levinson and concentrate on the unemployed miner sitting on the other side of her desk. The clean-cut young man was trying his best not to ogle, but his eyes kept returning to the front of her shapeless turtleneck sweater. Momma and her damned genetic engineering, Ferrer thought. I should have brought sloppy old sweatshirts, or, better yet, a space suit.

She kept their discussion strictly on business, without a hint of anything else. Humphries had sent her here to recruit crews for HSS ships and she had no interest in anything else.

"I don't understand your reluctance," she said to the miner. "We're offering top salary and benefits."

He looked a decent-enough fellow, Ferrer thought: freshly shaved and wearing well-pressed slacks and an open-necked shirt. His dossier, on her desktop screen, showed he had an engineering degree and had spent the past four years working as a miner under contract to Astro Corporation. He'd quit a month ago and hadn't found a new job yet.

Fidgeting nervously in his chair, he answered, "Look, Ms. Ferrer, what good will all that salary and benefits do me when I'm dead?"

She knew what he meant, but still she probed, "Why do you say that?"

Making a sour face, the miner said, "You want to hire me as a crewman on one of your HSS ships, right? Everybody knows HSS and Astro are fighting it out in the Belt. People are being killed every day, just about. I'd rather bum around here on *Chrysalis* and wait for a real job to open up."

"There are a lot of unemployed miners here," Ferrer said.

"Yeah, I know. Some got laid off, like me. Some just quit, 'cause it's getting too blamed dangerous out in the Belt. I figure I'll just wait until you guys have settled your war. Once the shooting stops, I'll go back to work, I guess."

"That could be a long wait," she pointed out.

With a frowning nod, he replied, "I'd rather starve slowly than get killed suddenly."

Ferrer admitted defeat. "Very well. If you change your mind, please contact us."

Getting up from the chair in a rush, as if happy to be leaving, the miner said, "Don't hold your breath."

Ferrer conducted two more interviews that afternoon with exactly the same results. Miners and prospectors were abandoning their jobs to get away from the fighting. *Chrysalis* was filling up with unemployed rock rats. Most of them had run through what little savings they had accumulated and were now depending for their living on the scanty largesse of *Chrysalis*'s governing board. Hardly any of them accepted employment aboard HSS ships. Or Astro's, Ferrer found with some satisfaction. Of the fourteen men and women she had personally interviewed, only two had signed up, both of them women with babies to support. All the others had flatly refused her offers.

I'd rather starve slowly than get killed suddenly. That was their attitude.

Sitting alone in her office as the day waned, Ferrer sighed heavily. I'm going to have to report to Humphries, she told herself. He's not going to like what I have to tell him.

Levinson was glad to be out of the space suit. In fact, he was whistling cheerily as he made his way from the airlock of the torch ship toward the compartment they had given him. In two days we'll be back at Ceres, and then Vickie and I ride a torch ship back to Selene. I'll bet we spend the whole journey shacked up together.

"Shouldn't whistle aboard ship," said one of the technicians, coming up the passageway behind him. "It's considered bad luck."

Levinson grinned at her. "That's an old superstition," he said.

"No it's not. It dates back to sailing days, when orders were given by playing a whistle. So they didn't want anybody whistling and messing up the signaling system."

"Doesn't apply here," Levinson said loftily.

"Still, it's considered—"

"EMERGENCY," the overhead speaker blared. "PRESSURE LOSS IN MAIN AIRLOCK COMPARTMENT."

The blood froze in Levinson's veins. The airtight hatch up the passageway slammed shut. His knees went rubbery.

"Don't piss yourself," the technician said, smirking at him. "It's probably something minor."

"But the hatch. We're trapped here."

"Naw. You can open the hatch manually and get to your quarters. Don't sweat it."

At that instant the hatch swung open and two of the ship's crew pushed past them, heading for the airlock. They looked more irritated than frightened.

Feeling marginally better, Levinson followed the tech through the hatch and toward his own compartment. Still, when the hatch automatically slammed shut again, he jumped like a startled rabbit.

He was opening the accordion-pleated door to his compartment when the overhead speaker demanded, "DR. LEVINSON REPORT TO THE BRIDGE IMMEDIATELY."

Levinson wasn't exactly certain where the bridge was, but he thought it was farther up the passageway that ran the length of the habitation module. With his pulse thumping nervously in his ears, he made his way past two more closed hatches and finally stepped into what was obviously the bridge. The ship's captain was standing with his back to the hatch, half bent over between the backs of two side-by-side chairs, both occupied by crew members. All three men were peering at readouts on the instrument panel.

The hatch slammed behind him, making him flinch again. The captain, grim-faced, whirled on him.

"It's those goddamned bugs of yours! They're eating up my ship!"

Levinson knew it couldn't be true. Pea-brained rocket jocks! Anything goes wrong, they blame the nearest scientist.

"The nanomachines are on the asteroid," he said, with great calm and dignity. "Or what's left of it. They couldn't possibly be aboard your ship."

"The hell they're not!" roared the captain, jabbing an accusing finger at the displays on the instrument board. Levinson could see they were swathed in red.

"They couldn't—"

"They were in that dust cloud, weren't they?"

"Well, yes, perhaps a few," he admitted.

"And the loose end of your fucking tether was flapping around in the cloud, wasn't it?"

Levinson started to reply, but his mouth went so dry he couldn't form any words.

"You brought the mother-humping bugs aboard my ship, damn you!"

"But . . . but . . ."

"They're eating out the airlock compartment! Chewing up the metal of the hull, for chrissakes!" The captain advanced toward Levinson, hands clenched into fists, face splotched with red fury. "You've got to stop them!"

"They'll stop themselves," said Levinson, backing away a step and bumping into the closed hatch. "I built a time limit into them. Once the time limit is reached they run out of power and shut themselves down."

The captain sucked in a deep breath. His face returned almost to its normal color. "They'll stop?"

"Yessir," Levinson said. "Automatically."

"How soon?"

Levinson swallowed and choked out, "Forty-eight hours."

"Forty-eight *hours*?" the captain bellowed.

Levinson nodded, cringing.

The captain turned back toward the two crewmen seated at the instrument panel. "Contact *Chrysalis*. Report our situation to them."

The crewman in the left-hand seat asked, "Anything else to tell them, sir?"

The captain fumed in silence for a moment, then muttered, "Yeah. Read them your last will and testament. We're going to die here. All of us."

Levinson wet his pants.

LAST RITES

Levinson had never been so terrified. He stumbled back to his compartment, slid the door shut after three trembling tries, then yanked his palmcomp out of his coveralls, tearing the pocket slightly, and called up the numbers he needed to calculate how long the torch ship would last.

The tiny corner of his mind that still remained rational told him the calculation was meaningless. He had no firm idea of how fast the nanomachines were disassembling the ship, and only the haziest notion of how massive the ship was. You're just rearranging the deck chairs on the *Titanic*, he told himself. But he knew he had to do something, anything, to try to stave off the terror that was staring him in the face.

We could make it to Ceres in less than forty-eight hours, he thought, if the captain pushes the engines to their max. If the nanomachines don't destroy the engines first. Okay, we get to Ceres, to the habitat *Chrysalis*. They won't let us in, though, because they'd be afraid of the nanos damaging them.

But the machines will shut themselves down in forty-eight hours, Levinson reminded himself. Less than that, now; it was about two hours ago that we dispersed them on the asteroid.

How fast are they eating up the ship? he asked himself. Maybe I can make some measurements, get at least a rough idea of their rate of progress. Then I could—

He never finished the sentence. The curving bulkhead of his compartment, formed by the ship's hull, suddenly cracked open. Levinson watched in silent horror as a chunk of metal dissolved before his goggling eyes. The air rushed out of the compartment with such force that he fell to his knees. His lungs collapsed as he sank to the metal deck of the compartment, blood gushing from every pore. He was quite dead by the time his nanomachines began taking him apart, molecule by molecule.

Martin Humphries was talking with his six-year-old son, Alex, in the family's estate in Connecticut.

"Van cries all the time," Alex said, looking sad. "The doctor says he's real sick."

"Yes, that's true," said Humphries, feeling nettled. He wanted to talk about other things than his stunted younger son.

"Can I come to see you?" Alex asked, after the three-second lag between Earth and Moon.

"Of course," Humphries replied. "As soon as your school year ends you can come up here for a week or so. You can take walks on the Moon's surface and learn how to play low-games."

He watched his son's face, so like the pictures of himself at that age. The boy blossomed into a huge smile when he heard his father's words.

"With you, Daddy?"

"Sure, with me, or one of my staff. They can—"

The amber light signaling an incoming call began blinking. Humphries had given orders that he was not to be disturbed except for cataclysms. He glared at the light, as if that would make it stop claiming his attention.

"I've got to go now, Alex. I'll call you again in a day or so."

He clicked off the connection, and never saw the hurt disappointment on his son's face.

Whoever was calling had his private code. And the message was scrambled as well, he saw. Scowling with impatience, Humphries instructed the computer to open the message. Victoria Ferrer's features appeared in three dimensions in the hologram above his desk. She looked tired, depressed.

"I'm on a torch ship on my way back to Selene," she said. "Still too far out for a two-way conversation, but I know you'll want to hear the bad news right away."

He started to ask what she was talking about, then realized that she wouldn't hear his question for a good twenty minutes or more.

"The nanomachine experiment backfired. The bugs got loose on the ship and totally destroyed it. Nothing left but a cloud of atoms. Everybody killed, including Levinson."

She gave a few more details, then added, "Oh, by the way, the recruiting was pretty much a flop, too. Those rock rats are too smart to volunteer for cannon fodder."

Her message ended.

Humphries leaned back in his desk chair and stared at the wall screen that displayed a hologram of Jupiter's colorful swirling clouds.

Completely destroyed the ship and killed everybody aboard, he repeated to himself. What a weapon those little bugs could make!

ORE CARRIER *STARLIGHT*

*S*tarlight was an independent freighter. For years it had plied between Ceres and Selene, taking on cargoes of ore in the Belt and carrying them on a slow, curving ellipse to the waiting factories on the Moon and in Earth orbit. Its owners, a married couple from Murmansk, had kept strictly aloof from the big corporations, preferring to make a modest living out of carrying ores and avoiding entanglements. Their crew consisted of their two sons and daughters-in-law. On their last trip to Selene they had tarried a week longer than usual so that their first grandchild—a girl—could be born in the lunar city's hospital. Now, after a trip with the squalling new baby to the Belt, they were returning to Selene, happy to be away from the fighting that had claimed so many Astro and HSS ships.

The Astro drone had no proper name, only a number designation: D-6. The *D* stood for "destroyer." It was an automated vessel, remotely controlled from Astro's offices in Selene. The controllers' assignment was to attack any HSS vessels approaching the Moon. The particular controller on duty that morning had a list of HSS ships in her computer, complete with their names, performance ratings, and construction specifications. She suspected that *Starlight* was a disguised version of a Humphries freighter and spent most of the morning scanning the vessel with radar and laser probes.

Astro's command center was kept secret from Humphries's people, of course; it was also kept secret from the government of Selene, which insisted that no hostilities should take place in its jurisdiction. So the controller watched *Starlight* passively, without trying to open up a communications link with the freighter or even asking the International Astronautical Authority offices about the ship's registration and identity.

To her credit, the Astro controller instructed D-6 to obtain close-up imagery of the approaching freighter. Unfortunately, the destroyer's programming was new and untried; the drone had been rushed into use too soon. The onboard computer misinterpreted the controller's order. Instead of a low-power laser scan, the destroyer hit *Starlight* with a full-intensity laser beam that sawed the vessel's habitation module neatly in half, killing everyone aboard.

Pancho was heading for the Moon's south pole when the news of the *Starlight* fiasco reached her.

She was flying in a rocket on a ballistic trajectory to the Astro power station set on the summit of the highest peak in the Malapert Mountains. Taller than Everest, Mt. Dickson's broad, saddle-shaped summit was always in sunlight, as were its neighboring peaks. Astro workers had covered its crest with power towers topped by photovoltaic cells. The electricity they generated was carried back to Selene by cryogenically cooled cables of lunar aluminum that ran across the rugged, crater-pocked highlands for nearly five thousand kilometers.

For the few brief minutes of the rocket's arcing flight southward, the handful of passengers hung weightlessly against their seat restraint straps. To her surprise, Pancho actually felt a little queasy. *You've been flying a desk too long, girl.* She thought about how the future growth of the Moon would almost certainly be in the polar regions. Water deposits were there, she knew, and you could build power towers that were always in sunlight, so you got uninterrupted electricity, except for Earth eclipses, but that was only a few minutes out of the year. *It was a mistake to build Selene near the equator,* she thought.

Back in those days, though, it started as a government operation. Moonbase. Some bean-counting sumbitch of a bureaucrat figured it'd be a couple of pennies cheaper in propellant costs to build near the equator than at either polar region. They picked Alphonsus because there were vents in the crater floor that outgassed methane now and then. Big lollapalooza deal! Water's *what you need, and the ice deposits at the poles are where the water is. Even so, it isn't enough. We have to import water from the rock rats.*

As the rocket vehicle fired its retros in preparation for landing at the Astro base, Pancho caught a glimpse through her passenger window of the construction already underway at Shackleton Crater, slightly more than a hundred kilometers distant. *Nairobi's found the money they needed,* she told herself. She had followed their progress in the weekly reports her staff made, but seeing the actual construction sprawling across the floor of Shackleton impressed her more than written reports or imagery. Where's their money coming from? she asked herself. Her best investigators had not been able to find a satisfactory answer.

She had brought one of the new nanomachine space suits with her, folded and packed in her travel bag. Stavenger had even supplied her with a nanofabric helmet that could be blown up like a toy balloon. Pancho packed it but firmly decided that if she had to use the softsuit she'd find a regular bubble helmet to go with it.

There was no need for a space suit. Once the ballistic rocket touched down, a flexible tunnel wormed from the base's main airlock to the ship's hatch. Pancho walked along its spongy floor to the airlock, where the director of the base was waiting for her, looking slightly nervous because he wasn't entirely sure why the company's CEO had suddenly decided to visit his domain.

Pancho allowed him to tour her through the base, which looked to her a lot like most of the other lunar facilities she had seen. It was almost entirely underground; the work on the surface of maintaining the solar cells and building new ones was done by robotic machines teleoperated from the safety of the underground offices.

"Of course, we're not as luxurious down here as Selene," the base director explained in a self-deprecating tone, "but we do have the basic necessities."

With that, he ushered Pancho into a tight, low-ceilinged conference room that was crowded with his senior staff people, all of them anxious to meet the CEO and even more anxious to learn why she had come to see them. The conference table was set with sandwiches and drinks, with a scale model of the base sitting in the middle of the table.

There weren't enough chairs for everyone, so Pancho remained standing, munched on a sandwich, sipped at a plastic container of fruit juice, and chatted amiably with the staff—none of whom dared to sit down while the CEO remained standing.

At last she put her emptied juice container back on the table. As if on signal, all conversations stopped and everyone turned toward her.

She grinned at them. "I guess you're wondering why I dropped in on y'all like this," Pancho said, reverting to her west Texas drawl to put them at their ease.

"It's not every day that the chief of the corporation comes to see us," the base director replied. A few people tittered nervously.

"Well," said Pancho, "to tell the truth, I'm curious 'bout what your new neighbors are up to. Any of you know how to get me invited over to the Nairobi complex?"

SELENE NEWS MEDIA CENTER

Despite its rather glitzy title, the news media center was little more than a set of standard-sized offices—most of them crammed with broadcasting equipment—and one cavernous studio large enough to shoot several videos at the same time.

Edith Stavenger stood impatiently just inside the studio's big double doors, waiting while the camera crew finished its final take on a training vid for the new softsuits. A young woman who actually worked a tractor on the surface was serving as a model, showing how easy it was to pull the suit on and seal its front.

Many years earlier Edith Stavenger had been Edie Elgin, a television news reporter in Texas, back in the days when the first human expedition to Mars was in training. She had come to the Moon as a reporter during the brief, almost bloodless lunar war of independence. She had married Douglas Stavenger and never returned to Earth. She still had the dynamic, youthful good looks of a cheerleader, golden blonde hair and a big smile full of strong bright teeth. She was still bright-eyed and vigorous, thanks to rejuvenation therapies that ranged from skin-cell regeneration to hormone enhancement. Some thought that she had taken nanomachines into her body, like her husband, but Edith found no need for that; cellular biochemistry was her fountain of youth.

She had served as news director for Selene for a while but, at her husband's prodding, semi-retired to a consultant's position. Doug Stavenger wanted no dynasties in Selene's political or social structure and Edith agreed with him, almost completely. She clung to her consultant's position, even though she barely ever tried to interfere with the operation of the news media in Selene.

But now she had a reason to get involved, and she waited with growing impatience for the head of the news department to finish the scene he was personally directing.

The young model took off her fishbowl helmet and collapsed the transparent inflatable fabric in her hands. Then she unsealed her soft-suit, peeled it off her arms and wriggled it past her hips. She'd be kind of sexy, Elgin thought, if she weren't wearing those coveralls.

At last the scene was finished, the crew clicked off their handheld cameras, and the news director turned and headed for the door.

"Edie!" he exclaimed. "I didn't know you'd come up here."

"We've got to talk, Andy."

The news director's name was Achmed Mohammed Wajir, and although he traced his family roots back to the Congo, he had been born in Syria and raised all over the Middle East. His childhood had been the gypsy existence of a diplomat's son: never in one city for more than two years at a time. His father sent him to Princeton for an education in the classics, but young Achmed had fallen in love with journalism instead. He went to New York and climbed through the rough-and-tumble world of the news media until a terrorist bomb shattered his legs. He came to Selene where he could accept nanotherapies that rebuilt his legs, but he could never return to Earth while he carried nanomachines inside him. Wajir soon decided he didn't care. The Moon's one-sixth g made his recovery easier, and at Selene the competition in the news business was even gentler than the gravity.

As they pushed through the studio's double doors and out into the corridor, Wajir began, "If it's about this *Starlight* accident—"

"Accident?" Elgin snapped. "It's a tragedy. Seven innocent people killed, one of them a baby."

"We played the story, Edie. Gave it full coverage."

"For a day."

Wajir had once been slim as a long-distance runner, but years behind a desk—or a restaurant table—had thickened his middle. Still, he was several centimeters taller than Elgin and now he drew himself up to his full height.

"Edie," he said, "we're in the news business, and *Starlight* is old news. Unless you want to do some sob-sister mush. But even there, there's no relatives left to cry on camera for you. No funeral. The bodies have drifted to god knows where by now."

Edith's normal cheerful smile was long gone. She was dead serious as they walked along the corridor past glass-walled editing and recording studios.

"It's not just this one terrible tragedy, Andy," she said. "There's a war going on and we're not covering it. There's hardly a word about it anywhere in the media."

"What do you expect? Nobody's interested in a war between two corporations."

"Nobody's interested because we're not giving them the news they need to get interested!"

They had reached Wajir's office. He opened the door and gestured her inside. "No sense us fighting out in the hallway where everybody can hear us," he said.

Edith walked in and took one of the big upholstered chairs in front of his wide, expansive desk of bioengineered teak. Instead of going to his swivel chair, Wajir perched on the edge of his desk, close enough to Edith to loom over her.

"We've been over this before, Edie. The news nets Earthside aren't interested in the war. It's all the way to hell out in the Asteroid Belt and it's being fought by mercenaries and you know who the hell cares? Nobody. Nobody on Earth gives a damn about it."

"But we should make them care about it," she insisted.

"How?" he cried. "What do we have to do to get them interested? Tell me and I'll do it."

Edith started to snap out a reply, but bit it back. She looked up at Wajir, who was leaning over her, his ebony face twisted into a frown. He's been a friend for a long time, she told herself. Don't turn him into an enemy.

"Andy," she said softly, "this disaster of the *Starlight* is only the tip of the iceberg. The war is spreading out of the Belt. It's coming here, whether we like it or not."

"Good. Then we can cover it."

She felt her jaw drop with surprise, her brows hike up.

"I'm not being cynical," he quickly explained. "We can't get news coverage from the Belt."

"If it's the expense, maybe I could—"

Shaking his head vigorously, Wajir said, "It's not the money. The Belt's controlled by the corporations. Astro and HSS have it sewn up between them."

"There are independents."

"Yeah, but the war's between Astro and HSS and neither one of them wants news reporters snooping around. They won't talk to us here and they won't ferry us out to the Belt."

"Then I'll go," Edith heard herself say.

Wajir looked genuinely shocked. "You?"

"I used to be a reporter, back in the Stone Age," she said, smiling for the first time.

"They won't take you, Edie."

"I'll fly out on an independent ship," she said lightly. "I'll go to *Chrysalis* and interview the rock rats there."

He pursed his lips, rubbed at his nose, looked up at the ceiling. "The big boys won't like it."

"You mean the big corporations?"

Wajir nodded.

"I don't really care whether they like it or not. I'll go out on an independent ship. Maybe Sam Gunn will give me a ride on one of his vessels."

"If he's got any left," Wajir muttered. "This war is bankrupting him."

"Again? He's always going bankrupt."

"Seriously, Edie," he said, "this could be dangerous."

"Nobody's going to hurt Douglas Stavenger's wife. There are *some* advantages to being married to a powerful man."

"Maybe," Wajir admitted. "Maybe. But I don't like this. I think you're making a mistake."

Damned if it isn't the same guy who came to see me in my office, Pancho thought as she looked at the holographic image of the handsome Nairobi executive. She was in the office of the Astro base's director, which he had lent her for the duration of her visit to the south polar facility. Leaning back in the creaking, stiffly unfamiliar chair, Pancho saw the man's name spelled out beneath his smiling, pleased image: Daniel Jomo Tsavo.

"Ms. Lane," he said, looking pleasantly surprised, "what an unexpected pleasure."

He was just as good-looking as she remembered him, but now instead of wearing a conservative business suit he was in well-worn coveralls, with the edge of a palmcomp peeping out from his breast pocket. He gets his hands dirty, Pancho thought, liking him all the more for it.

"You're the head of the Nairobi base?" Pancho asked him.

His smile turned brighter. "After my visit with you, my superiors assigned me to managing the construction of our facilities here."

"I didn't know," said Pancho.

"I suppose they thought it was cheaper to keep me here than fly me back home," he said, self-deprecatingly.

"So you've been down here at the south pole all this time."

"Yes, that's true. I had no idea you had come to the Mountains of Eternal Light," Tsavo said.

"Came down to check out how my people are doing here," she lied easily, "and thought maybe I could take a peek at how you're getting along."

"By all means! It would be an honor to have you visit our humble facility, Ms. Lane."

She arched a brow at him. "Don't you think you can call me Pancho by now?"

He chuckled and looked away from her, seemingly embarrassed. "Yes, I suppose so . . . Pancho."

"Good! When can I come over, Daniel?"

For a moment he looked almost alarmed, but he quickly recovered. "Um, our facilities are not very luxurious, Pancho. We weren't expecting illustrious visitors for some time, you see, and—"

"Can it, Danny boy! I can sleep on nails, if I have to. When can I come over?"

"Give me a day to tidy up a bit. Twenty-four hours. I'll send a hopper for you."

"Great," said Pancho, recognizing that twenty-four hours would give him time to check with whoever his bosses were and decide how to handle this unexpected visit.

"By the way," she added, "are you folks still interested in a strategic partnership with Astro Corporation?"

Now his face went almost totally blank. Poker-playing time, Pancho realized.

"Yes," he said at last. "Of course. Although, you realize, with this war going on, the financial situation has changed a good deal."

"Tell me about it!"

He smiled again.

"Okay, then, we can talk about it when I get to your base."

"Fine," said Daniel Jomo Tsavo.

DATA BANK: SOLAR FLARE

The minor star that humans call the Sun is a seething, restless million-kilometer-wide thermonuclear reactor. Deep in its core, where the temperature exceeds thirty million degrees, intact atoms cannot exist. They are totally ionized, their electrons stripped from their nuclei. Under those immense temperatures and pressures hydrogen nuclei—bare protons—are forced together to create nuclei of helium. This process of fusion releases particles of electromagnetic energy called photons, which make their tortuous way through half a million kilometers of incredibly dense ionized gas, called plasma, toward the Sun's shining surface.

Furiously boiling, gigantic bubbles of plasma rise and sink again, cooling and reheating, in an endless cycle of convection. Immense magnetic fields play through the plasma, warping it, shredding it into slender glowing filaments longer than the distance between the Earth and its Moon. Vast arches of million-degree plasma form above the solar surface, expanding, hurling themselves into space or pouring back down into the Sun in titanic cascades.

Over cycles of roughly eleven years the Sun's violence waxes and wanes. During periods of maximum solar activity the Sun's shining face is blotched with sunspots, slightly cooler regions that look dark compared to the surrounding chromosphere. Solar flares erupt, sudden bursts of energy that can release in a few seconds the equivalent of a hundred million *billion* tons of exploding TNT: more energy than the entire human race consumes in fifty thousand years.

The electromagnetic radiation from such a flare—visible light, radio waves, ultraviolet and X-rays—reaches the Earth's vicinity in about eight minutes. This is the warning of danger to come. Close behind, a few minutes or a few hours, comes the first wave of extremely energetic protons and electrons, traveling at velocities close to the speed of light.

The energy in these particles is measured in *electron volts*. One electron volt is a minuscule bit of energy: It would take five million electron volts to light a fifty-watt lamp. But protons with energies of forty to fifty million electron volts can easily penetrate a quarter-inch of lead, and particles from solar flares with energies of more than fifteen thousand *billion* electron volts have reached the Earth.

Yet the most violent effects of the solar flare are still to come.

The flare has ejected a gigantic puff of very energetic plasma into interplanetary space. The cloud expands as it moves outward from the Sun, soon growing to dimensions larger than the Earth. When such a cloud hits the Earth's magnetosphere it rattles the entire geomagnetic field, causing a magnetic storm.

The auroras at Earth's north and south poles flare dramatically, and the "northern lights" (and southern) are seen far south (and north) of their usual haunts. The ionosphere—the belt of ionized particles some eighty kilometers above Earth's surface—runs amok, making a shambles of long-range radio transmissions that are normally reflected off its ionized layers.

On the Moon and even out in the Asteroid Belt all surface activity is halted when a solar flare bathes the region in lethal radiation. All spacecraft that operate beyond the Moon carry protective electromagnetic shielding to divert the energetic particles of the flare's cloud. Otherwise the people in those spacecraft would swiftly die, killed by the invisible bullets of ionizing radiation.

Within a few days the deadly cloud wafts away, dissipates in interplanetary space. Earth's ionosphere settles down. The auroras stop flaring. Space-suited workers can return to the surface of the Moon and the asteroids. The solar system returns to normal. Until the next solar flare.

Jersey Zorach was a dour, dark, stolid astrophysicist who studied the weather in space. Despite his being a third-generation American, born and raised just outside Chicago, he had never outgrown his Latvian heritage of being burdened with a sense of impending doom.

He sat in his messy little cubbyhole of an office, a squat, untidy man built rather like a fireplug, with a thick thatch of unruly prematurely gray hair flopping down over his forehead, surrounded by beeping display screens, stacks of books, reports, video chips and the scattered remains of many meals he had eaten at his desk.

Since interplanetary space is a nearly perfect vacuum, most people smiled or even laughed when Zorach told them his profession, waiting for a punch line that never came. There was no rain or snow in space, true enough. But Zorach knew there was a wind of ghostly microscopic particles blowing fitfully from the Sun, a solar wind that sometimes reached hurricane velocities and more. There was a constant drizzle of cosmic particles sleeting in from the distant stars as well.

And there were clouds, sometimes. Invisible but quite deadly clouds.

For years he had worked to make precise predictions of solar flares. He studied the Sun until his eyes burned from staring at its seething, roiling image. He made mountains of statistical analyses, trying to learn how to forecast solar flares by matching existing data on earlier flares and making "backcasts" of them. He spun out holographic maps of the interplanetary magnetic field, knowing that those invisible threads of energy steered the radiation clouds that were thrown out by solar flares.

Nothing worked. His predictions were estimates at best. Everyone praised him and the results he was obtaining, but Zorach knew he had yet to predict a single flare. Not one, in all the years he had been working on them.

So he wasn't surprised when one of the display screens in his cluttered office suddenly pinged. Turning to it, he saw nothing unusual to the unaided eye. But the alphanumerics strung along the bottom of the screen told him clearly that a new solar flare had just erupted.

A big one, he saw. Big and nasty. He knew the automated system was already sending warnings to every human habitat and outpost from Selene to the colony in orbit around distant Saturn. But he pecked at his own phone and called Selene's safety office to make certain they started bringing everybody in from the surface. It was a point of honor with him. If I can't predict the bloody storms, he said to himself, at least I can make certain no one is killed by them.

Deep below the Moon's surface in his private grotto, Martin Humphries had no worries about solar flares or the radiation clouds that accompanied them.

He was ambling slowly through the colorful garden in the patio outside the elaborately carved front door of his mansion, with Victoria Ferrer at his side. The heady aroma of solid beds of roses and peonies filled the air, and he felt victory was close enough almost to touch.

"We're winning," Humphries said happily. "We've got Astro on the run."

Ferrer, walking slowly alongside him, nodded her agreement. But she warned, "This latest move of Astro's could cut off the ore shipments coming in from the Belt."

Humphries disagreed with a wave of his hand in the air. "Drones attacking our automated freighters? I'm not worried about that."

"You should be. This could be serious."

"Don't be stupid," Humphries sneered. "This fiasco with that *Starlight* vessel has brought Pancho's little scheme out into the open."

"But they could strangle your profits if—"

"I'm going to get rid of Astro's drones at one stroke," Humphries said confidently.

Ferrer looked at him questioningly.

"Set up a meeting for me with Doug Stavenger."

"Stavenger?"

"Uh-huh. Once Stavenger has his nose rubbed into the fact that

Astro's controlling those birds from inside Selene, he'll close down their operation."

"He will?"

"Yes indeed he will," said Humphries, smiling broadly. "He's made it clear to me and that little guttersnipe that he doesn't want any fighting in Selene. No fighting anywhere on the Moon."

"But does that mean he'll demand that Astro close down its control center for the drones?"

"Damned right he will. And he'll make it stick, too."

Ferrer was silent for a moment, thinking. Then, "Pancho will just move the control center off the Moon. Put up a space station."

"And we'll blast it to smithereens." Humphries clapped his hands together. "I only hope the damned greasemonkey is aboard when we wipe it out."

Ferrer thought it over and had to admit that her boss was correct. HSS mercenaries had scored major victories over Astro forces in the Belt. Astro had sprung a surprise with their drones attacking HSS freighters as they approached the Moon, but Humphries was probably right in thinking that Stavenger would force them to move that operation out of the safety of Selene. Of course, zapping that independent freighter and wiping out that family didn't help Astro's cause. Not at all.

Yet she heard herself ask, "What about Fuchs? He's still lurking out there somewhere."

"Fuchs?" Humphries snorted disdainfully. "He's a spent force. Once we've cleaned out Astro we can hunt him down at our leisure. He's as good as dead; he just doesn't know it yet."

For weeks, Lars Fuchs had been living in the machinery and storage spaces in Selene's "basement."

On the Moon, where the deeper below the surface you are, the safer you are from the radiation and temperature swings and the thin but constant infall of micrometeors that pepper the surface, Selene's "basement" was its topmost level.

Just below the Grand Plaza and its extensions, Selene's highest underground level was entirely devoted to the pumps and power converters and other life-support equipment that provided the city's air, water, light and heat. Living quarters were on the lower levels, the lower the more prestigious—and expensive.

The "basement" also held the warehouses that stocked spare parts, clothing, preserved foods, and the tanks of water that Selene's residents drank and washed in. In short, the "basement" had all the supplies that a renegade, a fugitive, a homeless exile would need to survive.

During the years he had lived at Ceres, Fuchs had listened for hours to Big George Ambrose talking about the "bad old days" when he had lived as a fugitive in Selene's shadowy underground economy, surviving on his wits and the petty pilfering that provided food and shelter for him and his fellow nonpersons. Even Dan Randolph had once spent a few months hiding from the authorities in Selene.

So Fuchs had politely checked out of the Hotel Luna, afraid that sooner or later he would be identified and forced to return to Earth, and toted his meager travel bag up toward the kilometer-long tunnel that led to Armstrong Spaceport. Instead of going to the spaceport, though, he found one of the access hatches marked MAINTENANCE AND SUPPLY SECTION: AUTHORIZED PERSONNEL ONLY, quickly decoded its simple security lock, and disappeared into the shadowy "basement," where machinery throbbed incessantly and the air was heavy with the odors of lubricating oil and ozone from the electrical machinery.

Color-coded pipes and electrical conduits ran overhead. Maintenance robots trundled back and forth along the walkways between the pulsating machinery and the warehouse stacks. Simpleminded machines programmed to alert human controllers of malfunctioning equipment or water leaks, the robots were fairly easy to avoid. Fuchs could see the red lights set into their tops flashing through the dimly lit passageways while they were still far enough distant to get out of range of their optical sensors.

There was a scattering of other people hiding there, too, a ragged handful of men and women who preferred to scratch out an underground living rather than submit to Selene's laws. Some of them were wild-eyed from drugs, or raving alcoholics; others were simply unable or unwilling to live by other people's rules. Fuchs met a few of them, barely avoided a fight when one of them pulled a knife and ordered him to swear loyalty. Fuchs bent his knee and agreed, then quickly moved as far away from the megalomaniac as he could and never saw him again.

Fuchs settled down in the "basement," content to sleep in a bedroll and eat canned foods pilfered from the warehouse stocks. He spent his waking hours peering at his palmcomp, studying the schematics of Selene's air ducts and water pipes, searching for a way to penetrate the lunar city's lowest level, where Humphries lived in his magnificent mansion.

As the weeks passed, Nodon, Sanja, and Amarjagal arrived at Selene one by one, each of them bearing identification as Astro Corporation employees, lowly technicians. Their one-room corporate apartments were sufficient for them, luxurious compared to Fuchs's hideout in the storeroom shelves in the "basement."

Fuchs visited his crew members, furtively making his way through Selene's corridors to spend long hours with them, planning how he might kill Martin Humphries.

SHINING MOUNTAIN BASE

Daniel Jomo Tsavo hated the three-second lag in communications between the Earth and Moon. It upset him to ask a question and then wait and wait and wait until the answer came back. Yet there was no way around the lag. And now the safety people have warned us that a solar storm is on its way; normal communications will be disrupted and all work on the surface will have to stop until the storm passes. Ah well, he said to himself, this call to Yamagata is on a tight laser-beam link. The storm should not affect it, unless it's powerful enough to fry the laser transmitter on the surface.

"Pancho Lane wants to visit your base?" Nobuhiko Yamagata replied at last.

Tsavo nodded vigorously. "She just called. She's at the Astro facility in the Malapert Mountains, no more than a hundred kilometers from where I sit."

Again the interminable lag. Tsavo used the time to study Yamagata. His round, flat face looked frozen, his eyes hooded, his expression unreadable. Yet he must be thinking furiously, Tsavo thought. Come on, come on. Tell me what I should do.

"This is a striking opportunity," Yamagata said at last.

Tsavo agreed heartily. "I took it on my own authority to invite her to come over tomorrow."

Yamagata again seemed lost in thought. At last he said, "Don't delay. Bring her to your base as quickly as you can. I will send an interrogation team immediately on a high-g burn. There is much we can learn from her."

Pancho felt slightly nervous being out on the surface with a solar flare cloud on its way. The scientists had estimated that it would take more than six hours for the radiation to even begin building up, but still she felt edgy about it. She was wearing a standard hard-shell space suit as she followed the Astro base director along the crest of Mount Randolph. Approaching storm or not, the director wanted to show off what his people were doing and Pancho had no intention of showing any fear in front of her own people.

I should be testing the softsuit I brought with me, she said to herself. Yet she answered silently, You know what they say about test engineers: more guts than brains. I'll wear a softsuit when they've been in use for a year or two. Momma Lane didn't raise any of her daughters to get themselves killed trying out new equipment.

She was being conducted on a quick walk through the small forest of gleaming white towers that reached up into the bright sunlight. Their wide, circular tops were dark with solar cells that drank in the Sun's radiant energy and converted it silently to electricity. They look like great big mushrooms, Pancho thought. Then she corrected herself. Nope, they look more like giant penises. She giggled inwardly. A forest of phalluses. A collection of cocks. Monumental pricks, all standing at attention.

"As you can see," the base director's voice rasped in her earphones, "another advantage of the power towers is that the solar cells are placed high enough above the surface so they're not bothered by dust."

It took an effort for Pancho to control her merriment. "You don't need to clean 'em off," she said, trying to sound serious.

"That's correct. It saves quite a bit of money over the long run."

She nodded inside her helmet. "What about damage from micrometeoroids?"

"The cells are hardened, of course. Deterioration rate is about the same for the ground arrays around Selene."

"Uh-hmm." Pancho seemed to recall a report that said otherwise. "Didn't the analysis that—"

A new voice broke into their conversation. "Ms. Lane, ma'am, we have an incoming call for you from the Nairobi base at Shackleton."

"Put it through on freak two," she said.

It was voice only, but she recognized Tsavo's caramel-rich baritone. "Ms. Lane, Pancho, this is Daniel. I'm sending a hopper over to your facility within the next half-hour. Please feel free to visit us whenever you're ready to."

Grinning, delighted, Pancho answered, "I'll get over there soon's I can, Danny."

"You know that a solar storm is approaching," he said.

Pancho nodded inside her helmet. "Yup. I'll get to you before it hits."

"Fine. That's wonderful."

Pancho cut her inspection tour short, apologizing to the base director, who frowned with undisguised disappointment.

Sure enough, there was a Nairobi Industries hopper standing on its spindly little legs, waiting for her at the launchpad. It was painted a vivid green with the corporate logo—an oval Masai shield and two crossed spears—stenciled just below the glassteel bubble of the cockpit.

She dashed to the room that the base director had given her for her quarters, picked up her still-unopened travel bag, and headed out toward the pad. She called Jake Wanamaker on her handheld to tell him where she was going and why. Then she buzzed her security chief and asked him why in the name of hell-and-gone he hadn't been able to locate Lars Fuchs yet.

"I want him found," she insisted. "And pronto."

At that moment, Lars Fuchs was huddled with his three crew members in a narrow, shadowy niche between one of the big electrical power converters and the open-shelved storehouse that he used as his sleeping quarters.

"This is where you live, Captain?" Amarjagal asked, in a whisper that was halfway between respect and disbelief.

"This is my headquarters," Fuchs replied evenly. "For the time being."

Nodon said, "You could move in with me, sir. There is no need for you—"

"I'll stay here. Less chance of being discovered."

The three Mongols glanced at one another, but remained silent.

Over the weeks since Fuchs had gone underground he had learned the pattern of the maintenance robots that trundled along the walkways set between the machinery and storehouses in Selene's uppermost level. It was easy enough to avoid them, and he swung up into the higher tiers of the warehouse each night to spread his bedroll for sleep. It was a rugged sort of existence, but not all that uncomfortable, Fuchs told himself. As long as he kept his pilfering of food and other supplies down to the bare necessities, Selene's authorities didn't bother to track him down. From what Big George had told him, it was easier for the authorities to accept a slight amount of wastage than to organize a manhunt through the dimly lit machinery spaces and storehouses.

The one thing that bothered Fuchs was the constant humming, throbbing that pervaded this uppermost level of Selene. He knew that Selene's nuclear power generators were buried more than a hundred kilometers away, on the far side of Alphonsus's ringwall mountains. Yet there was a constant electrical crackle in the air, the faint scent of ozone that triggered uneasy Earthly memories of approaching thunderstorms. Fuchs felt that it shouldn't bother him, that he should ignore the annoyance. Still, his head ached much of the time, throbbing in rhythm to the constant electrical pulse.

He had chosen this site for his headquarters because he could commandeer the big display screen that had been erected on one side of the storehouse shelving. It had been placed there to help the occasional human operator to locate items stacked in inventory. Fuchs used its link to Selene's main computer to study schematics of the city's water and air circulation systems. He was searching for a way into Humphries's mansion. So far his search had proved fruitless.

"The man must be the biggest paranoid in the solar system," Fuchs muttered.

"Or the greatest coward," said Amarjagal, sitting on the walkway's metal grating beside him, her sturdy legs crossed, her back hunched like a small mountain.

Nodon and Sanja sat slightly farther away, their shaved skulls sheened with perspiration in the overly warm air. This close together, Fuchs could smell their rancid body odors. They have showers in their quarters, he knew. Perhaps they're worried about their water allotments. Fuchs himself washed infrequently in water tapped from one of the main pipes that ran overhead. No matter how careful he was he always left puddles that drew teams of swiftly efficient maintenance robots, buzzing officiously. Fuchs feared that sooner or later human maintenance workers would come up to determine what was causing the leaks.

"Every possible access to his grotto is guarded by triply redundant security systems," Fuchs saw as he studied the schematics. "Motion detectors, cameras, heat sensors."

Nodon pointed with a skinny finger, "Even the electrical conduits are guarded."

"A mouse couldn't squirm through those conduits," said Sanja.

"The man is a great coward," Amarjagal repeated. "He has much fear in him."

He's got a lot to be afraid of, Fuchs thought. Then he added, But not unless we find a way into his mansion.

No matter how they studied the schematics, they could find no entry into Humphries's domain, short of a brute force attack. But there are only four of us, Fuchs reminded himself, and we have no weapons. Humphries must have a security force patrolling his home that's armed to the teeth.

Nodon shook his head unhappily. "There is no way that I can see."

"Nor I," Amarjagal agreed.

Fuchs took in a deep, heavy breath, then exhaled slowly, wearily. "I can," he said.

The three of them turned questioning eyes to him.

"One of you will have to change your job, get a position with Selene's maintenance department."

"Is that possible?" asked Amarjagal.

"It should be," Fuchs replied. "You're all qualified technicians. You have identity dossiers from Astro Corporation."

"I'll do it," said Nodon.

"Good."

"And after Nodon begins working for the maintenance department?" Amarjagal asked.

Fuchs eyed her dispassionately. Of the three, she was the feistiest, the most likely to ask questions. Is it because she's a woman? Fuchs wondered.

"I'll have to acquire an identification chip for myself, so I can get down to Selene's lowest level."

"How can you get one?"

"I'll need help," he admitted.

The three Asians looked at him questioningly.

"I'll call Pancho. I'm sure she can get an identification tag for me that will give me access to Humphries's grotto."

He was grasping at a straw and he knew it. Even worse, when he called Pancho from one of the phones set along the walkways of the machinery spaces, he was told that Ms. Lane was away from her office and unavailable.

"Where is she?" Fuchs asked.

"Ms. Lane is unavailable at present," the phone's synthesized voice answered. "Please leave your name and someone will get back to you as soon as possible."

Fuchs had no intention of leaving his name. "Can I reach her, wherever she is?"

"Ms. Lane is unavailable at present," the computer replied cheerfully.

"How long will she be gone?"

"That information is unknown, sir."

Fuchs thought swiftly. No sense trying to pry information out of a stupid machine, he thought. Besides, he didn't want to stay on the phone long enough to draw the attention of Selene's security monitors.

"Tell her that Karl Manstein called and will call again."

Feeling desperate, trapped, he punched the phone's OFF key.

It wasn't easy to surprise Douglas Stavenger. No matter that he had been officially retired from any formal office for decades, he still kept himself informed on everything that happened in Selene. And beyond, to a considerable extent.

He knew that his wife was pressing the news media chief for more coverage of the war raging out in the Belt. He knew that the corporations were pushing in the opposite direction, to keep the story as hushed up as possible. The *Starlight* tragedy had forced some light into the situation, but both Astro and Humphries Space Systems exerted every gram of their enormous power to move the media off the story as quickly as possible.

But now, as he sat at the breakfast table with his wife, Stavenger was truly shocked by her revelation.

"You're going to Ceres?"

Edith smiled prettily over her teacup. "Nobody else wants to open up this story, Doug, so I'm going to do it."

He fought down an impulse to shake his head. For several moments he said nothing, staring at his bowl of yogurt and honey, his thoughts spinning feverishly.

Yet when he looked up at her again all he could think to say was, "I don't like it, Edie."

"I'm not sure that I like it myself, darling, but somebody's got to do it and I don't see anyone else stepping up to the task."

"It's dangerous out there."

Her smile widened. "Now who's going to harm the wife of Doug Stavenger? That would bring Selene into the war, wouldn't it?"

"Not automatically, no."

"No?" She arched a brow at him.

He conceded, "I imagine the corporations would fear Selene's response."

"If anyone harmed me," she went on, quite seriously, "you'd see to it that Selene came into the war on the other side. Right? And that would throw the balance of power against the corporation that harmed me. Wouldn't it?"

He nodded reluctantly.

"And that would decide the war. Wouldn't it?"

"It could."

"It would, and you know it. Everybody knows it, including Pancho Lane and Martin Humphries." She took another sip of tea, then put the cup down with a tiny clink of china. "So I'll be perfectly safe out there."

"I still don't like it," he murmured.

She reached across the little table and grasped his hand. "But I've got to, Doug. You can see that, can't you? It's important: not just to me but to everybody involved, the whole solar system, for god's sake."

Stavenger looked into his wife's earnest eyes and knew he couldn't stop her.

"I'll go with you, then," he said.

"Oh no! You've got to stay here!"

"I don't think—"

"You're my protection, Doug. What happens if we both get killed out there? Who's going to lead Selene?"

"The duly elected governing council."

"Oh, sure," she sneered. "Without you pulling their strings they'll dither and shuffle and do nothing, and you know it."

"No, I don't know that."

She smiled again. "I need your protection, Doug, and I can only get it if you're here at Selene, keeping things under control."

"You give me more credit than I deserve."

"And you're the youngest éminence grise in the solar system."

He laughed. It was an old standing joke between them.

"Besides," Edith went on, "if you come out to Ceres all the attention will be on you. They'll fall all over themselves trying to show you that everything's all right. I'll never get a straight story out of anybody."

He kept the argument going for nearly another half-hour, but Stavenger knew that his wife would do what she wanted. And so would he. Edith will go to Ceres, he realized, and I'll stay here.

Nobuhiko was brimming with excitement when he called his father to tell him that Pancho Lane was walking into the Nairobi base on the Moon.

The elder Yamagata was in his cell in the monastery, a fairly sizable room whose stone walls were covered now with bookshelves and smart screens. The room was furnished sparsely, but Nobu noticed that his father had managed to get a big, square mahogany desk for himself.

Saito was sitting on his haunches on a tatami mat, however, directly under the big wallscreen that displayed an intricate chart that Nobu guessed was the most recent performance of the Tokyo stock exchange.

"She's going into the Nairobi base voluntarily?" Saito asked.

"Yes!" gushed Nobu. "I've ordered an interrogation team to get there immediately! The Africans can drug her and the team wring her dry and she'll never even know it!"

Saito grunted. "Except for her headache the next day."

Nobu wanted to laugh, but held back.

His father said nothing for long, nerve-racking moments. Finally, "You go to Shackleton. You, yourself."

"Me? But why—"

"No interrogation team knows as much about our work as you do, my son. You can glean much more from her than they could without you."

Nobu thought it over swiftly. "But if somehow she recognizes me, remembers afterward . . ."

"Then she must be eliminated," Saito answered. "It would be a pity, but it would be quite necessary."

COMMAND SHIP *SAMARKAND*

Since the battle that shattered Gormley's fleet, the HSS base at Vesta had been busy. Ships were sent out in groups of two or three to hound down Astro freighters and logistics vessels. Although Astro's crewed ships were armed, they were no match for the warships with their mercenary crews that Humphries was pouring into the Belt.

Sitting in the command chair of *Samarkand*, in charge of three attack ships, Dorik Harbin wondered how long the war could possibly go on. Astro's vessels were being methodically eliminated. It was clear that Humphries's mercenaries were on the verge of sweeping Astro entirely out of the Belt. Astro's pitiful effort to stop HSS freighters from delivering ores to the Earth/Moon region had backfired hideously with the *Starlight* fiasco.

Yet the rumor was that more Astro ships were heading for the Belt. Better-armed ships, vessels crewed by mercenaries who were smart enough to avoid massed battles. The war was settling down to a struggle of attrition. Which corporation could better sustain the constant losses of ships and crews? Which corporation would decide the war was costing too much and call it quits?

Not Humphries, Harbin thought. He had met the man and seen the tenacity in his eyes, the dogged drive to succeed no matter what the cost. It's only money to him, Harbin realized. He isn't risking his neck, he's in no danger of shedding his own blood. What does he care how many are killed out here in the empty silence of the Belt?

His communications technician flashed a red-bordered message onto the bridge's main screen. A solar flare warning. Scanning the data, Harbin saw that it would be several days before the cloud reached the Belt's inner fringes.

"Run a diagnostic on the radiation shield system," he commanded, thinking, Make sure now that the shield is working properly, and if it's not you've got three or four days to repair it.

"We have a target, sir!"

His weapons tech's announcement stirred Harbin out of his thoughts. The flare warning disappeared from the main screen, replaced by three small blips, nearly nine thousand kilometers away, too distant for their telescopic cameras to resolve into a clear optical image.

With the touch of a fingertip on his armrest keypad, Harbin called up the computer's analysis. Their trajectory was definitely not the Sun-centered ellipse of asteroids; they were moving in formation toward Ceres. Not HSS ships, either; the computer had all their flight plans in its memory.

"Three on three," he muttered.

As *Samarkand* and its two accompanying warships sped toward the Astro vessels, the display screen began to show details. One of them was a typical dumbbell-shaped freighter, toting a large, irregularly shaped mass of ores. The other two were smaller, sleeker, obviously escorts designed to protect the freighter. Both the escorts were studded with asteroidal rock, armor to absorb and deflect laser beams.

Harbin's ships, including *Samarkand*, were also covered with asteroidal rubble, for the same reason. He saw that the Astro freighter was not so armored. They probably hope to use their cargo as a shield, he thought.

"Parallel course," he commanded. "Remain at a distance of fifteen hundred klicks. No closer, for the present."

"It's a long shot for the lasers," his weapons tech said, her heavy, dark face looking decidedly unhappy. "And they're armored, too."

Harbin nodded. "It's the freighter we want. I don't care about the escorts."

The weapons technician gave him a puzzled frown, then returned her attention to her screens.

Harbin studied the image on the main screen. The Astro escort vessels look more like rock piles than warships, he thought. I suppose we do too. He smiled grimly. Between the two corporations, we must be using more ores as ship's armor than we're selling to the markets on Earth. Well, that will end sooner or later. No war lasts forever.

Unbidden, a couplet from the *Rubaiyat* came to his mind:

> One Moment in Annihilation's waste,
> One moment, of the well of life to taste—

"We've been pulsed by search radar," his pilot reported.

Harbin nodded. "They know we're here."

"They're making no move toward us."

"No," Harbin replied. "Two escorts are not going to come after the three of us. They'll stick close to their freighter and wait for us to make a move on them."

"What move shall we make, sir?"

"Just continue the parallel course at this distance." Turning to the communication tech, seated beside the pilot, Harbin added, "Make certain that our two other ships follow me closely."

As the comm tech relayed his orders, Harbin thought, How to separate those two escorts from the freighter? If we go in to attack we'll be moving into their massed fire. I've got to find a way to split them apart.

For long, nerve-stretching minutes the two little formations flew in parallel, too distant for either to waste power on laser shots that would be absorbed by the ships' protective shields of asteroidal rubble. The Astro ships were hurrying out of the Belt, heading Earthward, to bring the freighter's massive load of ores to the waiting markets.

"We'll be reaching fuel bingo in forty-five minutes, sir," the pilot announced.

Harbin acknowledged the warning with a nod. Fuel bingo: the turn-back point. The farthest distance from their refueling base at Vesta that *Samarkand* and its two accompanying ships could safely go.

How to separate those escorts from the freighter? Harbin asked himself, over and over. He played one scheme after another in his mind. He riffled through the tactical computer's preset plans. Nothing that he could use. He was pleased to see that the computer's data bank included his own tactics against Gormley.

And that gave him the idea he needed.

"You two," he said, jabbing a finger at the communications and weapons technicians. "Get to the main airlock and suit up. Now!"

They unbuckled their seat harnesses and scampered to the bridge's hatch. Once they announced that they were in their space suits, Harbin went back to the airlock to brief them on what they had to do. Neither of them relished the idea of going outside, he could see that on their faces even through the thick visors of their helmets. That didn't matter to Harbin. There was no other way for his scheme to work.

He made his way back to the bridge and resumed his position in the command chair. The executive officer monitored the two technicians as they left the airlock and followed Harbin's orders. Within half an hour they reported that they had successfully discharged the electrostatic field that held the rocks of their armor shield tightly around the hull of the ship.

"Some of the rocks are floating loose now," the weapons tech reported, her voice tense. "Most of 'em are holding in place against the hull, though."

"Good," Harbin said tightly. "Come back aboard."

"Yes, *sir*." He could hear the relief in their voices. They were technicians, not trained astronauts. Working outside was not a chore they enjoyed.

While they were wriggling out of their space suits back at the airlock, Harbin commanded his pilot to turn and commence a high-speed run at the Astro ships. The other two HSS vessels were to remain on their courses.

The two technicians struggled back into their seats as *Samarkand's* fusion engines accelerated the ship to a full g and then even beyond. Harbin heard metal groaning and creaking as the trio of Astro ships grew visibly bigger in the main screen.

The loosened rocks of the rubble shield were being pushed mechanically by the bulk of the accelerating ship. They were no longer held to the hull by the electrostatic field. Harbin heard thumps and bangs as some of the rocks separated entirely from the ship, but most of them obediently followed Newton's laws and hung on the ship's hull.

Harbin could see the Astro warships deploying to meet his solo attack. He felt sweat trickling down his ribs, cold and annoying. *Once we let loose the rocks we'll have no protection against their lasers,* he knew. *But they'll be too busy to fire on us.* He hoped.

"Decelerate," he ordered. "Reduce to one-half g."

The pilot tried to slow the ship smoothly, but still Harbin felt as if his insides were being yanked out of him. The comm tech moaned like a wounded creature and the entire ship seemed to creak and complain, metal screeching against metal.

As the ship slowed, though, the thousands of rocks of her rubble shield—fist-sized and smaller—kept on moving in a straight line, blindly following their own inertia as they hurtled toward the Astro vessels.

"Turn one hundred eighty degrees," Harbin snapped.

The sudden lurching turn was too much for the comm tech; she retched and slumped over the armrest of her chair. *Samarkand* was no racing yacht. The ship turned slowly, slowly toward the right. Some of the remaining rocks ground against the hull, a dull grating sound that made even the pilot look up with wide, frightened eyes.

Harbin paid no attention to anything but the main screen. The Astro vessels were in the path of a speeding avalanche of stones as most of *Samarkand*'s erstwhile shielding came plunging toward them.

"Keep the stones between us and them," Harbin told the pilot. "We can still use them to shield us."

The display screen was filled with the rubble now. Harbin saw a brief splash of laser light as one of the Astro warships fired into the approaching avalanche. With his armrest keyboard he widened the scope of the display.

The Astro captains knew what had happened to Gormley, too. For a heartstopping few seconds they maintained their formation, but then their nerve broke and the two escorting warships scattered, leaving the bigger, more ponderous freighter squarely in the path of the approaching stones.

The freighter tried to maneuver away from the avalanche but it was too slow, too cumbersome to escape. Its captain did manage to turn it enough so that its bulky cargo of asteroidal ores took the brunt of the cascade.

Harbin watched, fascinated, as the blizzard of rocks struck the freighter. Most of them hit the massive cargo of ores that the ship carried in its external grippers. Harbin saw sparks, puffs of dust, as the stones struck in the complete silence of airless space.

"I wouldn't want to be in that shooting gallery," the executive officer muttered.

Harbin glanced away from the screen momentarily, saw that the weapons tech was tending to the comm technician, who was sitting up woozily in her chair.

The rocks continued to pound the freighter. Harbin saw a flash of glittering vapor that quickly winked out. Must have hit part of the crew module, he thought. That was air escaping.

"Where are those two escort ships?" he asked aloud.

The pilot chuckled. "On their way back to Selene, from the looks of it."

Why not? Harbin thought. They don't have a ship to escort anymore. Why risk their butts in a three-against-two engagement?

He called his two other ships and told them to stand by in case the two Astro warships returned. Then he commanded his pilot to move *Samarkand* closer to the crippled freighter.

"We've got to finish her off," he said.

The pilot asked, "Do you want me to open a frequency to her? I can take over the comm console, sir."

Harbin shook his head. He had no desire to talk with the survivors, if there were any still alive aboard the freighter. His job now was to complete the destruction of the ship, which meant that anyone still breathing aboard her was going to die.

"No need to talk to them," he said to the pilot. Then, to the weapons tech, "Get back to your post and arm the lasers. Time to finish this job."

Admiral Wanamaker had expected his intelligence officer to be excited, or perhaps worried. Instead, she looked deadly calm. And determined.

"Willie," he said, "I can't let you go on this mission. I'm sure you understand why."

Tashkajian remained standing in front of his desk, her dark eyes unwavering. "This mission is my idea, sir. I don't think I should expect others to take risks that I'm not prepared to take myself."

Gently, trying not to injure her pride, Wanamaker said, "But I need you here, Willie. You're my intelligence officer, and a damned good one. I can't afford to risk you."

Her steadfast pose faltered just a little. "But, sir, it's not right for me to stay here while the crew dashes out to the Belt inside that radiation cloud."

He smiled slightly. "You assured me it was perfectly safe, Willie."

"It is!" she blurted. "But . . . well, you know, there's always a chance . . ." Her voice trailed off for a moment, then she snapped, "Dammit, sir, you know what I mean!"

"Yes I do," he admitted. "But you're not going. You've picked a crew and the ship is ready to go out inside the radiation cloud to attack the HSS base at Vesta. You are staying here, where you belong. Where I need you to be."

"That's not fair, sir!"

"I have no intention of being fair. This is a war we're fighting, not some playground game."

"But—"

"The ship goes without you," Wanamaker said, as firmly as he could manage. "That is final."

● ● ●

"Welcome to Shining Mountain Base," said Daniel Tsavo, beaming so widely Pancho thought she could see his molars.

He was standing at the end of the flexible tube that had been snaked out to the hopper from the airlock of the base structure.

Shifting the travel bag on her shoulder, Pancho took his extended hand, smiling back at him, and looked around. The interior of the Nairobi facility looked bare-bones, no-nonsense efficiency. Undecorated metal walls. Ribbed dome overhead. Tractors scuffed and grimy with lunar dust.

"Nice of you to invite me," Pancho said, knowing that she had actually invited herself.

"I'm glad you got here before the solar storm strikes. We'll be safely underground before the radiation begins to mount."

"Sounds good to me," said Pancho.

Tsavo led her to a pair of gleaming metal doors. They slid open to reveal an elevator.

"Most of our base is underground, of course," he said as he gestured her into the cab.

"Just like Selene."

"Just like Selene," he agreed as the doors slid shut and the cab began dropping so fast Pancho's stomach lurched.

Wanamaker had been dead-set against this visit. When Pancho had told him she was going to look over the Nairobi base, his holographic image had turned stony.

"Pancho, the head of the corporation shouldn't walk into a potential enemy base all by herself."

"Enemy?" Pancho's brows had shot up. "Nairobi's not an enemy of ours."

"How do you know?" Wanamaker had demanded. "You're at war, Pancho, and anybody who isn't an ally is potentially an enemy."

Pancho didn't believe it.

"At least take a security team with you," Wanamaker insisted.

"I can take care of myself."

As Tsavo guided her along the tunnels of the Nairobi base, though, Pancho began to wonder about her bravado. The place was larger than she had expected, much larger. Construction crews in dark blue coveralls seemed to be everywhere, drilling, digging, hauling equipment on electrically powered minitractors, yelling to each other, lifting, banging.

The noise was incredible and incessant. Tsavo had to shout to make himself heard. And everything smelled brand new: fresh paint, concrete dust, sprays of lubricants and sealants in the air.

Pancho smiled and nodded as Tsavo shouted himself hoarse explaining what they were walking through. Living quarters would be there, offices on the other side of that corridor, laboratories, storerooms, a big conference room that could be converted into a theater, the base control center: all still unfinished, raw concrete and lunar rock and plans for the future.

Many of the workers were Asians, Pancho saw.

"Contract labor," Tsavo explained, his voice getting rougher with each word. "They have the experience and skills, and they are cheaper than training our own people."

Deeper and deeper into the base they walked, down inclined ramps marked TEMPORARY ACCESS and through tunnels whose walls were still bare rock.

Jeeps, Pancho thought, this place is *huge*. They're really building a city here, sure enough.

She hoped that the minibeacon her communications people had planted under the skin of her left hip would be able to send its coded signal through the rock. Jake's put up a set of six of polar orbiting satellites to keep track of me, she reminded herself; there'd be one close enough to pick up my signal all the time. I'll be okay. They'll know exactly where I am.

Yet for the first time in years she found herself thinking about Elly. Pancho had always felt safe with Elly tucked around her ankle. The gengineered krait had been her faithful bodyguard. Nobody messed with her once they realized she had a lethally poisonous snake to protect her. No matter that Elly's venom had been replaced with a strong sedative. Very few people had enough nerve to push things to the point where the snake would strike. Little Elly had been dead for more than ten years now, and Pancho had never worked up the resolve to get another such companion. Blubbery fool, she chided herself. Sentimental over a slithering snake, for cripes sake.

She tugged at the asteroidal sapphire clipped to her left earlobe. Like the rest of her jewelry, Pancho's earrings held surprises, weapons to defend her, if need be. But damn, she thought, there's a miniature army down here. I'd never be able to fight my way through all these bozos.

•   •   •

Sitting in the little wheeled chair in her office, just off the master bedroom of her home in Selene, Edith Elgin Stavenger used the three-second lag between Earth and Moon to catch up on the dossier of the woman she spoke with. For more than a week she had been chasing down executives in the news media on Earth, trying to stir their interest and support for her upcoming flight to Ceres.

Edith's cozy office seemed to be split in two, and the head of the North American News Syndicate appeared to be sitting behind her massive, gleaming cherrywood desk, talking with Edith as if they were actually in the same room—except for that three-second lag. Edith had the woman's dossier up on the wallscreen to one side of her own petite, curved desk.

"It's not a story, Edie," the media executive was saying. "There's no news interest in it."

The executive's name was Hollie Underwood, known in the industry as Holy Underhand or, more often, Queen Hollie. Thanks to rejuvenation therapies, she looked no more than thirty: smooth skin, clear green eyes, perfectly coiffed auburn hair. Edith thought of *The Picture of Dorian Gray* and wondered how withered and scarred with evil her portrait might be. Her reaction to Edith's idea was typical of the news media's attitude.

"There's no interest in it," Edith replied smoothly, "because no one's telling the story to the public."

Then she waited three seconds, watching Underwood's three-dimensional image, wondering how much the woman's ruffled off-white blouse must have cost. Pure silk, she was certain.

"Edie, dear, no one's telling the story because there's no story there. Who cares about a gaggle of mercenaries fighting each other all the way out there in the Asteroid Belt?"

Edith held her temper. Very sweetly, she asked, "Does anyone care about the cost of electrical power?"

Underwood's face went from mild exasperation to puzzled curiosity. At last she asked, "What's the price of electricity got to do with this?"

Feeling nettled that an executive of Underwood's level didn't understand much of anything important, Edith replied patiently, "The greenhouse flooding knocked out more than half of the coastal power plants around the world, didn't it?"

Without waiting for a reply, she went on, "Most of the loss in generating capacity is being taken up by solar power satellites, right? And where do you think the metals and minerals to build those satellites come from?"

Before Underwood could reply, Edith added, "And the fuels for the fusion generators that the power companies are building come from Jupiter, you know. This war is driving up their prices, too."

By the time she answered, Underwood was looking thoughtful. "You're saying that the fighting out in the Asteroid Belt is affecting the price of metals and minerals that those rock rats ship back to Earth. And the price of fusion fuels, as well."

"And the price of those resources affects the ultimate price you flatlanders pay for electricity, yes." Edith grimaced inwardly at her use of the derogatory *flatlanders*, but Underwood seemed to pay it no attention.

"So it costs us a few cents more per kilowatt hour," she said at last. "That's still not much of a story, is it."

Edith sat back in her little desk chair. There's something going on here, she realized. Something circling around below the surface, like a shark on the hunt.

She studied Underwood's face for a few silent moments. Then she asked, "How much advertising is Astro Corporation buying from you? Or is it Humphries?"

Once she heard the question Underwood reddened. "What do you mean? What are you implying?"

"The big corporations don't want you to go public about their war, do they? They're paying for this cover-up."

"Cover-up?" Underwood snapped, once she heard Edith's accusation. "There isn't any cover-up!"

"Isn't there?"

Underwood looked furious. "This conversation is *over!*" Her image winked out, leaving Edith alone in her snug little office.

She nodded to herself and smiled. That hit a nerve, all right. The big boys are paying off the news media to keep the war hushed up. That's what's going on.

Then Edith's smile faded. Knowing the truth would be of little help in getting the story to the public.

How to break through their wall of silence? Edith wished she knew.

Jake Wanamaker actually banged his fist against the wall. He stomped past the row of consoles in the communications center and punched the wall hard enough to dent the thin metal paneling.

"She just waltzed in there all by herself and now you can't even make contact with her?"

The communications technicians looked scared. Old as he was, Wanamaker was still a formidable figure, especially when he was radiating anger. For several heartbeats no one in the comm center said a word. Console screens blinked and beeped softly, but everyone's attention was focused on the big admiral.

"Sir, we got good tracking data on her until she got to the Nairobi base."

"Those minibeacons are supposed to be able to broadcast through solid rock," Wanamaker snarled. "We hung a half-dozen satellites in polar orbits, didn't we? Why aren't they picking up her signal?"

"It must be the solar flare, sir," said another of the technicians. "It's screwing up communications."

Glowering, Wanamaker said, "You people assured me that the frequency the system uses wouldn't be bothered by a flare."

The chief comm tech, a cadaverous, sunken-eyed old computer geek, called across the room, "Their base must be shielded. Faraday cage, maybe. Wouldn't be too tough to do."

"Great!" Wanamaker snapped. "She's in a potential enemy's camp and we can't even track her movements."

"If she gets outside again the satellites'll pick up her signal," said the chief tech, hopefully.

"If she gets outside again," Wanamaker muttered.

"Not while the solar storm's in progress," said one of the younger techs, wide-eyed with worry. "Radiation level's too high. It'd be suicide."

Rumors spread through a tightly knit community such as Selene like ripples widening across a pond. One comm tech complained to a fellow Astro employee about the tongue-lashing Wanamaker gave to everyone in the communications center. The Astro employee mentioned to her husband that Pancho Lane had disappeared down at the Astro base near the south pole. Her husband told his favorite bartender that Pancho Lane had gone missing. "Probably shacked up with some guy, if I know Pancho," he added, grinning.

At that point the rumor bifurcated. One branch claimed that Pancho had run off with some guy from Nairobi Industries. The other solemnly insisted that she had been kidnapped, probably by Martin Humphries or some of his people.

Within hours, before Wanamaker or anyone in the Astro security office could even begin to clamp down a lid on the story, Selene was buzzing with the rumor that Pancho was either off on a love tryst or kidnapped and probably dead.

Nodon heard the story during his first hours of work as a maintenance technician in the big, echoing garage that housed the tractors and tour busses that went out onto the surface of Alphonsus's crater floor. He went through the motions of his new job and, as soon as his shift ended, hurried up into the "basement" to find Fuchs.

Fuchs was not at the stacks of shelving where Nodon and the others had met him before. Nodon fidgeted nervously, not knowing whether he should start searching through the dimly lit walkways or wait where he was for Fuchs to return. A maintenance robot came trundling along the walkway, its red dome light blinking. Nodon froze, plastering his back against the storeroom shelves. The robot rolled past, squeaking slightly. The maintenance robot needs maintenance, Nodon thought.

Half a minute behind the robot came Lars Fuchs, in his usual black pullover and slacks, and the usual dark scowl on his face.

"Kidnapped?" Fuchs gasped when Nodon told him the tale.

"Perhaps dead," the Mongol added.

"Humphries did this?"

To his credit, Nodon admitted, "I don't know. No one seems to know."

"It couldn't be anybody else," Fuchs growled.

Nodon agreed with a nod.

"Down at the south pole, you say? They captured her down there?"

"That is the story. Some say she has run off with a lover."

"Pancho wouldn't do that. She wouldn't have to. If she wanted a lover she'd do it right here in Selene, where she's safe."

Nodon said nothing.

"It's got to be Humphries," Fuchs muttered, as much to himself as his companion. "He's probably having her taken to his mansion, down below."

"Do you think so?"

"Even if he hasn't, that's where *he* is. We've got to get in there. And quickly."

Daniel Tsavo tried to hide his nervousness as he toured Pancho through the construction areas and finally down into the finished section of the Nairobi base, where he and the other corporate executives resided. It was blessedly quiet down at this lowest level; the constant battering noise of the twenty-four-hour-a-day construction was muffled by thick airtight hatches and acoustical insulation. As they walked along the carpeted corridor toward the executive dining room, Tsavo kept Pancho on his right, as he had done all through the brief tour, so that he could hear the microreceiver embedded in his left ear without being obvious about it.

It troubled him that Nobuhiko Yamagata himself was speeding to the base on a high-g rocket from Japan. The interrogation team had already arrived, but their work was suspended until Yamagata arrived.

Pancho, meanwhile, was trying to sort out in her mind everything she had seen in this brief tour of the unfinished base. It's enormous! she thought. They're not just building a phase-one facility here, they're putting up a whole city, all in one shot. This place'll be just as big as Selene.

Tsavo tried hard not to hold his left hand up to his ear. He was waiting for news that Yamagata had arrived, waiting for his instructions on what to do with Pancho.

"Pretty fancy setup you guys have for yourselves," Pancho teased as they walked along the corridor. Its walls were painted in soothing pastels. The noise of construction was far behind them. "Nice thick carpets on the floor and acoustic paneling on the walls."

"Rank has its privileges," Tsavo replied, making himself smile back at her.

"Guess so." Where are they getting the capital for all this, Pancho wondered. Nairobi Industries doesn't have this kind of financial muscle. Somebody's pouring a helluva lot of money into this. Humphries? Why would the Humper spend money on Nairobi? Why invest in a competitor? 'Specially when he's sinking so much into this goddamn war. I wouldn't be able to divert this much of Astro's funding; we'd go broke.

"Actually," Tsavo said, scratching at his left ear, "all this was not as expensive as you might think. Most of it was manufactured at Selene."

"Really?"

"Truly."

Pancho seemed impressed. "Y'know, back in the early days of Moonbase they thought seriously about putting grass down in all the corridors."

"Grass?"

"Yep. Life-support people said it'd help make oxygen, and the psychologists thought it'd make people happier 'bout having to live underground."

"Did they ever do it?"

"Naw. The accountants ran the numbers for how much electricity they'd need to provide light for the grass. And the maintenance people complained about the groundskeeping they'd have to do. That killed it."

"No grass."

"Except up in the Main Plaza, of course."

Tsavo said, "We plan to sod our central plaza, too. And plant trees."

"Uh-huh," said Pancho. But she was thinking, If Humphries isn't bankrolling Nairobi, who is? And why?

The receiver in Tsavo's ear buzzed. "Mr. Yamagata is expected in two hours. There is to be no interrogation of Ms. Lane until after he has arrived. Proceed with dinner as originally planned."

At that precise moment, Pancho asked, "Say, when's dinner? I haven't had anything to eat since breakfast."

"Perfect timing," Tsavo murmured, stopping at a set of double doors. Using both hands, he pushed them open. Pancho saw a conference room that had been transformed into a dining room. The central table was set for eight, and there were six people standing around the sideboard at the far end of the oblong room, where drinks had been set up. Two of them were women, all of them dark-skinned Africans.

Tsavo introduced Pancho to his Nairobi Industries colleagues, then excused himself to go to the next room for a moment, where the servers waited with a group of six Japanese men and women.

"No drugs," Tsavo told their chief. "We'll have a normal dinner. We can sedate her later."

TORCH SHIP *ELSINORE*

D oug Stavenger rode with Edith all the way up to the torch ship, waiting in a tight orbit around the Moon. He went with her through *Elsinore*'s airlock as the ship's captain personally escorted his passenger to her quarters, a comfortable little cabin halfway down the passageway that led to the bridge.

Once the captain had left them alone and had slid the passageway door shut, Stavenger took his wife in his arms.

"You don't have to do this, Edie," he said.

"Yes I do," she replied. She was smiling, but her eyes were steady with firm resolve.

"You could send someone else and have him report what he finds to you. You could stay here at Selene and produce the news show or documentary or whatever—"

"Doug," she said, sliding her arms around his neck, "I love you, darling, but you have no idea of how the news business works."

"I don't want you risking your neck out there."

"But that's the only way to get the story!"

"And there's a solar storm approaching, too," he said.

"The ship's shielded, darling." She nuzzled his nose lightly, then said, "You'd better be getting back to Selene before the radiation starts building up."

He frowned unhappily. "If something should happen to you . . ."

"What a story it would make!" She smiled as she said it.

"Be serious."

Her smile faded, but only a little. "I'm being serious, Doug. The only way to break this conspiracy of silence is for a major news figure to go to Ceres and report on the situation firsthand. If Selene broadcasts my story it'll be picked up by independents on Earth. Then the Earth-side nets will *have* to cover it. They'll have no choice."

"And if you get killed in the process?"

"I won't," she insisted. "I'm not going to go out into the Belt. I'll stay at Ceres, on the habitat the rock rats have built for themselves, where it's perfectly safe. That's one of the tricks of this business: Give the appearance of being on the front line, but stay at headquarters, where it's safe."

Stavenger tightened his grip around her waist. "I really don't want you to go, Edie."

"I know, dearest. But I have to."

Eventually he gave up and released her. But all the way back to Selene on the little shuttle rocket, all the way back to his home in the underground city's third level, Doug Stavenger could not shake the feeling that he would never see his wife again. He told himself he was being a foolish idiot, overly protective, overly possessive, too. Yet the feeling would not leave him.

Two ships left Selene, heading toward the Belt. *Elsinore*, carrying Edith Elgin, was going to the habitat *Chrysalis*, in orbit around the asteroid Ceres. *Cromwell*, an Astro Corporation freighter, was ostensibly going to pick up a load of ores that she would tote back to Selene.

Both ships turned on their electromagnetic radiation shielding as soon as they broke orbit around the Moon. The vast and growing cloud of energetic ionizing radiation that had been spewed out by the solar flare soon engulfed them both. Aboard *Elsinore*, the ship's crew and her sole passenger watched the radiation count climb with some unavoidable trepidation. Aboard *Cromwell*, the crew counted on the radiation cloud to shield their approach to Vesta. *Cromwell* carried no human passengers, of course. Its cargo was a pair of missiles that carried heavily insulated warheads of nanomachines, the type commonly called gobblers.

Unable to communicate with *Cromwell*, and equally unable to contact Pancho, Jake Wanamaker had nothing better to do but pace the communications center and glower at the technicians working the consoles. At last he thumped himself down at an empty console and pulled up Pancho's messages. Maybe there's something in here that can tell me what she thinks she's up to, he told himself, knowing it was just an excuse to engage in some busywork before he started smashing the furniture.

A long string of routine calls, mostly from Astro offices or board members. But one of the messages was highlighted, blinking in red letters. A Karl Manstein. No identification; just a call with no message attached. Yet it was highlighted. Wanamaker routed the call through Astro's security system, and the Mainstein name dissolved before his eyes, replaced by the name *Lars Fuchs.*

Lars Fuchs had called Pancho, Wanamaker realized. He remembered that she had wanted to contact Fuchs and was chewing out her security people because they couldn't find him.

The man's right under their noses, Wanamaker said to himself. Right here in Selene. But he left no callback number.

Wanamaker had the computer trace the origin of Fuchs's call. It had come from a wall phone up in the equipment storage area. Is he hiding up there? Wanamaker wondered.

He picked up the console microphone and instructed the communications computer to put through any call from Fuchs or Karl Manstein directly to him.

Nothing to do but wait, Wanamaker thought, leaning back in the console's little wheeled chair. Wait to see what's happening with Pancho. Wait to find out how *Cromwell's* mission to Vesta turns out. Wait for Fuchs to call again.

He hated waiting.

Then he realized that someone was standing behind him. Swiveling the chair he saw it was Tashkajian, looking just as somber and apprehensive as he felt.

Martin Humphries was strolling through his expansive underground garden when Victoria Ferrer hurried along the curving brick path, breathless with news of the rumors about Pancho.

"Who the hell would kidnap Pancho?" Humphries snickered.

Walking alongside him through the wide beds of colorful flowers, Ferrer said, "The betting upstairs is that you did."

"Me? That's ridiculous."

"Is it?" she asked.

"I wouldn't mind having her assassinated. But why kidnap her?"

Ferrer shrugged slightly. "She might have run off with some guy. They say this man running the Nairobi operation is quite a slab of beefcake."

"Pancho wouldn't do that," Humphries said, shaking his head.

"Well, the Astro security people are floundering around, wondering where she is."

Humphries stopped in the middle of the path and took in a deep breath of flower-fragrant air. "Well, let's hope that she's dead. But I doubt it. Pancho's a tough little guttersnipe."

SELENE: STORAGE CENTER FOURTEEN

Fuchs paced along the dimly lit walkway between storage shelves and humming, vibrating equipment, trying to avoid the scattering of renegades and outcasts that lived among the shadows, turning aside whenever he saw the flashing red light of an approaching maintenance robot. He rubbed at the back of his neck, which was tight with tension. Absently, his hand moved to massage the bridge of his nose. His head ached and he felt frustrated, angry, aching, and—worst of all—uncertain.

What to do? What to do? Humphries must have had Pancho kidnapped. Who else would do it? Right at this moment they're probably flying Pancho back here to his mansion. If they haven't killed her already. What can I do? How can I help her?

He knew the answer. Get to Humphries and kill him. Kill the murdering bastard before he kills Pancho. Kill him for Amanda. For all the rock rats he's killed out in the Belt. Execute him, in the name of justice.

He snorted at his own pretensions. Justice. No, what you want is vengeance. Don't talk of justice; you want revenge, nothing less.

Alone as he paced the walkway, he nodded his aching head fiercely. Vengeance. Yes. I will have vengeance against the man who destroyed my life. Who destroyed everything and everyone I hold dear.

And what risks are you willing to take for your vengeance? he asked himself. You have three people with you; Humphries has a small army of security guards down there in his mansion. How can you even think of getting to him? There is no one in Selene who will help you. No one in the entire solar system would lift a finger for you, except Pancho and she's a prisoner or perhaps already dead.

Fuchs abruptly stopped his pacing. He found himself in front of a large wall screen, set up against the side of a massive, chugging water pump that was painted bright blue. The screen was mounted on rubberized shock absorbers, to separate it from the pump's constant vibration. In the faint light from a distant overhead lamp Fuchs saw his reflection in the blank screen: a short, stocky man with a barrel chest, stubby arms and legs, a bristling black beard and deep-set eyes that glowed like twin lasers. He was dressed in shapeless black slacks and a pullover shirt, also black as death.

No more thinking, he told himself. No more planning. Get Sanja and the others and *strike*. Tonight. Humphries dies tonight or I do. He almost smiled. Possibly both of us.

His headache disappeared along with his uncertainty.

"It was a really great dinner," Pancho said as Tsavo walked her along the corridor. "You got some sharp people working for you. I enjoyed talking with them."

Tsavo beamed at her compliments. "I'm glad you enjoyed it."

During dinner he had learned that Nobuhiko Yamagata had landed, scant minutes ahead of the leading edge of the solar storm, and had gone immediately to his interrogation team. Now the voice whispering electronically in his left ear told him to take Pancho to her quarters and let her fall asleep. To help make her sleep, Yamagata's people had injected a strong sedative in the bottle of wine that waited on Pancho's bedside table.

"It's been a really good visit," Pancho was saying. "I'm glad I came."

Still smiling for her, Tsavo said, "You'll stay the night, of course."

Pancho grinned back at him. He was a centimeter or so taller than her own lanky height, and she liked tall men.

"I'd love to, Dan, but I've got to get back to my own people. They're expecting me."

"But the storm," he said earnestly. "All surface activities are suspended until the radiation goes down to normal."

Pancho teased, "Is that what your dinner was for? To keep me here long enough for the storm to hit?"

He looked shocked. "No! Not at all. But now that it's hit, you'll have to stay the night."

She said nothing as he led her a few more paces down the carpeted corridor and stopped at an unmarked door. Sliding it open, he ushered her into a spare but comfortable-looking bedroom, with a small desk set in one corner and a wallscreen that showed the view outside the base.

Pancho saw several hoppers standing out there, including the green one she had flown in on. And a transfer vehicle, the kind that brought people in from ships in orbit; that hadn't been there when she'd landed. In the bright sunlight outside she could see that it was anodized sky blue.

Then she noticed that her travel bag had been placed on the bed, unopened. And there was a bottle of wine sitting tilted in a chiller bucket on the low table in front of the cushioned sofa.

"Champagne," she noted. "And two glasses."

Tsavo put on a slightly sheepish look. "Even before the storm came up I had hoped you'd stay the night."

"Looks like I'll have to. I ought to call my people at Malapert, though, and let them know I'm okay."

He hesitated, as if debating inwardly with himself. Pancho couldn't hear the whispered instructions he was getting.

"All right," he said, flashing that killer smile again. "Let me call my communications center."

"Great!"

He went to the phone on the desk and the wallscreen abruptly switched to an image of a man sitting at a console with a headset clipped over his thick dark hair.

"I'm afraid, sir, that the solar storm is interfering with communications at this time."

Tsavo seemed upset. "Can't you establish a laser link?"

Unperturbed, the communications tech said, "Our laser equipment is not functional at this time, sir."

"Well get it functioning," Tsavo said hotly. "And let me know the instant it's working."

"Yes, sir." The wallscreen went dark.

Pancho pursed her lips, then shrugged. "Guess my people at Malapert will have to get along without me till the storm lets up."

Tsavo looked pleased. Smiling, he asked, "Would you like some wine?"

COMMAND SHIP *SAMARKAND*

arbin was heading back to the HSS base at Vesta. *Samarkand* had not escaped its one-sided battle against the Astro freighter unscathed. The loosed rocks and pebbles of his ship's armor shield had dented and buckled parts of the hull, and now *Samarkand* was totally unarmored, easy prey for any warship it should happen to meet.

He was worried about the ship's radiation shielding. Even though the diagnostics showed the system to be functioning properly, with a solar storm approaching he preferred to be safely underground at Vesta.

Still, he left his two other vessels to continue their hunt through this region of the Belt while he made his way back to Vesta for refurbishment.

It will be good to have a few days of R&R, he thought as he sat in the command chair. Besides, my medicinals are running low. I'll have to get the pharmacy to restock them.

He turned the con over to his executive officer and left the bridge, ducking through the hatch and down the short passageway to his private quarters. Making his way straight to his lavatory, he opened the medicine chest and surveyed the vials and syringes stored there. Running low, he confirmed. But there's enough here to get me through the next few nights. Enough to let me sleep when I need to.

He reached for one of the vials, but before he could take it in his fingers the intercom buzzed.

"Sir, we have a target," the exec's voice said. Then she added, "I think."

Harbin slammed the cabinet door shut. "You think?" he shouted to the intercom microphone set into the metal overhead of the lav.

"It's an odd signature, sir."

Incompetent jackass, Harbin said to himself. Aloud, "I'm on my way."

He strode to the bridge, simmering anger. I can't trust this crew to do anything for themselves. I can't even leave them alone long enough to take a piss.

But as he slid into the command chair he saw that the display on the main screen was indeed fuzzy, indistinct.

"Max magnification," he commanded.

"It is at maximum," the comm tech replied. She too was staring at the screen, a puzzled frown furrowing her pale Nordic countenance.

Harbin glanced at the data bar running across the bottom of the display. Just over twelve hundred kilometers away. The object was spinning slowly, turning along its long axis every few seconds.

"Size estimate," he snapped.

Two pulsating cursors appeared at each end of the rotating object. Blinking alphanumerics said 1.9 METERS.

"It's too small to be a ship," said the pilot.

"A robot vehicle?" the weapons technician asked. "Maybe a mine of some sort?"

Harbin shook his head. He knew what it was. "Turn off the display."

"But what is it?" the communications tech wondered aloud.

"Turn it off!"

The screen went dark. All four of his officers turned to stare at him questioningly.

"It's a man," Harbin said. "Or a woman. Someone in a space suit. Someone dead. Killed in a battle out there, probably months ago."

"Should we—"

"Ignore it," he snapped. "It can't hurt us and there's nothing more we can do to it. Just leave it alone."

The officers glanced at each other.

"A casualty of war," Harbin said grimly as he got out of the command chair. "Just forget about it. I'm going back to my quarters. Don't disturb me with any more ghosts."

He went back to his cabin, stripped off his sweaty uniform and stretched out on his bunk. It will be good to get back to Vesta, he thought. This ship needs refurbishment. So do I.

This war can't last much longer, he told himself. We've driven most of the Astro ships out of the Belt. They'll come back with more, I suppose, and we'll destroy them. We'll keep on destroying them until they finally give up. And what then? Do I retire back to Earth? Or keep on working? There's always money to be made for a mercenary soldier. There's always someone willing to pay for killing someone else.

He closed his eyes to sleep, but instead he saw a space-suited figure tumbling slowly through the star-flecked emptiness, silently turning over and over, for all eternity alone in the cold, dark emptiness, forever alone.

His eyes snapped open. Harbin thought about taking a shot that would let him sleep, but he didn't want to dream. So he lay on the bunk for hours, wide awake, staring at the hard metal of the overhead.

"Wish I could call my people and tell 'em I'll be spending the night here," Pancho said. "When's that laser link going to start working?"

Wine bottle in one hand, pneumatic corkscrew in the other, Daniel Tsavo suddenly looked uneasy.

"They'll know you're safe down here," he said, with a slightly labored smile. "Let's have some wine and stop worrying."

Pancho made herself smile back at him. "Sure, why not? You open the bottle while I freshen up a little."

She went to the lavatory and closed its door firmly. Pecking at her wristwatch, she saw that its link with the satellites that were supposed to be tracking her was dead. She tried the phone function. That was down, too.

Pancho leaned against the sink, thinking furiously. I'm cut off from the outside. He wants me to stay here overnight. Fun and games? Maybe, but there's more to it than just a romp in the sheets. This place is *huge*. They're spending more money on construction than Nairobi's got on its books. A lot more. Somebody big is bankrolling them.

And then it hit her. Tsavo said to me, "Welcome to Shining Mountain Base." That's what the Japanese call this mountain range: the Shining Mountains. And that transfer ship outside is painted in Yamagata Corporation's blue.

Yamagata's behind all this, Pancho finally realized. They're bankrolling Nairobi. And now they've got me here; I waltzed right in and they're not going to let go of me that easy.

She heard the pop of a champagne cork through the flimsy lavatory door. Ol' Danny boy's working for Yamagata, Pancho said to herself. And I'll bet there's enough happy juice in that wine to get me to babble my brains out to him.

I've got to get out of here, she told herself. And quick.

• • •

Nobuhiko Yamagata paid scant attention to the bows and self-effacing hisses of his underlings. He went straight from the transfer rocket that had landed him at Shining Mountain Base to the room where Pancho Lane would be interrogated. It was in the base's infirmary, a small room where his interrogation team surrounded an empty gurney.

Father is right, Nobu said to himself. I can learn much more from Pancho than these hirelings could.

The team was gowned and masked, like medics. Two young women were helping Nobu into a pale green surgical gown. Within minutes he was masked, gloved, and capped with one of the ridiculous-looking shapeless hats that came down over his ears.

Then he stood by the gurney, waiting. The members of the interrogation team flanked him in silence.

Well, Nobuhiko thought, everything is prepared. Everyone is here except Pancho.

SHINING MOUNTAIN BASE

Won't you have some champagne?" Tsavo asked smoothly, offering Pancho one of the crystal flutes that he had filled with the bubbly wine.

"Love to," said Pancho, smiling her best smile for him.

As he handed her the glass Pancho let it slip from her fingers. She watched with inner amusement as the glass tumbled slowly in the gentle lunar gravity, wine spilling from its lip in languid slow motion. Pancho could have grabbed the glass before it started spilling, but she watched it splash champagne over her coveralls while Tsavo stood there looking shocked.

"Aw gosh," she said as the glass bounced on the thick carpeting. "Sorry to be so clumsy."

Tsavo recovered enough to say, "My fault."

Looking down at the wine-spattered front of her coveralls, Pancho said, "I better dry this off." She headed for the lavatory, stopping momentarily to unclip one of her earrings and place it on the night table beside the bed.

There are many ways to incapacitate an opponent who's bigger and stronger than you are, Pancho reminded herself as she firmly closed the lavatory door. One of them is to blind the sumbitch.

She leaned her back against the door and squeezed her eyes shut, but still she saw the flash behind her closed eyelids. Tsavo screamed. By the time Pancho had the lav door open again he was staggering across the bedroom.

"I can't see!" he shrieked. "I'm blind!"

He crashed into the coffee table, knocking the bottle and chiller bucket to the floor and tumbled into the sofa with a painful thump, groaning, pawing at his eyes.

"I'm blind! I'm blind!"

"Sorry, Danny boy," Pancho said as she scooped her travel bag off the bed. "You'll get your sight back in a few hours, more'n likely."

She left him moaning in a tumbled sobbing heap on the floor by the sofa and dashed out into the corridor.

Now we find out how much security they got here, Pancho said to herself, actually grinning as she raced on her long legs up the carpeted corridor.

Fuchs had thought about calling Astro Corporate headquarters to try to speak with one of Pancho's aides, but decided against it. None of them would have the authority to give him the help he needed, nor the wit to see the necessity of it. With Pancho out of the picture, Fuchs realized he was on his own.

Just as well, he told himself as he rode the powered stairs down to Selene's bottommost level. It's better not to involve Pancho or anyone else. What I have to do I'll do for myself.

Nodon, Sanja and Amarjagal were waiting for him at the bottom of the last flight of stairs. The corridor down at this level was empty, as Fuchs had expected it to be. Only the very wealthiest lived down here, in the converse of penthouses on Earth. No crowds here, he said to himself as the four of them strode down the broad, empty, quiet corridor. Fuchs saw that the walls here were decorated with bas reliefs, the floor softly carpeted. Security cameras watched them, he knew, but they looked like a quartet of maintenance workers, nothing to set off an alarm.

So far.

"Have you set the maintenance computer?" Fuchs asked Nodon.

The younger man nodded, his big liquid eyes looking slightly frightened. "Yes, sir. The water will be shut off to this level in . . ." he glanced at his wristwatch, ". . . three minutes."

"Good," said Fuchs. He had no idea how long it would take the maintenance people to discover that the water to level seven had been shut off. Long enough to get the four of us inside Humphries's grotto, he hoped.

The corridor ended in a blank stone wall with a heavy metal hatch set in it. Beside the hatch was a keypad.

"Do you have the access number?" Fuchs asked Nodon.

"I haven't had enough time on my job with the maintenance

department to be assigned down here," Nodon said, his voice little more than an apologetic whisper. "But I know the emergency numbers that work on the upper levels."

"Try them."

Nodon hunched slightly before the keypad and began tapping numbers. Fuchs watched with gathering impatience. One of those numbers should override the security code, he told himself. Humphries has to allow Selene emergency crews inside his private preserve, he's got to. Not even he can refuse to allow emergency workers to enter his area. That's written into Selene's basic safety regulations.

The hatch suddenly gave off a metallic click. In the stillness of the empty corridor it sounded like a gunshot.

"That's it!" Fuchs hissed. He set a meaty hand against the cold steel of the hatch and pushed. It opened slowly, silently. A gust of soft, warm air brushed past him as the hatch swung all the way open.

Fuchs gaped at what he saw. A huge expanse filled with brilliant flowers, warm artificial sunlight glowing from the lamps high overhead, the very air heavy with scents he hadn't smelled since he'd left Earth. And trees! Tall, stately, spreading their leafy branches like arms open to embrace him.

"It's a paradise," Amarjagal whispered, her eyes wide with awe. Nodon and Sanja stood beside her, mouths agape. Fuchs felt tears welling up.

With an angry shake of his head he growled, "Come on. Their security alarms must be going off. Their cameras are watching us."

He started up the brick path that wound through beds of bright colorful flowers, heading for the mansion they could see through the trees.

Paradise, Fuchs thought. But this paradise has armed men guarding it, and they'll be coming out to stop us in a few minutes.

Nobuhiko pushed up the sleeve of his green surgical gown and looked at his watch. Turning to the chief of the interrogation team, he demanded, "Well, where is she? I've been waiting for more than half an hour."

The man's mask was slightly askew. He pushed back his shower-cap hat, revealing a line pressed into his high forehead by the cap's elastic band.

"Tsavo was to bring her here," he said.

"They should be here by now," said Nobuhiko.

The man hesitated. "Perhaps they are . . ."

"They are what?"

With a shrug, the man said, "They spent a night together back at Selene, when they first met. Perhaps they are in bed together now."

One of the gowned and masked women tittered softly.

Nobuhiko was not amused. "Send someone to find them. At once."

Her travel bag clutched under one arm, Pancho walked briskly along the corridor, trying to remember the route she had followed when Tsavo brought her down to this level. Cripes, she thought, it was only an hour or two ago but I'm not sure of which way we came. My memory's shot to hell.

She thought about the stealth suit she had used so many years ago to sneak into Humphries's mansion unseen. I could use a cloak of invisibility right about now, she told herself as she glanced up at the corridor's ceiling, searching for surveillance cameras. She couldn't see any, but she knew that didn't mean there weren't any watching.

She spotted a pair of metal doors at the end of the corridor. The elevator! Pancho sprinted to it and leaned on the button set into the wall.

Now we'll find out if they're watching me. If the elevator's working, it means they don't know I'm on the loose.

The elevator doors slid smoothly open and Pancho stepped into the cab. It wasn't until the doors shut again and the elevator started accelerating upwards that she thought it might be a trap. Jeeps! They could have an army of guards waiting for me up at the top level.

TORCH SHIP *ELSINORE*

An ordinary passenger riding out to the rock rats' habitat at Ceres would have been quickly bored in the cramped confines of the torch ship. *Elsinore* was accelerating at one-sixth g, so that its sole passenger would feel comfortable at the familiar lunar level of gravity. But like all the ships that plied between the Moon and the Belt, *Elsinore* was built for fast, efficient travel, not for tourist luxuries. There was no entertainment aboard except the videos broadcast from Selene or Earth. Meals were served in the neatly appointed but decidedly small galley.

Edith had dinner with the ship's captain and one of his officers, a young Asian woman who said little but listened attentively to the ship's passenger and her skipper.

"We'll be vectoring out of the radiation cloud tomorrow," the captain announced cheerfully, over his plate of soymeat and mushrooms. "Ceres is well clear of the cloud's predicted path."

"You don't seem worried about it," Edith said.

He made a small shrug. "Not worried, no. Respectful, though. Our radiation shielding is working, so we're in no danger. And by this time tomorrow we should be out of it altogether."

"Will the cloud reach the Belt at all?" she asked.

"Oh yes, it's too big and intense to dissipate until it's well past the orbit of Jupiter. Ceres is well clear of it, but a good half of the Belt is going to be bathed in lethal radiation."

Edith smiled for him and turned her attention to her own dinner of bioengineered carp fillet.

After dinner, Edith went to her cabin, sent a laser-beamed message to her husband back at Selene, then started working on the first segment of the documentary she had planned.

Sitting on the tiny couch of her cabin with the video camera perched on its mobile tripod by the bed, she decided to forgo the usual Edie Elgin cheerleader smile. Covering a war was a serious matter.

"This is Edie Elgin, aboard the torch ship *Elsinore*," she began, "riding out to the Asteroid Belt, where a deadly, vicious war is taking place between mercenary armies of giant corporations. A war that could determine how much you pay for electrical energy and all the natural resources that are mined in the Belt."

She got to her feet and walked slowly around the little cabin, the camera automatically pivoting to keep her in focus.

"I'll be living in this cabin for the next six days, until we arrive at Ceres. Most of the men and women who go out to the Belt to work as miners or prospectors or whatever travel in much less comfortable quarters."

Edith went to the door and out into the passageway. The camera trundled after her automatically on its tripod as she began to show her viewers the interior of the torch ship. As she spoke, she hoped that this segment wouldn't be too boring. If it is I can cut it down or eliminate it altogether, she thought. I don't want to bore the viewers. That is, assuming anybody wants to watch the show once it's finished.

Cromwell was cruising toward the Belt at a more leisurely pace, allowing the radiation cloud to engulf it. The ship's five-person crew could not feel the radiation that surrounded the ship nor see it, except in graphs the computer drew from the ship's sensors.

"The shielding is working fine," the skipper kept repeating every few minutes. "Working just fine."

His four crew members wished he'd change the subject.

Eventually, he did. "Set course thirty-eight degrees azimuth, maintain elevation."

Embedded in the radiation cloud, *Cromwell* headed toward Vesta.

Suddenly panicked, Pancho stabbed at the panel of buttons in the elevator. The cab lurched to a stop and the doors slid open. The pounding, growling, roaring sounds of construction immediately blasted her ears but she paid them no attention as she walked briskly out into the unfinished expanse.

She saw that she wasn't at the topmost level, the dome where there was an airlock that led to the rocket hoppers sitting outside. Must be a rampway that leads up, she thought hopefully. Better stay away from the elevators.

A construction worker driving an orange tractor yelled at her in Japanese. Pancho couldn't understand his words, but she recognized the tone: *What the hell are you doing here? Get back where you belong!*

With a grin she hollered back to him, "That's just what I'm trying to do, buddy. Which way is up?"

The head of base security was perspiring visibly. Nobuhiko glared at the black man and demanded, "Well, where is she? She has to be *someplace!*"

Yamagata had left his interrogation team in their silly green gowns and bustled off to the security chief's office, tearing off the surgical gown they had given him and throwing it angrily to the floor as his own quartet of bodyguards hastened along behind him.

The security chief was standing behind his desk, flanked by a wall of display screens, most of them blank.

"She *was* here," he said, punching a keypad on his desktop, "with Mr. Tsavo."

One of the screens lit up to show Pancho and Tsavo in the bedroom. Nobu watched Pancho spill her champagne, go to the lavatory—and then the screen flared with painful brilliance.

Blinking, a red afterimage burning in his eyes, Yamagata said through gritted teeth, "I don't want to know where she *was*. I want to know where she is now."

The security chief wiped at his tearing eyes. "She must have gone up into the construction area. The surveillance cameras on those levels haven't been activated yet."

Before the exasperated Yamagata could say anything, the security chief added, "I've ordered all the airlocks sealed and placed guards at all the space suit storage areas. She can't get outside."

Nobu thought, That's something, at least. She's trapped inside the base. We'll find her, then. It's only a matter of time.

We make an unlikely invasion force, Fuchs thought as he and his three crew members walked purposively through the flowering garden toward Humphries's mansion.

But that might be a good thing, he realized. The more unlikely we appear, the less seriously the guards will take us. We might still have surprise on our side.

Not for long, he saw. A pair of men were striding down the winding path toward them, both of them tall, broadshouldered, with the hard-eyed look of professional security guards. They were clad in identical slate-gray tunics and slacks: not quite uniforms, but close enough. Fuchs wondered what kinds of weapons they carried.

"What are you doing here?" the one on the left called, raising a hand to stop Fuchs and his people.

"Emergency maintenance," said Fuchs, slowing but not stopping. "Water stoppage."

"We didn't get any emergency call," said the other one. He was slightly shorter, Fuchs saw, and looked somewhat younger.

"It registered on our board," Fuchs lied. Stretching out an arm to point, he said, "You can see the problem from here, up on your roof."

The shorter one turned almost completely around. The other glanced over his shoulder. Fuchs launched himself at the older one, ramming his head into the man's midsection. He heard a satisfying "Oof!" and the two of them went down, Fuchs on top. Nodon kicked the man in the head and he went limp. Getting to his feet, Fuchs saw that Amarjagal and Sanja had knocked the other one unconscious as well.

Swiftly, they tied the two men with their own belts and dragged them into the bushes, but not before taking their guns and communicators.

Fuchs looked over one of the pistols as they ran toward the mansion. Laser pistols. Fuchs remembered how the rock rats had turned their handheld tools into makeshift weapons, years ago. These were specifically designed as sidearms. Nodon held the other gun.

"STOP WHERE YOU ARE!" boomed an amplified voice.

Fuchs yelled back, "This is an emergency! Quick! We haven't a moment to lose!"

The front door of the mansion opened as they raced up to it, and another pair of guards in identical slate-gray outfits—one of them a woman—stepped out, looking puzzled.

"What's going—"

Fuchs shot the man and before she could react Nodon shot the woman. The infrared laser beams were invisible but Fuchs saw the smoking little circular wound in his man's forehead as he slumped to the ground.

"Come on," Fuchs said, waving his crew forward. Amarjagal and Sanja stopped long enough to take the guns from the unconscious guards, then they stepped over their inert bodies and into the mansion's entryway.

I'm in his house! Fuchs marveled. I'm actually in Humphries's home! He realized he hadn't expected to get this far.

A woman in a black servant's dress came out of a door down the hall, carrying a silver tray laden with covered dishes. Fuchs rushed toward her. When she saw the gun in his hand she gave out a frightened squeak, dropped the tray with a loud crash, and fled back into the kitchen.

"Never mind her," Fuchs snarled. "Find Humphries."

Finally ending her video tour of the ship, Edith returned to her cabin. She felt tired, but decided to review what she had shot and mark the scenes for future editing.

Once her face appeared on the cabin's wallscreen, though, she studied it minutely for signs of aging. To her relief, she could find none. The rejuvenation therapies were still working.

Then she wondered if that might not be counted against her, back on Earth. They might think I'm filled with nanomachines, like Doug. That would prejudice them against me, maybe.

She shrugged to herself and shut down the display. Faced with a choice between flatlander prejudices and physical youth, she opted for youth. With a yawn she looked toward her bed. Time for some beauty sleep, Edith said to herself, wishing that Doug were here with her.

The house was huge, Fuchs realized, and divided into two sections. On one side of the hallway that extended from the entrance there seemed to be a warren of offices and laboratories. Fuchs and his crew glanced into a few of them; they were unoccupied, quiet, dark. Offices for his staff, Fuchs guessed, empty at this time of night.

Impatiently he waved his three aides back to the hallway.

"Sanja," he directed, pointing down the hall, "you find that woman. She must know where Humphries is. "We'll look through the other side of the house."

Humphries was upstairs, in the master bedroom suite, sitting at his computer desk. The war is going well, he said to himself as he studied the latest figures on battle casualties. In another couple of months we'll have booted Astro out of the Belt altogether.

Yet when he turned to his intelligence department's latest assessment, his face contorted into a frown. Astro's building more ships, gearing up for a counterattack. That damned greasemonkey doesn't know when she's beaten.

He heard a muffled clatter from downstairs. One of the servants must have dropped something. Leaning back in his yielding desk chair he realized that he had ordered a snack more than half an hour ago. Where the hell was it?

With a shake of his head he returned to his musings about the war. They claim Pancho's disappeared. More likely she's down at that Nairobi base trying to get their support. And I've got a board of directors meeting coming up. They'll yell bloody murder about the p-and-l figures. This war's bleeding us. But once we win it, they'll all shut up. They'll have to.

His thoughts returned to Pancho. The little guttersnipe. If she's building a new fleet of warships here at Selene it makes sense to attack the factories where they're being built. But that would bring Stavenger into the war on her side. I don't want Selene coming in against—

"The water turned off."

Annoyed, Humphries turned to see Victoria Ferrer standing in the doorway to his office, wrapped in a white full-length robe, its sash cinched around her waist. Her hair was glistening wet.

"What?" he snapped.

"The water turned off," she repeated, "right in the middle of my shower."

At that moment the report hovering above his desk abruptly disappeared, replaced by the intense face of his chief security guard.

"Sir, we have intruders on the premises."

"Inside the house?"

"Yessir. Downstairs. I suggest you go to top security mode immediately."

"Damned right! And you get them! Call everyone you've got. Get them!"

Down in his basement office, the security chief clicked off his phone, thinking furiously. Only twelve guards on night duty, he knew. Still, he glanced at the screen showing the duty roster. They've already knocked out four of them. He told the phone to call up every guard on the payroll—another two dozen of them—and get them to the mansion immediately.

Humphries has his suite sealed off, so they can't get to him unless they can cut through three centimeters of reinforced cermet, he thought. Even with laser pistols that will take some time. The boss is safe enough. He called for a view of the master suite and saw that Ferrer was in there with Humphries. He grinned to himself. Hell, he might even enjoy this, as long as she's sealed into the bedroom with him.

Then he turned his attention to the screen showing three of the four intruders making their way up the main staircase to the upper floor.

Fuchs was leading Nodon and Amarjagal cautiously up the main stairway, peering intently at the upper landing to see if any more security guards were up there. Suddenly he heard the heavy slamming of doors. A voice blared from speakers hidden in the ceiling:

"WE HAVE YOU ON CAMERA AND ARE AUTHORIZED TO USE LETHAL FORCE IF NECESSARY. THE HOUSE IS SEALED AND THERE IS NO WAY FOR YOU TO ESCAPE. DROP YOUR WEAPONS AND PUT YOUR HANDS ON TOP OF YOUR HEADS."

Fuchs hesitated for barely a fraction of a second, then rushed up the stairs, the two others behind him. As they reached the landing, Sanja started up the steps behind them.

"The front doorway has been sealed with a metal slab!" he called.

The windows, too, were covered with heavy metal grillwork, Fuchs saw as he glanced around the upstairs hallway. The hall was lined with real wooden furniture: tables and chests and sideboards. Actual paintings hung along the walls.

They think we're burglars or thieves, Fuchs thought. They're trying to make certain we can't get away. But I don't want to get away, I want to find Humphries.

"Where are you, Humphries?" he shouted at the ceiling. "Show yourself, coward!"

Nodon, his eyes so wide that Fuchs could see white all around the pupils, said in a tight whisper, "They must be sending more guards. We're trapped!"

All the lights went off, plunging them into almost total darkness. Within an instant, though, Nodon pulled a hand torch from his coverall pocket. Its feeble beam made the hallway look eerie, mysterious.

Fuchs rushed to a heavy walnut table against the wall. With one sweep of his arm he sent the flower vase and smaller porcelain pieces atop it crashing to the carpeted floor.

"Help me turn this thing over and drag it over to the top of the stairs. We can stop them from getting up here."

Sanja and Amarjagal tipped the table over with a heavy thud, and the four of them pushed it to the head of the stairs and wedged it there between the wall and the staircase railing. Down below they heard the pounding of running feet and saw the shadowy figures of security guards coming along the downstairs hall. They must have been stationed in the basement, Fuchs thought, straining to make out how many of them there were. No more than six, he estimated.

He whispered to the two men, "Get the statues, the chairs, any-thing you can lift and bring them here. Amarjagal, go down the hallway a few meters so you can fire on them as they come up the stairs."

If they think we're going to surrender, they have a big surprise com-ing, Fuchs thought grimly. I'm not leaving this house until I see Humphries dead at my feet.

ancho jogged up the rampway, long legs pumping easily as she made her way to the top level of the base. Trotting along the final section of ramp she could see the ribbed vaulting of the surface dome overhead. Almost there, she said to herself.

But she skidded to a halt when she spotted a quartet of men standing by the row of space suits that hung next to the airlock. They were all Japanese, their coveralls sky blue and bearing the white flying crane emblem of Yamagata Corporation. Each of them had an ugly-looking sidearm strapped to his waist.

They saw her, too. Two of them started to sprint toward her as Pancho reversed her course and started back down the ramp, back toward the noisy, bustling construction crews and the minitractors that were hauling loads of steel beams and drywall sheeting. She swung her legs over the ramp's railing and jumped lightly to the dusty floor several meters below.

The noise was an advantage to her, she thought. Nobody's going to hear those guards yelling, and these construction guys don't have comm units in their ears. She loped alongside one of the electric-powered minitractors and hopped into the cart it was towing, landing with a plop amidst coils of wire and bouncing, flexing lengths of plastic piping.

She lay flat, hoping that the guards didn't see her hitchhike maneuver. The minitractor trundled on for several minutes; all Pancho could see was the bare beams supporting the ceiling overhead.

She was thinking as hard and fast as she could. Airlocks are up on the next level, but they're all guarded. So are the suits. Even if I could grab a space suit the guards would grab me before I had time to put one on. And there's the damn-dratted solar storm outside, too. Not the best time for a walk on the surface.

I could use the softsuit, she reminded herself. It's right here, tucked into my travel bag. Never used the blow-up helmet before but Doug said it works okay. Yeah, maybe. Maybe not. What choice do I have?

The big problem was to get to an airlock without being seen. Suddenly Pancho broke into a fierce grin. No, the problem is how do I get some explosives so I can *make* a new airlock for myself!

Doug Stavenger tried to busy himself with catching up on the minutes of Selene's governing council meetings. But as he read the reports of the water board and the maintenance department and the safety office, the words blurred into meaningless symbols before his eyes. Irritated, nervous, he told his computer to show him the latest report on the solar storm.

One wall of the office in his home seemingly dissolved into a three-dimensional image of the Earth/Moon system. It was bathed in a hot pink glow that represented the radiation cloud. Stavenger muted the sound, preferring to read for himself the figures on radiation intensity and predicted time duration of the storm displayed across the bottom of the holographic image.

"Add traffic," he said quietly.

Several yellow dots appeared in the image. One of them was identified as *Elsinore*, the ship Edith was aboard.

"Project trajectories."

Slim green curving lines appeared, the one attached to *Elsinore* arcing out to the right and out of the cloud.

"Add destinations."

Elsinore's projected path ended at a dot labeled "Ceres." Stavenger noted almost subliminally that of all the ships in the region, there was one named *Cromwell* but that had no projected destination visible. No course vector for it showed at all. It was deep inside the radiation cloud, too.

As he watched, *Cromwell's* dot winked out. Stavenger stared at the display. Either the ship's suddenly been destroyed or they've turned off all their tracking and telemetry beacons. There were no other ships near it, as far as the imagery showed. So it can't have been attacked by somebody.

Why would they turn off all their beacons? Stavenger asked himself. It took only a moment's thought for him to understand.

• • •

Pancho jumped off the cart as the minitractor rolled past a jumbled pile of equipment and crates of supplies lying in what seemed a haphazard disorder on the dusty concrete floor. The driver saw her and yelled at her over his shoulder in Japanese as the tractor trundled away from her.

"Same to you, buddy," Pancho hollered back, bowing politely to the driver.

Slinging her travel bag over one shoulder, she ducked behind the nearest pile of crates and started searching through the trove. No explosives, but in the midst of the scattered pieces of equipment she saw something that might be almost as good: a welding laser. Kneeling beside the laser's finned barrel, she clicked its ON switch and felt her heart sink. The power supply's battery indicator was way down in the red. *I need a power source,* she told herself.

Suddenly the loudspeakers hanging on poles every fifty meters or so blared into harsh, rapid Japanese. Pancho didn't understand the words but she knew the tone: *There's an intruder sneaking around here. Find her!*

All the construction noise stopped. It was eerie, Pancho thought. The banging, buzzing, yelling construction site went absolutely still. It was as if everybody froze.

But only for a moment. Hunkered behind a crate, Pancho saw the blue-clad construction workers looking around uncertainly. Foremen and women strode out among them, snapping orders. The workers gathered themselves into parties of four, five and six and began methodically searching the entire floor. Pancho figured they were doing the same on the other levels, too.

Feeling like a mouse in a convention hall filled with cats, Pancho knelt behind the crate. The laser was within reach, but without a power supply it was useless. *And even if I get outside,* she told herself, *I'll have to sprint through the storm to get into one of the hoppers sitting out on the launchpad. The outlook ain't brilliant.*

Then she saw the same minitractor she had ridden on heading across the cement-dusty floor toward her. Two men were squeezed into its cab alongside the driver.

He remembers me hitching the ride, Pancho realized, *and he's bringing the goons to search the area.* She smiled. *The tractor could serve as a power supply for the laser,* she thought. *All I have to do is get* rid of those three guys. She unclipped her other earring and held it tightly in her palm.

Sitting on the bare concrete floor, her back pressed against the plastic crate, Pancho listened to the tractor coming up and stopping. Voices muttering in Japanese. They're getting out, she knew. Poking around.

She clambered to her feet. The three saw her immediately. Pancho noticed with some surprise that the hard-hatted driver was a young woman. The other two, bareheaded, were stony-faced men. And armed with guns.

"You!" one of the men shouted in English, pointing a pistol at her. "Don't move!"

Pancho slowly raised both hands above her head, the earring still clutched in her right palm. Wait, she said to herself, flicking the catch of the earring with her thumb. Let them get just a little closer.

Now! She tossed the earring at them and flung both arms over her eyes. The flash of light still seared through her closed lids and burned a red afterimage on her retinas. But once she opened her eyes she found that she could see well enough. The two goons were writhing on the ground, screeching in Japanese. The woman driver was staggering around blindly. Blinking painful tears, Pancho grabbed the laser in both hands, pushed past the dazed and groping driver, and dumped it into the back of the tractor. Even in one-sixth g, it was heavy.

Quickly she detached the cart and slipped into the tractor's cab. She put it in gear and headed for the nearest ramp, up to the top level.

HABITAT *CHRYSALIS*

Big George scowled at the display splashed across his wall screen as he sat in his favorite recliner, feet up, a frosty mug of beer at his side. Solar storm, he said to himself. Big one.

The IAA forecasters were predicting that the storm would not reach Ceres. The cloud of ionized particles followed the interplanetary magnetic field, and the field's loops and knots were guiding it across the other side of the solar system, far from Ceres's position. George felt grateful. *Chrysalis* was protected by electromagnetic shielding, just as most spacecraft were, but George had no great ambition to ride out a storm.

Poor bastards on Vesta are gonna get it, he noted. Hope they've got the sense to get their arses underground in time. George shrugged and reached for his beer. At least they've got plenty of warning.

The display showed spacecraft traffic. *Elsinore* was the only vessel George was interested in. Edith Elgin was aboard, coming to Ceres to do a video report on the war out here. About fookin' time somebody in the news media paid attention, George thought.

Elsinore was swinging clear of the radiation cloud, he saw. She'll be here in four days and some, George said to himself. Good. We'll be waitin' for her.

He took a long swallow of beer. There was nothing else for him to do, except wait.

HUMPHRIES MANSION

Fuchs crouched behind the makeshift barricade jammed at the top of the stairs, peering into the shadows. Some light from the garden outside was leaking through the grills covering the upstairs windows. He could hear movement downstairs, but it was almost impossible to see anything with all the indoor lights off. Nodon has a hand torch, he knew, but to turn it on would simply give the guards a target to shoot at.

"Nodon," he whispered, "pull down some of the drapes on the windows."

The crewman scuttled away, and Fuchs heard ripping noises, then a muffled thud.

A strong voice called from the first floor, "Whoever you are, you can't get out of here. You're trapped. Better give yourselves up and let us turn you over to the authorities."

Fuchs bit back the snarling reply he wanted to make. Nodon slithered up and pushed some bunched-up fabric into his hands. "Will this do, Captain?" he asked.

"We'll see," Fuchs whispered back.

A light flashed momentarily in the darkness and a man yowled with pain. Amarjagal, halfway across the landing, had fired her gun at someone creeping silently up the steps. But not silently enough. The Mongol woman had heard him and shot him with her laser pistol. Its beam was invisible, but the fabric of the guard's clothing flashed when it was hit. Fuchs heard the man tumbling down the carpeted stairs.

We need some light, Fuchs said to himself. If I can set this drapery afire we can use it as a torch.

Another spark of light splashed against the table, just past Fuchs's ear. He smelled burning wood.

"Behind us!" Sanja screamed in his native Mongol dialect.

Fuchs turned as both Sanja and Nodon fired blindly down the hallway. There's another staircase! he realized. Fool! Fool! You should have thought of that, should have—

Nodon screamed with pain as a bolt struck him and grabbed his shoulder. Fuchs snatched the gun from Nodon's fingers and fired blindly down the hall. In the corner of his eye he saw Amarjagal shooting at a pair of figures crawling up the steps.

Dropping Nodon's gun, Fuchs bunched the drapery fabric in one hand and fired his gun into it. The stuff smoldered. He fired again, and it burst into flame. So much for fire-retardant materials, he thought. Put a hot enough source on it and it will burn.

"Shoot at them," he ordered Sanja. "Keep their heads down."

Sanja obediently fired down the hallway, even picking up Nodon's gun and shooting with both hands.

Fuchs scrambled to his feet and plunged down the hall, bellowing like a charging bull, firing his own gun with one hand and waving the blazing drapery over his head with the other. Whoever was down there was still ducking, not firing back. Fuchs saw the back stairwell, skidded to a stop and threw the fiery fabric down the steps. For good measure he sprayed the stairwell with his gun.

He saw several men backing down the stairs as the drapery tumbled down. The carpeting on the steps began to smoke and an alarm started screeching in the flickering shadows.

Humphries had gone from his office into his adjoining bedroom, eyes wide with fright. He could feel his heart pounding beneath his ribs, hear the pulse thundering in his ears so loudly he barely heard Ferrer shouting at him.

Somebody's broken into my house, screeched a voice in his head. Somebody's gotten into my home!

The emergency lights were on and the cermet shutters had sealed off the bedroom from the office and the hallway beyond it. Nobody can get to me, Humphries told himself. There's two fireproof doors between me and them. I'm safe. They can't reach me. The guards will round them up. I'm safe in here.

Still in her white terrycloth robe, Ferrer grabbed him by both shoulders. "It's Fuchs!" she shouted at him. "Look at the display!"

The wall screen showed a stubby miniature bear of a man charging down the hallway outside, swinging a blazing length of drapery.

"Fuchs?" Humphries gasped. It was difficult to make out the man's face in the false-color image of the infrared camera. "It can't be!"

Ferrer looked angry and disgusted. "It is! The computer's matched his image and his voice. It's Fuchs and three of his henchmen."

"Here?"

"He's come to kill you!" she snapped.

"No! He can't! They'll—"

"FIRE!" the computer's emergency warning sounded. "FIRE IN THE REAR STAIRWELL."

Humphries froze, staring at the wall screen, which now showed the rear stairs blazing.

"Why don't the sprinklers come on?" he demanded.

"The water's off," she reminded him.

"No water?" Humphries bleated.

"The building's concrete," Ferrer said. "Seal off the burning area and let the fire consume all the oxygen and kill itself. And anybody in the burning section."

Humphries felt the panic in him subside a little. She's right, he thought. Let the fire burn itself out. He stood up straighter, watching the wallscreen's display.

"Anybody caught in there," he said, pointing shakily, "is going to get burned to death. Fuchs is going to roast, just as if he were in hell."

Hurrying back to the makeshift barricade at the top of the main staircase, Fuchs could smell smoke wafting up from the rear stairs.

"FIRE!" said a synthesized voice, calm and flat but heavily amplified. "FIRE IN THE REAR STAIRWELL."

"We've got to get out of here," Sanja hissed in his ear.

"No!" Fuchs snapped. "Not till we get Humphries."

Amarjagal crawled to them. "More guards down there," she said. "They will charge up the stairs."

From the corner of his eye Fuchs could see the flickering light of the flames in the rear stairwell. They can't attack us from that direction, he thought. Then he realized, And we can't retreat that way, either.

Laser bolts sizzled against the upturned table and scorched the wall behind them.

"Here they come!"

Even in the shadowy light Fuchs could see a team of guards charging up the stairs, firing their handguns as others down in the entryway also fired up at them.

Fuchs rolled to one side of the table, where his crew had laid a heavy marble bust from one of the tables down the hall. He noticed that one of the laser blasts had ignited a painting on the wall behind them. Grunting with the effort, he lifted the bust with both hands, raised it above the edge of the upturned table, and hurled it down the stairs. It bounced down the steps, scattering the approaching guards like a bowling ball. Sanja and Amargjagal fired at them. Fuchs heard screams of pain.

"We must get out of here," Amarjagal said flatly. There was no panic in her voice, not even fear. It was simply a statement of fact.

And Fuchs knew she was right. But they were surrounded, trapped. And Humphries was untouched.

B een a long time since I drove a tractor, Pancho said to herself as she puttered up the ramp toward the base's topmost level. They haven't changed much since my astronaut days, she thought. Haven't improved them.

The fact that the Nairobi base was so big was an advantage to her. They're scurrying all over the place looking for me; got a lot of territory to search. I'll be in good shape until those three blind mice down there start talking.

The tractor reached the top of the ramp and Pancho steered past a knot of blue-coveralled construction workers, heading for a quiet, empty spot along the base of the dome. She figured it would take the better part of half an hour to get the laser going and cut a reasonably sized hole in the dome's metal wall. Better get into the softsuit before then, she told herself. Unless you want to breathe vacuum.

Nobuhiko felt sorry for Daniel Tsavo. The man sat in a little folding chair in the base's infirmary, hunched almost into a fetal position, his fists balled up on his lap, his unseeing eyes aimed at the floor. It must be terrible to be blind, Nobu thought, even if it's only temporary.

A pair of doctors and three nurses were finishing their ministrations, taping a bandage across Tsavo's eyes while the man kept up a low angry mumble about what Pancho had done to him.

Keeping his face impassive as he listened to Tsavo's muttered story, Nobu couldn't help feeling some admiration for Pancho. She walked into the lion's den knowingly, he realized. She came here to learn what Nairobi is doing. I wonder if she understands now that Nairobi is a tool of Yamagata Corporation? And if she does, what should I do about it?

I should call my father, Nobuhiko thought. But not here. Not now. Not in front of these aliens. Wait. Have patience. You've come all the way to the Moon, be patient enough to wait until they capture Pancho. Then we'll find out how much she knows. Once we determine that, it will be time to decide what to do with her.

Pancho was thinking of Yamagata as she toted the laser from the back of the minitractor to the base of the dome's curving metal wall. This topmost level of the base was quieter than the lower levels. Construction here was nearly complete, except for small groups scattered across the dome's floor, painting and setting up partitions. There were guards at all the airlocks, though, and more guards stationed along the lockers where space suits were stored.

She kept low and stayed behind the tractor, hoping that anyone searching for her up at this level would see nothing more than a tractor parked near an empty section of the wall. Until the laser starts flashing sparks of molten metal, and by then it'll be too late to stop me. I hope.

Why is Yamagata backing Nairobi? she asked herself as she plugged the power cable into the tractor's thermionic generator. Nobuhiko told me Yamagata's not involved in space operations, they're concentrating all their efforts on Earth. Yeah, sure. What was it Dan Randolph used to say: "And rain makes applesauce." Nobu was lying through his teeth at me. Sumbitch is using Nairobi to get established on the Moon. But why?

It wasn't until she had the laser ready to go and was pulling the softsuit out of her travel bag that the answer hit Pancho. Yamagata's getting ready to take over the Belt! They're letting Astro and Humphries slaughter each other and they'll step over the bloody corpses and take control of everything! They're even *helping* us to fight this damned stupid war!

Suddenly Pancho felt angry. At herself. I should've seen this, she fumed silently. If I had half the smarts god gave a warty toad I would have figured this out months ago. Damn! Double damn it all to hell and back! I've been just as blind as I made those people downstairs.

Okay, she told herself. So you've been outsmarted. Just don't go and kill yourself. Check out this suit carefully.

The softsuit was easy to put on. You just stepped into it the same way you stepped into a pair of coveralls, put your arms through the sleeves, and sealed up the front like it was Velcro. The nanomachines are activated by the body's heat, she knew. Wriggling her fingers inside the skin-thin gloves, she wondered all over again how the virus-sized nanobugs could keep her safe from the vacuum of space without stiffening up the way normal gloves and fabric suits did.

She had never worn a nanotech helmet before. It hung limply in her gloved hands, like an empty plastic sack. Reading the illustrated instructions off her palmcomp, Pancho blew it up like a kid's balloon. It puffed out to a rigid fishbowl shape. It felt a little spongy to her, but Pancho pulled the helmet over her head and sealed it to the suit's collar by running two fingers along the seam. Same as sealing a freezer bag, she thought.

No life-support pack; only a slim green cylinder of oxygen, good for an hour. Or so the instructions said.

Okay, she told herself. You got one hour.

It was difficult for the Nairobi security woman to understand what the nearly hysterical Japanese woman was saying. She kept pawing at her eyes and sobbing uncontrollably. The two African guards, both men, were still sprawled on the concrete floor, unconscious.

She called her boss on her handheld and reported her finding: one tractor driver and two guards, all three of them incapacitated, blinded.

"Where's the tractor?" Her boss's face, even in the handheld's minute screen, scowled implacably at her.

"Not here," she replied.

The boss almost smiled. "Good. All tractors have radio beacons. Get the number of the tractor out of the driver, then we can track its beacon and find out where the fugitive is."

"Assuming the fugitive is with the tractor," she said, before thinking.

His scowl deepened. "Yes, assuming that," he growled.

It wasn't wise to second-guess the boss, she remembered too late.

Pancho hesitated as she held the laser's cutting head next to the curving metal wall. I cut a hole and the air whooshes out. None of the people up here are in suits. They could get killed.

Then she shook her head. This dome's too big for that. The air starts leaking out, they'll pop some emergency sheets that'll get carried to the hole and plug it up long enough for them to get a repair crew to fix it. Nobody's going to get hurt except you, she said to herself, if you don't get your butt in gear.

She thumbed the laser's control switch. Its infrared beam was invisible, but a thin spot of cherry-red instantly began glowing on the metal wall. Holding the laser head in both her gloved hands like an old-fashioned power drill, Pancho slowly lifted it in an arc-like shape. She felt nothing inside the softsuit, but noticed that dust was swirling along the floor and disappearing into the thin, red-hot cut. Punched through, she thought. Nothing but vacuum outside.

The wall was thick, and the work went slowly, but finally Pancho cut a hole big enough for her to crawl through. Dust and scraps of litter were rushing through it now. But as she turned off the laser and ducked the hole, she saw there was another wall beyond it. Drat-damn it! Meteor shield.

It was a flimsy wall of honeycomb metal set up outside the actual dome structure to absorb the constant hail of micrometers that rained down on the Moon's surface. Grumbling to herself, Pancho took up the laser again and started cutting once more. This one'll go a lot faster, she told herself.

She heard a voice bellowing in Japanese, very close, but ignored it, sawing frantically with the laser to cut through the meteor shield and get outside.

"You there!" a man's voice yelled in English. "Stop that or I'll shoot!"

ORE CARRIER *CROMWELL*

Despite his outward show of confidence as he sat in the command chair on the bridge, *Cromwell*'s skipper felt decidedly nervous as the creaking old ore ship cruised toward Vesta inside the radiation cloud. As surreptitiously as he could, he kept an eye on the console that monitored the radiation levels inside and outside his ship. A glaring red light showed that the sensors outside were reporting lethally high radiation, enough to kill a man in minutes. Next to that baleful red glow on the control panel a string of peaceful pale green lights reported that radiation levels inside the ship were close to normal.

Good enough, the captain said to himself. So far. We still have a long way to go.

He had worked out with the special weapons tech how close they would have to be to Vesta before releasing the twin missiles that contained the nanomachines. They had developed three possible scenarios. The first one was the basic plan of attack, the flight path they would follow if everything went as planned and they were not detected by Humphries's people. That was the trajectory they were following now, sneaking along inside the radiation cloud until they reached the predetermined release point.

If they were detected on their way in to Vesta, or if the ship developed some critical malfunction such as a breakdown of its radiation shielding (a possibility that made the skipper shudder) then they would release the missiles early and hope that they would not be seen or intercepted by Vesta's defense systems. The skipper and the weapons tech had worked out a release point for that contingency. It was only six hours from where they now were.

Their third option was to call off the attack altogether. That decision would be entirely—and solely—up to the captain. Only a major disaster would justify abandoning the attack, such as a serious malfunction of the ship's systems or an interception by HSS vessels.

Cruising blind and deaf inside the radiation cloud, watching the sensor readings on the control panel, the skipper thought that of the three options before him he much preferred number two. *Let's get to the early release point, fire the damned missiles at Vesta, and get the hell out of here before something goes wrong.*

He got up from the command chair. All four of his crew turned from their consoles toward him.

"I'm going to catch some zees," he said gruffly. "You take your normal relief, one at a time. Ms. Yamaguchi, you have the con. Wake me in five hours."

"Yes, sir. Five hours."

The captain ducked through the hatch. His quarters were immediately aft of the bridge. *Five hours,* he thought. *I'll make my decision after a good nap, when my mind is fresh.*

He knew what he wanted that decision to be.

HUMPHRIES MANSION

I n his basement office, Humphries's security chief watched the screens on the wall to one side of his desk with growing dismay. *Four guys are holding off two dozen of my people. The dumb bozos are just sitting there like a bunch of petrified chipmunks. And now the back staircase is on fire. Humphries is gonna fry my ass for this.*

Angrily he punched the keyboard on his desk. "What the hell are you punks doing, waiting for hot dogs so you can have a fuckin' barbecue?"

He had only a voice link with his team upstairs, no video. "I got six people wounded here."

"You got a dozen and a half untouched! Go get the intruders!"

"Why should we rush 'em and take more casualties? They're not goin' anywhere. We can wait 'em out."

"While the fuckin' house burns down?" the chief yelled.

"Then we'll burn 'em out!"

The chief thought it over swiftly. *Humphries is sealed into his master suite. They can't get to him. The fire's triggered the automatic alarms. That upstairs hallway is closed off by airtight doors. Windows are already sealed. Okay. We'll let the fire do the job.*

It was getting smoky in the upstairs hall. Leaning his back against the overturned table Fuchs peered down the hallway and saw flames licking at the carpet, spreading toward them.

"We must get out," Amarjagal repeated.

The flames reached the drapes on the farthest window. They began smoldering.

Coughing, Sanja added, "It is useless to die here, Captain."

Fuchs wanted to pound his fists on the floor. Humphries was a few meters away, cowering behind his protective cermet barrier. The coward!

Fuchs raged. The sniveling coward. But he's smarter than I am. He's pre-pared for this attack, while I've led my people into a stupid assault that will gain us nothing even if we live through it. He pictured Humphries's smirking face and felt the rage rising inside him even hotter than the flames creeping toward them.

"THE ENTIRE HALLWAY AREA IS SEALED OFF," the loud-speaker voice declared. "THE FIRE'S GOING TO SUCK ALL THE OXYGEN OUT OF YOUR AIR. YOU HAVE THREE CHOICES: SUFFOCATE, ROAST, OR SURRENDER."

Sitting cross-legged on his oversized bed, Humphries yelled at the wallscreen image of his security chief, "You're letting them burn up the second-floor hallway? Do you have any idea of the value of the artwork on those walls? The furniture alone is worth more than your salary!"

The security chief looked distinctly uncomfortable. "Sir, it's the only way to get them. They've wounded six of my people already. No sense getting more of them hurt."

"That's what I pay them for!" Humphries raged. "To protect me! To kill that sonofabitch Fuchs! Not to burn my house down!"

Ferrer was sitting on an upholstered chair on the far side of the spa-cious room, her robe demurely pulled down below her knees.

The security chief was saying, "You're perfectly safe inside your suite, Mr. Humphries. The walls are concrete and your door is fireproof reinforced cermet."

"And my hallway's going up in flames!"

"They started the fire, sir, my people didn't. And now they either surrender or the fire kills them."

"While your people sit on their asses."

Stiffly, the security chief replied, "Yessir, while my people keep the rest of the house secure and wait for the intruders to give themselves up."

Humphries stared at the chief's image for a long moment, panting with frustrated rage. Then he snarled, "Don't look for a bonus at Christmas."

"We're trapped here," Amarjagal said, still as unemotional as a wood carving.

Fuchs saw the flames licking up the window draperies, heard them hissing, edging along the carpeting toward them. But the smoke was no worse than it had been before: annoying, but not suffocating.

"Where's the smoke going?" he muttered.

"Captain, we must do something," said Sanja, his voice tense. "We can't stay here much longer."

Fuchs scrambled to his feet and took a few steps along the hall. He saw the smoke curling up from the blazing drapes and streaming across the ceiling in a thin, roiling layer. It grew noticeably thinner halfway along the hall.

"Help me," he called to Sanja as he grabbed a heavy chest of inlaid ebony. The two men wrestled it into the middle of the hall and Fuchs clambered up onto it.

A ventilator, he saw, its grillwork cleverly disguised to look like an ornamental design on the ceiling. It was closed, he realized, but not completely. Some of the smoke was being sucked up through it. He pushed against it with both hands. It gave, but only slightly.

Sanja immediately understood. He took a copper statuette from the nearest table and handed it up to Fuchs, base first. Fuchs pounded at the ventilator grill with the fury of desperation. It dented, buckled. With an animal roar he smashed at it again and the ventilator gave way with a screech of metal against metal. Immediately, the smoke slithering along the ceiling began pouring into the opening.

"It's big enough to crawl through!" he shouted.

"Nodon," said Amarjagal, on her feet now. "He's unconscious."

"Carry him. Come on."

Fuchs hauled himself up into the ventilator shaft. It was filled with smoke and utterly dark inside. Coughing, he reached down for Nodon's still-unconscious body. This shaft can't be too long, he thought. We're up near the roof. There must be an outlet nearby.

Crawling, coughing, eyes streaming with burning tears, he dragged Nodon's limp body through the shaft. Its metal walls felt hot to his fingers, but he slithered along, knowing that either he found his way out of the building or he would soon die.

The security chief was peering at his display screens, straining to see what was going on in the dim shadows of the upstairs hall. The only light came from the flickering flames. The intruders were moving around, he felt sure, but it was almost impossible to make out anything definite in the smoke. Even the infrared cameras were virtually useless now. Several of the window draperies were blazing; the flames over-loaded the surveillance cameras' light sensitive photocells. All he could see was overexposed flickers of flame and inky black shadows shambling around.

The fire's contained to the upstairs hall, he saw, checking the other screens. Thank god for small miracles. I'll probably have to resign after this. If Humphries doesn't fire me outright.

Pacing the length of the big bedroom, Humphries muttered, "I don't like this. I don't like being cooped up in here."

Victoria Ferrer suppressed an incipient smile. He's really frightened, she thought. Normally, if we were locked in his bedroom together he'd peel this robe off me and pop me between the sheets.

"I don't like waiting," he said, louder.

"Think of it this way," she suggested, not moving from the chair where she sat, "Fuchs is dying out there. When those fireproof doors open again you can go out and stand over his dead body."

He nodded, but it was perfunctory. The thought of victory over Fuchs obviously didn't outweigh his innate fear for his own life.

Fuchs's lungs were burning. The metal walls of the ventilator shaft were scorching hot now as he crawled along blindly, dragging Nodon's inert body with one pain-cramped hand. He couldn't see Amarjagal or Sanja behind him. He didn't even know if they were still there. His entire world had narrowed down to this smoke-filled, blistering hot purgatory.

Through tear-filled eyes he saw a light up ahead. It can't be, he told himself. I'm starting to hallucinate. The garden outside is still in its nighttime lighting mode. There can't be bright lighting out there—

His heart clenched in his chest. Unless the guards have turned up all the outdoor lights! Like a badger, Fuchs scuttled along the upward-slanting shaft, leaving Nodon and the others behind. Light! Air! He bumped his head against a metal grill, feeling blessedly cool air caressing his hot, sooty face. The smoke was streaming out. Fresh air was seeping in.

With his bare hands Fuchs battered the grill, punched it until his knuckles were raw and bleeding, butted it with his head, finally forced it open by wedging his feet against the sides of the shaft and leaning one powerful shoulder against the thin metal and pushing with all his strength. It gave way at last.

He took one huge gulp of fresh air, wiped at his eyes with grimy hands, then ducked back down the shaft to grab Nodon by the collar of his coveralls and haul him up onto the roof. Amarjagal's head popped up behind Nodon's booted feet. She too was grimy, soot-streaked. But she smiled and pulled herself out of the shaft.

"Stay low," Fuchs hissed. "The guards must be patrolling the grounds."

Sanja came up, and crawled on his belly to lay beside Fuchs. They looked out onto the splendid garden just beyond the mansion's wall and, farther, to the trees and green flowering shrubbery of this artificial Eden planted deep below the surface of the Moon.

And there were guards standing out there, armed with assault rifles, ready to shoot to kill.

SHINING MOUNTAIN BASE

Y ou there!" the guard yelled. "Stop that or I'll shoot!"

Pancho realized that her necklace was tucked inside the dratted softsuit. She couldn't reach it. Couldn't whip it off her neck and toss it at the goon. Prob'ly wouldn't have time to do it before he drilled me, anyway, she thought as she slowly climbed to her feet and raised both gloved hands over her helmeted head. She nudged the laser slightly with her boot. It was still on, still cutting away at the honeycomb shield outside the dome's wall.

"Who the devil are you?" the guard demanded, walking slowly around the minitractor, a pistol leveled at Pancho's navel. He looked African but spoke like an Englishman. "And what the devil do you think you're doing?"

Pancho shrugged inside the softsuit. "Nothin'," she said, trying to look innocent.

"My god!" the guard yelped, seeing that hole cut into the dome wall and the bright red hot spot the laser was making on the honeycomb shield. "Turn that thing off! Now! Don't you realize you could—"

At that instant the honeycomb cracked open and a rush of air knocked Pancho flat against the curving dome wall. The guard was staggered but kept his senses enough to realize what was happening. He turned and ran as fast as he could, which wasn't very fast because he was leaning against a gale-force wind trying to rush out of the hole Pancho had cut.

The loudspeakers started yammering in Japanese, then in another language Pancho didn't understand. She slid down to the floor and slithered out of the break, hoping the softsuit wouldn't catch or tear on the broken edges of the holes the laser had made.

Outside, she looked around the barren lunar landscape. The dome was on the crest of the ringwall mountains that surrounded Shakleton.

The ground sloped away, down toward the floor of the crater. Nothing to see but rocks and minicraters, some of them no bigger than a finger-poke into the stony ground. Damn! Pancho thought. I'm on the wrong side of the dome.

Without hesitation she began sprinting, looking for the launch-pads, happy to be able to run inside a space suit. Inside the old hard-shell suits it was impossible to do anything more than lumber along like Frankenstein's monster.

That guard'll be okay, she told herself. There's plenty of air inside the dome. They'll get the leak plugged before anybody's in any real danger. Jogging steadily, she grinned to herself. Meantime, while they're chasing around trying to fix the damage I've done, I'll get to one of the hoppers and head on home.

A sickly pale green splotch of color appeared on the left side of her helmet. The earphones said, "Radiation warning. Radiation level exceeding maximum allowable. Get to shelter immediately."

"I'm trying!" Pancho said, surprised at the suit's sophistication.

Before she took another dozen strides the color went from pastel green to bright canary yellow.

"Radiation warning," the suit said again. "Radiation level exceeding maximum allowable. Get to shelter immediately."

Pancho gritted her teeth and wondered how she could shut off the suit's automated voice synthesizer. The launchpads were still nowhere in sight.

Nobuhiko was back at the base's infirmary, this time in a screened-off cubicle barely large enough to hold a bed, looking down on a heavily sedated Daniel Tsavo. A spotless white bandage covered the upper half of the Kenyan's black face. He was conscious, but barely so, as the tranquilizing drug took effect.

". . . she blinded me," he was mumbling. "Blind . . . can't see . . ."

Yamagata glanced impatiently at the African doctor standing on the other side of Tsavo's bed. "It's only temporary," the doctor said, trying to sound reassuring. He seemed to be speaking to Yamagata, rather than his patient. "The retinal burns will heal in a few days."

"Failed," Tsavo muttered. "Failure . . . blind . . . nowhere to go . . . career ruined . . ."

Bending slightly over the bed, Nobuhiko said, "You haven't failed.

You'll be all right. Rest now. Everything will be fine in a day or two."

Tsavo's right hand groped toward the sound of Yamagata's voice. Nobuhiko instinctively backed away from it.

"Did you find her?" the Kenyan asked, his voice suddenly stronger. "Did you get what you wanted from her?"

"Yes, of course," Nobuhiko lied. "You rest now. Everything has turned out very well."

Tsavo's hand fell back to the sheets and he breathed a heavy sigh. The doctor nodded as if satisfied that the drugs had finally done their job. Then he made a small shooing gesture.

Nobuhiko understood. He turned away from the bed and stepped out of the tiny cubicle. He wrinkled his nose at the smell of antiseptics that pervaded this part of the infirmary. He had spent many hours in hospitals, when his father was dying. The odor brought back the memory of those unhappy days.

The pair of aides waiting for him out in the corridor snapped to attention almost like elite-corps soldiers, even though they wore ordinary business suits.

"Have they found her?" Nobuhiko asked in Japanese.

"Not yet, sir."

Nobu frowned as he started walking toward the exit, allowing his aides to see how displeased he was. To come all this way to the Moon, he thought, and have her slip away from us. Hot anger simmered through him.

The senior of the two assistants, noting the obvious displeasure on his master's face, tried to change the subject:

"Will the black man recover his sight?"

"Apparently," Nobuhiko snapped. "But he is not to be trusted with any important tasks. Never again."

Both aides nodded.

As they reached the double doors of the infirmary the handheld of the senior aide beeped. He flicked it open and saw a Yamagata engineer in a sky-blue hard hat staring wide-eyed in the miniaturized screen.

"The dome has been penetrated!" the engineer blurted. "We have sent for repair crews."

The aide looked stricken. He turned to Yamagata, wordlessly asking him for instructions.

"*She* did this," Nobu said. "Despite all our guards and precautions, Pancho has gotten away from us. She's outside."

"But the radiation storm!" the junior aide said, aghast. "She'll be killed out there."

Suddenly Nobu felt all his anger dissolve; all the tension that had held him like a vise for the past several hours faded away. He laughed. He threw his head back and laughed aloud, while his two aides gaped at him.

"Killed out there?" he said to them. "Not likely. Not Pancho. We couldn't hold her in here with a thousand guards. Don't think that a little thing like a solar storm is going to stop her."

His two aides said nothing even though they both thought that their master had gone slightly insane.

"Radiation warning," the suit repeated for the umpteenth time. "Radiation level exceeding maximum allowable. Get to shelter immediately."

Pancho made a silent promise to herself that when she got back to Selene she would rip the voice synthesizer out of this goddamned suit and stomp on it for an hour and a half.

The color splashed across the left side of her bubble helmet was bright pink now. I'm absorbing enough radiation to light a concert hall, she thought. Unbidden, the memory of Dan Randolph's death from radiation poisoning rose in her mind like a ghostly premonition of things to come. She saw Dan lying on his bunk, too weak even to lift his head, soaked in sweat, gums bleeding, hair coming out in bunches, dying while Pancho looked on, helpless, unable to save him.

You got a lot to look forward to, she growled to herself.

Her loping stride had slowed to a walk, but she was still doggedly pressing forward across the outer perimeter of the dome. You don't really appreciate how big something is until you have to walk around it, she told herself. Everything always looks bigger on foot.

And there it was! Around the curve of the dome she saw one, then two and finally three spacecraft sitting on concrete launchpads. She recognized the little green one that had brought her here from the Astro base, about a hundred klicks away.

Would they have guards placed around those birds? Pancho asked herself, without slowing her pace toward the launchpads.

Naw, she answered. Not in this storm. That'd be suicide duty. Not even Yamagata would ask his people to do that. Then she added, I hope.

Aside from the splotch of color in her helmet and the automated voice's irritating, repetitive warning, there was no visible, palpable sign of the radiation storm. Pancho was striding along the rocky, barren lunar crest, kicking up slight plumes of dust with each step. Outside the nanomachined fabric of her softsuit was nothing but vacuum, a vacuum thousands of times rarer than the vacuum just above Earth's atmosphere, nearly four hundred thousand kilometers away. Instinctively she glanced up for a sight of Earth, but the black sky was empty. Only a few of the brightest stars shone through the heavy tinting of her helmet. You can always see Earth from Selene, she said to herself. Maybe that's an advantage over this polar location that we hadn't realized before.

She started to hurry her pace toward the rocket hopper but found it was too tiring. Uh-oh, she thought. Fatigue's one of the first signs of radiation sickness.

She knew the vacuum out here wasn't empty. A torrent of subatomic particles was sleeting down upon her, mostly high-energy protons. The suit absorbed some of them, but plenty of others were getting through to smash into the atoms of her body and break them up. When she glanced at the color swatch in her helmet, though, it had gone down from bright pink to a sultry auburn.

Jeeps, Pancho exclaimed silently, the radiation level's going down.

"Radiation warning," the suit repeated yet again. "Radiation level exceeding maximum allowable. Get to shelter immediately."

"I'm goin'," Pancho groused. "I'm goin'."

Radiation's decreasing. The storm's ending. Maybe I'll make it through this after all. But then she thought that Yamagata might send some goons out to the launchpads if the radiation level's gone down enough. Despite the aches in her legs and back, she pushed herself to walk faster.

HUMPHRIES MANSION: ON THE ROOF

Smoke was billowing up through the ventilator that Fuchs had smashed open. The guards down in the garden below pointed to it. One of them pulled a handheld from his tunic pocket and started talking into it.

We've got to get off this roof and out to the exit hatch, Fuchs thought. And quickly, before they get all their guards out here and we're hopelessly surrounded.

Turning, he saw that Nodon was sitting by himself, his eyes open. He looked groggy, but at least he was conscious.

"Nodon," Fuchs whispered, hunkering down beside the wounded man, "can you walk?"

"I think so, Captain." Nodon's right shoulder had stopped bleeding, but the charred spot on his coveralls showed where the laser beam had hit him. The arm hung limply by his side.

Turning to Amarjagal, Fuchs gestured toward the two guards below. "Get those two when I give the word. Sanja, help me carry Nodon."

Sanja nodded wordlessly while Amarjagal checked the charge on the pistol in her hand. As Fuchs slid one beefy arm around Nodon's slim waist he saw the two guards looking up in their direction. One of them was still speaking into his handheld.

"Now!" he shouted, hauling Nodon to his feet.

Amarjagal shot the one with the handheld squarely in the forehead, then swung her aim to hit his companion in the chest. They both tumbled into the bushes that lined the garden walkway.

With Sanja helping to support Nodon, Fuchs yelled, "Jump!" and all four of them leaped off the roof to land with a thump amid the shrubbery that lined the mansion's wall. Lunar gravity, Fuchs thought gratefully. On Earth we would have broken our bones.

Half-dragging Nodon, they started up the bricked path, hobbling toward the heavy airtight hatch that was the only exit from the grotto. Fuchs heard shouts from behind them. Turning his head, he saw a trio of guards boiling out of the mansion's front door, pistols in their hands. A tendril of pale gray smoke drifted out of the open door.

"Stop while you're still alive," one of the guards shouted. "There's no way you can get out of here."

"Amarjagal, help Sanja," Fuchs commanded, slipping the wounded man out of his grasp and dropping to one knee. He snapped a quick shot at the three guards, who scattered to find shelter in the shrubbery. Fuchs fired at them until his pistol ran out of power. One of the flowering shrubs burst into flame and a guard leaped out from behind it.

Running back to the others Fuchs yelled, "Give me your guns! Quick!"

They obediently dropped their pistols onto the path, hardly breaking stride as they carried the wounded Nodon toward the hatch. Nodon's the only one who knows the emergency codes to open the hatch, Fuchs thought. He'd better be conscious when we get there or we're all dead.

He ducked behind the sturdy bole of a tree and peered up the pathway. No one in sight. They could be crawling through the shrubbery, Fuchs realized. He checked the three guns at his feet. Picking the one with the fullest charge, he began spraying the greenery, hoping to ignite it. Some of the plants smoldered but did not flame. Fuchs growled a curse as his pistol died; he picked up the next one.

In his bedroom, Humphries was screaming at his security chief.

"What do you mean, the whole house is burning? It *can't* burn, you stupid shit! The firewall partitions—"

"Mr. Humphries," the chief snapped stiffly, "the partitions have failed. The intruders opened a ventilator shaft and the fire is spreading through the eaves beneath the roof. You'll have to abandon your suite, sir, and pretty damned quick, too."

Humphries glared at the screen.

"I'm leaving," said the chief. "If you want to roast, go right ahead."

The phone screen went blank. Humphries look up at Ferrer. "This can't be happening," he said. "I don't believe it."

She was at the door, ready to make a break for it. "At least Fuchs and his crew have left the house," she said, trying to stay calm.

"They have?"

"That's what the guards outside reported. Remember? They're having a firefight out there right now."

"Firefight?" Humphries couldn't seem to get his mind working properly. Everything was happening too fast, too wildly.

"We've got to get out, Martin," she insisted, almost shouting.

Humphries thought it was getting warm in the bedroom. *That's my imagination*, he told himself. *This whole suite is insulated, protected. They can't get to me in here.*

Something creaked ominously overhead. Humphries shot a glance at the ceiling, but it all looked normal. He looked around wildly. *The whole building's on fire*, he heard the security chief's voice in his mind. I pay that stupid slug to protect me, Humphries said to himself. He's finished. I'll get rid of him. Permanently.

"How do you open this hatch?" Ferrer asked. She was standing at the bedroom doorway, the door itself flung open but the protective cermet partition firmly in place.

Humphries eyes were on the window, though. "My garden!" he howled, staring at the flames licking across the branches of several of the trees.

"We've got to get out—" Ferrer put a hand on the cermet hatch and flinched back. "It's hot!"

The phone was dead, Humphries realized. The controls for the fireproof partitions were automated. As long as the sensors detected a fire, the hatches would remain closed unless opened manually. But the controls are down in the security office, in the basement, Humphries realized. And that yellow little bastard has run away.

I could override the controls from my computer, he thought. But that's in the sitting room, and we're shut off from it!

He could feel the panic bubbling inside him, like the frothing waves of the sea rising over his head to drown him.

Ferrer was standing in front of him, shouting something, her eyes wide with fear. Humphries couldn't hear what she was saying. His mind was repeating, The whole house is on fire! over and over again. Glancing past her terrified face through the bedroom window he saw that the garden was blazing as well.

Ferrer slapped him. Hard. A stinging smack across his face. Instinctively Humphries slapped her back as hard as he could. She staggered back, the imprint of his fingers red against her skin.

"You little bitch! Who do you think you are?"

"Martin, we've got to get out of here! We've got to get through the window and outside!"

Perhaps it was the slap, or perhaps the sight of the always cool and logical Ferrer looking panicked, terrified. Whatever the reason, Humphries felt his own panic subside. The fear was still there, but he could control it now.

"It's burning out there," he said, pointing toward the window.

Her face went absolutely white. "The fire will consume all the oxygen in the air! We'll suffocate!"

"*They'll* suffocate," Humphries said flatly. "Fuchs and whatever riffraff he's brought with him."

"And the guards!"

"What of it? They're a useless bunch of brain-dead shits."

"But we'll suffocate too!" Ferrer shouted, almost screaming.

"Not we," he said. "You."

The six-hundred-meter-long concrete vault of Selene's Grand Plaza is supported, in part, by two towers that serve as office buildings. Selene's safety office is located in one of those towers, not far from Douglas Stavenger's small suite of offices.

This late at night, the safety office was crewed by only a pair of men, both relaxed to the point of boredom as they sat amid row after row of old-fashioned flat display screens that showed every corridor and public space in the underground city. On the consoles that lined one wall of their sizeable office were displayed the readouts from sensors that monitored air and water quality, temperature, and other environmental factors throughout the city.

They were playing chess on an actual board with carved onyx pieces, to alleviate their boredom. The sensors and displays were automated; there was no real need for human operators to be present. There was hardly ever any problem so bad that a plumber or low-rate electrician couldn't fix it in an hour or less.

The senior safety officer looked up from the chess board with a malicious grin. "Mate in three."

"The hell you will," said the other, reaching for a rook.

Alarms began shrilling and lurid red lights started to flash across several of the consoles. The rook fell to the floor, forgotten, as the men stared goggle-eyed, unbelieving, at the screens. Everything looked normal, but the alarms still rang shrilly.

Running his fingers deftly across the master console's keyboard, the senior of the two shouted over the uproar, "It's down at the bottom level. Temp sensors into overload."

"That's Humphries's area," said his junior partner. "We got no cameras down there."

Shaking his head, the other replied, "Either the sensors are whacked out or there's a helluva fire going on down there."

"A fire? That's im—"

"Look at the readings! Even the oxygen level's starting to go down!"

"Holy mother of god!"

The senior man punched at the emergency phone key. "Emergency! Fire on level seven. I'm sealing off all the hatches and air vents."

"There's people down there!" his assistant pointed out. "Martin Humphries himself! If we seal them in, they'll all die!"

"And if we don't seal them in," the senior man snapped, his fingers pecking furiously across the keyboard, "that fire'll start sucking the oxygen out of the rest of the city. You want to kill everybody?"

LUNAR HOPPER

oppers are meant for short-range transportation on the Moon. They are ungainly looking vehicles, little more than a rocket motor powered by powdered aluminum and liquid oxygen, both scraped up from the lunar regolith. Atop the bulbous propellant tanks and rocket nozzle is a square metal mesh platform no more than three meters on a side, surmounted by a waist-high podium that houses the hopper's controls. The entire craft sits on the ground on a trio of spindly legs that wouldn't be strong enough to hold its weight in normal Earth gravity.

Pancho felt bone-weary as she slowly climbed the flimsy ladder up to the hopper's platform. She felt grateful that this particular little bird had a glassteel bubble enclosing the platform. It'll gimme some protection against the radiation, she told herself. She got to the top, pulled herself up onto the aluminum mesh and let the trapdoor hatch slam shut. All in the total silence of the airless Moon.

There were no seats on the hopper, of course. You rode the little birds standing up, with your boots snugged into the fabric loops fastened to the platform.

The radiation sensor display on the side of her helmet had gone down to a sickly bilious green and the automated voice had stopped yakking at her. Pancho felt grateful for that. Either the radiation's down enough so the warning system's cut out or I've got such a dose the warning doesn't matter anymore, she thought.

She felt bilious green herself: queasy with nausea, so tired that if there had been a reclining seat on the hopper she would've cranked it back and gone to sleep.

Not yet, she warned herself. You go to sleep now, girl, and you prob'ly won't wake up, ever.

Hoping the radiation hadn't damaged the hopper's electronic

systems, Pancho clicked on the master switch and was pleased to see the podium's console lights come on. A little on the weak side, she thought. Fuel cells are down. Or maybe my vision's going bad.

Propellant levels were low. Nairobi hadn't refueled the bird after it had carried her here to their base. Enough to make it back to the Astro base? Despite her aches and nausea, Pancho grinned to herself. We'll just hafta see how far we can go.

Nobuhiko had followed one of the engineers to the base flight control center, a tight little chamber filled with consoles and display screens, most of them dark, most of the desks unoccupied. Still the room felt overly warm, stifling, even with Yamagata's retinue of bodyguards stationed outside in the corridor.

One console was alight, one screen glowing in the shadows of the control center. Nobu bent over the Nairobi flight controller seated at that console. He saw Pancho's lanky figure slowly climbing the ladder of the green-anodized hopper.

The Yamagata engineer standing at his side gasped. "She's not wearing a space suit!"

"Yes she is," Nobu replied. "A new type, made of nanomachines."

To the flight controller he asked, "Can you prevent her from taking off?"

Looking up briefly, the controller shook his head. "No, sir. She can control the vehicle autonomously. Of course, without a flight plan or navigational data, she won't be able to find her destination. And the vehicle's propellant levels are too low for anything but a very short flight."

"We could send a team out to stop her," suggested the Yamagata engineer.

Nobuhiko took a breath, then replied, "No. Why send good men out into that radiation storm?"

"The storm is abating, sir."

"No," he repeated. "Let her take off. If she is to die, let it be a flight accident. I'll have the Nairobi public relations people make up a plausible story that keeps Yamagata Corporation out of it."

Nobuhiko straightened up and watched the little lunar hopper take off in a sudden spurt of stark white gas and gritty dust, all in total silence.

He almost wished Pancho good fortune. An extraordinary woman, he thought. A worthy opponent. Too bad she's going to die.

•   •   •

As soon as the hopper jerked off the ground Pancho turned on its radio, sliding her finger along the frequency control to search for Malapert's beacon. She knew roughly which direction the Astro base lay in. The hopper had only limited maneuverability, however; it flew mainly on a ballistic trajectory, like an odd-looking cannon shell.

"Pancho Lane calling," she spoke into her helmet microphone. She wanted to yell, to bellow, but she didn't have the strength. "I'm in a hopper, coming up from the Nairobi Industries base at Shackleton crater. I need a navigation fix, pronto."

No reply.

She looked down at the bleak lunar landscape sliding by, trying to remember landmarks from her flight in to Shackleton. Nothing stood out. It all looked the same: bare rock pitted by innumerable craters ranging from little dimples to holes big enough to swallow a city. Rugged hills, all barren and rounded by eons of meteors sandpapering them to worn, tired smoothness. And rocks and boulders strewn everywhere like toys left behind by a careless child.

Pancho felt worn and tired, too. Her mind was going fuzzy. It would be so good to just fold up and go to sleep. Even the hard metal deck of the hopper looked inviting to her.

Stop it! she commanded herself. Stay awake. Find the base's radio beacon. Use it to guide you in.

She played the hopper's radio receiver up and down the frequency scale, seeking the automated homing beacon from the Malapert base. Nothing. Feeling something like panic simmering in her guts, Pancho thought, Maybe I'm heading in a completely wrong direction. Maybe I'm so way off that—

A steady warm tone suddenly issued from her helmet earphones. Pancho couldn't have been more thrilled if the world's finest singer had begun to serenade her.

"This is Pancho Lane," she said, her voice rough, her throat dry. "I need a navigational fix, pronto."

A heartbeat's hesitation. Then a calm tenor voice said to her, "Malapert base here, Ms. Lane. We have you on our radar. You're heading seventeen degrees west of us. I'm feeding correction data to your nav computer."

Pancho felt the hopper's tiny maneuvering thruster push the

ungainly bird sideways a bit. Her legs felt weak, rubbery. Bird's on automatic now, she thought. I can relax. I can lay down and—

A red light on the control console glared at her like an evil eye and the hopper's computer announced, "Propellant cutoff. Main engine shutdown."

Pancho's reply was a heartfelt, "Shit!"

BRUSHFIRE

F uchs backed slowly along the brick path, a nearly spent laser pistol in each hand, his eyes reflecting the lurid flames spreading across the wide garden that filled the grotto. Burn! he exulted. Let everything burn. His garden. His house. And Humphries himself. Let the fire burn him to death, let him roast in his own hell.

Coughing, he finally turned and sprinted heavily up the path toward the airlock hatch that they had come in through. The others were already there; Nodon was even standing on his own feet, although he looked pale, shaky.

Fuchs was panting as he came up to them. "Hard . . . to breathe," he gasped.

Amarjagal wasted no time on the obvious. "The airlock is sealed. The emergency code doesn't work."

Fuchs stared at her flat, normally emotionless face. Now she was staring back at him, cold accusation in her eyes.

Sanja said, "The fire . . . it's eating up the oxygen."

"Get the airlock open!" Fuchs commanded. "Nodon, try all the emergency codes."

"I have," Nodon said, almost wailing. "No use . . . no use . . ."

Fuchs leaned his back against the heavy steel hatch and slid down onto his rump, suddenly exhausted. Most of the garden was ablaze now, roaring with flames that crawled up the trees and spread across the flowering bushes, burning, destroying everything as they advanced. Gray smoke billowed up and slithered along the rough rock ceiling as if trying to find an opening, the slightest pore, a way to escape the inferno of this death trap.

Humphries was coldly logical now. The closet in his bedroom was built to serve as an emergency airlock. There was even a space suit stashed in there, although Humphries had never put it on. The Earthbound architect who had designed the mansion had been rather amused that Humphries insisted on such precautions, but the knowing smirk on his face disappeared when Humphries bought out his firm, fired him, and sent him packing back to Earth.

The mansion had been completed by others, and the emergency airlock built to the tightest possible specifications.

Knowing that there were two extra tanks of breathable air in there, Humphries headed for his closet.

"What are you doing?" Ferrer screamed at him. "We've got to get out!"

"You get yourself out," he said icily, remembering the slap she had given him. "I'll stay here until this all blows over."

He slid open the door to his closet. All that Ferrer could see was a row of clothing neatly arrayed on hangers.

"What've you got in there?" she demanded from the other side of the bedroom. She no longer looked smoothly sultry, enticing. Her dark hair was a disheveled tumble, her white robe rumpled, hanging half open. She seemed frightened, confused, far from alluring.

"Enough air to last for a day or more," he said, smiling at her.

"Oh thank god!" she said, rushing toward the closet.

Humphries touched the stud set in the closet's interior door frame and an airtight panel slid quickly shut. He saw the shocked surprise on her face just before the panel shot home and closed her off from his view.

He heard her banging on the steel panel. "Martin! Open the door! Let me in!"

He walked back deeper into his closet, trying to shut out her yammering. Pushing a row of slacks aside he saw the space suit standing against the closet's back wall like a medieval suit of armor.

"Martin! Please! Let me in!"

"So you can slap me again?" he muttered. "Go fry."

The chief of the emergency crew nearly dropped his handheld when he recognized who was coming up the corridor toward them.

"Mr. Stavenger!"

"Hello . . . Pete," Stavenger said, after a quick glance at the crew chief's nametag. "What's the situation here?"

Stavenger could see that a team of three men and four women were assembling a portable airlock and sealing it over the hatch that opened onto the grotto. The crew chief said as much.

"How long will this take?" Stavenger asked.

"Another ten minutes. Maybe twelve."

"Once it's ready, how many people can you take through it at one time?"

The crew chief shook his head. "It's only big enough for two."

"There are at least thirty people in there," Stavenger said. "They're running out of oxygen pretty quickly."

"We got another crew working on the water lines. If we can get the sprinklers working we oughtta be able to put the fire out pretty quick."

"But those people need air to breathe."

"I know," said the crew chief. "I know."

Fuchs saw dark-clad figures stumbling up the path, coughing, staggering. He scrambled to his feet and picked up one of the nearly spent pistols.

"Stop where you are!" he shouted, coughing himself.

The closest man tossed his pistol into the bushes. "Let us out!" he yelled. "The fire . . ."

The others behind him also threw their guns away. They all lurched toward Fuchs, coughing, rubbing at their eyes. Behind them the flames inched across the flowers and grass, climbed nimbly up the trunk of a tree. Its crown of leaves burst into flame.

"The hatch is locked," Fuchs told them. "We're all trapped in here."

The security guards didn't believe him. Their leader rushed to the hatch, tapped frantically at the keyboard panel.

"Jesus, Mary and Joseph," he growled. "Of all the sonofabitch fuck-ups . . ."

"It's automatic, I imagine," said Fuchs, resignedly. "Nothing we can do about it."

The security guard stared at him. "But they should have emergency teams. Something—"

At that moment a voice rumbled through the heavy hatch, "This is Selene emergency services. Is anybody there? Rap on the hatch."

Fuchs almost leaped with sudden joy and hope. He banged the butt of his pistol against the steel hatch.

"Okay. We're setting up an airlock. Once it's ready we'll be able to start taking you out. How many of you are there?"

Fuchs counted swiftly and then rapped on the hatch eleven times, thinking, We might live through this after all. We might get out of this alive.

FLIGHT PLANS

P
ancho knew she had to think swiftly, but the fog of fatigue and
radiation sickness made her feel as if she were wrapped in heavy
wet blankets.

Propellant bingo, she said to herself. There's still enough
juice for an automated landing. But not enough to reach the
base. Override the automatics and push this bird as far as she'll
go? Do that and you won't land, you'll crash on the landing pad—if you
get that far. Let the bird coast and come down wherever it reaches? Do
that and you'll land in the middle of nowhere. No, you won't land,
you'll crash on the rocks.

"We have a good track on you, Ms. Lane, and we're getting some
satellite imagery, as well," said the Malapert controller's voice. "You're
not going to reach the base, I'm afraid. We're gearing up a search and
rescue team. If you can find a reasonably flat place to set down, we'll
come out and get you."

"Copy search and rescue operation," Pancho said, her throat
painfully dry. "I'll set her down as close to the base as I can."

If I can stay on my feet long enough, she added silently.

"Malapert?" she called, her voice little more than a croak now.

"Malapert here, Ms. Lane."

"Better include some medics in the S&R team. I got me a healthy
dose of radiation."

The barest fraction of a second's hesitation. Then, "Understood,
Ms. Lane."

Okay, Pancho said to herself. Now all you gotta do is stay awake
long enough to put this bird on the ground without breaking your neck.

She wanted to smile. If I wasn't so pooped-out tired, this would be
kinda fun.

• • •

Some half a billion kilometers away, Dorik Harbin decided to leave *Samarkand*'s bridge and inspect the ship personally. They were fully enveloped by the radiation storm now, and although all the ship's systems were performing adequately, Harbin knew that the crew felt edgy about flying blind and deaf inside a vast cloud of high-energy particles that could kill an unshielded man in moments.

The monitors on the control panels were all in the green, he saw, except for a few minor pieces of machinery that needed maintenance. I'll get the crew working on them, Harbin thought as he got up from his command chair. It will be good for their morale to have something to do instead of just waiting for the radiation level to back down to normal.

He gave the con to his pilot and stepped to the hatch. Turning back for a moment, he glanced once more at the radiation shielding monitors. All green. Good.

Aboard *Cromwell* the skipper awoke minutes before his number one called on the intercom. He hauled himself out of his bunk, washed his face and pulled on a fresh set of coveralls. No need to brush his hair: It was shaved down to within a centimeter of his scalp.

He entered the bridge and saw that all the ship's systems were operating within nominal limits. And they were still sailing inside the cloud of ionized particles. Its radiation intensity had diminished, though, he noted. The cloud was thinning out as it drifted outward from the Sun.

"Are we still shielded against radar?" he asked his communication technician.

"Theoretically, sir," the man answered with a nod.

"I'm not interested in theory, mister," snapped the skipper. "Can the radars on Vesta spot us or not?"

The technician blinked once, then replied, "No, sir. Not unless they pump up their output power to two or three times their normal operational mode, sir."

Not unless, the captain grumbled to himself.

"You holler out loud and clear if we get pinged," he told the comm tech.

"Yes, sir. Loud and clear."

Pointing at the weapons technician, the skipper said, "Time for a skull session. In my quarters."

The weapons tech was actually a physicist from Astro Corporation's nanotechnology department, so tall he was continually banging his head on the hatches as he stepped through them, so young he looked like a teenager, but without the usual teenaged pose of sullen indifference. Instead, he was bright, cheerful, enthusiastic.

Yet he looked somber now as he ducked low enough to get through the hatch without thumping his straw-thatched head against the coaming.

"We'll be at the decision point in a few minutes," the captain said as he sat on his bunk and gestured the younger man to the only chair in the compartment.

"Eighteen minutes," said the physicist, "and counting."

"Is there any reason why we shouldn't release the missiles then?"

The physicist's pale blond brows rose questioningly. "The plan calls—"

"I know what the plan calls for," the captain interrupted impatiently. "What I'm asking is, are the missiles ready to be released?"

"Yessir, they are. I checked them less than an hour ago."

The captain looked into the youngster's cool blue eyes. I can fire off the missiles and get us the hell out of here, he told himself.

"But if we wait until the final release point their chances of getting to Vesta without being detected or intercepted are a whole lot better," said the younger man.

"I understand that."

"There's no reason I can see for releasing them early."

The captain said nothing, thinking that this kid was a typical scientist. As long as all the displays on the consoles were in the green he thought everything was fine. On the other hand, if I fire the missiles early and something goes wrong, he'll tell his superiors that it was my fault.

"Very well," he said at last. "I want you to calculate interim release points—"

"Interim?"

"Give me three more points along our approach path to Vesta where I can release those birds."

"Three points short of the predetermined release point?"

"That's right."

The kid broke into a grin. "Oh, that's easy. I can do that right here." And he pulled his handheld from the breast pocket of his coveralls.

SELENE: LEVEL SEVEN

t's getting warmer in here, Humphries thought. Then he told himself, No, it's just your imagination. This space is insulated, fireproof. He pushed through a row of suits hanging neatly in the closet and touched one hand to the nearest of the three green tanks of oxygen standing in a row against the back wall. I've got everything I need. They can't burn me out.

Slowly he edged past the suits and slacks and jackets and shirts, all precisely arranged, all facing the same direction on their hangers, silent and waiting for him to decide on using them. He brushed their fabrics with his shoulder, was tempted to finger their sleeves, even rub them soothingly on his cheek. Like a baby with its blanket, he thought. Comforting.

Instead he went to the door, still sealed with the cermet partition. Tentatively, he touched it with his fingertips. It wasn't hot. Not even very warm. Maybe the fire's out, he supposed. Ferrer wasn't pounding on the door anymore. She gave up on that. I wonder if she made it out of the house? She's tough and smart; could she survive this fire? He suddenly felt alarmed. If she lives through it, she'll tell everybody I panicked! She'll tell them I crawled into my emergency shelter and left her outside to die!

Humphries felt his fists clenching so hard his fingernails were cutting painfully into his palms. No, the little bitch will *threaten* to tell everything and hang that threat over my head for the rest of her life. I'll have to get rid of her. Permanently. Pretend to give her whatever she wants and then get Harbin or some other animal to put her away.

His mind decided, Humphries paced the length of his clothes closet once more, wondering how he would know when it was safe to leave his airtight shelter.

•   •   •

At least the flames aren't advancing as fast as they were, Fuchs thought as he lay sprawled on the brick pathway in front of the airlock. The grotto was a mass of flames and smoke that seemed to get thicker every second. Their heat burned against his face. Nodon had lapsed into unconsciousness again; Amarjagal and Sanja lay on the grass beside him, unmoving, their dark almond-shaped eyes staring at the fire that was inching closer. The black-clad security guards sprawled everywhere, coughing, their guns thrown away, their responsibilities to Humphries forgotten.

One of the women guards asked, "How long . . ." She broke into a racking cough.

As if in answer to her unfinished question, the voice from the other side of the hatch boomed, "We've got the airlock set up. In thirty seconds we'll open the hatch. We can take two people at a time. Get your first two ready."

Fuchs pawed at his burning eyes and said, "Amarjagal and Nodon."

The woman slung Nodon's good arm around her bulky shoulders and struggled up to her feet, with Sanja helping her. Some of the security guards stirred, and Fuchs reached for the laser pistol on the ground next to him.

"We'll all get through," he said sternly. "Two at a time."

The guards stared sullenly back at him.

"Which of you is in charge?" Fuchs asked.

A big-shouldered man with his gray hair cut flat and short rolled over to a sitting position. Fuchs noted that his belly hung over the waistband of his trousers.

"I am," he said, then coughed.

"You will decide the order in which your people go through the hatch," said Fuchs, in a tone that brooked no argument. "You and I will be the last two."

The man nodded once, as the heavy steel hatch clicked and slowly swung open.

Stavenger stood out in the corridor beyond the emergency airlock and watched the survivors of the fire come out, two by two.

Like Noah's Ark, he thought.

Most of them were Humphries security people, their faces smudged with soot as black as their uniforms. There were three Asians, one of them in the gray coveralls of Selene's maintenance department.

"The last two coming through," said one of the emergency team.

An odd couple, Stavenger thought. One tall and broad-shouldered, the other short and thickset. Both in black outfits. Then he recognized the dour face of the shorter man. Lars Fuchs! Stavenger realized. That's Lars Fuchs!

"Anybody else in there?" the emergency team's chief asked.

"Nobody alive," said the Humphries' security chief.

"Okay," the chief called to his team. "Seal the hatch and let the fire burn itself out."

Stavenger was already speaking into his handheld, calling for a security team to arrest Lars Fuchs. There's only one reason for him to be here in Humphries's private preserve, Stavenger knew. He's killed Martin Humphries.

If it weren't so infuriating it would almost be funny, Humphries thought as he sat huddled in his closet.

The idiotic architect who designed this for me never bothered to install a phone inside the shelter because everybody carries handhelds or even implants. I don't have an implant and I hate those damned handhelds beeping at me. So now I'm sitting here with no goddamned way to let anybody know I'm alive. And I don't dare go outside because the fire might still be burning. Even if it isn't, it's probably used up all the oxygen out there and I'd suffocate.

Damn! Nothing to do but wait.

Humphries detested waiting. For anything, even his own rescue.

CRASH LANDING

round's coming up awful fast, Pancho said to herself. She had allowed the little hopper to follow its ballistic trajectory, knowing it was going to come down way short of the Astro base in the Malapert Mountains. How short she didn't really care anymore. Her main concern—her *only* concern now—was to get this bird down without killing herself.

Any landing you can walk away from is a good landing, she told herself as the bare, rock-strewn ground rushed up at her. Find a flat, open spot. Just like Armstrong in the old Apollo 11 Eagle. Find a flat, open spot.

Easier said than done. The rolling, hilly ground sliding past her was pitted with craters of all sizes and covered so thickly with rocks and boulders that Pancho thought of a teenaged boy she had dated whose face was covered with acne.

Funny what the mind dredges up, she thought.

"Pay attention to the real world," she muttered.

She fought down a wave of nausea as the ground rushed up at her. It would be *sooo* good to just lay down and go to sleep. Her legs felt like rubber, her whole body ached. Without thinking of it consciously she ran her tongue across her teeth, testing for a taste of blood. Bad sign if your gums start bleeding, she knew. Symptom of radiation sickness, big time.

"Pay attention!" she screamed at herself.

"Say again?" came the voice of the flight controller at Malapert.

"Nothin'," Pancho replied, apologetically. They've still got me on their radar, she thought. Good. They'll know where the body's buried.

There! Coming up on the right. A fairly flat area with only a few dinky little rocks. It's sloping, though. On a hillside. Not so bad. If I can reach it.

Pancho nudged the tee-shaped control yoke and the hopper's maneuvering thrusters squirted out a few puffs of cold gas, enough to jink the ungainly little craft toward the open area she had spotted.

Shit! More rocks than I thought. Well, beggars can't be choosers. Only enough juice for one landing.

She tapped the keyboard for the automatic landing sequence, not trusting herself to do the job manually. The hopper shuddered as its main engine fired, killed its velocity, and the little craft dropped like a child's toy onto the stony, sloping ground. All in total silence.

Pancho remembered enough from her old astronaut training to flex her knees and brace her arms against the control podium. The hopper thumped into the ground, one flat landing foot banging into a rock big enough to tip the whole craft dangerously. For a wild moment Pancho thought the hopper was going to tumble over onto its side. It didn't, but the crash landing was violent enough to tear away the loop that held her right foot to the platform grillwork. Her leg flew up, knocking her so badly off balance that her left leg, still firmly anchored in its foot loop, snapped at the ankle.

Pancho gritted her teeth in the sudden pain of the broken bone as she thudded in lunar slow motion to the grillwork platform.

Feeling cold sweat breaking out of every pore of her body, she thought, Well, I ain't dead yet.

Then she added, Won't be long before I am, though.

ASTRO CORPORATION COMMAND CENTER

might as well move a cot in here, thought Jake Wanamaker as he paced along the row of consoles. A technician sat at each of them, monitoring display screens that linked the command center with Astro ships and bases from the Moon to the Belt. Lit only by the ghostly glow of the screens, the room felt hot and stuffy, taut with the hum of electrical equipment and the nervous tension of apprehensive men and women.

There were only two displays that Wanamaker was interested in: Malapert base, near the lunar south pole, and *Cromwell*, about to start its runup to the asteroid Vesta.

Wanamaker hunched over the technician monitoring the link with *Cromwell*. Deep inside the cloud of high-energy particles, radio contact was impossible. But the ship's captain had sent a tight-beam laser message more than half an hour earlier. It was just arriving at the Astro receiving telescope up on the surface of the Moon.

The screen showed nothing but a jumbled hash of colors.

"Decoding, sir," the seated technician murmured, feeling the admiral's breath on the back of her neck.

The streaks dissolved to reveal the apprehensive-looking face of *Cromwell*'s skipper. The man's eyes looked wary, evasive.

"We have started the final run to target," he stated tersely. "The radiation cloud is dissipating faster than predicted, so we will release our payload at the point halfway between the start of the run and the planned release point."

The screen went blank.

Turning her face toward Wanamaker, the technician said, "That's the entire message, sir."

His immediate reaction was to fire a message back to *Cromwell* ordering the captain to stick to the plan and carry the nanomachines all the way to the predecided release point. But he realized that it would take the better part of an hour for a message to reach the ship. *Nothing I can do,* he told himself, straightening up. He stretched his arms over his head, thinking, *The captain's on the scene. If he feels he needs to let the package go early it's for a good reason.* But Wanamaker couldn't convince himself. *The captain's taking the easiest course for himself,* he realized. *He's not pressing his attack home.*

Turning slowly, he scanned the shadowy room for Tashkajian. She was at her desk on the other side of the quietly intense command center. *This is her plan,* Wanamaker thought. *She worked it out with the captain. If there's anything wrong with his releasing the package early, she'll be the one to tell me.*

But what good will it do? I can't get the word to him in time to straighten him out.

Tashkajian got up from her little wheeled chair as he approached her desk.

"You saw the report from *Cromwell?*" Wanamaker asked.

"Yes, sir."

"And?"

She hesitated a moment. "It's probably all right. The missiles are small and Vesta's radars will still be jammed by the radiation."

"But he said the cloud was breaking up."

"Our reports from the IAA monitors—"

A whoop from one of the consoles interrupted them. "They found her!" a male technician hollered, his face beaming. "They found Pancho! She's alive!"

The first that Pancho realized she'd passed out was when the excruciating pain woke her up. She blinked her gummy eyes and saw that somebody in a bulbous hard-shell space suit was lifting her off her back, broken ankle and all.

"Jesus Christ on a Harley!" she moaned. "Take it easy, for chrissakes."

"Sorry," the space-suited figure said. Pancho heard his words in her helmet earphones.

"That leg's broken," she said. Nearly sobbed, actually, it hurt so badly.

"Easy does it," the guy in the space suit said. Through a haze of agony Pancho realized there were three of them. One holding her shoulders, another her legs, and the third hovering at her side as they carried her away from the wreck of the hopper.

"I'll immobilize the ankle as soon as we get you to our hopper," the guy said. "I'm a medic, Ms. Lane."

"I can tell," she groused. "Total indifference to pain. Other people's pain."

"We didn't know your ankle was broken, ma'am. You were unconscious when we reached you. Almost out of air, too."

Screw you, Pancho thought. But she kept silent. I oughtta be pretty damn grateful to these turkeys for coming out and finding me. Each step they took, though, shot a fresh lance of pain through her leg.

"We had to land more than a kilometer from your crash site," the medic said. "Not many places around here to put down a hopper safely."

"Tell me about it."

"We'll be there in ten-fifteen minutes. Then I can set your ankle properly."

"Just don't drop me," Pancho growled.

"The ground is very stony, very uneven. We're doing the best we can."

"Just don't drop me," she repeated.

They only dropped her once.

When the Selene emergency team brought Fuchs, his three crew, and the Humphries security people to the hospital, Fuchs had the presence of mind to give his name as Karl Manstein. Medical personnel put each survivor of the fire onto a gurney and wheeled them to beds separated by plastic curtains.

Fuchs knew he had to get out of the hospital as quickly as possible, with his crew. He lay on the crisp white sheets staring at the cream-colored ceiling, wondering how far away from him the others were. Nodon's wounded, he remembered. That's going to make an escape more difficult.

It's only a matter of time before they realize Manstein is an alias, a fiction. Then what?

But a new thought struck him and suddenly he smiled up at the ceiling, alone in his curtained cubicle.

When he and the Humphries security chief finally staggered through the hatch and the temporary airlock that the Selene emergency crew had erected, the head of the emergency team had asked them, "Anybody else in there?"

The security chief had shaken his head gravely. "Nobody alive," he had said.

Humphries is dead! Fuchs exulted. Lying on his hospital bed, his eyes still stinging and his lungs raw from the smoke, he wanted to laugh with glee. I did it! I killed the murdering swine! Martin Humphries is dead.

Martin Humphries was quite alive, but gnawingly hungry. He had never in his life known hunger before, but as he paced, or sat, or stretched out on the thick carpeting of his closet hideaway, his empty stomach growled at him. It *hurt*, this hollow feeling in his belly. It stretched the minutes and hours and drove his mind into an endless need for food. Even when he tried to sleep his dreams were filled with steaming banquets that he somehow could not reach.

Thirst was even worse. His throat grew dry, his tongue seemed to get thicker in his mouth, his eyes felt gritty.

I could die in here! he realized. A hundred times he went to the airtight panel, touched it gingerly with his fingertips. It felt cool. He pressed both hands on it. Flattened his cheek against it. The fire *must* be out by now, he thought. His wristwatch told him that more than twenty hours had gone by. The fire's got to be out by now. But what about the air? Is there any air to breathe on the other side of the panel?

Somebody will come, he assured himself. My security chief knows about this shelter. If he wasn't killed in the fire. If he didn't suffocate from lack of oxygen. Ferrer. Victoria might have gotten out. She'll tell them I'm here. But then he wondered, Will she? I wouldn't let her in here with me; she could be sore enough to let me rot in here, even if she got out okay. But even so, *somebody* will send people to go through the house, assess the damage. The Selene safety inspectors. The goddamned insurance people will be here sooner or later.

Later, a sardonic voice in his mind told him. Don't expect the insurance adjusters to break their butts getting here.

It's all that motherless architect's fault, Humphries fumed. Idiot! Builds this emergency shelter without a phone to make contact with the outside. Without sensors to tell me if there's air on the other side of the door. I'll see to it that he never gets another commission. Never! He'll be panhandling on street corners by the time I get finished with him.

There's not even a water fountain in here. I could die of thirst before anybody finds me.

He slumped to the floor and wanted to cry, but his body was too dehydrated to produce tears.

BALLISTIC ROCKET

From her seat by the narrow window Pancho could see out of the corner of her eye the rugged lunar highlands gliding swiftly past, far below. She was the only passenger on the ballistic rocket as it arced high above the Moon's barren surface, carrying her from Astro's Malapert base back to Selene. Her ankle was set in a spraycast; she was heading for Selene's hospital, and injections of nanomachines that would mend her broken bones and repair the damage that radiation had done to her body.

Pancho had precious little time to study the scenery. She was deep in conversation with Jake Wanamaker, whose craggy unsmiling face reminded her of the rocky land below.

". . . should be releasing the nanomachines right about now," Wanamaker was saying.

"And everybody on Vesta is belowground?" Pancho asked.

"Ought to be, with that radiation cloud sweeping over them. Anybody up on the surface is going to be dead no matter what we do."

Pancho nodded. "All right. Now what's this about Humphries's mansion burning down?"

Wanamaker grimaced with distaste. "A group of four fanatics infiltrated into the grotto down there on the bottom level. Why, we don't know yet. They're being held by Selene security in the hospital."

"And they burned the house down?"

"Set the whole garden on fire. The place is a blackened wasteland."

"Humphries?"

"No sign of him. Selene inspectors are going through the place now. Apparently the house is still standing, but it's been gutted by the fire."

Strangely, Pancho felt no elation at the possibility that Humphries was dead. "Have they found his body?"

"Not yet."

"And the people who attacked the place are in the hospital?"

"Under guard."

Pancho knew only one person in the entire solar system who would be crazy enough to attack Humphries in his own home. Lars Fuchs.

"Was Lars Fuchs one of the attackers?"

Wanamaker's acid expression deepened into a dark scowl. "He gave his name as Karl Manstein. I don't think Selene security has tumbled to who he really is."

For an instant Pancho wondered how Wanamaker knew that Manstein was an alias for Fuchs. But she put that aside as unimportant. "Get him out of there," she said.

"What?"

"Get him out of the hospital. Out of Selene. Send him back to the Belt, to Ceres, anywhere. Just get him loose from Selene security."

"But he's a murderer, a terrorist."

"I brought him to Selene to help in our fight against Humphries," Pancho half-lied. "I don't want Stavenger or anybody else to know that."

"How am I supposed to get him past Selene's security guards?" Wanamaker asked, clearly distressed.

Pancho closed her eyes for a moment. Then, "Jake, that's your problem. Figure it out. I want him off the Moon and headed back to the Belt. Yesterday."

He took a deep breath, then replied reluctantly, "Yes, ma'am." For an instant she thought he was going to give her a military salute.

"Anything else?" Pancho asked.

Wanamaker made a face that was halfway between a smile and a grimace. "Isn't that enough?"

Ulysses S. Quinlan felt awed, his emerald-green eyes wide with admiration, as he stood in the middle of the huge downstairs living room of the Humphries mansion. Or what was left of it. The wide, spacious room was a charred and blackened desolation, walls and ceiling scorched, floor littered with burned stumps of debris and powdery gray ash.

Born in Belfast of an Irish father and Irish-American mother, Quinlan had grown up to tales of civil wars. To please his father he played football from childhood, which eventually brought him an athletic scholarship to Princeton University, back in the States—which pleased his mother, even though she cried to be separated from her only child. Quinlan studied engineering, and worked long years on the frustrating and ultimately pointless seawalls and hydromechanical barriers that failed to prevent the rising ocean from flooding out most of Florida and the Gulf Coast regions as far south as Mexico's Yucatan peninsula.

He suffered a nervous breakdown when Houston was inundated, and was retired at full pension precisely on his fortieth birthday. To get away from oceans and seas and floods he retired to the Moon. Within a year he was working in Selene's safety department, as happy and cheerful as he'd been before the disastrous greenhouse floods on Earth.

Now he whistled through his breathing mask as he goggled at the size of the mansion's living room.

"The grandeur of it all," he said as he shuffled through the gray ash and debris.

"Like the old Tsars in Russia," said his partner, a stocky redheaded Finnish woman. He could hear the contempt in her tone, even through her breathing mask.

"Aye," agreed Quinlan, thudding the blackened wall with a gloved fist. "But he built solid. Reinforced concrete. The basic structure stood up to the flames, it did."

His partner reluctantly agreed. "They could have contained the fire to one area if somebody hadn't allowed it to spread to the roof."

Quinlan nodded. "A pity," he murmured. "A true pity."

They wore the breathing masks to protect their lungs from the fine ash that they kicked up with each step they took. The grotto had been refilled with breathable air hours earlier. Quinlan and his Finnish partner were inspecting the ruins, checking to make certain that no hint of fire reignited itself now that there was oxygen to support combustion again.

They spent a careful hour sifting through the debris of the lower floor. Then they headed cautiously up the stairs to the upper level. The wooden facings and lush carpeting of the stairway had burned away, but the solid concrete understructure was undisturbed by the fire.

Upstairs was just as bad a mess as below. Quinlan could see the broken and charred remains of what had once been fine furniture, now lying in shattered heaps along the walls of the hallway. The windows were all intact, he noticed, and covered with metal mesh screens. He must have built with tempered glass, Quinlan thought. Bulletproof? I wonder.

Following the floor plan displayed on their handhelds, they pushed through the debris at the wide doorway of the master bedroom suite. Quinlan whistled softly at the size of it all.

"That must have been the bed," his partner said, pointing to a square block of debris on the floor.

"Or his airport," muttered Quinlan.

"Hey, look at this." The Finn was standing in front of an intact door panel. "The fire didn't damage this."

"How could that be?" Quinlan wondered aloud, stepping over toward her.

"It's plastic of some sort," she said, running her gloved had along the panel.

"Ceramic, looks like."

The redhead checked her handheld. "Should be a closet, according to the floorplan."

"How in the world do you get into it, though?" Quinlan looked for a door latch or a button but could see nothing along the soot-blackened door frame.

He tried to slide the door open. It wouldn't budge. He tapped it, then rapped. "It's locked from the inside, seems like."

At that instant the door slid open so fast they both jumped back a startled step or two.

Martin Humphries stood tottering on uncertain legs, glaring at them with red-rimmed blazing in his eyes.

"About time," he croaked, his voice bricky-dry.

"Mr. Humphries!"

Humphries staggered past them, looked at the ruins of his palatial bedroom, then turned back on them fiercely.

"Water! Give me water."

Quinlan yanked the canteen from his belt and wordlessly handed it to the angry man. Humphries gurgled it down greedily, water spilling down his chin and dripping onto the front of his wrinkled shirt. Even through the breathing mask, Quinlan could smell the man's foul body odor.

Humphries put the canteen down from his lips, but still held onto it possessively. Wiping his chin with the back of his free hand, he coughed once, then jabbed a finger at Quinlan.

"Phone," he snapped, his voice a little stronger than before. "Give me a phone. I'm going to hang that murdering bastard Fuchs by his balls!"

ASTEROID VESTA

lthough the military base on Vesta belonged to Humphries Space Systems, its key personnel were mercenaries hired by HSS from several sources. Leeza Chaptal, for example, was a Yamagata Corporation employee. She was now effectively the base commander, since the HSS man nominally in charge of the base was a business executive, by training and education an accountant, by disposition a bean-counter.

Leeza left him to shuffle paperwork (electronically, of course) and he left her to run the two-hundred-odd men and women who made up the military strength of the base: engineers, technicians, astronauts, soldiers. It was a wise arrangement. The HSS man dealt with numbers, while Leeza handled the real work.

With the solar storm raging, though, there was very little real work being done. Leeza had called in everyone from the surface. Huddled safely in the caverns and tunnels deep underground, there was little for the military to do other than routine maintenance of equipment and that oldest of all soldierly pursuits: griping.

In truth, Leeza herself felt uncomfortable burrowed down like a mole in its den. Even though she seldom went to the surface of Vesta, it unnerved her to realize that she *could not* go up to the surface now, could not get out of these cramped little compartments carved out of the asteroid's rocky body, could not stand up on the bare pebbled ground—even in a space suit—and see the stars.

She paced slowly along the consoles in the base command center, looking over the shoulders of the bored technicians sitting at each desk. The storm was weakening, she saw. Radiation levels were beginning to decline. Good, she thought. The sooner this is over, the better. Four HSS vessels were hanging in docking orbits up there, waiting for the radiation to recede enough so they could begin shuttling their crews down to the base. And Dorik Harbin was approaching in his ship, *Samarkand*.

Dorik had been distant for weeks now; perhaps it was time to bring him closer. Leeza smiled inwardly at the thought. He doesn't like the fact that I outrank him, she knew. But a few of the right pills and he'll forget all about rank. Or maybe I should try something that will make him obedient, submissive. No, she decided. I like his passion, his ferocity. Take that away from him and there's nothing special left.

"Unidentified vehicle approaching," said the tech monitoring the radar.

Leeza felt her scalp tingle. Anything that the radar could spot through this radiation cloud must be close, very close.

"Two bogies," the technician called out as Leeza hurried to his chair.

They were speeding toward Vesta, and so close that the computer could calculate their size and velocity. Too small to be attack ships, Leeza saw, swiftly digesting the numbers racing across the bottom of the display. Nukes? Nuclear bombs couldn't do much damage to us while we're buttoned up down here. For the first time she felt grateful for the solar storm.

"They're going to impact," said the technician.

"Yes, I can see," Leeza replied calmly.

The two approaching missiles fired retrorockets at the last instant and hit the hard, stony ground almost softly. A crash landing, she thought. No explosion. Timed fuzing?

She walked a few paces to the communications console. "Do you have a camera in the vicinity where those two bogies landed?"

The comm tech already had the scene on her main display screen. It was grainy and dim, but Leeza saw the crumpled wreckage of two small missiles lying on the bare ground.

"Is that the best magnification you can get?" she asked, bending over the technician's shoulder to peer at the screen.

The technician muttered something about the radiation up there as she pecked at her keyboard.

The display went blank.

"Nice work," Leeza sneered.

"It shouldn't have done that," said the technician, defensively.

"Radar's out!" called the radar tech.

Leeza straightened up and turned in his direction.

"Radiation monitors have gone dead."

"No response from the surface camera at the crash site," the comm tech said. "Hey, two more cameras have gone out!"

Leeza turned slowly in a full circle. Every console was conking out, screens going dark while red failure-mode lights flared.

"What's going on up there?" Leeza asked.

No one answered.

No less than fourteen Humphries Space Systems employees attended Martin Humphries between his burned-out mansion and the finest suite in the decaying Hotel Luna, four flights above the fire-blackened grotto. Flunkies and lackeys ranging from his personal physician to a perky blonde administrative assistant with a brilliant smile from HSS's personnel department were already waiting for their CEO as Quinlan and his surprised partner helped Humphries through the temporary air-lock and into Selene's bottommost corridor.

The head of his security department, the never-smiling Grigor, fell into step alongside Humphries as they started toward the powered stairs.

"Your assistant, the woman Ferrer . . ."

"What about her?" Humphries asked, suddenly worried that Victoria had survived the fire and was ready to tell the world how he had abandoned her.

"They found her body in the upstairs hallway," said Grigor morosely. "Dead of smoke inhalation."

Humphries felt a surge of relief flow through him. But he growled, "Fuchs. He's responsible for this. I want Fuchs's balls on a platter."

"Yessir," said Grigor. "I'll see to it right away."

"And fire that dumb sonofabitch who was in charge of security for my house!"

"Immediately, sir."

"You've got to rest, Mr. Humphries," the doctor said, placing a placating hand on Humphries's arm. "You've been through an ordeal that would—"

"Fuchs!" Humphries raged, shaking loose of the doctor. "Find him! Kill the bastard!"

"Right away, sir."

Humphries fumed and ranted all the way up the power stairs and into the sumptuous hotel suite that the woman from the personnel department had reserved for him. A full dinner was waiting on a wheeled table set up in the sitting room. Humphries blurted orders and demands as he stormed into the suite and went straight to the lavatory. Even while he stripped off his sweaty clothes and stepped into the steaming shower he still yelled at the aides—including the blonde—swirling around him.

"And another thing," he called from the shower. "Get my insurance adjusters down to the mansion and see to it that they have a complete list of its contents. Goddamned fire ruined everything in there. Everything!"

Aides scurried and took notes on their handhelds. The doctor wanted to give Humphries an injection of tranquilizers, but he would have none of it.

"But you've got to rest," the doctor said, backing away from his employer's raging shouts.

"I'll rest when Fuchs's body is roasting over a slow fire," Humphries answered hotly while he struggled into a robe being held for him by the head of his public relations department.

He stormed into the sitting room, glared at the dinner waiting for him, then looked up at the small crowd of aides, assistants and executives.

"Out! All of you! Get the hell out of here and leave me alone."

They hurried toward the door.

"You!" He pointed at Grigor. "I want Fuchs. Understand me?"

"I understand, sir. It's as good as done. He can't get out of Selene. We'll find him."

"It's his head or yours," Humphries growled.

Grigor nodded, looking more morose than usual, and practically bowed as he backed away toward the door.

The doctor stood uncertainly in the center of the sitting room, a remote sensing unit in his hand. "I should take your blood pressure, Mr. Humphries."

"Get OUT!"

The doctor scampered to the door.

Humphries plopped himself down on the wide, deep sofa and

glowered at the covered plates arranged on the wheeled table. A bottle of wine stood in a chiller, already uncorked.

He looked up and saw that everybody had left. Everybody except the blonde, who stood at the door watching him.

"Do you want me to leave, too?" she asked, with a warm smile.

Humphries laughed. "No." He patted the sofa cushion beside him. "You come and sit here."

She was slim, elfin, wearing a one-piece tunic that ended halfway down her thighs. Humphries saw a tattoo on her left ankle: a twining thorned stem that bore a red rose.

"The doctor said you should rest," she said, with an impish smile.

"He also said I need a tranquilizer."

"And a good night's sleep."

"Maybe you can help me with that," he said.

"I'll do my best."

He discovered that her name was Tatiana Oparin, that she worked in his personnel department, that she was ambitious, and that she would be delighted to replace the late Victoria Ferrer as his personal aide. He also discovered that the rose around her ankle was not her only tattoo.

Grigor Malenkovich noted, in his silent but keen-eyed way, that Tatiana stayed behind in Humphries's suite. Good, he thought. She is serving her purpose. While she keeps Humphries occupied I can start the search for Fuchs without his hounding me.

The place to start is the hospital, he told himself. All four of the intruders have been brought there. They are under guard. One of them is undoubtedly Fuchs himself. Or, if not, then he knows where Fuchs is.

He went directly to the hospital, only to be told by Selene's security officers that all the people taken from the fire scene were under protective custody.

"I want to ask them a few questions," said Grigor.

The woman in the coral red Selene coveralls smiled patiently at him. "Tomorrow, Mr. Malenkovich. You can be present when we interrogate them."

Grigor hesitated a moment, then asked, "Why not now? Why wait?"

"The medics say they need a night's rest. One of them was wounded, you know, and all of them have had a pretty rugged time of it."

"All the better. Question them while they are tired, worn down."

The woman smiled again, but it seemed forced. "Tomorrow, Mr. Malenkovich. Once the medics okay it. We'll talk to them tomorrow."

Grigor thought it over. No sense getting into a quarrel with Selene security, he decided. Besides, Humphries is busy enjoying a good night's rest—or something of the kind.

"You can't take patients out of the hospital without authorization," said the doctor. He was young, with a boyish thatch of dark brown hair flopping over his forehead. Wanamaker thought he probably made out pretty well with the female hospital staffers.

He kept his thoughts to himself, though, and put on his sternest, darkest scowl.

"This is an Astro Corporation security matter," he insisted, his voice low but iron-hard.

They were standing at the hospital's admittance center, little more than a waist-high counter with a computer terminal atop it. The doctor had been summoned by the computer, which normally ran the center without human intervention. Wanamaker had waited until midnight to fetch Fuchs and his people out of the hospital. Minimal staff on duty. He had brought six of the biggest, toughest-looking Astro employees he could find. Two of them actually worked in the security department. The other four consisted of two mechanics, one physical fitness instructor from Astro's private spa, and a woman cook from the executive dining room.

The doctor looked uncertainly at the identification chip Wanamaker held out rigidly at arm's length. He had already run it through the admittance center's computer terminal and it had verified that Jacob Wanamaker was an executive of Astro Corporation's security department.

"I should call Selene's security department," the doctor said.

"Aren't they guarding the four?" Wanamaker demanded, knowing that they had been called off by one of his own people who had hacked into their computer system.

"Not on this shift," said the doctor. "They'll be back in the morning, at oh-eight-hundred."

"All right then," Wanamaker said. "I'll deal with them in the morning. Right now, I've been instructed to take the four to Astro headquarters."

Wanamaker was thinking, If this young pup doesn't cave in I'll have to slug him. He didn't want to do that. He wanted this extraction to be painless.

The young man's face was too bland to frown effectively, but he screwed up his features and said, "This hospital is run by the governing board of Selene, not Astro or any other corporation."

Wanamaker nodded knowingly. "Very well. You contact your governing board and get their okay."

The doctor glanced at the wall clock. "It's almost one A.M.!"

"Yes, that's right."

"They'll all be asleep."

"Then you'll have to wake them." Wanamaker hoped fervently that the kid didn't think of calling Selene's security department. That could create a problem.

Before the doctor could make up his mind, Wanamaker suggested, "Why don't you call Douglas Stavenger?"

"Mr. Stavenger?" The doctor's eyed widened. "He knows about this?"

"And he's given his approval," Wanamaker lied.

"Well . . ."

"Is there any medical reason to keep them hospitalized?" Wanamaker demanded.

The doctor shook his head. "No, they're supposed to be released in the morning."

"Very well then. Give me the release forms and I'll sign them."

"I don't know . . ."

Wanamaker didn't wait any further. He walked past the puzzled, uncertain young doctor. His six subordinates marched in step behind him, trying to look fierce, as Wanamaker had instructed them to do.

ARMSTRONG SPACEPORT

As the cart trundled to a stop at the end of the tunnel that led back to Selene, Wanamaker noticed that the lower half of Pancho's right leg was wrapped in a cast. She looked grim, almost angry, as she sat behind the cart's wheel with her leg sticking out onto the fender.

Fuchs was standing beside Wanamaker, also far from happy. His three aides were already on their way to the little rocket shuttlecraft that would take them up to the vessel waiting in orbit above the Moon's rugged, airless surface.

"Humphries is alive and well," said Pancho, without getting down from the electric cart. "No thanks to you, Lars."

His mouth a downcast slash, Fuchs answered, "Too bad. The world would be better off with him dead."

"Maybe so, but all you did was kill a dozen or so of his people. Now he's got a perfectly good excuse to go after your ass, ol' buddy."

Fuchs started to reply, thought better of it, and said nothing.

Turning to Wanamaker, Pancho asked, "What've you got for him?"

"The only available armed vessel is a new attack ship, *Halsey*."

Pancho nodded brusquely. "Okay, Lars. That's your new ship. Officially, you've hijacked it while it was sitting in lunar orbit waiting for a crew to be assigned to it."

"You're giving it to me?" Fuchs asked, flabbergasted.

"You're stealing it. We'll add it to your long list of crimes."

His broad, normally downcast face broke into a bitter smile. "Pancho . . . I . . . I don't know what to say."

She did not smile back at him. "Just get your butt up to the ship and get the hell out of here as fast as you can. Go back to the Belt and hide out with the rock rats. Humphries is going to come after you with everything he's got."

Fuchs nodded, understanding. "I'm only sorry that I didn't kill him. He deserves to die."

"So do we all, ol' buddy," said Pancho. "Now, *git*! Before a platoon of HSS security goons comes boiling down the tunnel."

Fuchs grasped her hand and, bending slightly, kissed it. Pancho's face turned red.

"Go on, git. There's gonna be plenty hell to pay; I've got to get busy."

Almost laughing, Fuchs turned and started trotting down the corridor that led to the waiting shuttlecraft, a thickset, sturdy little badger of a man clad in black, his short arms pumping as he ran.

Wanamaker shook his head. "When Humphries finds out you've helped him escape . . ."

Pancho grinned at him. "Hell, Jake, he got away from you. You're the one who sprang him out of the hospital. He got away from you and stole a brand-new Astro spacecraft. I might have to dock your pay or something."

Wanamaker broke into a craggy smile. "You are some piece of work, Ms. Lane. Really some piece of work."

"Come on," Pancho said, patting the plastic of the seat beside her. "I'll give you a ride back to town. We got a lot of work to do."

"What do you mean, he's disappeared?" Humphries demanded.

Grigor stood before him like a dark wraith, his eyes downcast. With a shrug, he repeated, "Fuchs is gone."

They were in the sitting room of Humphries's suite in the Hotel Luna. Tatiana Oparin had discreetly remained in the bedroom when Grigor had arrived, before Humphries's breakfast order had come from room service.

"He *can't* be gone!" Humphries shouted, pounding the pillows of the sofa on which he sat. Clad only in a silk hotel robe, his thin, almost hairless legs reminded Grigor of a chicken's.

Standing before the sofa, to one side of the coffeetable, Grigor reported, "He was under Selene's custody last night, in the hospital. This morning, when we went to interrogate him, he and his crew were gone."

"Gone? How could he be gone? Where did he go? How could he get out?"

"An Astro Corporation security detail removed him from the hospital shortly after one A.M.," Grigor replied, his voice as flat and even as a computer's. "There is no trace of him after that."

Leaping to his feet so hard that his robe flapped open, Humphries screamed, "Find him! Search every centimeter of the city and *find him!* Now! Use every man you've got."

"Yes, sir."

"Don't stand there! Find him!"

As Grigor turned toward the door, the phone chimed. Scowling, Humphries saw that the wallscreen displayed the name of the caller: Pancho Lane.

"Phone answer," he snapped.

Pancho's angular, light tan features took shape on the wallscreen, slightly bigger than life.

"Martin, I have some unpleasant news for you."

He glared at her image as he pulled the maroon robe tightly around himself.

"Lars Fuchs somehow stole our newest ship and lit out of lunar orbit a few hours ago. He's prob'ly heading back to the Belt."

"He stole one of your ships?" Humphries asked, his voice dripping sarcasm.

"Yup," said Pancho. "Slipped away from a phony security detail that sprang him out of the hospital last night."

Humphries's innards felt like a lake of molten lava. "He had lots of help, then, didn't he?"

Keeping her face immobile, Pancho admitted, "Well, he's got some friends among my Astro people, yeah. We're looking into it."

"I'm sure you are."

She almost smiled. "I just thought you'd want to know."

"Thank you, Pancho."

"Any time, Martin." The screen went dark.

Humphries stepped to the small table at the end of the sofa, yanked up the lamp sitting atop it, and heaved it at the wallscreen. It bounced off and thudded to the carpeted floor.

"Guttersnipe bitch! She helped him get away. Now he's running back to the Belt to hide out with his rock rat friends."

Grigor said, "We could intercept him."

Humphries glared at his security chief. "He'll be running silent.

You'd have to search the whole region between here and the Belt. There aren't enough ships—"

"He'll have to put in somewhere for supplies," said Grigor. "The *Chrysalis* habitat at Ceres is the only place for that."

Still glowering, Humphries said, "They won't take him in. They exiled him, years ago."

Nodding slightly, Grigor countered, "Perhaps. But he will contact a ship in the region for supplies."

"Or capture one, the damned pirate."

"Either way, *Chrysalis* is the key to his survival. If we control the habitat at Ceres, we will get him into our grasp, sooner or later."

Humphries stared at his security chief for a long, silent moment. Then he said, "All right. Tell our people at Vesta to send a force to Ceres and take control of *Chrysalis*."

An unhappy expression twisted Grigor's normally dour face. "We seem to have lost contact with Vesta," he said, the words coming out swiftly, all in a rush.

"What?"

"I'm sure it's only temporary."

"Lost contact?" Humphries's voice rose a notch.

"It might be the solar storm," said Grigor, almost to himself, "although the cloud is well past the Belt now."

"Lost contact with the whole base?" Humphries shouted. "The entire base?"

"For more than twelve hours," Grigor admitted, almost in a whisper.

Humphries wanted to scream. And he did, so loudly and with such fevered anger that Tatiana Oparin rushed into the sitting room. When she failed to calm him down she called the HSS medical department for Humphries's personal physician.

arbin hated these one-way messages. I have to sit here like an obedient dog while my master speaks to me, he grumbled silently. Yet there was no other way. Grigor was at Selene, Harbin in his private compartment aboard *Samakand*, so deep in the Belt that it took light the better part of an hour to span the distance between them.

Grigor's face, in the display screen, looked even dourer than usual. He's worried, Harbin thought. Frightened.

". . . completely wiped out Humphries's home here in Selene and killed four security guards," the security chief was saying, speaking rapidly, nervously. "They also killed Humphries's personal assistant, the woman Ferrer. The attack was led by Lars Fuchs."

Fuchs attacked Humphries in his own home! Harbin marveled. He felt some admiration for such daring. Strike your enemy as hard as you can. Strike at his heart.

Grigor was droning on, "Astro has apparently spirited Fuchs away. Most likely he's on his way back to the Belt. He must have friends at Ceres, allies who will give him supplies and more crewmen. Your orders are to find Fuchs and kill him. Nothing else matters now. Bring Fuchs's head to Mr. Humphries. He will accept nothing less."

Harbin nodded. This isn't the first time that Humphries has demanded Fuchs's life, he recalled. But this will be the last time. The final time. Fuchs has frightened Humphries. Up until now Humphries has fought this war in comfort and safety. But now Fuchs has threatened him, terrified him. Now he'll move heaven and Earth to eliminate the threat that Fuchs represents. Now it's time for Fuchs to die.

"Something else," Grigor added, his eyes shifting nervously. "The base on Vesta has gone silent. We don't know why. I've diverted one of our attack ships to the asteroid to see what's happened. You stay clear of

Vesta. Head directly for Ceres and the habitat *Chrysalis*. Get Fuchs. Let me worry about Vesta."

The security chief's morose face disappeared from Harbin's screen, leaving him alone in his compartment.

Let him worry about Vesta, Harbin thought sourly. And what do I do about supplies? Where do I get fuel and food for my crew? How do I get all the way over to Ceres on what's left in my propellant tanks? I've stripped this ship's armor, too. What if I run into an Astro attack vessel? Grigor can give orders, but carrying them out is up to me.

Doug Stavenger was also feeling frustrated about the long time lag between Selene and the Belt. Edith, aboard *Elsinore*, was approaching Ceres. She would be arriving at the *Chrysalis* habitat in less than twenty-four hours.

". . . so it turns out that if you'd stayed here," he was saying to her, "you'd have had a big story at your doorstep. Humphries isn't letting any news media into his home, not even inside his garden, or what's left of it. But from what the safety inspectors tell me the house is a burned-out shell and that big, beautiful garden of his is almost completely destroyed."

He hesitated, leaned back in his recliner and tried to group his thoughts coherently. It was difficult speaking to a blank screen. It was like talking to yourself.

"Edie, this war's gone far enough. I've got to do something to stop it. They're fighting here in Selene now and I can't permit that. If that fire had spread beyond Humphries's garden it could have killed a lot of people here. Everyone, maybe, if we couldn't get it under control. I can't let them pose that kind of a threat to us. I've got to stop them."

Yes, Stavenger told himself. You've got to stop them. But how? How can you stop two of the most powerful corporations in the solar system from turning Selene into a battleground?

When his message arrived at *Elsinore*, Edith Elgin saw the concern, the deep lines of apprehension creasing her husband's handsome face.

But in her mind a voice was exulting, Fuchs is heading here! He has to be. He has friends among the rock rats. One way or another he's going to sneak back to Ceres, at least long enough to refuel and restock his ship. And I'll be there to interview him!

She was so excited that she hopped up from the chair she'd been sitting in to view her husband's message and left her cabin, heading up the narrow passageway toward the bridge. I've got to find out exactly when we dock at *Chrysalis*, she told herself. And see if the captain can spot any other ships heading toward the habitat. Fuchs may be running silent, but his ship will show up on radar, now that we're clear of the radiation cloud.

Lars Fuchs was indeed heading for Ceres, running silently, all beacons and telemetry turned off. Hands clasped behind his back, mouth turned down in a sullen scowl, he paced back and forth across the bridge of the *Halsey*, his mind churning.

The ship was running smoothly enough, for its first flight in deep space. Its systems were automated enough so that the four of them could run it as a skeleton crew. Nodon's shoulder was healing, and Sanja had assured Fuchs that there were more crewmen waiting for them at *Chrysalis*.

Fuchs was officially exiled from the rock rats' habitat, and had been for nearly ten years. But they'll let me take up a parking orbit, he thought. Just for a day or so. Just long enough to take on more crew and supplies.

Then what? he asked himself. I have *Nautilus* waiting for me in the Belt, and now this new ship. Can I find enough people to crew them both? Humphries will be coming after me with everything he's got. Fuchs nodded to himself. Let him. Let him chase me all through the Belt. I'll bleed him dry. I failed to kill him, but I can hurt him where the pain is greatest: in his ledger sheets. Every ship he sends after me is an expense that drains his profits. Every HSS ship that I destroy will pour more red ink on him. I'll bleed him dry.

Until he kills me, Fuchs realized. This war between us can end in only one way. I'm a dead man. He told me that years ago.

He caught a glimpse of himself reflected in one of the blank screens on the bridge. A bitter, angry face with a thin slash of sneering lips and deepset eyes that burned like hot coals.

All right, he said to his image. He'll kill me. But it will cost him plenty. I won't go easily. Or cheaply.

Big George Ambrose was fidgeting uncomfortably at the conference table. His chair was just a tad too small for his bulk, its arms just high enough to force him to hunch his shoulders slightly. After a couple of hours it got painful.

And this meeting had been going on for more than a couple of hours. The governing board of *Chrysalis* was having one of its rare disagreements. Usually the board was little more than a rubber stamp for George's decisions. None of the board members really wanted any responsibility. They were all picked at random by the habitat's personnel computer, and required to serve a year on the governing body. Each of the eight men and women wanted to be back at their jobs or at home or taking in a video or at the pub. Anywhere but stuck in this conference room, wrangling.

George thought the pub was a good idea. Maybe we should have our fookin' meetings there, he said to himself. Get them all half blind and then take a vote.

But this was a serious issue, he knew. It had to be faced squarely. And soberly.

Pancho had warned George that Lars Fuchs was in a spacecraft heading for the Belt. It didn't take a genius to realize that he'd have to get supplies from somewhere, and Ceres was the only somewhere there was.

"He might not come here at all," said one of the board members, an edgy-looking woman in a high-mode pullover that sported more cutouts than material. "He might just hijack a ship or two and steal the supplies he needs. He *is* a pirate, after all."

"That's why we exiled him in the first place," said the bland-looking warehouse operator sitting next to her.

"That's not entirely true," George pointed out.

"But we did exile him," the warehouseman retorted. "So we don't have to allow him to dock here."

"That all happened ten years ago," said one of the older board members, a former miner who had started a new career as an armaments repairman.

"But he was exiled for life, wasn't he?"

"Right," George admitted.

"So there."

The woman sitting directly across from George, a plumpish redhead with startling violet eyes, said, "Listen. Half the HSS ships in the Belt are going to be looking for Fuchs. If he puts in here they'll grab him."

"This is neutral territory," George said. "Everybody knows that. We've established it with HSS and Astro. We service any ship that comes to us, and they don't do any fighting within a thousand klicks of our habitat."

"That doesn't mean we have to service Fuchs. He's an exile, remember."

"There's something else involved," George added. "We have a news media star heading here. She'll arrive tomorrow. Edith Elgin."

"I've watched her shows from Selene!"

"Isn't she married to Douglas Stavenger?"

"What's she coming here for?"

"To do a documentary about the war," George explained.

"Do we want to have a documentary about the war? I mean, won't that be bad publicity for us?"

"She'll want to interview Fuchs, I bet."

"That'd be a great way to get everybody's attention: an interview with the notorious pirate."

"It'll make us look like a den of thieves."

"Can we stop her?"

All eight of them looked to George.

Surprised at this turn, George said, "We'd have a helluva time shooing her away. She's got a right to report the news."

"That doesn't mean we have to help her. Let her interview Fuchs somewhere else."

But George was thinking, Humphries's people are smart enough to watch her and wait for Fuchs to show up. Wherever she interviews Fuchs, it's going to be fookin' dangerous for both of them.

ASTEROID VESTA

A n individual nanomachine is like an individual ant: mindless but unceasingly active. Its blindly endless activity is of little consequence by itself; even the most tireless exertions of a device no bigger than a virus can be nothing but invisibly minuscule in the human scale of things.

But while an individual ant can achieve little and has not enough brain to accomplish more than instinctual actions, an ant *colony* of many millions of blindly scurrying units can strip a forest, build a city, act with a purposefulness that seems little short of human intelligence.

So it is with nanomachines. An individual unit can accomplish little. But strew millions of those virus-sized units over a restricted area and they can build or destroy on a scale that rivals human capacities.

The asteroid Vesta is a spheroid rich in nickel-iron, some 500 kilometers in diameter. The Humphries Space Systems base on Vesta was burrowed, for the most part, more than twenty meters below the asteroid's pitted, airless, bare surface.

The nanomachines that were strewn across a small area of the asteroid's surface operated in a far different regime of scale and environment. Their world was a universe of endlessly vibrating, quivering molecules where electromagnetic forces held atoms in tight clusters, and Brownian motion buffeted atoms, molecules and nanomachines alike. On that scale of size, the nanomachines were giant mechanical devices, like huge bulldozers or derricks, bulling their way through the constantly jostling, jiggling molecules.

Each nanomachine was built with a set of grippers that fit the shape of the molecule that made up high-grade steel. Each nanomachine had the strength to seize such molecules and pull them apart into their constituent atoms of iron, carbon, chromium, and nickel.

Drawing their energy from the unceasing Brownian vibrations of the molecules themselves, the nanomachines patiently, mindlessly, tirelessly chewed through every molecule of steel they could find, tearing them apart. On the molecular scale of the nanomachines this was a simple operation. It would end only when the quantum-dot timing devices built into each individual nanomachine told it to stop and disassemble itself.

Or when the nanos ran out of steel to chew on. Whichever came first.

Leeza Chaptal was the first to understand what was happening. As she stood in the control center deep underground and watched the monitor screens go blank, one by one, she realized that only the sensors and other equipment up on the surface were failing.

The technicians seated at their consoles around her had gone from surprise to irritation to outright fear.

"Something's wiping out everything up on the surface," one of them said, needlessly. They could all see that.

"Those missiles," said Leeza. "They must be responsible for this."

"But what . . . how?"

"There wasn't any explosion," said one of the puzzled technicians. "Nothing seismic registered except their crashing on the surface."

"And then everything started blanking out."

"Nanomachines," Leeza guessed. "They must have brought in nanomachines that are eating up our surface installations."

All the techs turned to her in wide-eyed fear. Nanomachines. They had all heard stories about how they could chew up everything, including people, and turn everything in their path into a dead, formless gray goo.

"Somebody's got to go up the surface and see what's going on up there."

Nobody budged.

Leeza hadn't expected volunteers. "I'll go myself," she said.

Leeza's heart was already thumping loudly as she clumped to the hatch in the awkward, bulbous hard-shell space suit. Then she saw that the display on the hatch opening onto the vertical shaft that led up to the surface showed that there was nothing but vacuum on its other side.

Omygod, she gasped silently. They've eaten through the hatch at the top of the shaft.

Should I go through? What if they infect my suit? What if they start chewing on me?

Yet she had to know what was going on, had to learn the nature and depth of the attack they were undergoing.

Turning to the two maintenance engineers who had helped her into the suit, she said through its fishbowl helmet, "Get back on the other side of the hatch down the corridor."

They didn't need to be told twice. Both of them scampered down the corridor and squeezed through the hatch together, neither one of them willing to wait for the other. Leeza heard the metallic thud when they slammed the hatch and sealed it.

Okay, she told herself. Just a quick peek. A fast reconnaissance. Nothing heroic.

With gloved fingers she tapped the code on the hatch's control panel. It popped open slightly, and she noticed a puff of gritty dust from the floor swirl through the crack.

Breathing heavily inside her helmet, she pushed the hatch all the way open and stepped tentatively through. The lamps fixed to the shoulders of her space suit reflected light off the steel wall of the shaft.

"Looks all right so far," she said into her helmet microphone to the techs in the control center watching her progress in the corridor's surveillance camera.

"Some dust or dirt accumulated on the floor of the shaft," she reported, kicking up little lingering clouds of dust as she turned a full circle.

She had to crane her neck painfully to look up the length of the shaft. Sure enough, the hatch up at the top was gone. She could see a swatch of stars in the circular opening up there. Feeling jumpier with every heartbeat, Leeza unclipped the hand torch from her waist and shone it up the shaft. The gleaming reflection from the smooth steel lining ended about halfway up.

"The metal lining of the shaft seems to have been eroded or

something," she said. A pebble pinged on her helmet. She would have jumped halfway out of her skin if she hadn't been inside the cumbersome suit.

"It's eating the metal!" she yelped.

"Get back inside," said one of the techs from the control center. "Get back before they start chewing on you!"

Leeza didn't wait to be told twice.

There was no nanotech expert among the HSS crew at the Vesta base. And no way to call for advice or information, with all the surface antennas gone. Leeza ordered the entire team into the galley, the only room large enough to hold the nearly two hundred men and women in the base at the same time.

"It's nanomachines," she concluded, after reporting to them what was happening. "They seem to be attacking metal. Maybe they're specifically programmed to destroy steel, maybe it's any metal at all. We don't know. But either way, we're in deep trouble."

"They could eat out all the hatches and open the whole complex to vacuum!" said one of the mercenary soldiers.

"That's what they're in the process of doing," Leeza admitted.

The head of the logistics storeroom, a soft-looking sandy-haired man with a bold blue stylized wolf tattooed across his forehead, spoke up:

"They're coming down the shaft and eating at the airtight hatch, right?"

"Right," said Leeza.

"And when they've gone through that first hatch they'll come along the corridor toward the next hatch, right?"

"We all know that!" snapped a dark-haired woman in pale green coveralls. "They'll eat up anything metal."

"Well," said the logistics man, "why don't we spray the corridors and hatches with something nonmetallic?"

"Spray?"

"We've got sprayguns, ceramics torches, butterknives, for chrissakes. Cover every square millimeter of exposed metal with something nonmetallic. Slather it on good and thick. Maybe that'll stop the nanos."

"That's ridiculous!"

"Maybe not."

"It's worth a try."

Leeza agreed that it was worth a try. If nothing else, it would keep everybody busy, instead of waiting in dread for the nanomachines to kill them.

COMMAND SHIP *SAMARKAND*

A great way to go into battle, thought Dorik Harbin: out of fuel, stripped of armor, and low on rations.

Sitting in the command chair on *Samarkand*'s bridge, Harbin turned his gaze from the main display screen to the thick quartz port set into the bulkhead on his left. They were close enough to the *Chrysalis* for him to see it without magnification; the habitat's linked circle of metal-skinned modules glinted faintly in the light from the distant Sun, a tiny spark of human warmth set against the cold, silent darkness of infinite space.

"I have contact with *Chrysalis*, sir," his communications technician said, turning halfway in her chair to look at Harbin.

"Main screen," he ordered.

A woman's face appeared on the screen, ascetically thin, high cheekbones, hair cropped down to a bare fuzz, almond-shaped dark eyes full of suspicion.

"Please identify yourself," she said, her voice polite but hard-edged. "We're not getting any telemetry data from you."

"You don't need it," Harbin said, reflexively rubbing one hand over his fiercely dark beard. "We're looking for Lars Fuchs. Surrender him to us and we'll leave you in peace."

"Fuchs?" The woman looked genuinely puzzled. "He's not here. He's an exile. We wouldn't—"

"No lies," Harbin snapped. "We know Fuchs is heading for your habitat. I want him."

Her expression turned from surprise to irritation. "How can we produce him when he's not here?"

"Who's in charge there?" Harbin demanded. "I want to speak to your top person."

"That'd be Big George. George Ambrose. He's our chief administrator."

"Get him."

"He's not here."

Harbin's jaw clenched. "Are you joking, or do you want me to start shooting?"

Her eyes widened. "George is aboard the *Elsinore*. Greeting some VIP from Selene."

"Patch me through to him."

Sullenly, the woman said, "I'll try."

The screen went blank. Harbin turned to his comm tech. "Did she cut me off?"

The technician shrugged. "Maybe it wasn't deliberate."

Harbin thought otherwise. They're playing a delaying game. Why? Do they know we're almost out of propellant? Why are they being stubborn?

Aloud, he commanded, "Show me the ships parked at the habitat."

The technician murmured into the pin microphone at her lips and the main screen lit up. *Chrysalis* showed up as a circle in the middle of the display. Harbin counted eleven ships co-orbiting nearby. One of them was identified as *Elsinore*, a passenger-carrying torch ship. The others appeared to be freighters, ore carriers, logistics supply vessels.

We'll have to take the propellants and supplies we need from them, Harbin said to himself. After we've found Fuchs.

He called up *Elsinore*'s manifest. Registered to Astro Corporation. Just in from Selene. No cargo. Carrying only one passenger, someone identified as Edith Elgin, from Selene.

From Selene, he thought. Who would pay the expense of sending a torch ship from Selene to Ceres for just one passenger? Lars Fuchs must be aboard that ship. He has to be. The passenger they've identified on their manifest, this Edith Elgin, must be a front for Fuchs.

It must be.

Harbin rose from his command chair. "Take the con," he said to his pilot. "I'll be back in a few moments. If *Chrysalis*'s chief administrator calls, let me know immediately."

He ducked through the hatch and walked the few steps to the door of his private quarters. They're not going to give up Fuchs willingly, Harbin thought. They might know that we're low on supplies, or guess it. Maybe they think they can wait us out. They could be calling for more Astro attack ships to come to their aid.

He looked at his bed. How long has it been since I've slept? he asked himself. With a shake of his head he answered, No matter. This is no time for sleep. He went past the bed and into his lavatory. There he opened the slim case that housed his medications. I'll need to be alert, razor-sharp, he told himself. He picked one of the vials and fitted it to the hypospray. Rolling up the sleeve of his tunic, he pressed the spray-gun against his bare skin and pushed the plunger.

He felt nothing. For good measure he fitted another vial to the hypospray and shot the additional dose into his bloodstream.

Big George was walking Edith Elgin down the passageway to *Elsinore's* main airlock, where his shuttlecraft had docked.

"You won't need a space suit," George was saying. "We'll go straight into the shuttle and then we'll dock with *Chrysalis*. Shirtsleeve environment all the way."

Edith smiled, delighted with this big, shaggy mountain of a man with the wild brick-red hair and beard. He would look terrific on video.

"I'm looking forward to seeing how the rock rats live," she said, secretly berating herself for not having a microcam attached to her and slaved to wherever her eyes focused. Always be ready to shoot, she reminded herself. You're letting an opportunity slip away.

"Aw, there aren't many ratties in the habitat. Mostly clerks and shopkeepers. The real rock rats are out in the Belt, workin' their bums off."

"Even with this war going on?" she asked.

George nodded. "No work, no eat."

"But isn't it dangerous, with ships being attacked?"

"Sure it is. But—"

"URGENT MESSAGE FOR MR. AMBROSE," the overhead intercom speakers blared.

George swiveled his head around, spotted a wall phone, and hurried to it. Edith followed him.

A bone-thin woman's face showed in the wall phone's little screen.

"An unidentified ship has taken up a parking orbit. They're demanding we surrender Lars Fuchs to them."

"Lars isn't here," George said.

"I told him that but he said we either give him Fuchs or he starts shooting!"

"Bloody fookin' maniac," George growled.

"He wants to talk to you."

"Right. I want to talk to him. Put me through."

Harbin felt perfectly normal. Bright, alert, ready to deal with these miserable rock rats or whatever other enemies came at him.

For the moment, though, he was sitting in his command chair and staring into the sky-blue eyes of a man sporting a thick mane of blazing red hair and an equally wild-looking beard.

Stroking his own neatly cropped beard, Harbin said, "It's very simple. You surrender Fuchs to me or I'll destroy you."

"We don't have Fuchs," George Ambrose said, obviously working hard to hold back his temper.

"How do I know that's true?"

"Come aboard and look for yourself! He's not here."

"He is aboard *Elsinore*, don't deny it."

"He isn't. He's not here. You're welcome to come aboard and search the ship from top to bottom."

"I'm not such a fool. You've already spirited him away to your habitat."

"Search the habitat then!"

"With a dozen men? You could hide him from us easily."

Ambrose started to say something, thought better of it, and sucked in a deep breath. At last he said, "Look, whoever the fook you are. *Chrysalis* is neutral territory. We're not armed. We have no weapons. You're welcome to search the habitat to your heart's content. We'll resupply your ship and fill your propellant tanks for you. What more can I offer you?"

"Lars Fuchs," said Harbin, implacably. This stubborn fool is beginning to anger me, he realized. He could feel the rage building, deep within him, like a seething pit of hot lava burning its way toward the surface.

"Lars isn't here!" Ambrose insisted. "He's not anywhere near here!

We exiled the poor bloody bastard years ago. He's persona non grata."

Harbin leaned forward in his chair, his eyes narrowing, his hands clenching into fists. "You have one half-hour to produce Fuchs. If you haven't given him to me by then, I will destroy your precious habitat and everyone in it."

SELENE: DOUGLAS STAVENGER'S QUARTERS

Doug Stavenger sat tensely in the armchair at one end of his living room's sofa. At the matching chair on the other end sat Pancho Lane. Between them, Martin Humphries was on the sofa, beneath a genuine Bonestell painting of a sleek rocket sitting on the Moon's rugged surface.

Pancho looks wary, Stavenger thought, like a gazelle that's been caught in a trap. The trousers of her trim sea-green business suit hid the cast on her left ankle.

Humphries looks worried, too, he realized. I've never seen him so uptight. Maybe being nearly killed has finally knocked some sense into his head.

"This war has gone far enough," Doug Stavenger said, leaning forward earnestly. "Too far, in fact. It's got to stop. Now."

Neither Pancho nor Humphries said a word. They look like two schoolkids who've been sent to the principal's office for discipline, Stavenger thought.

He focused on Pancho. "Despite Selene's demands, and my personal request to you, Astro has used its facilities here to direct military operations."

She nodded, lips tight. "Yep, that's true."

"And you produced a disaster."

Pancho nodded again.

Turning to Humphries, he said, "And that fire in your personal preserve could have wiped out all of Selene."

"I didn't start the fire," Humphries snapped. "It was that murdering sonofabitch Fuchs."

"And why was he trying to get to you?" Pancho interjected.

"He's a killer! You know that. Everybody knows it. He even killed one of my assistants, Victoria Ferrer!"

"And how many have you killed?" Pancho retorted. "You've tried to kill Lars more'n once."

For the first time in long, long years Stavenger felt angry. Truly angry. These two stubborn idiots were threatening Selene and everyone living in it.

"I don't care who started the fire," he said coldly, "the fact is that you're running your war from here. It was inevitable that the fighting would spread to Selene."

"I'm sorry for that," Pancho said. "Really sorry. But I had nothing to do with Fuchs's attack on the mansion."

Humphries glared at her. "Didn't you? You brought Fuchs here to Selene, didn't you? You protected him while he plotted to kill me!"

"I brought him to Earth to save his hide from your hired killers," Pancho countered, with some heat.

"Enough!" Stavenger snapped. "You want to fight your war, then fight it elsewhere. You're both leaving Selene."

"What do you mean?" Humphries demanded.

"Both Humphries Space Systems and Astro Corporation will move out of Selene. That includes the two of you, all your employees, and all your equipment. I want you both out, lock, stock and barrel. Within the week."

"You can't do that!"

"Can't I?" Stavenger said, meeting Humphries's angry gaze. "The governing council of Selene will formally declare both your corporations to be outlaw operations. If you don't move out by the deadline they will seize all your assets and forcibly exile any of your people still remaining here."

"That's illegal," Pancho blurted.

"It won't be by this time tomorrow," said Stavenger. "I guarantee it."

Humphries jabbed an accusing finger at him. "You can't expect me to—"

"I do expect you to clear out of Selene. Now. Immediately. I don't care where you go. I don't care if you slaughter each other out in the Belt or in the pits of hell. But you will *not* drag Selene into this war. And you will not endanger this community. Is that clear?"

Humphries glowered at him for a silent moment, then seemed to relax and lean back into the sofa's ample cushions.

"So I'll go to Hell Crater," he said, with a smirk.

Stavenger turned to Pancho. "And you?"

She shrugged. "Maybe Malapert. Maybe we'll set up shop in one of the habitats at L-4 or L-5."

Humphries sneered at her. "Good idea. I can wipe you out with a single nuke, then."

Stavenger suddenly shot out of his chair, grabbed Humphries by the collar of his tunic and hauled him to his feet.

"Why don't I just break your damned neck here and now and get this war over with?" he snarled.

Humphries went white. He hung limply in Stavenger's grasp, not even able to raise his hands to defend himself.

Stavenger pushed him back onto the sofa. "Martin, I can see that you're not going to stop this war of your own volition. It won't stop until you're stopped."

Some color returned to Humphries's face. With a trembling hand he pointed to Pancho. "What about her? She started it!"

"*I* started it?" Pancho yelped. "That's the biggest motherhumping lie I ever heard."

"You started arming your ships!"

"You tried to assassinate me!"

"I did not!"

"The cable car from Hell Crater, remember? You're saying you didn't do that?"

"I didn't!"

"Liar."

"I didn't do it!"

"Then who the hell did?"

"Not me!"

Stavenger's phone chimed, interrupting their finger-pointing.

"Phone answer," Stavenger called.

Edith Elgin's face appeared on the screen. She looked tense, worried, almost frightened. "Doug, I know you're going to hear about this one way or the other. The rock rats' habitat at Ceres is being threatened by somebody who wants Lars Fuchs. It must be a Humphries operation. I'm safe on the *Elsinore* so far, but we don't know what's going to happen. This could get ugly."

The screen went blank.

"Edith!" Stavenger called.

The screen remained gray, but a synthesized voice said, "Transmission was interrupted at the source. The system will attempt to reconnect."

Stavenger whirled on Humphries. "If anything happens to my wife I'll kill you. Understand me? I'll kill you!"

W ell at least lemme get back to *Chrysalis*," Big George was saying to the image on the screen, "and show you that Fuchs isn't there."

The fierce, dark-bearded man shook his head grimly. "No one will transfer from your ship to the habitat. How do I know that you won't smuggle Fuchs in with you?"

With obvious exasperation, George replied, "Because Fuchs isn't here! Come and see for your fookin' self!"

"I am not leaving my ship," said the intruder. "You will produce Lars Fuchs or face the consequences."

Big George and Edith were in her quarters aboard *Elsinor*, trying to reason with the scowling image on the screen. As George fumed and attempted to explain the situation to the intruder, Edith surreptitiously went to the travel kit resting on the shelf above her bed. Hoping she was out of the comm screen camera's view, she slipped one of the microcams she had brought with her out of the kit and attached it to the belt of her dress. It looked like an additional buckle, or perhaps a piece of stylish jewelry.

"I know Fuchs is with you," the dark-bearded man was saying, his voice flat and hard. "Don't try to tell me otherwise."

"But he's not," George replied for the umpteenth time. "Send a crew over here and inspect the ship."

"So that you can overpower them and cut my forces in half?" The man shook his head.

He's paranoid, Edith thought as she stepped to George's side, hoping the microcam was focused on the wall screen.

"Look," George said, straining to remain patient, "this ship isn't armed. The habitat isn't armed—"

"You provide weapons to the rock rats," said the intruder.

"No," George answered. "We provide mining equipment. If the rats get any weapons it's from logistics ships that the corporations send to the Belt."

"That's a lie. Where is Fuchs? My patience is running thin."

"He's not fookin' here!" George thundered.

In truth, Lars Fuchs was aboard *Halsey*, cruising past the orbit of Mars, nearly 200 million kilometers from Ceres. At his ship's present rate of acceleration, he would reach the *Chrysalis* habitat in a little more than three days.

He knew nothing of the circumstances unfolding at Ceres. As his ship traveled through the dark emptiness toward the Belt, Fuchs had plenty of time to think, and remember, and regret.

A failure. A total failure, he accused himself. Humphries killed my wife, destroyed my life, turned me into a homeless wandering exile, a Flying Dutchman doomed to spend my life drifting through this eternal night, living off whatever scraps I can beg or steal from others. I talk of vengeance, I fill my dreams with visions of hurting Humphries again and again. But it's all futile. All in vain. I'm a beaten man.

Amanda, he thought. My beautiful wife. I still love you, Amanda. I wish it had all turned out differently. I wish . . .

He squeezed his eyes shut and strove with all his might to drive the vision of her out of his thoughts. You're alive, he told himself sternly. You still exist, despite all he's done to you. Humphries had driven you into a life of piracy. He's made me into an outcast.

But I still live. That's my only true revenge on him. Despite everything he's done, despite everything he can do, I still live!

Aboard *Samarkand*, Harbin stared with dilated eyes at the floundering, fuming image of the red-bearded George Ambrose.

"You will produce the man Fuchs," Harbin said tightly, "or suffer the consequences. You have less than fifteen minutes remaining."

He cut the connection to *Elsinore*. Turning to his weapons technician, sitting at his console to Harbin's right, he asked, "Status of the lasers?"

"Sir, we have full power to all three of them."

"Ready to fire on my command?"

"Yessir."

"Good," said Harbin.

The executive officer, a blade-slim Japanese woman, suggested, "Perhaps we should send a boarding party to the ships parked around the habitat."

"To search for Fuchs?" Harbin asked lazily. He was starting to feel calm, almost tranquil. The injection must be wearing off, he thought. Too much stress burns the drug out of the bloodstream. I need another shot.

"If he's aboard any of those ships we can find him," the exec said.

"How many troops could we send, do you think? Six? Ten? A dozen?"

"Ten, certainly. Armed with sidearms and minigrenades. Those civilians in the ships wouldn't dare stand in their way."

Harbin felt just the slightest tendril of drowsiness creeping along his veins. It would be good to get a full night's sleep, he thought. Without dreams.

Aloud, he asked, "And what makes you think that there are nothing but civilians in those ships?"

The exec blinked rapidly, thinking, then replied, "Their manifests show—"

"Do you believe that if *Elsinore*, for example, were carrying a company of armed mercenaries they would show it on their manifest?"

She gave Harbin a strange look, but said nothing.

He went on, "Why do you think that red-bearded one is so anxious to have us search his ship? It's an obvious trap. He must have troops there waiting to pounce on us."

"That's—" The exec hesitated, then finished, "That's not likely, sir."

"No, not likely at all," Harbin said, grinning lopsidedly at her. "You would have done well against Hannibal."

"Sir?"

Harbin pushed himself out of the command chair. "I'm going to my quarters for a few minutes. Call me five minutes before their time is up."

"Yes, sir," said the exec.

Harbin knew something was wrong. If the drug is burning out of my system I ought to be feeling withdrawal symptoms, he thought. But I'm tired. Drowsy. Did I take the right stuff? I can't direct a battle in this condition.

Once he popped open the case that held his medications he focused blurrily on the vials still remaining, lined up in a neat row along the inside of the lid. Maybe I'm taking too much, he considered. Overdosing. But I can't stop now. Not until I've got Fuchs. I've got to get him.

He ran his fingertips over the smooth plastic cylinders of the medications. Something stronger. Just for the next half hour or so. Then I can relax and get a good long sleep. But right now I need something stronger. Much stronger.

HABITAT *CHRYSALIS*

Yannis Ritsos was the last of a long line of rebels and poets. Named after a famed Greek forebear, he had been born in Cyprus, lived through the deadly biowar that racked that tortured island, survived the fallout from the nuclear devastation of Israel, and worked his way across the Mediterranean to Spain where, like another Greek artist, he made a living for himself. Unlike El Greco, however, Yanni supported himself by running computer systems that translated languages. He even slipped some of his own poetry into the computers and had them translate his Greek into Spanish, German and English. He was not happy with the results.

He came to Ceres not as a poet, but as a rock rat. Determined to make a fortune in the Asteroid Belt, Yanni talked a fellow Greek businessman into allowing him to ride out to the Belt and try his hand at mining. He never got farther than the *Chrysalis* habitat, in orbit around Ceres. There he met and married the beautiful Ilona Mikvicius and, instead of going out on a mining ship, remained at Ceres and took a job in the habitat's communications center.

Sterile since his exposure to the nuclear fallout, totally bald for the same reason, Yanni longed to have a son and keep the family line going. He and Ilona were saving every penny they could scratch together to eventually pay for a cloning procedure. Ilona knew that bearing a cloned fetus was dangerous, but she loved Yanni so much that she was willing to risk it.

So Yannis Ritsos had everything to live for when Dorik Harbin's ship came to the *Chrysalis* habitat. He had suffered much, survived much, and endured. He felt that the future looked, if not exactly bright, at least promising. But he was wrong. And it was his own rebellious soul that put an end to his dreams.

•　　•　　•

"Sir," the comm tech called out, "someone aboard *Elsinore* is sending a message to Selene."

Harbin, fresh from a new injection of stimulant, turned to his weapons technician. "Slag her antennas," he commanded. "All of them."

The technician nodded and bent over his console.

In her compartment aboard *Elsinore*, Edith Elgin stopped in mid-sentence as the wall screen suddenly broke into jagged, hissing lines of hash.

"Something's wrong," she said to Big George. "The link's gone dead."

George frowned. "He doesn't want us talkin' to anybody. Prob'ly knocked out the antennas."

"You mean he attacked this ship?" Edith was shocked.

Nodding, George said, "And he'll do worse in another fifteen minutes if we don't produce Lars."

"But Fuchs isn't here!"

"Tell it to him."

Yannis Ritsos was alone on duty in *Chrysalis*'s communications center when Harbin's ultimatum came through.

It was a dull night shift; nothing but boringly routine chatter from the far-scattered ships of the miners and prospectors, and the coded telemetry sent routinely from their ships. With everything in the center humming along on automatic, and no one else in the comm center at this late hour, Yanni opened the computer subroutine he used to write poetry.

He had hardly written a line when the central screen suddenly lit up to show a dark-bearded man whose eyes glittered like polished obsidian.

"Attention, *Chrysalis*," the stranger said, in guttural English. "This is the attack vessel *Samarkand*. You are harboring the fugitive Lars Fuchs. You will turn him over to me in ten minutes or suffer the consequences of defiance."

Annoyed at being interrupted in his writing, Yanni thought it was some jokester in the habitat pulling a prank.

"Who is this?" he demanded. "Get off this frequency. It's reserved for incoming calls."

The dark-bearded face grew visibly angry. "This is your own death speaking to you if you don't turn Fuchs over to me."

"Lars Fuchs?" Yanni replied, only half believing his ears. "God knows where he is."

"I know where he is," the intruder snapped. "And if you don't surrender him to me I will destroy you."

Irritated, Yanni shot back, "Fuchs hasn't been here for years and he isn't here now. Go away and stop bothering me."

Harbin stared at the comm screen in *Samarkand's* bridge. They're stalling for time, he thought. They're trying to think of a way to hide Fuchs from me.

He took a deep breath, then said with deadly calm, "Apparently you don't believe me. Very well. Let me demonstrate my sincerity."

Turning to the weapons tech, Harbin ordered, "Chop one of the habitat's modules."

The man swallowed hard, his Adam's apple bobbing up and down. "Sir, there are civilians in those modules. Innocent men and women—"

"I gave you an order," Harbin snapped.

"But—"

"Get off the bridge! I'll take care of this myself."

The weapons tech glanced at the others on the bridge, looking for support.

"*Chrysalis* is unarmed, sir," said the pilot softly, almost in a whisper.

Cold fury gripped Harbin. "Get out. All of you," he said, his voice hard as ice. "I'll tend to this myself."

The entire bridge crew got up and swiftly went to the hatch, leaving Harbin alone in the command chair. He pecked furiously at the keyboards on his armrests, taking control of all the ship's systems.

Fools and weaklings, he raged to himself. They call themselves mercenaries but they're no good for anything except drawing their pay and pissing their pants in fear. *Chrysalis* is unarmed? I'll believe that when pigs fly. They're harboring Fuchs and they're stalling for time, trying to hide him, trying to lure me into sending my crew over there so they can ambush and slaughter them. I've seen ambushes, I've seen slaughters. They're not going to do that to me or my crew.

He called up the weapons display for the main screen, focused on the module of the *Chrysalis* closest to his ship and jabbed a thumb against the key that fired the lasers. Three jagged lines slashed across the thin skin of the module. Puffs of air glittered briefly like the puffs of a person's breath on a winter's day.

"Give me Fuchs," he said to the comm screen.

Yanni heard screams.

"What's going on?" he asked the empty communications center.

The face on the screen smiled coldly. "Give me Fuchs," he said.

Before Yanni could reply, the comm center's door burst open and a woman in bright coral coveralls rushed in. "Module eighteen's been ripped apart! They're all dead in there!"

Yanni gaped at her. She was from the life support crew, he could see by the color of her coveralls. And she was babbling so loud and fast that he could barely understand what she was saying.

"We're under attack!" she screamed. "Call for help!"

"Call who?" Yanni asked.

The executive officer stepped through the hatch into the bridge.

"Sir," she said crisply, her face a frozen expressionless mask, "I have a squad of twenty ready to board *Chrysalis* and search for Fuchs. They are armed with pistols and minigrenades, perfectly capable of dealing with whatever resistance the rock rats may try to offer."

Harbin stared at her. Why are these fools trying to undermine me? I know what to do. You kill your enemies. Kill them all. Men, women, children, dogs, cattle, all and every one of them. Burn down their village. Burn their crops. Blast the trees of their orchards with grenades. Leave nothing alive.

"Sir, did you hear me?" the exec asked, stepping closer to him.

Harbin swiveled the chair slightly toward her. "My hearing is perfect," he said calmly. "Tell your troops to stand down. I won't need them."

"They can search the habitat—"

"No," Harbin said softly, almost gently. "That won't be necessary. Why risk them when we can destroy the habitat from here?"

"But Fuchs—"

"Fuchs will die with the rest of the rock rats," Harbin said. He wanted to laugh. It was all so simple. You killed your enemies and then they will never be able to hurt you again. Why can't she see that? It's so logical, so beautifully clear.

He dismissed the executive officer and began to calmly, methodically, thoroughly destroy *Chrysalis* and everyone in it.

TORCH SHIP *ELSINORE*

The wall screen in Edith's compartment lit up to show the ship's captain. He looked shaken.

"You'd better come up to the bridge and see this," he said, his voice trembling. "They're destroying the habitat."

Big George boiled out into the passageway and charged up toward the bridge, Edith running hard behind him.

The captain and the two crew members on the bridge looked ashen, dazed.

Through the observation port Edith could see *Chrysalis*; three of its modules were ripped apart, chunks of metal and structure floating aimlessly. As she watched, invisible laser beams began slicing through another module. Air burst into the vacuum of space in glittering wisps of ice and dissipated in an eyeblink. All in silence: total, deadly, complete silence. Shapes came tumbling through one of the gouges torn in the module's skin. Bodies, Edith realized. Those are human bodies.

"The bloody fookin' bastard," George growled. He pounded both fists against the thick quartz of the observation port. "Bloody fookin' BASTARD!" he bellowed.

"Can't we do something?" Edith asked the captain.

He shook his head. "Not a thing."

"But there must be *something*! Call for help!"

"Our antennas are out. Even if we had Fuchs aboard or knew where he is, we wouldn't be able to tell him now."

Edith felt the strength ebbing out of her. I'm watching a thousand people dying. Being killed. George looked on the verge of tears. The captain was a white-faced statue.

"There's nothing we can do?" she asked.

"Nothing except wait," said the captain. "We're probably next."

● ● ●

Once he realized what was happening, Yanni bolted from the useless comm center and down the habitat's central passageway. Ilona! I've got to find Ilona! Their quarters were three modules down the passageway; at this time of night she should be in their bedroom, asleep.

He had to fight his way past a screaming mob at the module's air-lock, fighting to grab the pitifully few space suits stored there.

Why is this happening? Yanni asked himself as he ran toward the hatch that led to his wife. Why are they killing us?

Then the bulkhead ahead of him split apart and a blast of air like a whirlwind lifted him off his feet and out into the dark cold emptiness beyond. He had just time enough to understand that it didn't matter why or who or anything else. He was dead and Ilona was too.

The exec simply stood by Harbin's side as he carefully, precisely cut up the modules of the *Chrysalis* habitat. When the last unit was reduced to a broken shambles he looked up at her and saw fear in her eyes: fear and shock and disgust.

"There," Harbin said, lifting both hands from the armrest key-boards. "It's done. Fuchs is dead. I've accomplished my mission."

The exec seemed to stir, as if coming out of a trance. "Are . . ." Her voice caught, and she coughed slightly. "Are you certain he was in the habitat?" Then she added, "Sir?"

Harbin ignored her question. "They're all dead. Now we can go home and be safe."

He got up from the command chair slowly, almost leisurely, and stretched his arms up to the metal overhead.

"I'm rather tired. I'm going in for a nap. You have the con."

"Yes, sir," she said. As she watched him go to the hatch and duck through it, she thought about the ships in parking orbits around *Chrysalis*. Witnesses to the slaughter. And Fuchs might in reality be aboard any one of them.

She shook her head. I can testify that he did it on his own. He even dismissed the rest of us from the bridge. I returned to try to dissuade him, but he wouldn't listen to me. I couldn't disobey a superior officer, and I certainly couldn't overpower the man. He acted alone, she rehearsed her testimony. It was entirely his doing.

She slipped into the command chair and summoned the rest of the bridge crew. One of the ships parked nearby was an HSS logistics vessel. We'll refuel and reprovision from her, the exec thought, and then double back to Vesta.

Harbin saw several of his troopers idling in the galley, down at the end of the passageway from the bridge. Still in full armor, bristling with guns and grenades.

"Stand down," he called to them. "We won't be boarding the habitat." And he giggled. There's no habitat to board, he added silently.

As he entered his privacy compartment he seemed to recall that there was an incoming ship that might be harboring Fuchs. He shook his head foggily. No, that can't be. I killed Fuchs. I killed them all. All of them.

He tottered to the lav and splashed cold water on his face. Drug's wearing off, he realized. They wear off quicker and quicker. I must be building a tolerance to them. Have to tell the medics when we get back to Vesta. Need something stronger, better lasting.

He flopped onto his bed and closed his eyes. Sleep, he told himself. I need sleep. Without dreams. No dreaming. Please don't let me dream.

Doug Stavenger would not allow either Pancho or Humphries to leave his living room. They sat there and watched him desperately trying to reestablish contact with his wife, at Ceres.

Pancho offered him the full resources of Astro Corporation. After checking with her handheld she told Stavenger, "We've got three ships docked at Ceres. I've sent an order for them to report to me here."

"That will take an hour or more," Stavenger said.

Pancho shrugged. "No way I can make it happen faster."

Humphries remained on the sofa, silent, his eyes following Stavenger's every move, every gesture. Pancho felt contempt for the man. And a certain tiny speck of pity. Doug'll kill him, she knew, if anything's happened to his wife. All of Humphries's money can't help him one little iota now. Doug'll tear him apart.

They waited, Stavenger sending urgent, desperate messages to every ship in the Belt, Humphries sitting frozen with fear, Pancho churning the entire situation over and over in her mind, time and again, going over every detail she could think of, reliving the chain of events that had led to this place, this moment, this fearful point in spacetime.

"There's somebody else who oughtta be here," she said at last.

Stavenger froze the image on the wall screen and turned to look at her, obviously annoyed at her interruption.

"Yamagata," Pancho went on, despite his irritation. "Nobuhiko Yamagata should be here, if you want to stop this war."

Humphries stirred himself. "Just because his corporation provides mercenary troops—"

"He's behind this whole thing," Pancho said.

Stavenger gave her his full attention. "What do you mean?"

"Yamagata's the money behind the Nairobi base at the south pole," said Pancho. "He's been renting mercenaries to Astro and HSS, both."

"So?"

She jabbed a finger at Humphries. "You say you didn't set up that accident with the cable car?"

"I didn't," Humphries said.

"Then who else would've done it? Who's sittin' fat and happy while you and me bleed ourselves to death? Who stands to take over if Astro and HSS go broke?"

"Yamagata," Humphries breathed.

"Yamagata?" Stavenger echoed, still not believing it.

"Yamagata," Pancho insisted.

Stavenger turned back to his wall screen. "Phone, get Nobuhiko Yamagata. Top priority."

Leeza Chaptal was back in her space suit, but this time it was covered in slick, shining oil. Still, she was trembling inside it as the airlock hatch swung open.

The metal cladding of the circular shaft was obviously eaten away down almost to the level of her eyes. But no further, she saw. In the twelve hours since she'd last been in the shaft, the nanomachines had progressed only a meter or so down the shaft.

"I think they've stopped," she said into her helmet microphone.

"How can you be sure?" came the reply in her earphones.

Leeza unhooked the hand laser from her equipment belt. "I'm going to mark a line," she said, thumbing the laser's switch. A thin uneven line burned into the steel coating. She realized that her hands were shaking badly.

"Okay," she said, backing through the hatch and pushing it shut. "I'll come back in an hour and see if they've chewed past my mark."

She clumped in the ungainly suit back to the next hatch and rapped on it. "Fill the tunnel with air and open up," she ordered. "I've got to pee."

"They're leaving," Edith saw.

Still standing in the bridge of *Elsinore* with the captain and Big George, she saw the ship that had destroyed the habitat accelerate away from the area, dwindling into the eternal darkness, its rocket thrusters glowing hotly.

"Running away from the scene of the crime," said the captain.

George said nothing, but Edith could see the fury burning in his eyes. Suddenly he shook himself like a man coming out of a trance. Or a nightmare.

He started for the hatch.

"Where are you going?" the captain asked.

"Airlock," George replied, over his shoulder. Squeezing his bulk through the hatch, he said, "Space suits. Gotta see if anybody's left alive in *Chrysalis.*"

Edith knew there couldn't be any survivors. But George is right, she thought. We've got to check.

And she stirred herself, realizing that she had to record this disaster, this atrocity. I've got to get this all on camera so the whole human race can see what's happened here.

T hree days after the *Chrysalis* atrocity, the conference took place in Doug Stavenger's personal office, up in the tower suite that housed Selene's governing administrators and bureaucrats. It was very small, very private, and extremely well-guarded.

Only four people sat at the circular table in the center of the office: Pancho, Humphries, Nobuhiko Yamagata and Douglas Stavenger himself. No aides, no assistants, no news reporters or anyone else. Selene security officers were stationed outside the door and patrolled the corridors. The entire area had been swept for electronic bugs.

Once the four of them were seated, Stavenger began, "This meeting will be held in strict privacy. Only the four of us will know what we say."

The others nodded.

"None of us will leave this room until we have come to an agreement to stop this war," Stavenger added, his face totally grim. "There will be no exceptions and no excuses. There's a lavatory through that door," he pointed, "but the only way out of here is through the door to the corridor and no one is leaving until I'm satisfied that we've reached a workable understanding."

Humphries bristled. "What gives you the right to—"

"Several thousand dead bodies scattered across the Asteroid Belt," Stavenger snapped. "I'm representing *them*. You are going to stop this damned war or you are going to starve to death right here at this table. There is no third option."

Yamagata smiled uneasily. "I came here voluntarily, at your request, Mr. Stavenger. This is no way to treat a guest."

Gesturing in Pancho's direction, Stavenger replied, "Ms. Lane was your guest at the Nairobi base at Shackleton crater, wasn't she? And you damned near killed her."

Nobuhiko's brows knit momentarily. Then he said, "I could call for help, you know."

Without any change in his expression, Stavenger said, "There's no way to get a message out of this room. I've had it shielded. Your hand-helds won't get a signal past these walls."

Pancho leaned back in her chair and stretched her legs beneath the table. "Okay, then. Let's start talking."

Harbin had spent the three days since the attack on *Chrysalis* drifting in and out of a drug-induced stupor. His executive officer ran the ship while he slept and dreamed eerily distorted fantasies that always ended in blood and death.

By the time they reached Vesta, he had run out of medications and was beginning to sober up.

He was washing his bearded, pouchy-eyed face when someone tapped at his door.

"Enter," he called, mopping his face with a towel.

The exec slid the door back and stepped into his compartment. Harbin realized the bed was a sweaty, tangled mess, and the cramped compartment smelled like the hot insides of an overused gym shoe.

"We're about to enter a parking orbit around Vesta, sir," she said stiffly.

"The base is back in operation?" he asked. As he spoke the words he realized that he didn't care if the base was operating again. It meant nothing to him, one way or the other.

"Yes, sir. The nanomachine attack was limited to the surface installations, for the most part. No one was killed or even injured."

Harbin knew from the look on her face that there was more to come. "What else?"

"I have received orders to relieve you of command. Mr. Humphries personally called and demanded to know who was responsible for the destruction of the *Chrysalis* habitat. When he found out it was you he went into a rage. Apparently he knows you from an earlier experience."

Harbin felt as if he were watching this scene from someplace far away. As if he was no longer in his body, but floating free, drifting through nothingness, alone, untouched, untouchable.

"Go on," he heard himself say.

"He wants you brought to Selene to stand trial for war crimes," the exec said, her words stiff, brittle.

"War crimes."

"The *Chrysalis* massacre. He also said that you murdered an employee of his, several years ago."

"I see."

"I've been ordered to relieve you of command and confine you to your quarters. Sir."

Harbin almost smiled at her. "Then you should follow your orders."

She turned and grasped the door handle. Before she stepped through the doorway, though, she said, "It's on all the news nets. They've been playing it for the past two days."

She left him, sliding the door shut. There was no lock on the door. It didn't matter, Harbin thought. Even if it were locked the accordion-fold was so flimsy he could push through it easily. If he wanted to.

Harbin stood in his musty, messy compartment for a moment, then shrugged. *The moving finger writes*, he thought. *Nor all thy tears wash out a word of it.*

Why can't I feel anything? He asked himself. I'm like a block of wood. A statue of ice. The *Chrysalis* massacre, she called it. Massacre?

Shrugging his shoulders, he told the wall screen to display a news broadcast.

A woman's shocked, hollow-eyed face appeared on the screen, her name—Edie Elgin—spelled out beneath her image. She wore no makeup, her hair was disheveled, her voice little more than a shaky whisper.

". . . been working for several hours now," she was saying, "trying to determine if there are any survivors. So far, none have been found."

The scene suddenly changed to show the shattered remains of the *Chrysalis* habitat: broken, crumpled cylinders of metal glinting against the blackness of space, jagged pieces floating nearby, bodies drifting.

And Edie Elgin's voice, choked with sorrow and horror, nearly sobbing, was saying, "Nearly eleven hundred people were living in the habitat when it was attacked. They had no weapons, no defenses. They were methodically slaughtered by their unidentified attacker."

Harbin sank down onto his bed, staring at the screen. The icy armor that had surrounded him began to melt away. For the first time in many days he felt an emotion. He felt pain.

"Yamagata Corporation is not responsible for the *Chrysalis* tragedy," Nobuhiko said sternly. "Our employees were working under a contract with Humphries Space Systems."

"I never ordered them to attack the habitat," Humphries replied, with some heat. "I just wanted them to find Fuchs."

Pancho said, "Lars is somewhere in the Belt by now. You'll never find him."

"Yes I will. He tried to kill me!"

"That wasn't my doing," Pancho said.

Stavenger slapped a palm on the table, silencing them. "I don't care who did what to whom. The past is over and done with. We're here to prevent this kind of thing from happening again. I want an end to this fighting."

"Sure," Humphries said easily. "I'm willing to stop it. But I want Fuchs's head on a platter."

"What you want," said Pancho, "is total control of the Belt and all its resources."

"Isn't that what you want, too?" Humphries countered. Turning to Yamagata, he added, "And you, as well?"

Keeping his face expressionless, Nobuhiko replied, "Now that you have introduced nanomachine processing to mining the asteroids, there is good economic sense in having one corporation establish a monopoly in the Belt."

"But which corporation?" Humphries asked.

The three of them stared at each other.

"Wait a minute," Stavenger interrupted. "You're all forgetting something that's important."

They turned toward him.

"There's more to mining the asteroids than making profits," he said. "More involved in this than acquiring power."

Humphries smirked. "I can't imagine what it could be."

But Pancho's face lit up. "It's what Dan Randolph wanted in the first place! Back when we made the flight out to the Belt in the old *Starpower!*"

"And what was that?" Nobuhiko asked.

"To help the people on Earth," said Pancho. "Help 'em recover from the greenhouse cliff. Bring 'em the raw materials for rebuilding. Bring 'em the fuels for fusion power generators. *That's* what Dan started out to do!"

"And that's what you've all lost sight of," said Stavenger.

"Well, that's our principal market, I agree," Humphries said. "But that doesn't mean—"

Pancho cut him off. "We oughtta be selling the ores from the asteroids at the lowest possible price. And the fusion fuels, too."

"And building more solar power satellites," Stavenger added.

"To help rebuild Japan," Yamagata murmured.

"To help rebuild the world," said Pancho.

Stavenger smiled gently. "And to help expand human habitats on the Moon and elsewhere, in deep space."

"We can do that!" Pancho agreed eagerly.

"But not with the three of you cutting each other's throats," Stavenger said.

"Only one corporation should manage the resources of the Belt," Yamagata said firmly. "Competition is pointless, once nanoprocessing reduces the prices of asteroidal ores."

"Not ores," Humphries reminded him. "The nanomachines will produce pure metals."

"And minerals," Pancho added.

Humphries gave her an exaggerated bow of his head.

"But which corporation will gain the monopoly?" Yamagata asked.

"None of us," said Pancho.

"What?" Humphries snapped. "It's got to be one of us. Nobody else has the capability."

"Selene does," Pancho said, staring straight at Stavenger.

Looking back at her, he admitted, "I've been thinking that way, too."

Humphries exploded, "If you think you're going to muscle me out of what's rightfully mine—"

Pancho waved him down. "Don't pop your cork, Martin. I know how we can do this and keep our shareholders happy."

"I don't see how that can be done," Humphries groused.

"Nor do I," Nobuhiko added.

Grinning, Pancho clasped her hands together and leaned them on the conference table. "It's simple. We each sign a contract with Selene for them to operate our asteroid business. We get the profits, minus a small percentage to Selene."

"A manager's fee," said Stavenger.

"Right," Pancho agreed. "Selene manages our operations and sets the market prices for the asteroidal products. The three of us just sit back and collect the profits."

Yamagata took in a deep breath. Then, "I presume that Selene will set the prices as low as possible."

"Very likely," Stavenger said. "Those people on Earth need the resources. We won't put power trips ahead of the people's needs."

"Power trips?" Humphries snarled. "You'll have all the power."

"That's right," Stavenger replied amiably. "Selene will be the arbiter for the rest of the solar system. No more competition. No more killing. No more war."

"I don't like it," said Humphries.

Yamagata asked, "Can Selene be trusted with such power?"

"Can anyone else in this room?" Stavenger retorted.

A heavy silence fell across the conference table.

Finally Pancho said, "I'm willing to try it—on a five-year time limit. That way, if we're not happy with Selene's performance when the time's up, we don't have to renew the contract."

"But only if two of the three corporations refuse to renew," said Stavenger. "No single corporation can back out of the contract, it will take a majority vote."

"Agreed," said Pancho.

"I would like to consult my people back on Earth before agreeing," Yamagata said.

"I still don't like it," Humphries grumbled.

"C'mon, Martin," Pancho reached over and shook him slightly by the shoulder. "It'll make life a lot easier for you. You'll still be the richest sumbitch in the solar system. All you'll have to do is sit back and pull in the profits. No more worries."

"No more slaughters," Stavenger said, his face still deadly serious. "Regardless of your intentions, Martin, it was your orders that led to the *Chrysalis* massacre."

"That would never hold up in a court of law."

"Don't be too certain of that. War crimes courts can be very harsh."

Humphries leaned back in his chair, his mouth a tight line, his eyes closed. At last he sat up straight and asked Stavenger, "Will you still exile me?"

Stavenger smiled. "No, I don't think that would be necessary, Martin. You can rebuild your home down below. Besides, I rather think I'd like to have you close by, where I can keep an eye on you."

FINAL ADJUSTMENTS

The three-second lag in communications between Earth and the Moon did not irritate Nobuhiko Yamagata. He found it useful; it gave him a few moments to think before responding to his father.

Saito's face grew solemn when Nobu told him of the tentative agreement they had hammered out.

"But this will keep Yamagata from moving back into space operations," the older man complained.

"Not entirely," Nobuhiko replied. "We will gain only a small share in the profits from asteroidal mining, true enough. But the price for asteroidal resources will become so low that we will be able to continue our rebuilding programs and invest in new space ventures, as well."

"Lower our costs," Saito muttered. "H'mm. I see."

In the end, the elder Yamagata agreed that his son's best course was to accept the agreement. By the time Nobuhiko ended his conversation with his father, Saito was already talking about building solar power satellites in orbit about the planet Mercury.

"The sunlight is much more intense that close to the Sun," he said. "Perhaps I will leave this dreary monastery and lead the Mercury project myself."

Soaked with well-earned perspiration, Martin Humphries held Tatiana Oparin's naked body close to his own and contemplated his future.

"Maybe I won't rebuild the house," he said, gazing up at the darkened ceiling of the hotel bedroom. It sparkled with a thousand fluorescent flecks of light, like stars on a summery evening back on Earth.

"Not rebuild it?" Tatiana murmured drowsily.

"I could go back to Connecticut. That's where my boys are living. The runt's nothing much, but Alex is turning into a real son. Just like his father." He laughed at his private joke.

"You'd leave the Moon?"

"Just for a visit. To see the kids. And there's other family still down there. Can't take too much of them."

"But you'll still live here at Selene, won't you?"

"Maybe. Maybe not. Hell Crater's an interesting place. Maybe I'll buy into one of the casinos there. Be a playboy instead of a captain of industry. Might make a nice change for me."

"You would make an excellent playboy," said Tatiana, snuggling closer to him.

Humphries laughed in the darkness. This is a lot easier than running a corporation, he thought. Let the others do the work. I'll spend the profits.

Stavenger spent much of his evening sending a long, detailed report to his wife about the peace conference.

"I think it could work," he concluded. "I think we can make it work."

Edith was on her way back to him, he knew. She had survived the atrocity at Ceres unscathed, physically. Her news coverage, complete with computer-graphic simulations of the actual attack based on her eye-witness description, had been the biggest news event since the green-house floods had first struck. There was already talk of a Pulitzer for her.

None of that mattered to Stavenger. Edith's all right, he thought. She's on her way back. She wasn't hurt. It was an emotional trauma for her, but she wasn't physically harmed. She'll be all right. I'll help her recover.

Edith's news reporting had been the key to making the peace agreement, Stavenger realized. With the *Chrysalis* massacre in full view of every person in the solar system, Humphries and the others had no choice except to come to some sort of an agreement to end the fighting.

Now comes the hard part, Stavenger told himself. Now we have to make the agreement work.

Pancho was packing her travel bag when the call from Jake Wanamaker came through. She invited him to come to her residence.

By the time he buzzed at the front door, Pancho was packed and ready to go. She carried her travel bag to the door and let it drop to the floor, then opened the door to let Wanamaker in. In the languid lunar gravity, the bag thumped on the carpeting as Wanamaker stepped into the entryway.

"Going somewhere?" he asked.

"Yep," said Pancho, ushering him into the sitting room. "But I got lots of time. Want a drink?"

The room's décor was set to the Mediterranean isle of Capri: steep, green-clad cliffs studded with little white-walled villages clinging here and there, and the placid sea glittering beneath a warm Sun.

Wanamaker asked for a bourbon and water. Pancho had the auto-bar pour her an ice-cold *lemoncello*, to go with the scenery.

She gestured him to a comfortably wide armchair, and perched herself on the smaller upholstered chair next to it. They clinked glasses. Pancho noticed that Jake took a healthy swig of his bourbon, rather than a polite little sip.

"What's on your mind?" Pancho asked.

He gave her a sheepish grin. "Looks like I'm out of a job."

"Guess so," she said. "Your contract runs to the end of the year, though."

"I don't feel right taking money for doing nothing."

Pancho considered this for a moment, then heard herself say, "So why don't you come with me? Be my bodyguard."

His brows shot up. "Bodyguard? Where are you going?"

With a shrug, she admitted, "Dunno. Just want to get away from all this. I'm going to resign from Astro Corporation."

"Resign?"

"Yep. I sorta fell into this job by accident. Took me a lotta years to realize I don't really want to be a corporate executive."

"So you're going to travel?"

"For a bit. My sister's out at the Saturn habitat. Thought maybe I'd have a look-see out there."

"You don't need a bodyguard for that," Wanamaker said.

Pancho grinned at him. "Okay then, I'll be your bodyguard. How's that?"

Realization dawned on Wanamaker's face. He broke into a wide grin.

Shanidar was in orbit around Vesta. There was a delay getting the crew transferred down to the base because most of the surface facilities had been eaten away by the nanomachine attack. Just as well, Harbin thought. He was in no hurry to leave the ship.

He had remained in his quarters, as ordered by the executive officer. He had not slept for several days. Without his medications, sleep brought dreams, and Harbin did not like what his dreams showed him.

He replayed the news broadcasts of his attack on *Chrysalis* over and over. Each time it seemed worse to him, more horrifying, more damning.

What does life hold for me now? he asked himself. They'll send out some troops to arrest me. Then a trial, probably back on Earth. And then what? A firing squad? More likely a lethal injection. Or perhaps life in prison.

I can save them the trouble, he thought.

His mind resolved, Harbin slid open the pleated door to the passageway and headed toward the rear of the ship, away from the bridge. I've got to do this quickly, he knew, before they realize I've left my quarters.

He went straight to the weapons locker, unattended now that the ship was in orbit and the crew waiting to transfer to their base. The grenade storage bins were locked, but Harbin knew all the combinations. He tapped out the proper sequence and the lock clicked open.

A small one, he told himself. You don't want to damage the ship too much.

A minigrenade, hardly larger than his thumbnail. Enough explosive in it, however, to blast open an airlock hatch. Or something else.

"Hey, what're you doing?"

Harbin whirled to see one of his crewmen coming down the passageway.

"Oh, it's you, Captain." The man looked suddenly embarrassed. "Sir, eh—you're supposed to be confined to your quarters."

"It's all right, trooper," Harbin said reassuringly. "Nothing to worry about. *For all the Sin wherewith the Face of Man is blackened . . .*"

"Sir?" the crewman asked, puzzled. Then he saw the minigrenade in Harbin's hand. His eyes went wide.

"Nothing," Harbin muttered. He flicked the grenade's fuse with his thumbnail as he spun around to place his body between the crewman and the blast. The explosion nearly tore him in half.

What do you mean, Dorn's not available?" Humphries shouted at the blank phone screen. "Get me the officer on watch aboard the Humphries Eagle."

"All exterior communications are inoperable at the present time," replied the phone.

"That's impossible!"

"All exterior communications are inoperable at the present time," the phone repeated, unperturbed.

Humphries stared at the empty screen, then turned slowly toward Elverda Apacheta. "He's cut us off. We're trapped in here."

Elverda felt the chill of cold metal clutching at her. Perhaps Dorn is a madman, she thought. Perhaps he is my death, personified.

"We've got to do something!" Humphries nearly shouted.

Elverda rose shakily to her feet. "There is nothing that we can do, for the moment. I am going to my quarters and take a nap. I believe that Dorn, or Harbin or whatever his identity is, will call on us when he is ready to."

"And do what?"

"Show us the artifact," she replied, silently adding, I hope.

Legally, the artifact and the entire asteroid belonged to Humphries Space Systems. It had been discovered by a family—husband, wife, and two sons, ages five and three—that made a living from searching out iron-nickel asteroids and selling the mining rights to the big corporations. They filed their claim to this unnamed asteroid, together with a preliminary description of its ten-kilometer-wide shape, its orbit within the asteroid belt, and a sample analysis of its surface composition.

Six hours after their original transmission reached the commodities market computer network on Earth—while a fairly spirited bidding was going on among four major corporations for the asteroid's mineral rights—a new message arrived at the headquarters of the International Astronautical Authority, in London. The message was garbled, fragmentary, obviously made in great haste and at fever excitement. There was an artifact of some sort in a cavern deep inside the asteroid.

One of the faceless bureaucrats buried deep within the IAA's multi-layered organization sent an immediate message to an employee of Humphries Space Systems. The bureaucrat retired hours later, richer than he had any right to expect, while Martin Humphries personally contacted the prospectors and bought the asteroid outright for enough money to end their prospecting days forever. By the time the decision-makers in the IAA realized that an alien artifact had been discovered they were faced with a fait accompli: the artifact, and the asteroid in which it resided, were the personal property of the richest man in the solar system.

Martin Humphries was something of an egomaniac. But he was no fool. Graciously he allowed the IAA to organize a team of scientists who would inspect this first specimen of alien intelligence. Even more graciously, Humphries offered to ferry the scientific investigators all the long way to the asteroid at his own expense. He made only one demand, and the IAA could hardly refuse him. He insisted that he see this artifact himself before the scientists were allowed to view it.

And he brought along the solar system's most honored and famous artist. To appraise the artifact's worth as an art object, he claimed. To determine how much he could deduct from his corporate taxes by donating the thing to the IAA, said his enemies. But over the days of their voyage to the asteroid, Elverda came to the conclusion that buried deep beneath his ruthless business persona was an eager little boy who was tremendously excited at having found a new toy. A toy he intended to possess for himself. An art object, created by alien hands.

For an art object was what the artifact seemed to be. The family of prospectors continued to send back vague, almost irrational reports of what the artifact looked like. The reports were worthless. No two descriptions matched. If the man and woman were to be believed, the artifact did nothing but sit in the middle of a rough-hewn cavern. But they described it differently with every report they sent. It glowed with light. It was darker than deep space. It was a statue of some sort. It was formless. It overwhelmed the senses. It was small enough almost to pick up in one hand. It made the children laugh happily. It frightened their parents.

When they tried to photograph it, their transmissions showed nothing but blank screens. Totally blank.

As Humphries listened to their maddening reports and waited impatiently for the IAA to organize its handpicked team of scientists, he ordered his security manager to get a squad of hired personnel to the asteroid as quickly as possible. From corporate facilities at the Jupiter station and the moons of Mars, from three separate outposts among the Asteroid Belt itself, Humphries Space Systems efficiently brought together a brigade of experienced mercenary security troops. They reached the asteroid long before anyone else could, and were under orders to make certain that no one was allowed onto the asteroid before Martin Humphries himself reached it.

"The time has come."

Elverda woke slowly, painfully, like a swimmer struggling for the air and light of the surface. She had been dreaming of her childhood, of the village where she had grown up, the distant snowcapped Andes, the warm night breezes that spoke of love.

"The time has come."

It was Dorn's deep voice, whisper-soft. Startled, she flashed her eyes open. She was alone in the room, but Dorn's image filled the phone screen by her bed. The numbers glowing beneath the screen showed that it was indeed time.

"I am awake now," she said to the screen.

"I will be at your door in fifteen minutes," Dorn said. "Will that be enough time for you to prepare yourself?"

"Yes, plenty." The days when she needed time for selecting her clothing and arranging her appearance were long gone.

"In fifteen minutes, then."

"Wait," she blurted. "Can you see me?"

"No. Visual transmission must be keyed manually."

"I see."

"I do not."

A joke? Elverda sat up on the bed as Dorn's image winked out. Is he capable of humor?

She shrugged out of the shapeless coveralls she had worn to bed, took a quick shower, and pulled her best caftan from the travel bag. It was a deep midnight blue, scattered with glittering silver stars. Elverda had made the floor-length gown herself, from fabric woven by her mother long ago. She had painted the stars from her memory of what they had looked like from her native village.

As she slid back her front door she saw Dorn marching down the corridor with Humphries beside him. Despite his slightly longer legs, Humphries seemed to be scampering like a child to keep up with Dorn's steady, stolid steps.

"I demand that you reinstate communications with my ship," Humphries was saying, his voice echoing off the corridor walls. "I'll dock your pay for every minute this insubordination continues!"

"It is a security measure," Dorn said calmly, without turning to look at the man. "It is for your own good."

"My own good? Who in hell are you to determine what my own good might be?"

Dorn stopped three paces short of Elverda, made a stiff little bow to her, and only then turned to face his employer.

"Sir: I have seen the artifact. You have not."

"And that makes you better than me?" Humphries almost snarled the words. "Holier, maybe?"

"No," said Dorn. "Not holier. Wiser."

Humphries started to reply, then thought better of it.

"Which way do we go?" Elverda asked in the sudden silence.

Dorn pointed with his prosthetic hand. "Down," he replied. "This way."

The corridor abruptly became a rugged tunnel again, with lights fastened at precisely spaced intervals along the low ceiling. Elverda watched Dorn's half-human face as the pools of shadow chased the highlights glinting off the etched metal, like the Moon racing through its phases every half-minute, over and again.

Humphries had fallen silent as they followed the slanting tunnel downward into the heart of the rock. Elverda heard only the clicking of his shoes at first, but by concentrating she was able to make out the softer footfalls of Dorn's padded boots and even the whisper of her own slippers.

The air seemed to grow warmer, closer. *Or is it my own anticipation?* She glanced at Humphries; perspiration beaded his upper lip. The man radiated tense expectation. Dorn glided a few steps ahead of them. He did not seem to be hurrying, yet he was now leading them down the tunnel, like an ancient priest leading two new acolytes—or sacrificial victims.

The tunnel ended in a smooth wall of dull metal.

"We are here."

"Open it up," Humphries demanded.

"It will open itself," replied Dorn. He waited a heartbeat, then added, "Now."

And the metal slid up into the rock above them as silently as if it were a curtain made of silk.

None of them moved. Then Dorn slowly turned toward the two of them and gestured with his human hand.

"The artifact lies twenty-two point nine meters beyond this point. The tunnel narrows and turns to the right. The chamber is large enough to accommodate only one person at a time, comfortably."

"Me first!" Humphries took a step forward.

Dorn stopped him with an upraised hand. The prosthetic hand. "I feel it my duty to caution you—"

Humphries tried to push the hand away; he could not budge it.

"When I first crossed this line, I was a soldier. After I saw the artifact I gave up my life."

"And became a self-styled priest. So what?"

"The artifact can change you. I thought it best that there be no witnesses to your first viewing of it, except for this gifted woman whom you have brought with you. When you first see it, it can be—traumatic."

Humphries's face twisted with a mixture of anger and disgust. "I'm not a mercenary killer. I don't have anything to be afraid of."

Dorn let his hand drop to his side with a faint whine of miniaturized servomotors.

"Perhaps not," he murmured, so low that Elverda barely heard it.

Humphries shouldered his way past the cyborg. "Stay here," he told Elverda. "You can see it when I come back."

He hurried down the tunnel, footsteps staccato.

Then silence.

Elverda looked at Dorn. The human side of his face seemed utterly weary.

"You have seen the artifact more than once, haven't you?"

"Fourteen times," he answered.

"It has not harmed you in any way, has it?"

He hesitated, then replied, "It has changed me. Each time I see it, it changes me more."

"You . . . you really are Dorik Harbin?"

"I was."

"Those people of the Chrysalis . . . ?"

"DORIK HARBIN KILLED THEM ALL. YES. THERE IS NO EXCUSE FOR IT, NO PARDON. IT WAS THE ACT OF A MONSTER."

"But why?"

"Monsters do monstrous things. Dorik Harbin ingested psychotropic drugs to increase his battle prowess. Afterward, when the battle drugs cleared from his bloodstream and he understood what he had done, Dorik Harbin held a grenade against his chest and set it off."

"Oh my god," Elverda whimpered.

"He was not allowed to die, however. Yamagata Corporation's medical specialists rebuilt his body and he was given a false identity. For many years he lived a sham of life, hiding from the authorities, hiding from his own guilt. He no longer had the courage to kill himself; the pain of his first attempt was far stronger than his own self-loathing. Then he was hired to come to this place. Dorik Harbin looked upon the artifact for the first time, and his true identity emerged at last."

Elverda heard a scuffling sound, like feet dragging, staggering. Martin Humphries came into view, tottering, leaning heavily against the wall of the tunnel, slumping as if his legs could no longer hold him.

"No man . . . no one . . ." He pushed himself forward and collapsed into Dorn's arms.

"Destroy it!" he whispered harshly, spittle dribbling down his chin. "Destroy this whole damned piece of rock! Wipe it out of existence!"

"What is it?" Elverda asked. "What did you see?"

Dorn lowered him to the ground gently. Humphries's feet scrabbled against the rock as if he were trying to run away. Sweat covered his face, soaked his shirt.

"It's . . . beyond . . ." he babbled. "More . . . than anyone can . . . nobody could stand it . . ."

Elverda sank to her knees beside him. "What has happened to him?" She looked up at Dorn, who knelt on Humphries's other side.

"The artifact."

Humphries suddenly ranted, "They'll find out about me! Everyone will know! It's got to be destroyed! Nuke it! Blast this whole asteroid to bits!" His fists windmilled in the air, his eyes were wild.

"I tried to warn him," Dorn said as he held Humphries's shoulders down, the man's head in his lap. "I tried to prepare him for it."

"What did he see?" Elverda's heart was pounding; she could hear it thundering in her ears. "What is it? What did you see?"

Dorn shook his head slowly. "I cannot describe it. I doubt that anyone could describe it—except, perhaps, an artist: a person who has trained herself to see the truth."

"The prospectors—they saw it. Even their children saw it."

"Yes. When I arrived here they had spent eighteen days in the chamber. They left it only when the chamber closed itself. They ate and slept and returned here, as if hypnotized."

"It did not hurt them, did it?"

"They were emaciated, dehydrated. It took a dozen of my strongest men to remove them to my ship. Even the children fought us."

"But—how could . . ." Elverda's voice faded into silence. She looked at the brightly lit tunnel. Her breath caught in her throat.

"Destroy it," Humphries mumbled. "Destroy it before it destroys us! Don't let them find out. They'll know, they'll know, they'll all know." He began to sob uncontrollably.

"You do not have to see it," Dorn said to Elverda. "You can return to your ship and leave this place."

Leave, urged a voice inside her head. Run away. Live out what's left of your life and let it go.

Then she heard her own voice say, as if from a far distance, "I've come such a long way."

"It will change you," he warned.

"Will it release me from life?"

Dorn glanced down at Humphries, still muttering darkly, then returned his gaze to Elverda.

"It will change you," he repeated.

Elverda forced herself to her feet. Leaning one hand against the warm rock wall to steady herself, she said, "I will see it. I must."

"Yes," said Dorn. "I understand."

She looked down at him, still kneeling with Humphries's head resting *in his lap. Dorn's electronic eye glowed red in the shadows. His human eye was hidden in darkness.*

He said, "I believe your people say, Vaya con Dios."

Elverda smiled at him. She had not heard that phrase in forty years. "Yes. You too. Vaya con Dios." *She turned and stepped across the faint groove where the metal door had met the floor.*

The tunnel sloped downward only slightly. It turned sharply to the right, Elverda saw, just as Dorn had told them. The light seemed brighter beyond the turn, pulsating almost, like a living heart.

She hesitated a moment before making that final turn. What lay beyond? What difference, she answered herself. You have lived so long that you have emptied life of all its purpose. But she knew she was lying to herself. Her life was devoid of purpose because she herself had made it that way. She had spurned love; she had even rejected friendship when it had been offered. Still, she realized that she wanted to live. Desperately, she wanted to continue living no matter what.

Yet she could not resist the lure. Straightening her spine, she stepped boldly around the bend in the tunnel.

The light was so bright it hurt her eyes. She raised a hand to her brow to shield them and the intensity seemed to decrease slightly, enough to make out the faint outline of a form, a shape, a person . . .

Elverda gasped with recognition. A few meters before her, close enough to reach and touch, her mother sat on the sweet grass beneath the warm summer sun, gently rocking her baby and crooning softly to it.

Mamma! she cried silently. Mamma. The baby—Elverda herself— looked up into her mother's face and smiled.

And the mother was Elverda, a young and radiant Elverda, smiling down at the baby she had never had, tender and loving as she had never been.

Something gave way inside her. There was no pain; rather, it was as if a pain that had throbbed sullenly within her for too many years to count suddenly faded away. As if a wall of implacable ice finally melted and let the warm waters of life flow through her.

Elverda sank to the floor, crying, gushing tears of understanding and relief and gratitude. Her mother smiled at her.

"I love you, Mamma," she whispered. "I love you."

Her mother nodded and became Elverda herself once more. Her baby made a gurgling laugh of pure happiness, fat little feet waving in the air.

The image wavered, dimmed, and slowly faded into emptiness. Elverda sat on the bare rock floor in utter darkness, feeling a strange serenity and understanding warming her soul.

"Are you all right?"

Dorn's voice did not startle her. She had been expecting him to come to her.

"The chamber will close itself in another few minutes," he said. "We will have to leave."

Elverda took his offered hand and rose to her feet. She felt strong, fully in control of herself.

The tunnel outside the chamber was empty.

"Where is Humphries?"

"I sedated him and then called in a medical team to take him back to his ship."

"He wants to destroy the artifact," Elverda said.

"That will not be possible," said Dorn. "I will bring the IAA scientists here from the ship before Humphries awakes and recovers. Once they see the artifact they will not allow it to be destroyed. Humphries may own the asteroid, but the IAA will exert control over the artifact."

"The artifact will affect them—strangely."

"No two of them will be affected in the same manner," said Dorn. "And none of them will permit it to be damaged in any way."

"Humphries will not be pleased with you, once he recovers."

He gestured up the tunnel, and they began to walk back toward their quarters.

"Nor with you," Dorn said. "We both saw him babbling and blubbering like a baby."

"What could he have seen?"

"What he most feared. His whole life has been driven by fear, poor man."

"What secrets he must be hiding!"

"He hid them from himself. The artifact showed him his own true nature."

"No wonder he wants it destroyed."

"He cannot destroy the artifact, but he will certainly want to destroy us. Once he recovers his composure he will want to wipe out the witnesses who saw his reaction to it."

Elverda knew that Dorn was right. She watched his face as they passed beneath the lights, watched the glint of the etched metal, the warmth of the human flesh.

"You knew that he would react this way, didn't you?" she asked.

"No one could be as rich as he is without having demons driving him. He looked into his own soul and recognized himself for the first time in his life."

"You planned it this way!"

"Perhaps I did," he said. "Perhaps the artifact did it for me."

"How could—"

"It is a powerful experience. After I had seen it a few times I felt it was offering me . . ." he hesitated, then spoke the word, "salvation."

Elverda saw something in his face that Dorn had not let show before. She stopped in the shadows between overhead lights. Dorn turned to face her, half machine, standing in the rough tunnel of bare rock.

"You have had your own encounter with it," he said. "You understand now how it can transform you."

"Yes," said Elverda. "I understand."

"After a few times, I came to the realization that there are thousands of my fellow mercenaries, killed in engagements all through the asteroid belt, still drifting where they were killed. Miners and prospectors, as well. Floating forever in space, alone, unattended, ungrieved for."

"Thousands of mercenaries?"

"The Chrysalis massacre was not the only bloodletting in the Belt," said Dorn. "There have been many battles out here. Wars that we paid for with our blood."

"Thousands?" Elverda repeated. "Thousands of dead. Could it have been so brutal?"

"Men like Humphries know. They start the wars, and people like me fight them. Exiles, never allowed to return to Earth again once we take the mercenary's pay."

"All those men—killed."

Dorn nodded. "And women. The artifact made me see that it was my duty to find each of those forgotten bodies and give each one a decent final rite. The artifact seemed to be telling me that this was the path of my atonement."

"Your salvation," she murmured.

"I see now, however, that I underestimated the situation."

"How?"

"Humphries. While I am out there searching for the bodies of the slain, he will have me killed."

"No! That's wrong!"

Dorn's deep voice was empty of regret. "It will be simple for him to send a team after me. In the depths of dark space, they will murder me. What I failed to do for myself, Humphries will do for me. He will be my final atonement."

"Never!" Elverda blazed with anger. "I will not permit it to happen."

"Your own life is in danger from him," Dorn said.

"What of it? I am an old woman, ready for death."

"Are you?"

"I was . . . until I saw the artifact."

"Now life is more precious to you, isn't it?"

"I don't want you to die," Elverda said. "You have atoned for your sins. You have borne enough pain."

He looked away, then started up the tunnel again.

"You are forgetting one important factor," Elverda called after him.

Dorn stopped, his back to her. She realized now that the clothes he wore had been his military uniform. He had torn all the insignias and pockets from it.

"The artifact. Who created it? And why?"

Turning back toward her, Dorn answered, "Alien visitors to our solar system created it, unknown ages ago. As to why—you tell me: Why does someone create a work of art?"

"Why would aliens create a work of art that affects human minds?"

Dorn's human eye blinked. He rocked a step backward.

"How could they create an artifact that is a mirror to our souls?" Elverda asked, stepping toward him. "They must have known something about us. They must have been here when there were human beings existing on Earth."

Dorn regarded her silently.

"They may have been here much more recently than you think," Elverda went on, coming closer to him. "They may have placed this artifact here to communicate with us."

"Communicate?"

"Perhaps it is a very subtle, very powerful communications device."

"Not an artwork at all."

"Oh yes, of course it's an artwork. All works of art are communications devices, for those who possess the soul to understand."

Dorn seemed to ponder this for long moments. Elverda watched his solemn face, searching for some human expression.

Finally he said, "That does not change my mission, even if it is true."

"Yes it does," Elverda said, eager to save him. "Your mission is to preserve and protect this artifact against Humphries and anyone else who would try to destroy it—or pervert it to his own use."

"The dead call to me," Dorn said solemnly. "I hear them in my dreams now."

"But why be alone in your mission? Let others help you. There must be other mercenaries who feel as you do."

"Perhaps," he said softly.

"Your true mission is much greater than you think," Elverda said, trembling with new understanding. "You have the power to atone for the wars that have destroyed your comrades, that have almost destroyed your soul."

"Atone for the corporate wars?"

"You will be the priest of this shrine, this sepulcher. I will return to Earth and tell everyone about these wars."

"Humphries and others will have you killed."

"I am a famous artist, they dare not touch me." Then she laughed. "And I am too old to care if they do."

"The scientists—do you think they may actually learn how to communicate with the aliens?"

"Someday," Elverda said. "When our souls are pure enough to stand the shock of their presence."

The human side of Dorn's face smiled at her. He extended his arm and she took it in her own, realizing that she had found her own salvation. Like two kindred souls, like comrades who had shared the sight of death, like mother and son they walked up the tunnel toward the waiting race of humanity.

My son, if sinners entice you,
Do not consent. . . .
Keep your feet from their path;
For their feet run to evil,
And they hasten to shed blood. . . .
But they lie in wait for their own blood;
They ambush their own lives.
So are the ways of everyone who gains by violence.
It takes away the life of its possessors.

—The Book of Proverbs
Chapter 1, verses 10–19